EVE
OF
MAN

Also by TOM FLETCHER

The Christmasaurus

There's a Monster in Your Book

There's a Dragon in Your Book

Also by GIOVANNA FLETCHER

Billy and Me

You're the One That I Want

GIOVANNA AND TOM FLETCHER

EVE
OF
MAN

Random House New York

Text copyright © 2018 by Giovanna and Tom Fletcher
Jacket images copyright © Getty Images and Shutterstock

All rights reserved. Published in the United States by Random House Children's Books, a division of Penguin Random House LLC, New York. Originally published in hardcover by Penguin Random House UK, London, in 2018.

Random House and the colophon are registered trademarks of Penguin Random House LLC.

Visit us on the Web! GetUnderlined.com

Educators and librarians, for a variety of teaching tools, visit us at RHTeachersLibrarians.com

Library of Congress Cataloging-in-Publication Data
Names: Fletcher, Tom, author. | Fletcher, Giovanna, author.
Title: Eve of man / Tom and Giovanna Fletcher.
Description: First American edition. | New York: Random House, [2019] | Summary: In a world where no girls had been born in fifty years, Eve arrived and, having been protected from the dangers of a ruined world, is now sixteen and expected to renew the human race.
Identifiers: LCCN 2018012941 | ISBN 978-1-9848-3011-1 (hardcover) | ISBN 978-1-9848-3012-8 (hardcover library binding) | ISBN 978-1-9848-3013-5 (ebook)
Subject: | CYAC: Fantasy.
Classification: LCC PZ7.F6358 Eve 2019 | DDC [Fic]—dc23

Printed in the United States of America
10 9 8 7 6 5 4 3 2 1
First American Edition

For our boys

EVE
OF
MAN

Prologue

ON THE FIRST DAY NO ONE REALLY NOTICED. PERHAPS THERE was a chuckle among the midwives at the sight of all those babies wrapped in blue blankets, not a pink one in sight. Individual hospitals would've thought nothing of it. They wouldn't have known that this day of blue was only the beginning.

On the second day they frowned, confused, at another twenty-four hours of blue.

Just boys.

How baffling. Still, they assumed it was nothing more than coincidence. The Y chromosome was just making more of an appearance than usual.

On the third day the media made light of it—*It Really Is a Man's World.* That brought the situation to everyone's attention. Doctors and nurses realized theirs wasn't the only hospital to go blue. Blue was taking over. Not just entire hospitals, not just entire countries, but the entire world.

Where had the pink gone?

With approximately two and a half million babies born each week, half of whom were usually girls, the sudden imbalance couldn't be ignored. World leaders were called together with the most respected scientists to try to understand what was happening and discuss measures they could take to monitor the situation. They had to find an ethical way of working—they didn't want to strip people of their human rights. That was what they said.

Initially.

At first it was a phenomenon, but soon it was threatening the survival of humanity, leaving us all on the brink of extinction. That was when governments stopped being nice. When women became more controlled and oppressed than ever before.

Compulsory tests were carried out. To start with, pregnant women were screened to identify the sex of their unborn children. Then, as more time passed with no females born, all women under the age of fifty were examined in an attempt to determine the cause of the blue generation.

Sex was encouraged—those in power wanted lots of babies in the hope that the odds would eventually favor girls. And there were girls—they were spotted in utero, bouncing around in the amniotic fluid and nudging their mommies with their flailing arms and legs.

Not one survived.

Eventually those cases disappeared. There was no pink to be seen . . . or lost.

Science battled for years. And years. And years. No cause was found. There was no breakthrough. Without a cause there could be no cure. The future of humanity was ticking away with the biological clocks of any remaining fertile women.

They would never give up, the world was told. They would save the human race. Somehow.

And the people played their part. They prayed. Prayed to many gods to grant them the rebirth of their kind. For a long time it seemed no one was listening. The people prayed harder, for longer, calling on different all-powerful beings with urgency. They unearthed old religions, forged new ones, and muttered their worshipful chants with longing.

Then, after a fifty-year female drought, a miracle happened—and it didn't occur in a sterile science lab.

Corinne and Ernie Warren had been married for twenty-five years. They'd always wanted children, but it seemed Mother Nature wasn't on their side. Corinne suffered miscarriage after miscarriage until eventually the couple gave up their dream to become parents. She was struck off as a potential carrier when she was forty-three. They accepted the failure with much sadness and a hint of relief. They'd been beaten down by grief so many times. They were broken, but at least they had each other to cling to.

Eight years later, at fifty-one, Corinne unexpectedly fell pregnant. Naturally. She and Ernie were thrilled, but full of fear. What if this baby was taken from them like all the others? They couldn't face another miscarriage.

Like every woman, Corinne was screened—but, unlike other women, she and Ernie welcomed the tests. They wanted to be sure their baby was fit and healthy—they wanted to do all they could to ensure the safe arrival of the little being they already loved so much and for whom they would do anything.

Their hearts leaped when they saw their creation stretching on the ultrasound. Their baby. Their joy.

For the midwife dealing with Corinne, the screening process had become routine—a monotonous series of tests, invariably with the same outcome. She didn't expect to see anything but blue.

But there it was.

Pink.

And *her* appearance made quite an impact.

It caused a panic. The result in that examination room sent shockwaves of hysteria rippling around the globe. People couldn't believe that good news had come at last. They were longing to be told more about the couple who offered them a glimmer of light.

But Corinne's medical history of miscarriages, her age, and the fact that no girls had survived in utero in decades were causes for concern. Corinne and Ernie were moved into a specialized medical facility to maximize the chances of the pregnancy going full-term. Other than daily scans, no tests were carried out. This time Mother Nature was allowed to take her course—at least until there was any reason to interfere. Perhaps it was time to trust the human body again.

Corinne and Ernie understood the need for monitoring their baby's development and the desire to keep their daughter safe. They were happy their child was as special to others as she was to them. They didn't resent the restrictions placed on them. Or that they were allowed no visitors at all. They agreed they'd do whatever it took to bring their baby safely into the world.

There were complications in the delivery room. Mother and daughter were left fighting for their lives. Corinne died soon after giving birth, having fulfilled her life's ambition to become a mother.

Ernie was grief-stricken, unable to deal with the loss of his wife. Incapable of being a father.

He never held his daughter.

Never kissed her.

Never told her he loved her.

And what of the baby girl?

The world had waited for her arrival with bated breath, longing for the news that their hopes had been realized, that their girl had been born.

She had.

Against all odds, she survived.

She was the first girl born in fifty years.

They called her Eve.

She represented the rebirth of the human race. She was the answer to their prayers. She was all they cared about, their final hope.

Eve was the savior of humanity.

I am Eve.

1

EVE

GOOD TOES, NAUGHTY TOES. GOOD TOES, NAUGHTY TOES.
Good toes, naughty toes . . .

I watch my feet as they extend into a perfect point, then
flex them, feeling the pull of my calf muscles and enjoying the
breeze on my skin as I sit with my legs dangling over the Drop.

I love it here. Outside. Basking in the warmth of the sun.
Heights don't bother me, which is a good thing: I can't remember a time when I didn't live above the clouds in the sanctuary
they built for me in which I sleep, eat, learn, and grow. Everything I could ever need is here, within the vast half-bubble of
the Dome, where the glass lets the beauty of outside in. Sun-
beams bounce off every surface.

Up here in my home above the clouds, I can't be seen, or
see, thanks to the white cloud lying between us. A constant veil
hides the world and me from each other. Occasionally I'm sure
I can see shapes from the city below, but that might be my
imagination.

Still, I need to be closer to it. I need to experience it. That's
why I love sitting on the Drop. This is my spot, my place to

escape to at the end of a walkway to nowhere. It is the perfect quiet space in which to mull over the day and my future.

Our future.

The future.

"There you are," Holly says, walking through the glass doors several meters behind me, as though there's anywhere else I'd be.

I'm rarely completely alone out here. Or, rather, I'm never out here for long before she shows up. Without tearing my eyes from the beautiful view, I raise a welcoming hand. It's not her fault she interrupts my quiet time. She's only doing as she's told. They want to hear my thoughts—especially now, ahead of tomorrow. So they send her to find me. Holly. My best friend. My constant companion. My anchor. I was in class with her a few minutes ago discussing William Shakespeare's ability to turn tragedy into near comedy. She had some interesting thoughts, which I found intriguing and insightful—sometimes I learn as much from her as I do from whoever is teaching.

Holly is different now, though. She's less studious and more . . . accessible.

"Nice shoes," I say, spotting the orange slip-ons as she sits beside me. Her honey-blond hair is unmoving in the wind, yet she pulls her denim jacket a little tighter, as though she feels a chill.

It amuses me that they don't keep her in the same outfit all the time. They select what she wears each day or at each session. Why bother? Perhaps it's to show what's expected of me, or to inspire my own fashion sense, because it's not as though I can learn from others like me. I am the only girl.

I'm never directly told what to wear. I can choose from any

of the items they've placed in my wardrobe: mostly vintage garments collected from decades past—geometric prints, bell-bottom pants, shoulder-padded jackets, or pretty shirtdresses.

Yes, I still have the freedom of choice. Take today. This morning I opted for a floaty turquoise summer dress with a dainty white floral pattern. It falls below my knees, exposing an inch or two of naked flesh above the lace-up brown boots I've teamed it with. I've seen photos of similar dresses worn with a wedged heel, sandals, or espadrilles, but my footwear must always be laced and tied when I'm out on the Drop. No slip-ons for me. Not here.

It isn't the same for Holly, which irritates me, although only in the sense that it's a sloppy move on their part. Why implement a regulation, give her to me, then leave a murky area where we aren't tied to the same rules? It makes a mockery of her, and I don't like that.

I try not to sigh too heavily, and avert my eyes. I weave my fingers through the ends of my long brown hair, which has become tangled in the breeze.

The Mothers used to style it for me when I was younger. Their designs were too intricate for me to grasp back then, but now I have hours to play with my hair and I've become quite the expert. I can twist, knot, braid, pin . . . The possibilities are endless. For which I'm thankful. It gives me something to do. I used to be allowed to experiment with makeup, but now I wear it on special occasions to ensure it's not wasted. As the demand for these products isn't what it once was, there are no new supplies. What I have has to last me.

"So, tomorrow," Holly starts, breaking the silence.

"Wow, straight in there." I half laugh, turning to see her

pale green eyes twinkling as she stares straight ahead. Sometimes she tiptoes around these subjects, leaving me on edge and defensive, as I'm unsure where she's leading the conversation. Other times, like in class, all focus is on the work. I prefer it when it's like this. I like her more. It feels more genuine. Almost real.

"It's a big day," she states, shrugging her slender shoulders.

"Biggest of my life." I nod in agreement, my expression serious now. I want her to think she's pulled me in and that I'm ready for a deep and meaningful chat. "Well, apart from my birth—that was monumental."

"No big deal, really," she replies, trying to hide the smile lurking at the corners of her mouth.

"Hardly breaking news," I quip.

"Exactly," she breathes. "Tell me about him, then."

"I've got a whole file on him inside. You can go and have a look if you like. Or you could bring it out here?" I suggest cheekily, knowing she's already aware of what's in it and that she couldn't bring it out here even if we were allowed objects on the Drop.

"Are you trying to get rid of me?" she asks, wide eyes sparkling.

"Now, why would I do that?" I laugh, my thoughts turning to the stranger I'm set to meet. Potential Number One. "His name is Connor . . . From the pictures I've seen he looks pleasant enough."

"That's good, although looks aren't everything," she replies.

"Of course not—they can be deceiving." The irony is not lost on either of us. I notice her lips thin as she tries to hold in another smile. I love her for that little glimpse of something other.

"Anything else stand out about this one?" she asks, looping loose hair behind her ear as though it's an innocent question between two friends. As though she's not digging for information and hoping to gain insight into my thoughts—because as far as I know, they've not been able to control, test, or tap into them yet. I'd like to keep it that way.

But it's *this* Holly, I remind myself. I know from her eyes that *she* genuinely cares, that she's more than a messenger sent to manipulate my worries or delights out of me.

"Hard to tell, from what I've seen and read so far. I'll know more when I meet him in the morning," I say, sounding calmer than I feel.

We've been working toward this point for years. I've always known there'd be three Potentials. Not two or four, but three. A handful of short-listed males who've already proven themselves worthy of the task ahead. I haven't been told how that was done, but I can only imagine they've been tested, trained, and challenged as much as I have. Now it's time for me to have my say. To meet the three men and choose a life mate. A partner. A male to coexist with. I'm not here to repopulate the world in one fell swoop, but rather to give it a gentle reboot, to allow us to start again and right our wrongs. That is the hope and the plan they've entrusted me with.

"And how do you feel about meeting him?" she asks, her eyes on mine.

Nothing gets past her.

"Nervous, excited, scared, thrilled, terrified . . ." I trail off, my fingers tracing the outline of the rough moon-shaped patch of hard skin on my left wrist. A permanent reminder of how exposed I've been in the past, and why I've felt safe here, with only the company of those who can be trusted. "It's the un-known."

Holly smiles, as though she understands instantly. A notion that should be true after more than a decade of being my best friend, but she could never fathom the weight I carry. No one could. In that sense I'm totally alone, no matter what tricks they use to persuade me otherwise. These strangers look at me as though I hold the answers to their prayers, but what if I don't?

"He knows all about me. I know nothing about him, aside from what's in that file," I confide, sharing the tip of my concern and trying to ignore the self-doubt underneath.

"He only knows what he's been shown too," she replies matter-of-factly, reminding me of the times when they've stuck a camera in my face and asked me to say a few words to en-courage humanity in its plight. I know my sixteenth-birthday celebrations were captured last week too. Between the raucous games, singing, and dancing, they made me say a few words on how it felt to have reached this milestone. I didn't complain, as I'm used to it. The world has always rejoiced when I add another year to my age.

When I was younger I felt embarrassed in those moments. Now I feel a real connection with the public, as though I travel through the lens and speak directly to each person watching. I feel united and empowered, not quite so alone.

"What he's seen is better than the stupid video of him run-ning around a track and playing the cello—albeit very well," I moan, thinking about the clips of Connor that Vivian Silva, the woman in charge, showed me—as though I should be grateful for a stranger's musical talent and the speed at which his legs can move. "I wanted to see more of him."

"So you liked what you saw, then? It whetted your appetite?" She smirks, her head hanging low so that she's peering up at me, eyelashes batting.

"Yes. No . . . I don't know. I need more," I say. "I want to know what his life is like. What makes him smile and cry. Whether he has siblings, or a mother. What it's like to have a life outside the Tower and lots of friends."

"He might not have *lots*."

"He'll have more than I do. Real ones."

"Ouch. Cheap shot." She groans, putting a hand on her chest and rubbing it.

"Sorry," I mumble.

"It's okay to be nervous, Eve," she says, her voice more serious, her jokey manner slipping.

"I'm not. I'm just—" I stop as my face starts to burn. "I might hate him."

"That's why there are two more Potentials to choose from," she reminds me. "You have options. You're Eve."

"I know," I say. "Eve, the savior of humanity." The words seem thick in my mouth.

"No," she says firmly. "Strong, talented, funny, beautiful, unique. It's he who should be nervous. You're the one in control here. Remember that. There are plenty like him. There is only one of you."

"Thank you," I mutter, aware that my face has quickly gone from pink to red. A bubble of nervous energy floats in my stomach. "After years of waiting, of discussions and preparation, of wondering and worrying, tomorrow is the day. It's arrived. I'm going to meet a Potential. A boy . . . a man."

"I think 'boy' is more accurate." She laughs, burying her face in her hands.

"It's a new beginning."

Connor's youthful face flashes before me. Having studied it obsessively, I recall the pimples on his chin, his floppy light brown hair, and his smile, which slants to one side. It's all surface viewing, though. I want to know what's underneath.

Ever so briefly, Holly's face registers pain before her perfect smile reappears and she continues: "Did you see the way he kept flicking his hair out of his face before he talked? I thought it was endearing . . ."

"I did." The corner of my mouth is twitching.

I'm dissatisfied with the information they have given me on Connor, because it's not enough. I want more. The truth is, I've spent hours watching the same three minutes and twenty-two seconds of footage over and over again. I've watched it on repeat, taking in every detail, rewinding to watch him tug at his vest and seeing how his fingers connect with the fabric, glide effortlessly over the strings of his cello, and how his eyes squint at the sheet music. It's far more spellbinding than anything else they've let me see, do, or read. It's life. From out there.

I know they watch me watch.

I know they'll have assumed I've fallen for the first male I've ever been allowed to interact with, but I'm simply fascinated. I've wanted to soak up his every movement and inflection. They haven't let him say much, yet it is all information—all knowledge of a world below that I know barely anything about. We share the same beautiful night sky, but otherwise our lives are totally different. I spend the majority of my time up here in the Tower, out of harm's way, while he is free to roam. Free to live his life. Unless tomorrow is a success, of course. Then his life will be more like mine, or, in a more hopeful world, mine will be more like his . . .

"I think you'll have a great time," Holly says, looking me straight in the eye. "I'll be thinking of you."

"Will you?" I cringe as I hear neediness in my voice. Sometimes she really does seem tangible and real. Like she's an actual companion and my only ally. I long to cling to her for fear she'll leave.

"Yeah. Of course. It's—it's an important day for us all," she stammers. "Who's not going to be thinking about how you're getting on?"

"Right." I sigh.

2

EVE

WE'VE BEEN SITTING IN THE SAME SPOT FOR AT LEAST AN HOUR, in our usual way, talking of everything and nothing. Sometimes she lets me natter on about one of the Mothers, my confusion over a mathematical theory, or my difficulty in mastering Mandarin. Sometimes there's just silence. And that's fine too. There's such ease between us. It's effortless.

My heart spasms at the thought of tomorrow and how much effort will be required. How awkward, stilted, and clumsy I may be, not through any fault of my own but, rather, the situation we'll be in.

Without thinking I reach into my pocket and pull out my multicolored Rubik's Cube—like my wardrobe, it's a link to a bygone era in which life must've been so much simpler. That's why I've always been so fascinated by it. I find comfort in the way my fingers move around the cube, and the squeak as the plastic pieces rub together.

Gripping it with both hands, I twist and turn the movable faces so that the colored squares swap positions. It's a puzzle I've always loved solving. It was so difficult at first. When I was little, I would stare at it for hours, twisting randomly while getting frustrated. I'd dream about the thing! I remember Holly teasing me, "Just peel off the stickers and put them back in the right places," she'd say, knowing I would never cheat. Now I can do it easily, matching all the sides while barely thinking about it. It used to still my mind, but now the calm comes from having something to do with my hands.

"What are you doing with that?" Holly gasps, her voice shooting up an octave. She instantly looks panicked at the sight of the retro toy in my hands, glancing to the glass doors behind us.

"It was in my pocket from earlier and I forgot I had it on me," I lie, acting as though it's no big deal. Truth is, I knew it was in my pocket, but her reaction has shocked me enough to make me wish I could rewind the last thirty seconds and leave it where it was hidden.

"You know you shouldn't have brought it out here. It's against the rules!" she hisses, her eyebrows knotting.

"Holly, relax!" I laugh. I throw the cube a few inches into the air and catch it with both hands. It's a risky move and my stomach flips, but it's worth it for the look on Holly's face. She can hardly believe I'd break a tiny rule like this. I'm usually so obedient. There aren't many opportunities to rebel up here, and it's thrilling to feel the blood racing through me.

"Don't," she pleads, bringing her palms to her face as though she can't bear to watch. Imploring me to stop.

"I can't believe you're being such a wimp."

"Eve, inside. Now!" a voice booms, making us both jump.

"Really? It's only a—" My head swivels toward the doors behind us.

Vivian Silva is standing there, one hand on her hip, the other pointing in the direction she's commanding I go. Her stature never fails to make me cower. Her height, her strength—she's unlike any of the Mothers. There's not an ounce of femininity or softness in her, thanks to her chiseled features, gray pantsuits, and matching gray hair, which is short and sharp, the front touching her cheekbones, the back almost razored away completely.

The sternness of her face, which is always unfriendly but currently more thunderous than usual, stops my talking. There's no point in trying. Not with her.

My bravado slips away and I find myself rooted to the spot, feeling torn, not to mention humiliated.

"I said *now!*" she barks, her brown eyes boring into my own.

"We're just talking about tomorrow," I state, keeping my voice low and steady, wanting to quash her anger and turn her focus to the bigger task ahead. A toy making its way out to the Drop is trivial in comparison.

"Vivian, she didn't mean to—"

"Holly, off," she orders, without taking her eyes from mine.

My jaw drops as my friend literally disappears, like she's simply evaporated into thin air.

They've never done that before. Usually Holly leaves through an open door, helping to maintain the illusion they've created for me.

This is bad.

Very bad.

My throat feels tight as I scramble to my feet and walk up the concrete pathway of the Drop toward Vivian. I extend my hand, offering my Rubik's Cube for confiscation, hoping she'll take it and the whole thing can be forgotten. She doesn't. Instead she rejects my bid for peace, turning her head away from me.

"Inside," she says quietly in the cold, authoritative, and measured voice I'm used to hearing.

"Sorry," I mumble, feeling stupid as I follow her indoors and into the upper garden zone—a maze of leafy green trees, plants, and shrubs. Millions of species all housed under the Dome. This was made for me. It's my greenhouse in the sky, where I can watch living forms thrive and grow. They've been thoughtful like that . . . Caring.

The guilt creeps up on me.

Vivian takes us along one of the stone paths that meander through the garden and down a staircase into the working quarters. She stops outside the closed door of her office and turns to me, her face more composed than before, the walk having calmed her.

"Do you understand how serious this is?" she asks, her voice barely above a whisper.

"I forgot it was in my pocket," I lie, the clasp on my throat making it difficult to speak. I've never been good at reprimands and they rarely have cause to issue them. Not really.

"One little slip of the hand and you'd have killed someone below. You've not forgotten how high up we are, have you?" Her question makes me feel dim and foolish.

"No, of course not." I squirm.

"We give you so much freedom, Eve. Do you want that taken away?" she asks, sweeping her hair off her face with the back of her hand.

"No," I plead, realizing the Mothers will probably be

ordered to search me before I go out there in the future and cursing myself for my stupidity.

"Perhaps we should lock the doors from now on," she says, as though pondering her varying modes of punishment. She's playing with me, toying with her power. I'm aware of that, but it still fills me with fear.

"Please don't," I say, trying to strip my voice of emotion so that I sound more grown up and in control.

"Or we could get rid of the Drop altogether," she suggests.

"You wouldn't . . . ," I gasp.

"If you can't follow simple instructions, Eve . . ." The side of her mouth lifts a fraction. She knows she's got me where she wants me. All I can do is act with the appropriate amount of sorrow and regret in the hope she'll go easy on me.

"I promise I won't do it again," I say, bowing my head.

When I look up I find her staring at me so intently I have to drop my gaze back to my laced brown boots.

"You are a cog," she growls, her voice low and deep as she moves closer to me. "A significant one, I'll give you that, but you are still a cog. Without us protecting you, you are nothing."

I nod, my cheeks burning. I may be the one weighed down with the ultimate responsibility of continuing life on this planet, but she's entrusted to make sure I carry out the duties bestowed on me. She can't physically hurt me, of course, but she can take away the things I love to ensure I live up to my own potential. The Drop is my daily connection to the outside world. She knows I'd be crushed to see it go and that I'd do anything to keep it.

"I promise I won't disobey you again," I squeak.

"Good." She pauses, letting my misery linger as her nostrils flare in disgust. "Now go to your room and prepare yourself for the first encounter. I don't want you to disappoint me two days in a row," she warns. "The public is counting on you."

"Yes, Vivian." I almost curtsy before I turn away and run to my sleeping quarters.

3

BRAM

THE SIRENS WAKE HARTMAN. MY BEST FRIEND. MY PARTNER. MY copilot. It's two a.m. I'm not sleeping.

"Storm?" he croaks, scratching the stubble that covers the lower half of his round face. Storms were forecast, but the sound of boots running past our dormitory heralds something more.

"Protesters," I reply.

"Damn Freevers. Go home!" he grunts.

Sleep.

I've had so little of it that I'm starting to forget what it feels like. Hartman's never had trouble in that area. Even when we were just kids at the academy and I was still afraid of the dark, his mind would switch off as soon as they called "Lights out!" while mine continued whirring, trying to work all this out. Trying to figure out my place in the mess. It's nice to know that some things never change.

The sirens are still wailing. My guess is they'll be pulsing for a while. I try to imagine what sort of chaos is taking place down at water level.

Thousands of people braving the weather, knee-deep in the freezing floodwater that drowned their city years ago. It forced them inside, to build upward into the storm clouds, searching for warmth and safety. But this lot? These deluded rebels have strayed from their cloudscrapers in Central and, once again, found themselves outside our walls with only the fire of their anger to keep them warm.

Why?

Her, of course. Their savior. The future of mankind.

Eve.

Protesters are nothing new around here. The Tower has seen millions of passionate faces, heard millions of voices call up to the sky, millions of pointless soggy cardboard signs nailed to damp wooden sticks marched back and forth outside the armored walls, all wanting one thing: to free Eve.

"I hate Freevers . . . ," Hartman mumbles into his pillow. I think he's sleep-talking.

Tonight's protests will turn to riots. They always do. They'll get nowhere, though. A fire quickly extinguished. Quickly forgotten.

There have been one or two close calls over the years, but what do you expect? She is the most important human in history. Kidnapping attempts when Eve was a child were frequent. Assassination plots from religious extremists, terror threats around every one of her early public appearances. That was a long time ago. When she still went outside. Into the real world. She was just a little girl being paraded around to give hope to the hopeless, strengthen the weak, convince the nonbelievers.

She doesn't remember any of that, of course, and we don't

remind her. That was another life, before the Extinction Prevention Organization tightened its grip. Before it moved her permanently to the Dome.

The Dome.

My mind moves from the water nine hundred floors below me to Eve, five floors above. The Dome is her world. Self-sufficient on every level. If the Tower were a country, the Dome would be its capital.

Population: one.

Eve.

What is she doing right now? Of course she can't hear the sirens, not up there, but I know Eve. She won't be sleeping. Her head will be full of tomorrow. Like mine.

Our dorm shakes.

An explosion from below.

The riots have begun.

Hartman snores. He's as oblivious to the riots as Eve is, except he doesn't have the luxury of shock absorbers, motion stabilizers, or the largest suspension system ever created to keep him peacefully dreaming.

The water inside my transparent canteen ripples as another deep rumble shakes the Tower. Eve wouldn't have felt a thing. The Dome is constant, always perfectly calm and tranquil. It is never still, though. It subtly ebbs and flows, like a boat on an ocean, allowing the storms—or in this case the shock waves caused by explosives—to pass around it while keeping its precious occupant blissfully ignorant.

Another explosion. The Freevers must be putting on quite a show tonight.

I decide to take a look. I climb out of my bunk. As my feet

touch the cold floor it emits a soft orange glow so I can see where I'm walking without waking Hartman. The holo-display at my desk illuminates as I walk past, trying to tempt me to work by displaying my most viewed image—a tree.

I ignore it, and the screen returns to sleep mode. As I approach the dorm window, it senses my body heat and powers up. Funny that we still call them windows. There's not a single pane of glass on the outside of the Tower. It is a fortress. Our windows are realiTV monitors, repurposed and redesigned for the Tower, made to look and feel like the windows we were once so familiar with. One of the many things around here that my genius father invented. Dr. Isaac Wells. Definitely more genius than father.

I look out of the window and it shows me thick, dark storm clouds. Default setting: reality. I swipe my hand and a burst of red blinds me.

"Jeez, Bram," grumbles Hartman, turning his face away from the light.

"Sorry," I whisper, twisting my hand in the air, adjusting the brightness.

When it settles and the clouds have gone, I'm looking down on what remains of Central, our city, dark red patches representing the colder, more flooded areas. It amazes me that people still live out there. I step closer and look down. It makes my stomach turn every time. I've never been great with heights, and this is beyond high.

Directly beneath my window a hot red glow is fizzing at the base of the Tower. The body heat of thousands of Freevers bubbles like lava. I raise a fist in front of my face and spread my fingers wide. The window obeys and magnifies the view. The lava turns into fire ants as they try to swarm and invade our nest to take back their queen.

They will fail.

I gesture again. Now I can see their faces. The red heat of their anger. Some are crying. All are men, of course. Most will never have seen a woman in the flesh. There are some women out there, most of them in female-only safe houses and secluded sanctuaries. The youngest, other than Eve, are sixty-six, the last born before the fifty-year drought. I never met one on the outside when I lived out there. Other than my mother, of course. I hardly see any in the protests these days—most are either too old or too scared. Scared of us. Scared of men. Scared of this world we live in. We are an endangered species now, and women are the rarest of all.

The window flashes a hot white. The dorm vibrates. It's not one of their explosions this time; it's one of ours. Nonlethal, of course: we're an endangered species, after all. Fear Gas usually does the trick at dispersing even the most determined Freevers, filling them with their most dreaded fear while we watch them run home crying.

I swipe both hands, and the window returns to reality. Storm clouds. Always storm clouds. I look for a moment at what we have done to this planet. Idiots. So this is what happens to a world inhabited by fifty years' worth of men, generations of boys without hope of a future. They destroy it. Of course. Three world wars and this is what's left.

That was all before I was born.

Before Eve.

By the time Eve came along this was all that was left for our "savior" to save. I'm too young to remember anything BE, but I've read the Before Eve reports. With no future generation to inherit our world, we abused it beyond anyone's imagining.

Overconsumption of fossil fuels accelerated global warming beyond even the most pessimistic predictions. War. Greed. What we didn't destroy ourselves the weather finished off for us. *The most severe weather conditions in our planet's history,* they claim.

Selfish. It's in our nature.

Our savior has a lot of work to do.

A thick cloud presses against the window and I can see my face in the reflection, one of my two faces. This face takes me by surprise: it's the one I was born with. I run my hand over my cropped head, and my scalp tingles as the sensation relieves some of the stress of a day at work. My eyes are dull from lack of sleep. This face is tired. I'm seeing less and less of him these days, and more of my second face. *Her* face.

Holly.

My work hours have almost tripled in preparation for tomorrow and I'm spending most of my time suited up in the studio—or, as we pilots prefer to call it, the Cage. It's where we step out of ourselves and become Holly, Eve's best friend.

Holly still blows my mind, even after all these years. She is truly state-of-the-art. There's no other technology like her. Of course, when an organization becomes responsible for the most important human on the planet, it gains control of endless resources, unlimited funds to plow into developing anything that may have a positive benefit on Eve's life. My dad's technology was on their radar for years, but I don't think even the great Vivian Silva could ever have predicted Holly or that she would become so useful. Social interaction with a female her own age quickly became the key to understanding Eve.

Unlocking her thoughts.

Influencing her.

Controlling her.

There's no one more influential than your best friend.

Influence/manipulation. That's a fine line, and Holly walks it—*I* walk it—daily.

Of course Eve knows Holly isn't real. She's fully aware of her own uniqueness. Most of us would have trouble telling Holly from a real human, but Eve called it on week one of Holly's introduction, when we were just little kids.

"It's her eyes," I can still remember her insisting. "They keep changing."

It's the only flaw in an otherwise perfect program. Nine out of ten people can't spot it, but Eve is perceptive. Holly's eyes have to be directly linked to the person controlling her: the pilot—me. My father designed her that way: it's what makes her so lifelike. It's what makes you trust her. But no two pilots' eyes are exactly the same. Three of us control Holly, and Eve's worked out our differences.

Of course, we don't talk about it. It's forbidden. We never break protocol. When you are piloting Holly, you *are* Holly. You're not yourself anymore. It's what we train for.

Sometimes I forget where Bram ends and Holly begins. Maybe that's what makes me Eve's favorite. Why I'm the one she opens up to. That must be why I'm given all the difficult missions. Or maybe it's because I'm the boss's son. I dunno.

I run my fingers across my head again and my mind wanders. I was just a young boy when Dad first created Holly—he practically designed the hardware around me. Close in age to Eve, I was the perfect guinea pig for his latest creation. The EPO went nuts for it. It was a real game changer. His masterpiece. It put his name on the scientific map. He's like royalty around here now. Shouldn't that make me a prince? Hardly. We are knights and Eve is our queen.

Lightning flashes in the distance. From the way the clouds glow blue I know it hit flood level, charging the water and illuminating Central momentarily. I wonder what Eve would make of all this if she could see it.

What must it be like for her, knowing none of it? Up there in the Dome right now, underneath a perfect starry sky. Soon one of a thousand preprogrammed sunrises is scheduled to wake her and she'll look out over a blanket of soft white cloud. Her belief that the world is peaceful and wonderful will continue; her faith in the humanity she needs to save will be kept alive for another day. That is the purpose of the Dome. That is Eve's reality. I guess reality is just the world with which we are presented.

The sirens stop.

It's over.

I return to my bunk, switch on the reading light, and reread Connor's file. Tomorrow is a big day for us all. The first Potential.

I scan the scientific jargon about his genetic makeup that describes how perfectly suited he is to breed with Eve. It makes it all seem so sterile, so cold. Like she's some sort of zoo animal in a mating program. Do I agree with it? No. Is it necessary? Yes. Does my opinion matter? Hell, no.

My concern isn't so black and white. Human nature.

Emotion. Attraction. Love. There is no scientific formula for that, and Eve is, well, Eve. She's never predictable.

Eve.

I realize I'm smiling as my pillow takes me to that unfamiliar place called sleep.

Good luck, Connor. Tomorrow could change the world.

4

EVE

AFTER A RESTLESS NIGHT I'M AWAKE TO WATCH THE SUNRISE through the glass of the Dome. Oranges and pinks spread slowly across the sky, declaring a new dawn, the hope of a new beginning.

The day has come.

It is here.

It's time for me to fulfill the purpose of my existence.

I look around at my childhood bedroom and feel surprised to see it's remained as it was the night before—a tower within a tower set within the upper garden zone. Two glass walls give me a glorious view of our greenery, a fraction of the beauty in the world we're trying to save. I fall in love with it every time I look out—which is the first thing I do each morning from my wooden four-poster bed.

Yet today that feeling has shifted.

I've woken with a sense of change: I'm on the brink of adulthood, yet my bedroom is just as it was. I'm edging closer to the adult I'm not quite sure how to be. I just know I've got to be her and that her responsibilities rest on my shoulders.

Before long I hear a knock at my door. She's always standing there within minutes of my eyelids opening, as though she's been waiting outside.

"Come in," I call, sitting up while straightening my silk nightdress.

Mother Nina steps into the room in the formal uniform the Mothers wear in public—a dark khaki floor-length gown, with a matching shawl draped over her head that hides the long white hair she usually wears in a loose ponytail. At the moment her wrinkled face is visible, but she'll cover it later. Her tight little mouth, pink cheeks, and slightly hooked nose will be veiled before she takes me in to meet the first Potential, just as we've rehearsed. She must not be seen. She must appear invisible.

"Morning, Mother Nina," I say, attempting to smile like I usually do, but finding it difficult. This is not an ordinary day, and my tummy is churning.

The smile she gives me in return is far warmer than the one I've mustered. It's hopeful, which isn't surprising, as I know she's in favor of the mission at hand. All the Mothers are. That's why they've come here.

Her dress swishes around her ankles as she carries my breakfast tray to me and lays it across my lap. A healthy bowl of fruit and a mug of peppermint tea. You'd think the importance of the day would cause them to give me something special—like the pancakes with syrup I was allowed on my birthday last week, or the bacon-and-cheese sandwich I was given last Christmas, but they don't. Not today. They wouldn't want a bloated tummy pulling the Potential's attention from the magic of the moment. Today is all about me being a woman—a perfect one at that.

It is a historic event for our population, which comes charged with emotion and pressure.

I imagine the people will be glued to the news, waiting to hear if the meeting has gone well—or perhaps the event will be screened live for them to witness so they can draw their own conclusions as to whether or not Connor is my ideal match. Then again, maybe they aren't too fussed. After all, I'm told they have no part in the selection process. I wonder what it must be like for them, having to put all their faith in me. I try to forget that thought.

I can't.

I push the tray of food away from me. I can't eat right now anyway. Not with my insides cramping.

"Thank you," I say as Mother Nina hands me a plastic cup containing my morning pills, the first batch of the day: my daily dose of vitamins. There are five tablets, which vary in color and size. I tip them into my mouth and swallow.

"Are you not going to eat anything?" Mother Nina asks, the earlier joy turning to apprehension as she notices the untouched tray. Her dark eyes shoot me a look of dismay.

"Not hungry," I say sheepishly, picking up the peppermint tea and taking a sip.

"But you must eat, Eve. You need your energy."

She looks panicked and I feel sorry for her. Mother Nina has been my main caregiver for as long as I can remember—she was here long before Holly arrived. My childhood memories are peppered with images of her. Her kind face has always been the first to greet me in the morning and to offer the final goodnight. Her duty is to keep me fed, clothed, healthy, educated, and happy. By not complying with her offer of breakfast, I'm making her fail in her first task on the most important day of my adult life.

Her worried expression forces me to pick up my fork and pop three pieces of chopped pear into my mouth. My throat constricts and I gag, yet I continue.

"Thank you." Mother Nina bows, relief flitting across her face. "And perhaps some banana? You know how privileged you are to have such food. It doesn't grow outside anymore . . ."

I sigh but fork some into my mouth. Mother Nature has cut out bananas as well as girls. I'm pretty sure Mother Nina only says such things to spur me into eating. It's a regular tactic she employs.

"Good girl." She smiles, picking up the tray and placing it on my bedside table—she'll be hoping I decide to graze on it later. She turns back to me with her hands on her chest. "We're all ready when you are."

"Then let's begin." I half smile, taking another gulp of my tea, then throw back the bedcovers and head to the bathroom.

My feelings about today are complex, although one thing is clear: I want to get through it as painlessly as possible. I want it over with. I'm not being dismissive of what's planned: my whole life has been gearing up toward these encounters—but they'll be easier to deal with once I know what I'm walking into. Now it's the unknown. Today's will be the worst of the three meetings.

Once I'm showered, several of the Mothers venture in to help. Mother Kadi, petite at just over five foot, works on my hair. Her tiny hands—marked with tattoos from her previous life—work their magic. She gives me a braid similar to the one into which she weaves her own gray-streaked black hair.

It loops across the front like a band, taking hair away from my face, but the rest is left loose in waves. Mother Kimberley assists Mother Tabia with my makeup, handing her a variety of brushes and pots so seriously that I feel as though I'm on an operating table—in a life-or-death situation. Mother Kimberley is the youngest of the Mothers at sixty-seven, and the only one to have flaming-red hair. Her personality is usually just as bright, but not today when Mother Tabia is bossing her around. I'll lovingly refer to Mother Tabia as the strict one, but she's nowhere near as cold as Vivian, although she takes pride in having been chosen to report back to those in charge. I know this is so because the others clam up whenever she's around.

Mother Tabia's hand moves across my face, buffing, dabbing, and stroking, expertly accentuating my finer features and diminishing my flaws.

Everyone is intensely focused on doing their jobs to perfection. They have played a huge part in my upbringing, but now I sense disconnection in them because today is about so much more than raising a little girl.

One by one they complete their tasks and leave.

I slip out of my robe and stand in my underwear. Today I don't get a say in my outfit. It was designed many months ago specifically for this occasion.

I'm not in a shapeless sack, like the dresses the Mothers have been ordered to wear. Instead my womanly form is celebrated in a cream A-line gown with a scoop neckline and short sleeves. It's floor-length, like the Mothers', but the skirt is beautifully swishy. The bodice is beaded, and a diamanté belt fastens around my waist, making it look tiny. I turn from side to side to take it all in, then slip my feet into the pink ballet pumps Mother Nina has placed on the floor in front of me.

"Gosh . . . ," she breathes, her hands covering her mouth as she straightens and looks at me.

There are moments when Mother Nina feels less like my first maid and more like my mother, or at least what I imagine a mother to be. This is one of those moments. Pride colors her face. She cares about me.

And for that, I love her.

I turn to the mirror and see myself in my special dress. I marvel at the effort the Mothers have put into this version of me. Made up. Made better. Improved. I don't recognize the woman before me but, rather, everything she symbolizes. She's not me. She's theirs, and this is part of the show they long to see.

The Mothers have poured their love and time into me.

Please, let it not be in vain.

It's time to meet the first Potential and move one step closer to survival.

As I walk out of my room all of the Mothers are waiting expectantly. They gasp, voicing their admiration with tears in their eyes and shaking their heads in disbelief that this day has finally arrived.

"Feels like only yesterday I was getting ready for my first date," weeps Mother Kimberley, sniffing into her sleeve.

"Certainly reminds me of my youth," whispers Mother Kadi, her wise eyes filling with memories from a time I'll never know.

"Very beautiful." Mother Tabia nods, curt yet kind.

I chuckle as I wave away their compliments. With a nervous wobble in my step, I walk through them and hit my mark on the floor, standing exactly where we practiced in rehearsals. They fall into formation around me, Mother Nina standing to my right, the others branching out, giving me wings. I hear the fabric of their dresses rustling as they cover their faces. Only their eyes may show. Nothing else.

Once there is silence I lead us into the elevator. As soon as we're all inside, the doors close automatically, my tummy somersaulting as the elevator lurches us downward.

For the most part I'm held in the Dome upstairs and people come to me, but men are forbidden. I've never even seen the male security team in our safe haven. I'm told temptation is an evil that many fail to resist. I'm frequently warned about it. Apparently it's best for men and women to be kept apart so that the risk isn't there. They give me the Mothers and Holly. Seeing anyone else is a treat—especially real humans under the age of sixty-five.

When the doors slide open we find a small security team waiting to escort us the rest of the way. Their presence tells me we are away from the Dome, although I doubt we've traveled far: they'll be wanting to keep everything as controlled as possible, without too many variables added into the mix. Again I wonder what the people are being shown.

I don't recognize the space around me, but I know the faces of the men standing to attention. I've spent hours piecing them together from what I've seen in my peripheral vision. Talking to or looking directly at them is strictly forbidden, of course. I've been told it could give the wrong impression to pay any attention to them, or their focus on their task might slacken. Their duty is to serve me.

"He's waiting," barks Vivian Silva as soon as she spots us, as though we're late. I know we're not, but perhaps it's her own impatience or apprehension over the meeting that is causing her irritation . . . Or she might still be annoyed over my misbehavior on the Drop. I wonder how long she'll make me grovel for it. She never used to be quite so stern or unyielding. We were closer when I was younger, but things have become strained between us over the years.

Vivian marches ahead, gesturing for us to follow. The security team divides into two—half walking in front of me, the rest behind the Mothers. Vivian stops abruptly outside a closed door and steps aside.

"I'll be watching," she says, glancing along the corridor to where a door stands ajar, allowing me to see the many screens depicting various angles of the room I'm about to enter. As I expected, I shall be watched. It has to be documented. If Connor and I have a future together, today will be the making of history: the footage taken will be shown again and again to future generations. Our story will be sacred and cherished, or used as a stern warning to ensure the same doesn't happen again.

I take a deep breath and my muscles loosen a touch.

I give Vivian a nod—I could've done with being in her favor today, but instead she seems to be viewing me as a child who's ruining her hard work. I want this to go well as much as she does.

Ketch has always been the head of my security personnel. I've never set foot out of the Dome without him being there. We never speak, of course, but it's as though I know him, so it's a comfort to have him with me now.

He touches the door handle in front of us, pausing momentarily, then standing a little taller.

The door opens into a sparsely furnished dark room. There are no windows to the outside world, so there's no natural light. Instead the room is lined with screens, each displaying the familiar logo of the women's pictorial entwined with a lower-case *e*. My symbol. My branding.

Floppy-haired Connor, who is sitting in the middle of the room at a table, leaps to his feet as my entourage and I enter. I'd rather have tiptoed in with grace and femininity, but with so many of us it's impossible. Ketch's team and the Mothers line the walls, as they would have rehearsed without me present, and there is quiet once more.

Silence.

Expectation.

Suspense.

Everyone is waiting for something to happen, for the magic to occur.

Suddenly I find myself unsure of how to be. Part of me wants to flounce around the room with a welcoming smile, attracting my first Potential with my irrepressible charm, yet a bigger part of me wishes I were one of the Mothers and could blend into the line of women behind me. Unnoticed.

It seems Connor is also experiencing trepidation. At first he hops from foot to foot, rubbing his palms down his thighs in the navy pants. But when he looks up at me, when our eyes meet, he visibly shrinks. His chest becomes concave, his knees knock inward, and he seems to squirm. He stares at me, his dark eyes wide and disbelieving.

"You're real." He swallows, finding it difficult to speak.

"Of course," I reply, my voice sounding higher and lighter than normal, now that I've got his pleasant bass tones to compare it with. "It's such a pleasure to meet you, Connor," I say, moving toward him.

"I—I—I . . ." Looking horrified, he grips the table beside him and bends over, a hand cradling his stomach.

"Are you unwell?" I ask, my eyes flicking toward the cameras I can see all around us, catching our every move.

He shakes his head. "I'm fine," he mutters through gritted teeth.

Instinctively I place my hand on his slim shoulder to reassure him—it's an alien environment for us both, and it's all I can do to offer him comfort. It's what the Mothers would do for me, yet it doesn't prompt the same reaction.

His body convulses beneath my touch, his knees buckling as he gulps for air. Suddenly he throws his head backward as his hands fly to his lips.

The vomit spatters my face and clothes.

The stench stings my nostrils.

The bile burns my eyes.

I close them, willing the whole thing away. I'm at a total loss as to what to do next.

"I'm so sorry," he whispers, his breathing as labored as my own.

"No. I shouldn't have . . ." I'm humiliated.

"You're Eve," he says softly, as though he's offering an explanation.

"So I'm told," I reply, wanting the exchange to be over and wondering what's taking those around us so long to abort my first encounter.

While the silence engulfs us, I'm hit with an overwhelming sense of failure. Before it consumes me, I wipe my hands across my face, then rub my eyes. Connor is blurred, but I can still register the horror on his face.

"Thanks for coming, Connor," I manage to say, with as pleasant a smile as I can muster, then turn on my heel and head out of the door.

No one stops me or tries to make me go back into the room. It would be callous of them to do such a thing, given the state of me, but the world is a strange place.

In an instant Mother Nina is at my side. We don't say a word as we get into the elevator.

Back in my room, I can't look at her wounded face as she helps me out of my stained dress. I try to ignore the sight of her shaking with silent sobs as I shower away the evidence of what occurred.

I feel for her.

I cannot shift the foul odor, no matter how hard I scrub. Likewise, I know I'll never be able to remove the ghastly memories now that they've been etched into our world's history.

5

BRAM

THE CORRIDORS OUTSIDE OUR DORM ARE UNUSUALLY BUSY for this time of night. News spreads fast inside the Tower. Rumors spread faster.

"Apparently he didn't last five seconds in the same room as her before showing her his breakfast," Hartman blurts. I roll my eyes at him. I know what happened. I was watching live in the gallery, where Eve's movements are monitored twenty-four/seven. I watched as Potential Number One blew his chance at saving the world. The now-infamous Connor, a.k.a. Puketential Number One.

I might have found it funny if it weren't for the years of work, thousands of hours of research, and an unthinkable amount of money that were wasted in a few seconds.

Events like this are hard to conceal in here. They travel from the Dome to the ground faster than the elevator, and some version of today's incident will be whispered through the streets tonight.

Of course, a fabricated photo is now being broadcast across all public realiTV stations to keep up appearances. Connor's and Eve's perfect smiling faces projecting progress. To quash any rumors. Besides, any glimpse of Eve looking happy keeps the Freevers at bay for a while, perhaps long enough for the EPO to come up with a plan for Potentials Two and Three.

"What's your old man going to say, then?" Hartman asks as he chucks a handful of his favorite mini cheese crackers into his mouth, wipes his greasy hands on his tight-fitting jumpsuit, and picks up his notes on Eve's behavioral patterns since the meeting with Connor. I've skimmed them, but my instincts know more about Eve than her ECG can tell me. I'm ready for tonight's emergency briefing.

"He must be pretty pissed off, right?" Hartman continues when I don't reply.

"Yeah." I shrug. "So what's new?"

Our dorm door swishes open automatically, the signal for us to leave. Our room floods with the raucous voices of my fellow pilots. Here we go.

"Bram, is it true?" Jackson barks as we gather in the corridor. "About Connor?"

I don't answer.

"Aw, come on. You can't keep this from us. You can't have special privileges and not share the *juicy* stuff."

The whole squad cracks up as we walk down the metallic corridor toward the briefing room.

Jackson's always given me shit about my situation. About being the boss's son.

"I'm sure we'll find out what happened in a few minutes," I say calmly, knowing they're all aware that I was in the gallery, watching. Pilots aren't permitted there, but security turns a blind eye to Dr. Wells's son.

"Okay, I see. Same old story with *Daddy's boy,* isn't it?" Jackson teases as he speeds up to walk next to me. "Keep all the inside knowledge for yourself. Don't want any of us getting closer to your precious Eve." He winks. The squad laughs. He's such a dick.

"I don't know why they don't just scrap the Potentials, open up the Dome, and let us all have a go at her. One of us is bound to—"

My fist connects with his jaw and Jackson hits the floor. Hard. Shit.

I shouldn't have done that. It was automatic.

The whole squad has stopped, and before I know what's happening, Jackson has my throat in his bear-sized hand and slams my face against the steel-plated wall.

Ouch.

Oh, and now I can't breathe.

This is going well.

I can't feel the floor under my feet anymore as he lifts me into the air, and I feel the blood struggle to pass through the veins in my neck under the pressure of his grip.

I instinctively try to pull his hand away, but his fat fingers feel more like biceps, and my own hands flap uselessly as the color fades from my vision. Don't faint, Bram. Don't faint.

"Jackson." I hear a voice cut calmly through the chaos. "If you'd be so kind as to kill my son quickly so we can get on with the more important task of saving humanity, I would very much appreciate it," says my father, Dr. Isaac Wells, before turning his back on us and entering the briefing room.

Jackson gives my neck one last squeeze, then drops me into a heap on the floor. I've never felt so grateful for oxygen.

"That was stupid," Hartman whispers as he grabs my elbow and helps me up.

"Yeah," I agree, and we follow the squad into the darkened room. Thanks, Dad.

We take our seats at the back left of the briefing room. Same seats we've sat in for years, slightly elevated so we can see over the heads of our colleagues.

I try to nurse the feeling back into my neck and catch a glimpse of Jackson rubbing the inside of his stubbled cheek with his tongue. At least I hit him hard.

"Good evening, gentlemen—or not so gentle, it would seem." My father flashes me a look over his frameless spectacles as he takes his position at the lectern in front of Squad H.

I feel like a child.

"I'm sure you've all heard the news about the disappointing result from Potential Number One—Connor Dobbs."

He gestures with his hand, and a video file from the meeting flickers to life on the realiTV monitor behind him. The pilots all watch what I saw happen earlier—Connor sitting nervously in the cold, soulless meeting room. Whispers and giggles flutter around the room as we watch the footage. It's like being back at the academy.

My father doesn't even blink.

On the screen, Eve's security detail bursts through the door and then she appears, practically floating into the room in her white dress. I'd never seen her in something like that before today.

The room falls silent at the sight.

That's the problem.

Even we pilots who see Eve on a daily basis are dumbstruck

at the sight of her. Her hair. That dress. Those eyes. Eve. She's mesmerizing.

The room watches Connor struggle before the inevitable moment, but none of my fellow pilots are laughing now. I guess we're all protective of Eve. A new natural instinct. Apart from Jackson. He's still just a dick.

My father waves his hand and the footage stops. "As you can see, we have a problem," he says. "These Potentials aren't like you and me. We constantly see and interact with Eve, so we are relatively immune to the effects of female presence, but most of these young men have never seen a woman in the flesh in their entire lives." His brown eyes scan the room and observe the faces now attentively staring at him. His graying hair curves backward as if floating on invisible waves as his head darts between us, his team of six—Locke, Jackson, Kramer, Watts, Hartman, and myself, all sworn to obey his commands.

"Can you imagine being told you're potentially going to be a mate for *the savior of humanity*? All those emotions, those fantasies and nerves building up in you. Then imagine how it would feel coming face to face with *her* for the first time." He motions to the screen, and Eve's photo appears, her flawless skin glowing in the light as her image rotates. "It's no surprise that someone might have a physical reaction, and we should have foreseen it."

"So where do we come into this?" calls Locke eagerly from the front, voicing the question on everyone's mind. "We just control Holly. We're not even permitted in the room when the encounters take place. What can we do?"

My father smiles and removes his glasses.

Cue story.

"Do you know how I invented Holly?" he asks, and I immediately know where he's going. The squad glances around the room. "Bram, why don't you tell your fellow pilots?"

Thanks again, Dad.

"Holly was designed as Eve's social—" I stop as Dad interrupts me by holding up his hand, pausing me like I'm one of his screens.

"Before that, Bram. How did I invent the technology—or, better than that, *why*?"

I sigh. I can't believe he's making me say this. "To satisfy the desires of men," I say as professionally as I can.

The room laughs.

"Well, that's partially correct. My technology has been sold for explicit uses in the past. How else could I fund my research?" my father says.

Squad H applauds and cheers him in jest.

"That's right. My dad, the virtual pimp," I add, and the team cracks up.

"I designed a hologram technology so real, so lifelike, that it could convince even the keenest observer of its authenticity."

The room falls silent, ready to listen.

"Imagine the most highly skilled surgeon in the world able to operate on someone from the other side of the planet just by interacting with a hologram of the patient. That was what my technology could do. It required the hologram to be so precise, so exact, that to tell it apart from a real human you would need to run your hands through its light. It was from this technology that I created the Projectant Program."

"Projectant Program?" Locke asks. I can't believe he doesn't know this stuff. They've all been in here too long. My father studies his glasses and cleans each lens with a single swipe as he considers delving into the program he was forced to abandon.

"The Projectant Program." He sighs, his mind somewhere wonderful. "Not computer-controlled holograms but projections of *real* personality, using *real* thoughts of *real* humans."

The squad listens intently. At one time these ideas were like wild science fiction and people thought my father was insane, but his Projectants actually worked.

"Back before most of you were born, my Projectants were a serious consideration for what the EPO called Existence Extension. The idea that our minds could potentially continue to exist without the need for a physical body meant that the human race, in some form, would never become extinct. The female sex didn't need to die out if their minds could live forever."

Mouths hang open.

"But that was all BE," he says, bringing himself back into the room. "And before all of you." He chortles.

"Wait—what happened?" Locke calls, desperate for more information. "To the Projectants?"

"Once Eve was born, the Projectant Program was scrapped. All the focus turned to what was necessary to protect and nurture her."

"But, Dr. Wells—" Locke says.

"Perhaps we'll discuss the Projectant Program another time," my father interrupts, obviously wanting to get back on track. "Holly. Vivian feels it would be beneficial for the remaining Potentials to spend a little quality time with Holly, as a sort of stepping-stone to Eve." He finishes and looks around the room.

Silence.

"You want us to use Holly to flirt with these guys?" asks Jackson, looking confused.

"The virtual pimp returns," jokes Kramer.

"I ain't doing that shit," Jackson scoffs, ever the alpha male.

"Dude, you've made a career out of pretending to be a girl—get over it," Hartman heckles beside me, then slouches in his chair. I roll my eyes at him to shut up.

"When you've all quite finished, you'll find new briefing notes when you return to your dorms outlining the revised procedure with Potential Number Two. As usual, there will be no questions or debates. Thank you very much. You are all dismissed except Bram and Hartman. You two, remain in your seats, please." My father finishes the emergency briefing and the members of Squad H rise to their feet and file out of the room.

It's not unusual for me and Hartman to stay behind, which Jackson can't stand. I'm sure he's not the only one. I may not be the team leader, but my long history with Eve makes our connection more natural. I know her and she knows me. Or at least she knows my Holly. This means that occasionally Hartman and I are given different assignments from the rest of the squad.

My father walks toward us and leans against the back of the seat in front of us. I see myself in his face. Behind the deep wrinkles in his pale, drooping skin, under the wisps of gray in his hair, I'm there. It's almost unheard of in this day and age to know who your true father is, let alone have any sort of relationship with him. I'm lucky. Or at least that's how I'm supposed to feel.

It's how I used to feel when I'd wander the walkways of Central a few paces behind him, seeing the fatherless abandoned boys begging for scraps, back when we lived out there.

It's cloudy through the window of our apartment in the forest of concrete cloudscrapers. I'm young, four or five.

"Where's your bag?" my father barks. The gray hasn't appeared in his hair yet, but the wrinkles have begun to crease his face.

"Please! Don't take him—he's too young!" my mother screams, tears pooling in the wrinkles around her lower eyelids. "Take one of your others, one from the streets! Take any of them, but not my boy. Not my boy!"

My father pushes past her. Emotionless. "He is my son. He stays with me. You have a direct order from the EPO to hand him over. If you wish to say goodbye you must do it now," he barks.

My mother runs to me. Drops to her knees. She swallows hard and won't let the tears fall. "Never forget me, my son," she whispers, leaning her forehead on mine, letting her dark curly hair close like curtains around our faces as she breathes in, like she's smelling me. She lifts a silver chain from around her neck, pulls it over her head, and slips it over mine. A small cross swings from the bottom.

"That's enough!" My father pulls my mother out of the way and edges me out of the front door. Once it slides shut behind us I still hear her cry echoing in my mind.

"Bram, Hartman, how are you feeling?" my father asks.

Hartman shoots me a look.

"Huh? Sorry! I was . . . thinking. What did you say?" I stutter, forcing the memories out of my head. Lack of sleep must be catching up with me.

"Dr. Wells asked how we're feeling," Hartman says with a subtle squint of his eye in my direction. Dad never asks personal questions unless there's a specific reason. There's always a motive. For my father, a conversation is a scientific experiment to which he already has a desired result: he just needs to find the right method to achieve it. Right now he's trying kindness. It doesn't suit him. "I'm fine, sir," Hartman says. I nod in agreement.

"So, you're both fit and rested?" he probes. We look at each other and nod. "Then suit up and make your way to the studio. Eve is awake and expecting Holly." He drops a file on my lap and leaves the room.

I glance at Hartman. "Open it!" he says, so I peel off the red tape and open the brown folder.

A dozen photos slip onto my lap. Photos of Eve. She's wearing a white dressing gown, her wild hair is refusing to be tamed by the band holding her braids, and her face is red and blotchy. The room around her is completely trashed and the feathers from inside her pillow hang in the air.

Hartman states the obvious: "This must be after the meeting."

It's going to be a long night.

6

BRAM

THE LOCKER ROOM IS DESERTED. NO ONE ELSE IS WORKING SO late. It's me and Hartman. Just how we like it. I walk past my copilots' lockers—Jackson, Locke, Kramer, Watts. They'll all be back in their dorms, reading through their new assignments, but they'll be wondering what Hartman and I are up to.

It's nothing new, me and Hartman getting summoned out of hours for unscheduled meetings with Eve. Life isn't always predictable. Sometimes Eve needs us and we have to be there. Tonight is one of those nights. There's no agenda for Holly on tonight's assignment. She's simply going to be who Eve needs her to be—her friend.

There is no script. No key messaging. Pure improvisation. That's why I'm here, not Jackson or Kramer. They may outrank me, but they don't know Eve like I do. If Eve wants to talk about her childhood, I know it. I was there. They have to wait for Locke or Watts to load up a history file and find the information they require to have a successfully convincing conversation. Not me.

We open our lockers and I pull out my thin black kinetic

suit. It's well worn, but still as state-of-the-art as they come. Millions of microscopic sensors line flexible fabric, ready to capture my every movement. I strip naked and slip it on. It forms around my muscles like a second skin. Being a pilot requires a certain level of physical fitness, and the job itself keeps me in shape. It's demanding. I grab my visor, head-strap, and pressure gloves and turn to face Hartman, who's been busy programming tonight's assignment on his laptop on the bench next to me, a strip of red licorice poking out of his thick lips. His job is more mentally demanding than physical.

It takes two people to pilot Holly: the programmer and the pilot. Hartman is my programmer, my copilot. If Holly walks out onto the Drop and Eve grabs a jacket, Hartman programs one for me too, and it appears in Holly's hands. If Eve wants to gossip over a late-night snack, Hartman makes me a virtual mug of tea. He controls every aspect of Holly's appearance and everything she digitally interacts with during a session with Eve. Is he the best at it? Maybe not. He'd be the first to admit that. But he makes up for what he lacks by finding ways around the system. Are they always legal? Hell, no. But if it gets the job done the EPO are usually happy to overlook his hacking tendencies. They want results. They don't care how they get them.

My job? I am Holly. My movements, my mannerisms, my physicality: it's all captured by the hypersensitive pressure points that are woven into the kinetic suit. My facial expressions are analyzed, adapted, and applied to Holly's face in real time, as is my voice. When I'm suited up, I am Holly. When I enter the studio, two floors below the Dome, Bram stays at the door. This is my duty, my part in the future. I am Holly.

"I've loaded up the night program we used a few months back. It's not perfect, but it's the best I've got on short notice," Hartman says, swiveling his screen around to show me Holly's appearance, how Eve will see me.

"That'll work fine," I say, my mind already shifting. I'm numbing Bram's emotions, Bram's feelings. Switching off from my father, ignoring the ache in my neck from Jackson's fist. They are not Holly's issues; they are Bram's.

I am Holly.

We enter the darkened studio and I hear the electric hum of the scanners warming up, and the static electricity in the air emits small blue sparks on my visor as I slip it over my cropped dirty-blond hair. The room is large. Big enough to run in if I need to. It can simulate any event or environment that Holly might encounter in the Dome with Eve.

I flip the visor down in front of my eyes and prepare for connection. Whatever Holly sees up there, I see down here. Whatever I do down here, Holly does up there. We are connected. We are the same person. I am Holly.

"Okay, Holly is loaded and ready for connection." I hear Hartman in my earpiece. "Ready, Bram?"

I don't reply.

"Sorry . . . ready, Holly?" he corrects himself. Four years together and he still can't get the basics right.

"Ready. Idiot," I reply, and shoot him a look through my visor as he sits behind his control station illuminated by a subtle red light in the corner of the studio.

"Good luck. Rendering Holly now. Connection in three . . . two . . . one," he says in my ear as the Dome appears in front of me.

I look around at the dark greenery. I'm standing in the upper garden zone, a little walk from Eve's sleeping quarters, and I remember the night program Hartman has loaded from a few weeks back.

His voice crackles in my ear: "Sorry I forgot to change the location."

A few weeks ago Eve and I took a late-night stroll through the garden. She was anxious about the Potentials and wasn't sleeping well. Holly's assignment was to help her relax.

I walk past the trees and flowers as they glow in the blue light cast by the incredibly large full moon looming over my head on the other side of the hexagonal canopy. It's nothing like the real moon, more like the one you see in your dreams, the perfect kind that floats effortlessly, magically, over the world. This is Eve's moon.

I see the light from her room at the top of a small spiral staircase and walk up it. The studio floor beneath my feet reacts to what I'm doing and moves silently to simulate the experience of walking upstairs.

I reach the top and stand in front of a full-length glass door. I stop for a moment and take in my reflection. Pastel-pink pajamas. Natural blond hair with a subtle wave. Piercing green eyes. Thin lips and a pointy jaw make Holly elfishly pretty. Then my focus adjusts from my programmed pretty features to the naturally beautiful Eve.

I can see her sad eyes staring out at me. She hides her face in what remains of her pillow.

I press my thumb to my little finger, which holds Holly's position momentarily and mutes my voice from the Dome, allowing me to speak to Hartman without Eve hearing.

"Don't open the door," I tell him, pre-empting what he was about to do. *"She'll let me in."*

I release my fingers and raise a hand to tap on the glass. My kinetic gloves vibrate as I knock. It feels real.

I hear the sound of my simulated knock echo around the inside of Eve's small bedroom.

"Not tonight, Hols." Eve's voice is muffled by the pillow.

I don't reply. I give her a moment.

She turns her head and looks at me again. "I just want to—to be alone." She sniffs as more tears run sideways down her face.

"Come on, Eve. Let me in?" I ask.

She doesn't move. "I don't want to . . ."

"We don't have to talk. Let's just . . . sit," I suggest.

She looks at me. She's thinking. She knows I could just come in if they wanted me to. The doors can be unlocked with the click of a button. Everything can be controlled remotely in the Dome. But I like giving her the control. This is her place, not mine, not the EPO's.

"Eve, you can trust me. It's me," I say.

Through the translucent visor I see Hartman's head give me a look. Perhaps I emphasized *me* a little too much.

Eve looks more closely this time. She stares through the glass door into Holly's eyes. It's like she's looking through my visor and into my own.

She knows.

She immediately climbs down from her bed, steps over the mess she's created, and swings the glass door open. She raises her arms, places them around my neck, and sobs.

She can't feel me. Not *really*. Touching Holly is like touching a ball of static. They made us do it repeatedly at the academy.

It's warm, fizzy, but not real. We're not supposed to touch Eve physically. Vivian thinks it breaks the illusion of reality, but tonight's an exception. Tonight Eve needs it. She holds the weight of her own arms, places her cheek on my shoulder and accepts the sensation on her face. My suit reacts and lets me feel the weight of her and the soft tremor of her chest as she cries. My stomach jumps at this simulated embrace. Holding her: this isn't something many people get to do.

I say nothing and wait for her to run out of tears as we stand in the light of her moon.

"Let's walk," she says as she takes my hand and leads me down the staircase. I know where she's going, and as we reach the bottom step, I speed up to walk alongside her. We silently move through the greenery toward the opening in the canopy. I see the wind blow through the strands of her curly brown hair that have broken free of the braids and glance at my wrist. In a matter of seconds Hartman has understood my gesture, and the next time I look at my wrist a hairband is waiting there. I let go of Eve's hand for a moment, pull it off, and tie my blond hair away from my face to match hers as we step through the opening on to the Drop.

"So . . ." She sighs.

"Good day, then?" I say sarcastically.

"Fab." She smirks, giving me a thumbs-up. "All went according to plan. I can already hear those wedding bells."

I chuckle and she looks out over the sea of clouds below us. "It won't be like that again, Eve," I say.

"Won't it?" she asks. "You should have been there, Hols. He could barely look me in the eye. It was like my face was . . ." She stops and shakes her head.

"It wasn't anything to do with your face. It wasn't anything you did. It wasn't your fault in any way at all."

She looks at me in disbelief.

"This was a complete and utter screw-up by *them*." I nod toward the nearest camera invading our conversation. "And believe me, they know it! I mean, of course these guys are gonna be dumbstruck when they see you—you're the only girl on the planet! It's pretty obvious, if you ask me, and *they* should have taken that into consideration before marching you into a room with a Potential."

Eve smiles.

I know I shouldn't have referenced the camera or insulted the EPO's actions, but I have the authority here to do what needs to be done to gain Eve's cooperation.

"I don't think they're going to be happy with you saying things like that," Eve teases.

"Yeah, well, sometimes you've got to peel the stickers off the cube," I joke, and stick my middle finger up at the camera.

Eve cracks up and covers my hand with her own. "That's what you've always said."

"It's true."

She's back.

We sit on the Drop for hours as Eve's moon creeps overhead. We talk about life, about the world, the future, men, love, everything. She's interested, inquisitive, smart.

"So who's next?" she asks.

"I'm sorry?" I reply, wondering what she's talking about.

"Potential Number Two, who is he?"

"Oh. Erm, he's nice," I tell her, raising my eyebrows knowingly.

"Hmm."

"No, really. I think you'll like this one," I say as convincingly as I can, knowing that the next Potential is about as dull as cardboard.

"Why can't they just be like you?" She's taking in the view.

"Well, not everyone's perfect," I joke. "Besides, I think we'd find the whole repopulating-the-planet thing a little tricky, if you know what I mean!"

"No, I mean *you*," she says, turning to look straight through Holly's eyes, down two stories, past my visor, and into my own.

My heart stops. The hairs on my skin stand on end and I freeze. Is she talking to *me*?

I'm speechless. Completely blindsided. My mind slips from Holly and I'm myself, face to face with Eve.

She's never done this before.

"Bram!" I hear Hartman calling into my earpiece, snapping me back to reality, Eve's reality.

"Is it morning already?" Eve asks as we shield our eyes from the intense sunrise creeping over the distant horizon.

The answer is no. This is Vivian ending our meeting.

"I think you should get some sleep, Eve. Go back, shut the blinds, and rest. Forget about today. It won't happen again."

She looks into my eyes once more and I nervously tuck my hair behind my ears, forgetting that I've already tied it back. Shit, I'm shaking.

"Okay, night, Hols. Thanks," she says as she walks toward the doorway. She waves over her head as she yawns and disappears inside, leaving me alone on the Drop.

I turn and gaze at the sunrise, which hasn't moved since it first appeared. It's paused. I chuckle to myself as the display in my visor begins to fade and Hartman's voice irritates my eardrum.

"Disconnection in three . . . two . . . one. You're clear."

I sit on the floor, pull off the headset, and unzip my kinetic suit. I'm sweating.

"That girl's going to get us into trouble," I say as Hartman closes his laptop and walks over to where I'm slumped.

"No, she's not," he replies. "She's going to get *you* into trouble."

7

EVE

"AND ONE, TWO, THREE, FOUR, FIVE, SIX, SEVEN, EIGHT. BRUSH through the floor and into fifth. Lovely, Eve," says Mother Jacqui in her soothing voice, which she modulates to enhance the direction she's giving. Not only is she one of the youngest of the Mothers, but she's also the most agile—even though she's almost seventy she can still touch her toes and bring her foot up behind her ear. Until recently she could also outrun me. I'm not sure whether I've become faster or she's become slower, but either way, those qualities have made her responsible for Holly's and my physical education. This covers everything from swimming to ballet, netball to gymnastics, karate to running, all to keep me fit and active. To make sure my body is in full working order and prepared for what's to come.

I've never complained. There's no denying the release that comes with exerting myself. The buzz makes me feel alive as the blood rushes through me, into my fingers and toes, especially when I'm boxing: they hang up a bag and let me hook, jab, kick, and punch to the rhythm of the music. I always feel exhausted when I leave, and more alive than ever.

In contrast to the aggression I love in boxing, they give me dancing—which always leaves me exhilarated, sometimes even enchanted. Especially ballet, which is such an emotive form of storytelling. When I was younger I used to sit and watch Mother Jacqui twirl and spin around the room in awe.

I'm allowed to watch old footage of staged productions every now and then. They were grand affairs in huge theaters, where everyone got dressed up as though it was quite the event. I understand why. The emotion, the detail, the magic—a body can express so much in the way it moves. It takes me somewhere else. It's captivating.

I'm not at that level, but in many ways I *feel* like I am when I'm in class. In those moments, when I close my eyes, I'm transported. Not to a stage where I'm watched by an audience of thousands—I'm watched enough already—but to an empty auditorium where I perform only for me. Where I dance to the beat of my own drum. Occasionally I open my eyes and am surprised to be in the dance studio.

This is exactly what I've needed to calm my mind after the incident with Connor. In this room none of that matters.

I sense Holly behind me, breathing deeply after an intense class of pointe work. I always feel sorry for her in these classes. She's not a natural.

"Now bring your right arm up and over, and lean slowly into the barre." Mother Jacqui's voice is low and breathy as she demonstrates what she's asking of us. "Feel that *puuuuuull* . . . Keep your arm long, Holly."

Holly grunts in response.

"Plié and stretch," Mother Jacqui sings. "And lower into a révérence."

I do as she instructs, my body thankful as it bows into the curtsy and welcomes the end of the session.

"Well done." She smiles, giving a little clap, clearly happy with our progress. She walks to the corner of the room and pulls her uniform gray pants over her ballet tights, then slips her feet into her black shoes and her pale pink blouse over her head—plain except for the embroidered white logo to the left of her chest. This is the everyday uniform of the Mothers. It's practical and nondescript. That's another reason why I love to see Holly walking into a room; with her ever-changing wardrobe choices, she gives me something new to look at.

"That was a tough one," I puff once Mother Jacqui has left the room. I grab the barre with both hands, then lean over to lengthen my spine.

"You're improving," Holly says.

I look up to see her wearing a patronizing grin.

"They've been working me hard," I say matter-of-factly, straightening up. Holly's wearing an identical outfit to my own—pink tights and a black crossover leotard. "They've even made me have another go at Mandarin."

"Again? If you haven't mastered it by now you never will."

"Thanks for the encouragement."

"No, I . . . ," she falters. She never fluffs, which makes me think she pities me for what happened at the first encounter.

I clench my jaw. Then I open my mouth and out comes some broken Mandarin.

"What?" she asks, her brow dipping in confusion.

"Exactly." I laugh, amused that I managed to quote Sylvia Plath in Mandarin.

"Potential Number Two looks decent," she says, jumping on my good mood.

"He does," I say dismissively. Soon I have to meet Diego.

I was distraught after Connor. Holly came to see me afterward, but not *this* Holly. I can't be as open and raw with this one.

There are three Hollys. This is a fact that has never been confirmed or spoken about, but I know it's true. They look and sound the same, but aside from the minute differences in their eyes, there are also tiny traits that give them away and help me to tell them apart. This one talks *at* me, not *to* me. As though she knows best. Arguably she does know more than I do on subjects they like to keep from me, but still . . . It's irritating to see her enjoying that. She wears a permanent smirk. In my head I refer to her as Know-it-all Holly. She's the one I'm usually a little more cautious with.

Next there's I-concur Holly, who just agrees with everything I say, no matter how ludicrous. She usually joins me in my academic classes, but I hardly ever see her in my downtime.

And finally there's Holly. Just Holly. The one who's always been here. The one I trust above anyone I've ever met, even though I've never actually met her.

There were others too, before Know-it-all and I-concur, Hollys I formed heartfelt bonds with. I was sad to see them replaced, hurt that they'd been taken in that way. I think about them every so often and wonder what became of them.

As for these three, there's no denying I have my favorite, but I'm always pleased whenever Holly turns up. No matter which version she is, I'm always glad of her company. Even *this* one. Most of the time.

"What happened with Connor was unfortunate," she says,

choosing her words carefully while rearranging the strap of her leotard.

"Hmmm . . ."

It's a conversation I'd rather not have with her. I don't want to rehash it.

"I like his curly hair," I say quickly, turning her focus back on Diego, preferring the conversation to be steered forward rather than backward.

"I know, dark and gorgeous. It looks so soft."

Her comment is as pathetic as my own, but I ignore the voice in my head telling me so.

"He's good with numbers, apparently. And knows a lot about history," I tell her. Even though I hadn't been too keen to find out more about the next Potential, too embarrassed to go through it again so soon, he'd caught my attention when I heard of his interests.

"Really?"

"So I've been told. I wonder whether he studies the same history as us."

"Of course he does. What else would he study?" She laughs as though I'm daft.

"We study ancient history," I remind her, my tone flat.

"And?" she asks, as though anything that occurred after the Greeks and Egyptians is worthless.

"I wonder how it'll work," I mumble, fighting the urge to roll my eyes at her.

"Well, you've been talked through the new procedure." She almost tuts, as though she's irritated at having to explain it when Vivian already has. "You'll be wearing a veil this time and stay behind Mother Nina. I'll be up front leading the convers—"

"I meant me hearing of things I shouldn't know about the outside world," I interrupt.

"You know everything."

"You think?" I challenge, almost laughing at her statement.

"Did you see he's from Peru?" she asks, her eyebrows rising.

"And where are you from?"

She shakes her head disparagingly. "Don't make things so difficult, Eve."

"It was an innocent question," I shoot back, even though I know I'm pushing boundaries. "You've never told me," I mutter, sitting on the floor to take off my pumps, my toes reveling in their freedom.

Holly doesn't pander to me. Instead we stretch in silence until she deems that enough time has passed for her to probe again.

"Is there anything in particular you want me to ask him tomorrow?" she replies, taking us back to the topic they want her to focus on as she mirrors my action on the floor.

It's been decided Holly will sit in my place while I blend in with the Mothers and observe. It's an arrangement I'm more than happy with.

To blend.

To be a part of the Motherhood.

To be rid of the burden of being engaging and desirable.

"I'd like to know his first thought when he wakes up in the morning," I say. This was the one question I wanted to ask Connor before our meeting was cut short.

"Really?"

"Yes. That initial thought, when your eyes open and you take in a new day, cannot be controlled," I say, pulling my ankles into my bottom and enjoying the tug on my inner thigh muscles. "It's pure. I wonder if he wakes up feeling lucky to be alive or grateful for the earth's beauty . . ."

Holly looks perplexed.

"That's okay to ask, right?"

I rarely ask her advice, not this one, but on this occasion the bewilderment on her face leads me to do so.

"You can ask whatever you like," she says softly. "What's your first thought? In case he asks in return."

"Each morning I open my eyes to the most beautiful sunrise. I see the wonder that is nature and experience a thrill at the thought of being the one who can keep us here."

Holly nods, seemingly in a daze, her gaze fixed on her ankles.

"That thrill quickly turns into an overwhelming weight of responsibility, and I long to go back to sleep," I admit, revealing a touch more bitterness than I mean to.

"I'll leave that bit out," she says flatly.

"If you like." I get to my feet. "I'd better go. I have to shower before we have the next round of Mandarin."

"I'll see you there," she calls as I leave the room.

Holly will.

She won't.

8

EVE

A BONY HAND SQUEEZES MY SHOULDER, WAKING ME. AS I OPEN my eyes I'm confused to find Mother Nina hovering above me. Her mouth stretches wide while her cheeks wrinkle into a smile. In my sleepy state she's like an angel, her snow-white hair illuminating the top of her head like a halo in the darkness.

Darkness.

The observation startles me as I look past her to the sky outside. It's pitch black, not the dawn I'm used to being greeted with. It's nighttime. Somewhere between yesterday and tomorrow. Tomorrow. Today . . . It's almost time to meet the second Potential.

But not just yet.

"Come," Mother Nina whispers, waving an armful of clothes at me.

I frown, taking in the scene, my brain slow. "But the meeting?" I find myself mumbling.

"We'll be back in time."

"We're going out?" I ask in surprise, waking up properly.

Mother Nina smiles, confirming my conclusion.

I throw back the covers, energized at this unexpected turn of events. It takes me seconds to get dressed in the black top and joggers she has selected for me. I don't wait for her to fuss as she usually does. I reject our usual formalities.

I want to go.

As soon as I finish tying the shoelaces on my trainers I turn to Mother Nina with a nod, letting her know I'm ready.

She leads me to the steps out of my bedroom, down the stairs, through the dimly lit gardens, and to the elevator. I've rarely been out here at this hour. The place seems eerily quiet without the other Mothers milling around and getting on with their daily tasks. The silence is almost deafening.

I take a deep breath as the doors close on us and the elevator drops. The descent feels never-ending, as though we're going down for ages. But, of course, we are. We're going down, down, down to the ground. Down to the outside world. Something in my chest expands at the thought, my lips stretching into a smile that I try to suppress.

The doors open onto the cold gray collection bay—not quite outside in the elements, but it's one step closer. The chill of the morning air is tickling my cheeks.

Ketch is standing at attention next to a black car. Its solid back door has been left open for us to climb inside. We do so willingly, longingly, expectantly.

It's always like this. I'm happy and content in the Dome—of course I am—but when I think of being outside I long to explore a world I rarely see. A hunger bubbles up and I want to ingest as much as I can before they take me back to the home they chose for me.

Once Mother Nina and I are in our black leather seats,

Ketch shuts the door with a bang, putting us into darkness, thanks to the windowless bubble we're caged in. The inside of the car becomes a heavily padded cell. Within seconds subtle lights fade up, allowing us to see a little more—although there's not much to look at.

Sitting in our comfortable spots at the back, we hear Ketch getting into the driver's seat and closing the door with a dull thud. That tells me it's just the three of us: our trip isn't a big state affair. It's more personal—special and intimate. My heart sings at the realization of where we're going.

The car moves forward and I hug myself because I know we're on our way to the happiest of places. I envisage us moving away from the Dome, through the city and the towns on its outskirts, enjoying the way my body sways as Ketch turns corners or hits the brakes. The rhythm is calming yet thrilling. I lean my head back and close my eyes.

As usual we seem to drive for hours, which makes me wonder what time it is if we need to get back for the next encounter. I don't ask Mother Nina. I don't want her cutting our trip short or, worse, changing her mind and having us turn back before we reach our destination. It's been so long since they last brought me here.

The roads beneath us become more uneven—I can feel it in the way the car moves. What's more, I recognize the dips and turns. We're getting closer. Eventually we slow down. We stop. My heart flutters.

The mechanics keeping me in the back of the car moan as Ketch opens the door and sets me free. It's not as dark as it was when Mother Nina woke me. The sky is lightening. It must be nearing dawn now.

I climb out, feeling the crunch beneath my feet as my shoes hit the gravel. The sound causes my lips to twitch into a smile. While I step away from the vehicle I breathe in the familiar smells of jasmine, rose, bluebell, and lily of the valley wafting around me. I hear birds chirping and water trickling, which fills me with joy.

I've been coming here for years. Vivian brought me here first. When we got into the car she revealed they'd found me a garden outside, a place in the real world that was for me alone. When she first told me, I didn't care what it looked like. It could've been a patch of dirt, for all I cared. I was simply overwhelmed that a patch of something out here was going to be mine. I was blown away when I arrived to find a meadow in full bloom, with a stream trickling through the middle.

I asked why they'd allowed me to come here, but all the while I couldn't stop smiling as I took it all in. I could tell Vivian was pleased by my reaction. I was so grateful that I hugged her. She let me, and whispered into my hair that it was all for me. All mine.

We ran through the shrubs and played for hours. I can picture Vivian here, smiling, as we played hide-and-seek. I hear our laughter, rising to the leaves high above. I felt closer to her than ever before.

She's not been back here with me since, even though I know she felt as I did. Her joy wasn't faked or forced. It was genuine. She was kind, friendly, and affectionate. But after that day she distanced herself from me. A veil dropped between us and she became an authority figure, judging my every move. Our day here together has become a memory I find myself questioning. It was so different from how we are now.

Holly has never come either, but that makes sense, of course. She couldn't. She wouldn't function in the open air of the real world. The Drop is her limit.

I open my eyes and keep walking. I lose myself in the leafy green, the comfort of the scent, and the sound of running water. When I get to the stream I drop to the ground. The air seems richer here, damp and dewy in the morning light that's slowly creeping upon us. I sit and listen, watching the birds fly overhead. The trees dance in the breeze, and the water ripples.

In the Dome I have the Drop to escape to. I love it up there, perched above the clouds with Holly at my side. Here, amid nature, I feel less isolated but stronger than ever. I'm empowered to do all I can to ensure that humanity survives, surrounded by such beauty. This is nature's doing. Here, no one prunes the overgrown bushes, like we do in the Dome. Instead everything's allowed to grow as it likes. It flourishes of its own accord. Sometimes I feel I'd like to be a single bloom here. A rose allowed to follow her own course . . .

Mother Nina has followed me from the car and perched behind me. Her eyes are closed as she too loses herself in the tranquility of a peaceful morning setting. What must it be like for her to be so far from the world she grew up in? At least I don't know anything different.

Her forehead creases in thought, half a dozen lines becoming deeper than usual. Perhaps a memory from that time long ago.

"Thank you for bringing me here."

She nods, her eyes remaining shut. We stay like that for a few moments until she says, "I've got a gift for you." She pulls a little package, wrapped in brown paper, from her bag.

"A book?" I predict with excitement. I've always imagined that books out here are like the clothes they give me in the Dome, a gargantuan quantity just waiting for me. They don't give me a limitless stream of books. I know they hold some back from me, because most of the ones I've read were written hundreds of years ago—I've made a note of their publication dates. I've not read anything written within the last seventy years or so, maybe more.

I asked about it once. I wanted to know why there was such a gap in literature. Naturally I was curious—there is so much I don't know. Vivian told me that many decades before, technology had taken over, so there had been no need to produce actual books. But that was all. I've learned to be thankful for what I receive and keep certain thoughts in my head. Greed is an ugly sin and I know I should want no part of it . . . yet I experience a surge of joy when I receive something new.

"It's not a book, exactly," she says.

"Oh?"

"Well, it is, it's just . . . Open it."

I laugh at her uncharacteristic loss for words and rip apart the paper eagerly.

"What's this?" I ask, inspecting the object in my hands. It's more like a notebook, like the ones I use in the schoolroom, although with its black leather finish it's far more luxurious.

My hand grips its spine while I thumb the pages, glimpsing what's inside. My heart stops at the handwriting.

"It's your mother's," Mother Nina says quietly.

I turn to the first page and a lump forms in my throat.

• • •

Letters to my baby, by Corinne Warren.

You don't know me yet, but I am your mother. You might not call me Mother, you might choose Mama, Mommy, or Mom—but whichever it is will more than suffice. I can't wait to hear you call to me. I can't wait to see you grow. But more than anything, I can't wait to hold you in my arms and to know you're safe.

My life will be complete when you're in the world with your father and me, but until then this is a little gathering of letters from me to you, from mother to babe.

"Why haven't I seen this before?" I ask.

Mother Nina's face is pensive but stern. "It's best to focus on the fact that you have it *now*, Eve. Please learn that not all battles should be fought, especially those that start with good intentions."

I look back to the book in my hands and run my fingers over my mother's words. Words she wrote for me to read. I could sit and read all of it in one go, thinking about how her hand must have glided across the page as she dreamed of our future together. I could soak up every little detail of who she was, what she wanted for me, and ponder whether anything has been realized, but I don't want to rush through the only tangible thing that's passed between us. The opening paragraph is enough for now. I place the book against my chest and hold it there. I feel more complete, almost whole.

I take Mother Nina's hand in mine, stroking her thin and wrinkled skin with the other. She may not be my real mother, but she is here and has bridged the gap.

This isn't how I'd expected the day to start, but I'm glad it has.

Time passes while I enjoy the setting, the warmth of Mother Nina's hand in mine, and the feeling of promise that swells inside me at the thought of what awaits me.

For once, everything feels real.

9

EVE

I FALL ASLEEP IN THE CAR ON THE WAY BACK, WHICH ISN'T SUR-prising in view of the early start, the overload to my senses of being outside, and the emotion that's flooded me.

The first thing I do when I'm back in my room, sitting on my bed, is open the book of letters, reread the first paragraph, kiss the page, and bury it under my pillow. I'm desperate to carry on, but it's getting late. The Mothers will come in soon to get me ready and I don't want them seeing it or talking about it. Not yet. For a second I find myself wondering whether Vivian knows I've got it, but, of course, she knows everything. Does that matter? That's a question for another day. I have been handed an unexpected gift from my mother. In lots of ways wise old Mother Nina was right about choosing where to channel my energy. My chest swells at the thought of coming back to my mother's handwriting a little later, but now I must focus on the day ahead and the encounter with Potential Number Two.

The Mothers enter en masse and start to get me ready. It's noticeably calmer than last time. There's less of a buzz as they go about their tasks. Or perhaps I'm setting the tone: I'm more relaxed than before. Being at the stream has conquered my nerves, and the gift of my mother's words has propelled me into the day ahead. I'm eager for the meeting, of course, but I'm looking forward to afterward and spending time alone with my mother's notebook.

Perhaps the Mothers are mirroring what I'm projecting. We fall into silence as I'm handed a pretty dress, similar to the one I wore for my last meeting. Only this time it's hidden beneath the uniform of the Mothers. Similarly, my hair is styled and then hidden. My makeup is perfected.

As Mother Nina pins my headscarf into place she lets out a sigh of dismay. My longest-serving friend has been pensive since we got back. Her wrinkled face is a little tighter than usual, making her look almost stern. Something is on her mind—that's not an expression I'm used to seeing on her.

"It's such a shame to be covering you," she mumbles, the hooded skin over her eyes creasing further.

"It's only for the first meeting," I say reassuringly, our roles reversing as I try to put her mind at ease. We've had a great morning and I'm buoyed on the strength of it.

"It's just so unnatural this way," she continues in no more than a whisper, her face screwing up in agitation.

"Can we really call any of this natural?" I ask, my voice low and measured.

"Maybe not," she agrees, gently brushing my cheek. The affectionate gesture makes me smile.

Her disappointment in the change of procedure is understandable. After last time, I know how much these meetings mean to the Mothers: I saw their disappointment etched on their faces and heard it in Mother Nina's sobs. Not only are these encounters a promise of the future, they're a reminder of the past.

The thought of the outside world creates fire at my core. Soon Mother Nina's old world could be a part of my future if the final encounters go well. Reading my mother's letters has brought an excitement, belief, and renewed sense of hope for what's to come.

"Where did you meet your husband?" I ask.

Mother Nina takes a deep breath as she debates whether to answer or not.

"Go on," I whisper.

"At a bar in the city," she blurts before she can stop herself. She blushes as she turns to the dressing table and busies herself with packing away her beautifying tool kit. "It was before they stopped allowing us into such places."

"Why did they stop you?"

"They thought it wasn't a good idea. They were right," she concedes, snapping shut an eye shadow to emphasize her point.

"What was it like? When you first met?" I sit on my bed, unsure that I'll get a response. I want to hear more now that she's started to open up. She's talked of her husband before, of course. Just little bits here and there—enough for me to know how smitten they were and how heartbroken she was to lose him. That's the thing about the Mothers: the majority are here because they have a tragic tale to share, although they rarely tell it. Not to me, anyway. I know she loved and lost, and that her loss brought her to me. To have Mother Nina, who knows so much about me, telling me more about herself has me rapt.

"It was electric," she says plainly, flinching as she lets the memories in. "I knew there was no way I was leaving that night without the promise of seeing him again. He asked me to marry him two weeks later."

"Two weeks?" I gasp.

She giggles. "It was a different time. It felt good to be spontaneous. Even though . . ." She trails off, her face caving just a little. "I still wouldn't change it. We were born to be together. Even if it ended far sooner than it should have. His heart was mine, and mine his. My life became full because of him."

"It sounds so romantic."

"It was," she whispers, zipping up the last bag and looking me over once more. Her face is serene despite the sadness. "He made my life full, but you've made it complete. The future will be filled with connections like that because you're here and doing what you're doing. Thank you," she adds. "Look for that special something, Eve. Seek out love . . . Or, rather, allow love to seek out you."

I smile at her. What is love? I've read about it in books and expressed it in dance classes while stretching my limbs, but what does it feel like?

"Our girl," Mother Nina says, reaching over and stroking my cheek so that I'm looking directly at her. "You're everything we could've wished for, far more than we prayed for. Now, let's go."

She turns away. I follow her out of the room and stand in my new position within the formation, behind Mother Nina, in front of the other silent Mothers. This time there's no muttering of excitement. Rather, it's as if there's a job to do, and everyone wants to execute it to perfection.

I hear a rustle of clothing as faces are obscured.

I follow suit, my fingers clumsy with the fabric.

We go.

Ketch and his team are waiting for us when we walk out of the elevator, causing a wave of heat to crawl up my neck to my face as I have a flashback to my meeting with the first Potential. The sight of them makes me feel ashamed and embarrassed. Even though I know they can't be, I feel like they're all staring at me, maybe even sniggering.

As we walk past their formation an urge comes over me and I steal a glance at the closest guard. It's something I've never done before, but today I can't help it. Curiosity and paranoia force my eyes toward the stranger whose job is to protect me. He's young, maybe a couple of years older than me. He's incredibly tall, with dark hair and a muscular physique, his cheeks chiseled, his eyes focusing straight ahead. It's like he's unaware I'm just a few feet away from him.

He blinks and swallows, his Adam's apple jolting upward. Then, as though he can sense someone looking at him, his eyes flick nervously in my direction and lock with mine.

I gasp, my whole body tensing in alarm.

That wasn't meant to happen.

That isn't *allowed* to happen.

"Everything okay?" Mother Nina whispers.

"I must have a stray pin in my dress or something," I lie as I rub my thigh, taking a deep breath to steady my pounding heart.

I've certainly been testing the rules lately, but taking a toy onto the Drop and challenging Holly are nothing in comparison to disregarding orders put in place to keep us all safe.

"Want me to look?" Mother Nina offers, slowing her pace. There's a scuffle behind us as the rest of the Mothers realize that something's occurred. I hear Mother Kimberley apologize and Mother Tabia tut.

"No. I'm fine," I mutter, her kindness adding to my guilt.

We press on. This time I keep my eyes on the floor in front of us because I'm scared of them landing on anyone else.

As before, Vivian steps out of her spy hole and strides over as soon as we're outside the chosen meeting room, the heels of her boots making hardly any sound on the marble floor.

"Are you clear on everything?" she barks.

"Yes. Let Holly do the talking."

"Correct." She sniffs. "She'll enter once you're seated. Diego doesn't know you're here. He thinks it's another training exercise before the meeting later. To reiterate from our earlier discussion, do not let yourself be known until I say so."

She's always telling me what to do, and I hate that. This is my encounter, my Potential. None of this would be happening if I didn't exist. Vivian used to understand that, but now she's nothing like the woman who chased me through the meadow. Instead it's sometimes as though she looks at me with disgust, and I'm not sure how to process that shift.

"I'll be watching," she says, gesturing for Ketch to open the door and let the meeting commence. "Go."

Diego is shorter than I imagined. This is the first thing I notice as I walk into the room. He's not far off my height. His skin is rough and dark, his eyes small and beady. He wears a plain white shirt over brown pants with matching brown leather shoes. His mustard blazer gives him an earthy appearance, as though he's at one with nature. I like that. He's also wearing a straw hat, trimmed with a wide length of red fabric and a piece of white ribbon to keep it in place. It jars with the rest of his outfit. I've seen something similar in history books, so I imagine it has something to do with his Peruvian heritage. It's touching that he's honoring his ancestors.

He doesn't look nervous like Connor did. He looks controlled and centered. He barely moves as we all enter.

Shuffling in as one of the Mothers is entirely different from walking in as myself. It's the first time I've been *part* of the group rather than *with* it, which makes me sad: this is an isolated occasion, and soon I'll just be Eve again. Diego doesn't even register our existence. I'm not used to that: Eve gets pandered to wherever she goes. To be ignored is an alien sensation. It's a little thrilling to go unnoticed. To blend.

We find our seats quickly and without fuss.

"I hope you've not been waiting long," Holly calls as she enters the room wearing a floor-length pink gown and cream wedge heels.

My heart soars when I see the subtle, delicate glint behind her eyes—my Holly. I wasn't sure which one it would be, but now that I've seen her I know this'll go smoothly, that we're all in safe hands.

Diego shrugs despondently.

"Did you have a nice dinner last night?" Holly asks, not discouraged, as she sits on the chair opposite him with her back to us.

"Richer than I'm used to, but it was food," Diego replies, his voice lacking any warmth or kindness. Perhaps he's annoyed at having to speak to Holly again rather than meeting me. Or, like myself, he may not be in the mood for small talk, with the weight of humanity's future on his shoulders. Either way, it's surprising he hasn't succumbed to Holly's upbeat personality. She always puts a smile on my face.

"Let's use this as a rehearsal for later, shall we?" She's clearly trying to warm him up so that this meeting isn't another waste of time. It's funny being in the room like this, knowing that Holly is working for Vivian. I wonder if they're communicating in some way and whether they use the same tactics when they're with me. The thought sobers me a little. I look to Diego and will him to perk up, to give us something.

"Let's pretend that I'm Eve," continues Holly. "Feel free to talk to me as you'd talk to her. You can use this time to practice."

Diego's eyes go from Holly and drift to the floor in front of the Mothers and me. His gaze trails along our line of shoes and continues to the steel-toed boots of the other males in the room. The action makes my breath catch in my throat.

"It is a pleasure to meet with you," he says slowly, his words clear through his thick accent.

He lifts his eyes so that they're back on Holly, his face relaxing.

"That's better," Holly says, and I hear the smile in her voice, a look Diego mirrors as one side of his mouth inches up a fraction.

"Forgive me, this is new for me," he says, shaking his head.

"This is new for everyone." Holly laughs kindly. "None of us really know what we're doing, so let's just keep this casual and friendly. Yes?"

Diego nods and shifts in his seat, getting himself into a comfier position.

She's won him over, as I knew she would.

"Tell me about your life in Peru."

"I study math and history. I like learning."

"That's good. Eve is always picking up new skills and knowledge. It's good you have that in common," she sings.

It's odd hearing her talk about me as though I'm not in the room. I can't help but wonder what else she's going to tell him about me.

"I have a family," he goes on.

"Yes."

"Four brothers," he continues. "Our family owned a farm. The crops died. Our animals died."

"Sorry to hear that."

"My father died," he says without emotion—perhaps because he doesn't want to break down in a roomful of strangers. Even though I didn't know my own parents, I still feel full of sorrow that they're not here with me. "I study and learn to help my family," he continues earnestly. "I want a good job."

"That's great. It's always important to be ambitious."

"That I am," he concurs.

"How did you find the process of becoming a Potential?" Holly asks, tilting her head to one side while her elbows slide across the desk, moving her closer to Diego. It's a look she gives me when she wants me to confide in her—so open, friendly, and sympathetic. "I imagine it hasn't been easy so far. Perhaps your ambition has helped."

I know very little about how the three Potentials were selected. Genetic compatibility, of course, psychological profiling, physical studies, beliefs perhaps—I imagine they were subjected to every possible testing method the EPO could think of to whittle the population down to the chosen few. However, studying Diego, a simple man who doesn't seem extraordinary in any way, it's hard to imagine what they saw in him. Or what attributes they felt would be beneficial to any future offspring.

"I studied hard," Diego agrees, propping his elbows on the table and resting his chin in his palms. "This is an honor. To be here. To be chosen. I've taken it very seriously. I've prayed. Asked for guidance. Become all I can be," he says passionately, now spreading his hands across his chest. "Earth needs us to be strong. To give ourselves over for the cause."

In appearance Diego is small and uninteresting, but inside him there's a fire that draws me to him. His words are impassioned. He makes sense.

"What is your first thought when you wake up in the morning?"

I stop breathing as my question is asked, longing to hear his answer.

"I think of my father. How proud he would be to see me here. He taught me that in life we must seize every opportunity. I wake in the morning wanting to make him proud. He had courage. A strong heart. I am the same. I will always be grateful to him."

So he does think regularly of his loss.

I think of my own parents once more, and the book of letters hidden in my room. I have no idea if I inherited my mother's eyes or my father's love of all things sweet, but I'm about to find out. Soon I'll know what their dreams were for me. I hope that one day I too will be able to think of my parents and know that I have made them proud.

I catch myself absentmindedly rubbing the scar on my wrist. My father.

I stop myself and slowly place my hands on my thighs.

When I look up, Diego is gazing at me.

"Planet Earth is fragile. It needs us to fulfill our duties," he continues.

"Indeed, we all have a role to play," says Holly, with a beaming smile.

"I want to help her."

"Earth?" Holly asks, sounding confused. "Mother Nature?"

"Eve," he corrects as he hangs his head toward us seated ladies. "I know she's here. I know she's heard what I've said."

My breath catches in my throat. I want to hear more from this unlikely character.

"Together we can make a difference," he goes on, his hand softly tapping at his heart. "Together we can ensure the future for humanity as it should be. Eve, tell me you're here. Stand and show me. Tell me you want the same as I do."

I inhale deeply, his words touching me and holding me captive, my body aching to move in agreement.

"I do," Mother Nina declares unexpectedly, sensing that I was about to speak. Her veiled chin rises with youthful pride, imitating me.

I sense all eyes in the room turning to my impersonator, taking everyone by surprise as she steps beyond duty to protect my identity.

I glance back into the center of the room just as Diego's empty seat crashes to the floor. He's no longer there. Instead he looms over Mother Nina and stops her from standing tall.

My heart freezes as I see her head jolt violently, his hands gripping her throat and squeezing the soft flesh.

Screaming fills the room. I've never heard a sound like it before. Now that she's weakened, his hands move to either side of her beautiful face, jolting her around so that she's facing us, her friends, her family—watching in horror. Not one of the dozen armed members of Ketch's security team can get to her in time. In one swift movement he grabs her by the mouth and wrenches her jaw skyward. Her eyes lock onto mine as they bulge in pain. Fear. Relief.

Before I can get to her, two strong arms grab me from behind, hands covering my mouth, stifling the scream as I'm dragged away from the horror unfolding before me.

10

BRAM

I LOSE SIGHT OF EVE IN THE COMMOTION. I YANK OUT MY EAR-
piece and drop it on the studio floor to stop Hartman's yelling
at me. *Focus, Bram.*

My heart pounds under the kinetic suit as I scan the encounter room through my visor, and my eyes catch the lifeless
body of Mother Nina and the hands that are still around her
throat. The Mothers are beating helplessly at Diego, but their
frail, seventy-year-old fists make no impression on him.

Half of Ketch's security team are uselessly clicking the
triggers on their weapons. Idiots. Every gun in the building is
chipped, programmed not to fire when pointing at Eve.

Eve. Where is she?

I jump the table and move Holly through the mass of veiled
women. As I scan the chaos I see her.

Her blue eyes flash in my direction through the thin strip
of her black veil. One of Ketch's men has his arms around her
waist and is pulling her away from the danger, out of the line
of fire, so the weapons will reactivate and eliminate the threat.

When I turn back, Diego's face is barely a meter away from

my own. He is muttering something under his breath, sounds like a prayer. He's not fazed by the chaos around him, by the armed men scrambling frantically toward him through the sea of Mothers. He is focused as he releases his grip and pulls off the veil, revealing the face of the woman he's killed.

His muttering stops.

He has failed.

He drops the body and lunges at the nearest veiled Mother. He knows Eve is still in the room.

There is a sudden metallic click that echoes around the walls. Every gun is armed—Eve is out of the line of fire.

I turn back in time to see her hands clawing at the open door as she's pulled from the room toward the elevator—but not before she witnesses the execution of Potential Number Two.

The room lights up as a dozen guns open fire on Diego. I only see it through the reflection in Eve's horrified eyes before she's dragged into the corridor.

Run, Bram.

I bolt as fast as Holly can be projected, ignoring every obstacle in her way, moving through the table and chairs, through the Mothers and Ketch's security team, taking full advantage of being made of light. My kinetic suit pulses and vibrates, indicating the objects and people I'm running through, but I ignore it. This is no time for illusion.

I reach the hallway in time to see the elevator doors closing on Eve and her guardian.

My heart stops at what I'm seeing. Everything about this is wrong. Eve backs into the edge of the small, spherical space, terror on her face.

The security officer is staring at the doors, visibly willing them to close faster. His eyes flick up and lock with my own.

In that fraction of a second I read his thoughts. It's as though all his inner demons scream at me, revealing the true intention of his rescue.

The doors close on them as I bolt toward the elevator, arms reaching out for Eve. I'm two feet away when it begins to descend, a deafening shriek from inside making the walls vibrate.

"Holly!"

11

EVE

HER NAME RINGS IN MY EARS AS MY VOICE REVERBERATES around the elevator, my throat hoarse from terror as I stare at the closed doors between us. I'm too disoriented to tell which direction we're moving. Up, down—it makes no difference, as we barely have time to travel anywhere before I see his hand reach out for the emergency stop lever, halting us. We're suspended between floors. We're alone.

I cower. Squeeze myself into the elevator's wall and will the metal to absorb me. I shouldn't be here. I should still be in the meeting, hearing all about the Potential they carefully selected for me. I should still be in that room.

That room.

Diego.

Mother Nina.

My body convulses, jerking me forward as I gag.

No time to dwell. No time to think.

Not now.

I look at the black boots as they turn in my direction.

It's him. The one from before. The one I looked at. The one

who looked at me. He grabbed me around the waist. Dragged me out of that room. Pulled me to safety.

Safety.

When his hands first found me I thought that was the case. I thought it was part of another plan I'd not been briefed on, but there was too much going on. Too much commotion, too much confusion. I was veiled, blended. Some of them might've thought she *was* me, but he knew where I was as he peeled me away from my friend and the bloody chaos.

My eyes slowly travel over his boots, his uniform to his heaving chest.

"Take off your veil," he says, swallowing hard, his fingers clenching.

"No," I whimper, my voice barely audible.

His hand reaches up and snatches it away, causing the fabric to rip.

I look up at him then. The relief, delight, pleasure, and horror crossing his face tell me he wasn't part of Diego's plan, that he acted spontaneously, but also reveal that it wasn't part of anyone else's plan either. Not Ketch's or Vivian's, the company's, or even his own.

He looks as surprised and confused as I feel, which frightens me.

"What are you going to do to me?" I'm trembling with fear—hoping the imploring look on my face will stop him from spoiling me, stealing the part of me that's not meant for him. Vivian has told me of men's natural instinct. It's their weakness. I used to have special classes with her. I've known of our physical differences for quite some time, and of what our bodies will have to do to bring about the rebirth. It's a sacred act, yet one that men yearn for through no fault of their own. It's why we're kept apart, why I'm never put into situations like this. They want the rebirth, but it must be done in the correct way.

I stare at the man before me. He doesn't look evil or deviant, although right now it's hard to see any softness. He's big. He's strong and solid. I felt the tightness of his grip when he pulled me from the chaos, and I'm aware that he could hurt me. I'm not sure I have the power to stop him.

He frowns at me as his tongue wets his lips. Perhaps, I think, he's still torn between logic, duty, and his human desire. His apparent doubt spurs me on.

"It's not worth it," I say, my voice quiet. I try to remain calm and composed, even though I can feel my heart pounding frantically against my ribs.

"Isn't it?" he growls, rocking on the heels of his feet.

"You saw what happened up there." I wish I could create some distance between us so that I can't feel his hot breath hitting my face. "You saw what they did to him. They'll do the same to you. Eventually."

He gives me a quizzical look.

He lifts his hands slowly, his fingertips moving over my clothes. They stop below my throat. For a split second I think he's about to complete Diego's mission and throttle me, but instead I hear the pop of a clip, and the fabric around my head drops. I stop breathing when his hands move to cup my face and he leans closer, his eyes shutting as he breathes me in, releasing a sound of pleasure.

"Your smell. It's so—"

"You shouldn't be doing this," I interrupt.

"Doing what?"

"This. You shouldn't be here with me. They forbid it."

"I was protecting you."

"Were you?"

"Yes. Of course." His face is ashen as he lowers his head, his hands moving away from my face and down to the uniform of the Mothers, which he fingers in distaste. "You shouldn't be in this."

He releases each button with deep concentration. He sucks in a new lungful of air when the dark khaki material falls away, revealing my dress.

I am Eve.

I stand a little taller and he bows his head, although I'm uncertain whether he does so out of habit or respect. Maybe it's a bit of both.

"What's your name?" I ask, his action making me feel more confident.

"Turner," he replies, his face seeming kinder than before, the hardness in his eyes dissipating.

"Your first name?" I push. I know the Mothers by their given names and it occurs to me that this was probably because it seems more familiar and caring.

"Michael."

"Michael," I repeat. "How long have you worked here?"

"Years."

I nod. "Thank you for keeping me safe during that time. I know—"

"I wouldn't have hurt you," he interrupts. His forehead creases in concern as his eyes search mine. "I swore an oath to protect you. I meant it. I would never—could never . . . I had to get you out of there."

My breathing becomes a little easier. For years it's been drummed into me that this is wrong. That I cannot look. Must not look or interact. They told me nothing good could come of it. They made me fearful of the devil within our ranks . . .

"Thank you," I breathe, deciding to believe him. "I'm glad you did."

And there she is in my mind, surrounded by everything that crashed into my life mere moments before I got into this elevator. Mother Nina, Diego, and that room flash before my eyes. Grief and horror consume me and I feel powerless.

"What's going on?" I whimper. A sob escapes. A cry. A wail.

Michael puts an arm around my shoulders and guides me into his embrace. I don't feel fearful of the action. I want it. I need it. I'm thankful for it. I gain comfort from it.

One thought echoes through my mind: Mother Nina is gone, and it's all because of me.

I failed her.

12

BRAM

I'M RUNNING. NO, I'M SPRINTING. I'VE NEVER MOVED SO FAST IN my entire life. Hartman can barely keep up as we fly through the locker room. I rip the visor from my face and cast it to the ground, where it skitters across the metallic hallway outside the studio.

Sirens are screeching. Emergency lighting casts deep red streaks across the smooth walls as we round the corner toward the elevator shaft. I can still see that last image of Eve reaching out to Holly, to me, before the doors closed on her . . . on *them*.

She's inside the metal ball with that guard. That soldier. That *man*. Alone.

All at once I think of every possibility. Every outcome. Every eventuality.

I need to get to Eve.

I feel a tidal wave of adrenaline roll through my body.

I *must* get to Eve.

My eyes see only the elevator. My body slams against the cold metal-and-glass doors, but I feel nothing. I push my fingers into the thinnest crack between them, the metal frame ripping through the pressure gloves still covering them. These doors are designed not to be breached.

"You won't get them open like that," Hartman yells as he arrives next to me. I ignore him and keep trying to pry the doors open with my fist.

"They're magnetically sealed, Bram!" he continues as he unravels wires from something small and electronic. "Do something useful and unscrew the cover—" He stops mid-sentence, interrupted by the sound of me tearing the metallic front panel off the wall like it's made of cardboard. "Or that works too."

He begins to replace the wires with more from the device in his hands. As the last clicks into place, he punches a button on the box in his hands and we hear the elevator spring to life behind the thick transparent doors.

Hartman and I catch each other's eyes, both trying not to think about what we might find when those doors open.

I bounce on the spot as my mind tries to analyze the situation.

An armed soldier has kidnapped the most precious human on the planet, is now trapped in a confined space with her—and we are about to confront him. The very future of our species depends on what we do next. We are unarmed and I'm wearing skintight Lycra. If he's hostile we're screwed.

"Where is it?" I snap at Hartman, looking through the sheets of glass, waiting for the spherical chamber to appear. It's taking forever. He looks at the display on the device he wired into the wall.

"Three floors away. Two . . . one . . ." He stops as we hear the soft swish of the approaching elevator. Then we see it descend on the other side of the doors, its chromatic outer walls distorting our reflections as it halts in front of us.

There are no voices inside.

No screams.

My heart stops as my brain flashes horrific images of the worst possible outcome. I shake them out of my head.

The doors open and instinct takes over.

13

EVE

MICHAEL IS YANKED AWAY FROM ME AT A FEARSOME SPEED before I see a fist fly into view, striking his jaw. He's knocked out cold, his masculine body splayed lifelessly across the floor.

"Don't hurt him," I yelp, holding out an arm to stop the attacker as I crouch next to Michael on my knees, instinctively becoming a barrier between him and the other while I check that he's okay. I brush my hand across his face, careful not to touch the painful-looking welt that's already forming. It was quite a punch. "He was trying to help," I scold, sounding like one of the Mothers.

"He'll be fine," a voice says, sounding irritated.

I turn and see two men—boys, rather. They must be my age or close to it, both red-faced and out of breath. One wears the familiar uniform of the guards, although it's blue and has what I assume is his name stitched into the fabric across his chest—*Hartman.* The other wears a shiny black sports suit that highlights his athletic frame—he's the one who threw the punch.

I'm wondering whether I'm in danger at someone else's hands when I take in the second guy's features and my eyes lock with his.

Hers.

I gasp. I've looked into those eyes almost every day for as long as I can remember. I know their almond shape and the soul that lies beyond them. I'm gawking as I take in the alien features that surround the familiar. I've often wondered what she looked like in her true form. Of course, there was always the possibility that she was one of the Mothers, and I had considered it but reasoned against it: she just seemed younger.

I'm struck by how different he is from Holly, my blond-haired, green-eyed companion, with her delicate frame and beautiful face. He too is beautiful, but in a very different way. His dark blond hair is clipped short in what I'm guessing is their uniform style—he and his companion both sport it. His smooth skin has a subtle olive tone. I notice little beads of sweat on his wide nose and across his cheeks. His eyes are enchantingly dark—a rich, velvet brown that glistens in the light. The color may be different from Holly's but those eyes are the same.

He's nothing like her, yet he *is* her.

He averts his gaze and shifts, his foot nudging Michael's leg. There is no response.

"Are you okay?" he asks without raising his eyes to meet mine.

"I'm not sure," I say, thinking of everything that's happened since I woke up this morning.

"He didn't hurt you," he says quietly. It's more an observation than a question.

"No—I thought he was going to, but no. He was confused," I tell him, feeling protective of Michael even though I'm aware the outcome could have been different. If Vivian's words held some truth it should have been. Or maybe Michael is unique in his willpower and more dedicated to the cause than other men are.

"Right," he says in a disbelieving tone, a frown forming as the muscles in his jaw tighten.

"It all happened so fast. Mother Nina. She's dead," I tell him, the words spilling from my mouth.

He winces, but of course he isn't surprised. "I'm sorry," he says.

"You didn't—"

"No, but I should have—"

"Maybe," I conclude.

"You couldn't have," his friend cuts in.

I look up at him and study his face, wondering if he's another of my Hollys, but I don't recognize anything about him. I wonder what he's doing here and what his connection is to her.

A groan from the floor shifts my attention. Michael stirs, putting his hand over his face.

I start to go to him, but an arm is raised to prevent it.

I give "Holly" a withering look.

"Don't, Eve."

"I don't think he had any intention of hurting me," I tell them.

"It didn't look like that," he says.

"You saw," I say slowly, remembering that she was there as the elevator doors shut, that I was shouting for Holly to help. I was terrified of the unknown and hysterical over Diego.

He'd shed himself of Holly's form and run to help me. I hadn't needed him. I might've thought it at first, but Michael wasn't a threat. If the opposite were true, though, if Michael had been trying to take advantage of the situation, I would've been saved. Helped. Rescued. The words circulate in my brain. I don't like the sense of fragility that's crept up on me today. Yet, in reality, I am weak. Weaker than I'd thought.

"I . . ." He's shaking his head, as though he's finding the situation as bizarre as I am and doesn't know how to react. There's clearly no protocol for meeting me away from his disguise, away from her.

"You *are* Hol—"

"He just needs some ice," he says quickly, cutting across me. "And to sleep it off."

"It was quite a punch," grumbles his friend, rolling his eyes as he crosses his arms, assessing the damage in front of us.

"I could've hit him harder," he mutters under his breath.

We hear the sound of feet hammering on the floor before Ketch and his team sprint into view, swarming along the corridor, accompanied by several of the Mothers, their faces frantic and fearful.

I note the absence of Mother Nina, and my chest tightens.

"Hartman. Bram." Ketch nods at them, gesturing for them to step aside while the area is secured.

Bram.

His name is Bram.

"Are you all right?" wails Mother Kimberley, throwing her arms around me with such force that I'm almost winded. "He didn't . . ."

"No," I say, my cheeks reddening. "He— They—they just helped."

"Of course that's all *we* did!" Bram scoffs, bemused that they'd think anything different.

Mother Kimberley exhales with relief. "Let's get you back upstairs. Vivian will be coming to see you shortly."

I'm crushed at the prospect. She is the very last person I want to see. Not one part of me wants to hear what she has to say about what has happened and my involvement in it.

Within seconds Michael is removed from the elevator and I'm ushered back in, flanked by the Mothers.

As the doors close I search him out and find those eyes once more.

Bram.

His name is Bram.

Sitting on my bed, I wait. Not only am I waiting for Vivian to come in and reprimand me—somehow making out it was my fault—I'm waiting to become submersed in feelings. Guilt. Fear. Grief. Despair. Anger. Hope. Delight. Anything.

Nothing comes. I thought it would and feel it should. I was full to the brim with overwhelming emotion while I was in that elevator, but now there is a big black gap where I ought to be feeling something.

I am numb.

My body is an empty void.

My brain is frozen.

I can barely move.

Hardly think.

My eyes are drawn to my dressing table, the bags of makeup and brushes Mother Nina packed away just a couple of hours ago when we were talking affectionately. I remember the warmth of her fingers as she touched my face and am haunted by what happened a short while later. The same action repeated, but this time so violent. I see her wrinkled face in Diego's hands and the numbness intensifies. I'm unable to make sense of the horror I've witnessed. I should have been the victim. Instead he stole my old friend's life. What was the point?

This room. This space. I used to feel safe here. Oppressed, trapped, and controlled perhaps, but I have a great responsibility, and they've been here to help me do all I can to save our race. This sanctuary has given me support, kindness, and security while I've been growing up. They've given me comfort, stimulation, an education, and friends. Mother Nina.

And then there was Holly. She was a gift, I see now. To keep me engaged with people of my own age, to keep me connected. Because one day all my real companions will perish and I'll be here alone . . . What then? What is to become of me?

I think of Holly and I see him—Bram, full of passion, anger, and fire.

I wonder how long it'll be before his image fades, or before my brain revises the arches of his nostrils or the wave of his hairline, makes him taller or gives him a more muscular physique. How long will it be before the image I have of him is turned into a work of fiction?

I can't believe I've actually met a Holly.

They'll be livid, of course. Even if they're aware I can distinguish between her variations and know she's just their puppet, she works. That's why they keep sending her to me. I engage with her, confide in her . . . If they think I've seen completely through the lie, it's possible they'll stop sending me that version of Holly. My Holly.

It dawns on me that that's why Bram stopped me before I blurted out that I knew who he was. If I'd got those words out it would be over. Now I just have to wait and see if he returns. Pray that our little moment was lost within the spectacular devastation of the morning.

"I'm sorry," says a low voice behind me.

My heart constricts and shrivels.

I turn to Vivian, who is as composed as ever at my bedroom door.

Suddenly I'm overcome with anger and hate. I grip my bedsheets to stop myself from lurching at her, because that's what I want to do. I want to run at her and let this feeling go, but I can't do that.

"I know how fond you were of Mother Nina," she continues.

"I was," I respond, hating how quickly we're able to talk about her in the past tense and wishing we didn't have to.

"She did the right thing," Vivian says, walking unashamedly into my room and looking me up and down, as though examining me for any physical injuries. She won't find any.

"Did she?" I snap.

"Of course," she says, her voice chillingly cold, considering she is talking about the loss of an innocent life and someone she has spent at least a decade working alongside.

"And what makes you say that?" I ask, the anger still bubbling inside.

"She knew you were about to expose yourself."

I can't deny it.

"She saved you."

"So it's my fault?" I shout.

"I didn't say that," she says, her face like stone.

"You implied it!" I shriek.

"Eve, control yourself," she warns, her voice remaining

calm, unlike my own. "Mother Nina clearly sensed something that the rest of us had failed to spot. She'll have died happy knowing she was saving you."

"Why didn't you notice it?" I ask, jumping up from the bed. "How was he chosen over every other man screened? How was he allowed in here?" Blood rushes to my head as the words fire from my mouth.

"The matter is being looked into." She blinks with a pursed mouth, not giving the slightest indication that my reaction is bothering her. "It won't happen again."

"And that's it?" I ask, my voice cracking.

"I think you're forgetting the bigger picture here, Eve," she retorts, her eyebrow rising just enough to be condescending but not enough to be completely inhumane, given the circumstances. "You're becoming too sentimental at a time when the focus should be on the cause and what we're set to gain—or lose. Choose your battles. Focus on the path ahead. It's tragic about Mother Nina, of course it is, but hers was just one life."

"Why should my life be deemed more important than hers?" I ask, a lump forming in my throat.

"You are called the savior for a reason. Do you pay any attention in your history lessons?" she quips.

"I thought I was just a cog," I say drily.

"Eve . . ." She sighs with impatience, tugging on the cuffs of her shirt. "Mother Nina served the greater good by sacrificing herself. We should be grateful to her, but let's not dwell."

I remain silent, my gaze falling to the floor between us.

"And what happened in the elevator?"

"Nothing," I tell her, my voice barely audible as sadness niggles away at me. "I was saved."

"The guard was found unconscious."

"It was a misunderstanding."

Her eyes are on me, trying to read whether or not I'm telling her the truth. I don't know why she's bothering to ask. There must be cameras everywhere—surely she's seen the whole thing already.

"So no further action is necessary, with any of the young men involved?"

I shake my head, unable to lift my eyes from the floor. "You said they would hurt me. That temptation would be too much."

"Temptation can either strike instantly or grow over time, Eve. Don't be tricked into sloppy behavior or you may not be so lucky next time," she warns, her eyes sharp. "Understand?"

I nod.

"Very well," she says, making for the door.

"A funeral!" I call after her. "Will there be one?"

Vivian sighs at the inconvenience. "I'll make sure it's marked in some way," she says. "I'll get the other Mothers to . . . address it."

"Thank you," I say, almost to myself. "She really was the most remarkable woman."

In that moment all I want is a pair of arms around me. Michael's, Bram's—Mother Nina's . . . Even Vivian's would bring a certain level of comfort. Yet she gives me nothing. Vivian takes a breath, lifts her chin, and silently walks out of the room. Leaving me to cry a swamp of tears on my own.

14

BRAM

I CLOSE THE DOOR TO THE DORM AND HIT THE LOCK WITH MY trembling fist. I can't stop the shakes. I managed to contain them a few moments ago outside the elevator, but now that I'm alone my body is free to react as it wants.

I stumble backward. A grayish blur is forming a frame around the edge of my vision, like the vignette of an old photograph. The dorm spins. Bunk, window, door. Bunk, window, door. My balance fails as my legs give in to the weight of my thoughts, which are dedicated to one thing.

Eve.

I'm dragging my case through the corridor of my home in the cloudscraper. We're high, somewhere on the upper floors. Clouds press on the glass wall, turning it gray.

As I stare out at the hazy world, the clouds start to glow. A pair of huge luminous eyes suddenly appears outside the window, staring back at me.

Your savior. *A kind voice echoes through the air outside, muffled by the glass.* Our future. *The mist dissipates, revealing the pretty face projected across the side of the cloudscraper opposite.*

"Do you know who that is?" my father asks.

Of course I do.

"Eve," I say, but my eyes are drawn back down the hallway toward the sound of my mother's sobs behind the door.

"Eve is going to be your new friend," my father says, then notices where my attention has drifted.

"Don't look back," he drones. He stands at the elevator door, waiting for it to arrive. "This is your one chance at a better life. You'll thank me for it one day. For getting you out of this place."

"I want Mama." The sound of my voice makes me realize I'm crying. Sobbing. "I want Mama!"

"You will not see that woman again and you'll certainly not be needing that, not where we're going." He tugs the small silver cross, and the chain breaks, falling from my neck. "Foolish beliefs for a foolish woman. You will not speak of her."

Eve!

I sit up suddenly. It's cold. My cheek is stinging as if I've been slapped repeatedly. My vision is blurry and has no color, but I can make out Hartman standing over me, hand raised. His mouth is moving, but I can't hear him over the high-pitched ringing that's vibrating inside my skull.

He pulls his hand back and slaps me. The stinging in my cheek becomes a burn.

"Bram!" he whispers in a hushed panic. "Bram, if you don't come out of this soon I'm calling the medic."

"N-no . . . ," I mumble as I pull my cold, clammy body off the floor. "I don't need it. I'm okay."

"Are you?" he asks.

Am I?

What the hell just happened to me? The color slowly returns to my sight, and with every deafening beat of the pulse in my ears I feel normality returning.

"Just take some deep breaths and drink this." Hartman hands me his flask. Without hesitation I take a gulp, and the boiling liquid hits the back of my throat. I spit it out instantly.

"What's that?" I say, handing the flask back to him.

"Tea." He shrugs.

"You could have told me it was hot!"

"Sorry. I just thought it might help calm you down."

"Did I black out?" I ask, although I already know the answer.

"I dunno. All I know is that you bolted the second they escorted Eve away. When I got here the door was locked, so I had to hack in again, and when I finally got it open you were sprawled out on the floor, eyes in the back of your head, mumbling all sorts of weird stuff." He swigs his tea. "Shit, that *is* hot!"

I don't bother asking what I was mumbling. Not because I'm afraid of what it might have been, but because I already know what it was. The last thing I was thinking of before I blacked out and the first thing I thought of when I came around.

Eve.

My stomach convulses, and within a split second, my throat is full of its contents. I projectile-vomit onto our dorm floor. Hartman jumps out of the way just in time.

"What the actual f—" He doesn't get a chance to finish before a second round erupts from my mouth.

"Yuck!" He hands me a towel.

I rip off my kinetic suit and fall back onto my lower bunk with a heavy sigh. What's happening to me? I close my eyes. Eve.

I've seen her face thousands of times, but never like that. Never with my own eyes. I've never breathed the same air as her or caught the flowery scent of her hair.

I take a breath and fill my lungs, trying to remember what breathing next to her felt like. Her smell. She smelled real.

I suddenly remember her gazing into my eyes. No one has ever looked at me like that before. It's like she was staring through me, into my mind, trying to see the person inside—the way she looks at Holly, except she found no one but me there this time.

She saw me.

She recognized me.

She knows.

"We have an emergency meeting in thirty minutes, but you're staying here," Hartman says as he mops up my mess with a towel.

"No, I'm fine. I need to hear what's happening," I argue.

"You're in shock, Bram. You need to rest."

"Shock?" I almost laugh.

"You witnessed something horrific earlier, man. This is your body reacting to it."

Something horrific? What's he talking about?

Then it hits me. The memories flash in my brain, cutting like glass. Mother Nina's body, motionless on the floor. The cold stare of Diego and the blood on his hands, filling the creases of his knuckles and congealing under his fingernails.

Horrific.

"Yeah. I guess you're right," I lie.

"You're not a soldier, Bram. Things like that don't happen every day. At least not up here. I mean, shit, is this what they're all like out there? Are they that messed up?"

"Don't you remember it?" I ask.

"My life before this place? Barely. Thank God."

"I do," I admit. "Bits of it. Just flashes, really. It wasn't that bad."

"Not that bad?" Hartman gawks. "You must be ill, mate. It was a bloody war zone for about thirty years."

"Yeah, that was all BE, before we were born. Things got better after she came along, more stable."

"Damn right it got better, better for us! If it weren't for her we'd be out in Central, in the storm with the rest of them, counting down the days to extinction."

"We could have been frozen, our bodies preserved for the future," I joke.

"Ha, yeah. Or upload our brains into one of your dad's Projectants," Hartman replies. "No. Thank. You!"

"I thought you might like that. Your mind living forever as a projection," I say. "You love computers!"

"Er, I'd rather not be turned into one." Hartman blows on his tea and takes a sip. "Right, you. Stay. Rest."

I keep silent. It's best he thinks I'm struggling with the death of Mother Nina rather than knowing the truth. He was right about one thing, though: my body is in shock. My mind is in shock. But mostly my heart. I've never felt it beat as hard as it did today. Beating for a purpose. Beating for someone.

Eve.

"I'm going to find out what's going on. If you start crashing again, you call the medics," Hartman says, throwing the filthy towel into the laundry chute, then going to wash his hands in the basin.

"I will," I say, knowing I won't.

"I'm serious," he replies, also knowing I won't. He shoots me a look as he opens our door and disappears.

I lay my head on the pillow and stare up at the bunk above. With every blink of my eyes I see a flash of blue. Deep blue. Eve's eyes. They're in my head, staring back at me as if they are permanently burned onto my retinas.

I hear the soft swish of our door sliding open.

"I'm fine, you don't have to worry about me," I say.

"That's good to know," replies a deep voice.

"Dad?" I sit up instantly, banging my head on the top bunk. Great.

"Lie down before you do yourself some damage," he says, obviously unimpressed. "Shall we discuss today's events?" He was never one for small talk.

"Yeah. Shall we start with what the fuck happened and how a complete psychopath was allowed into a room with Eve?" I snap. Maybe I am in shock. My father certainly looks as though he is.

"Mistakes have been made," he replies calmly, not rising to my anger. "We're addressing and researching how and why Diego slipped through our net."

"Slipped through your net? I'd say it must have a pretty big hole in it. She could be dead now. Gone."

"We're all aware of the severity of the situation—"

"Really? Because I'm not sure you are," I interrupt, anger and frustration bubbling inside my chest. "The future of our species was almost erased in that room today and it must have been more than an accident. Someone has to be held responsible." My passion has brought me to my feet and I'm standing face to face with my father.

"And who do you suggest takes that responsibility, Bram?" he barks. "Me?"

"Yes, you. You and Vivian."

His palm connects with my throat faster than I can react, and he slams my head against the steel frame of the upper bunk.

I don't fight it. He's too strong. Physically and mentally. We've had fights before. I have the scars, physical and mental.

"That's enough from you. Did you really think I came here to discuss the flaws in our system? To hear your opinion? Do you think I care to know what goes on inside your insignificant mind?"

I feel his hand relax, and my throat is free of his grip.

"I'm sorry," I mutter. "It's just that . . ."

I hesitate and he shoots me a look. "That what?"

"It's just Vivian. Dad, she's—"

"Enough. I would be very careful of the path your mind is wandering down. Vivian is not a tolerant woman, and questioning her motives is not something you have the authority or the intelligence to do."

I'm a child again in his presence.

He moves to the window and touches his palm against the glass. The monitor scans his hand and grants him access to any file or program he wishes. He begins flicking through security footage from the afternoon.

He fast-forwards through the meeting. I watch it all unfold again at twice the speed. I see myself in the room, disguised as Holly, Eve disguised among the Mothers. Both there and not there at the same time.

"I came here to discuss Eve," my father says, turning his hand in the air as though winding an invisible cog while the footage plays out on the realiTV screen.

"What do you want to know?" I ask, watching Mother Nina die for the second time that day. My father's face doesn't change. It's hard. Emotionless.

The screen flicks to a different camera. Eve is being dragged toward the elevator. Holly chases after them, her nearly perfect projection only faltering slightly in the flashes of gunshots in the room behind.

"Here we are," my father says, nodding at the screen.

It's me. Not as Holly. The real me. We both stare at the screen as I burst into the elevator and land a perfect punch on the security guard's jaw. The footage pauses.

"And so you meet."

There it is. A historic moment, at least for me. On permanent record. I'm standing over the unconscious body of her kidnapper, she's kneeling next to him, and, for the first time, we look into each other's eyes.

"Did she recognize you?" my father asks.

"No," I say without hesitation.

My father says nothing.

"No," I repeat. "At least I don't think so."

He turns his wrist, flicks his finger, and the footage plays. Our recorded voices cut through the air of my room.

"*You* are *Hol—*"

"*He just needs some ice.*"

My father flicks and it repeats.

"*You* are *Hol—*"

"*He just needs some ice.*"

"*You—*are*—Hol—*"

115

He doesn't look at me, just stares straight ahead and adjusts the thin glasses on his nose, the way he does when he's pretending to think about what to say next.

"I think we both know what she was going to say before you cleverly interrupted her."

I stay silent.

"This footage will not be kept on file for obvious reasons," he says as he makes a cross with his fingers and erases the best moment in my life so far.

"Be very careful, Bram," he warns. Or maybe threatens. It's hard to tell as he makes his way toward the door. "You might be the best pilot we have, but you are by no means irreplaceable. Should you become problematic, the fact that you are my son will be irrelevant."

The door swishes open and he leaves me alone to ponder.

15

EVE

IT'S LIKE WE'VE PRESSED PAUSE IN THE DOME. A CLOUD HAS descended upon us and refused to clear. It feels wrong to laugh, smile, eat—to hold a single meaningless conversation that might lighten our hearts and encourage normality. Mother Nina's murder has given us a serious reality check in terms of what's at stake; it's also hit me with a grief I've never experienced before. Not only had I never witnessed the horror of a human dying before my eyes, but I'd never had anyone so close to me taken away like that. Even though I've experienced the loss of other Mothers, women who were in their eighties or nineties, none was as important to me as Mother Nina. Our bond was special.

My mother, Corinne, died during childbirth, and my father, Ernie, was committed after a breakdown following my mother's death. I did not and do not feel the same emotional turmoil over their absences as I do over Mother Nina's. Maybe it's because it's fresher and raw. Or maybe because it's real, not something I've been told about as though I'm in a history class learning of my past.

I remember the day Vivian told me of my own parents and what happened to them. I'd been asking the Mothers which of them was my "real" mother, so the topic needed to be addressed.

My birth had put "too much of a physical strain" on Corinne's body, which shouldn't have come as a huge surprise: she was older than most childbearing women from decades before. Vivian told me how hard they'd tried to save her. She was the first woman in fifty years to bear a female, so it stands to reason that they would do all they could to keep her alive, but sadly she slipped away. I'm told it was peaceful and that I was placed in her arms at the time. I've always found comfort in that, even though I have no recollection of it.

The situation with my father is slightly different. I don't really remember him either, but I know he tried to kidnap me when I was three, which led to him being cut off entirely. I'm regularly reminded of the incident because of the moon-shaped scar he caused on my wrist—a little rough patch that I always catch myself rubbing. Probably out of habit. I don't remember much about the episode other than a door creaking open in the dark, a hand grabbing mine and pulling me from my bed, lots of shouting and confusion, a scuffle, and then his tormented face at the sight of my bloodied arm as they dragged him away. I don't know how much of it is true or whether I dreamed it. Dreams distort, stretch, and obscure the line between what is real and what is not. All I can say with complete certainty is that I dream of my father most nights.

Vivian has briefed me on him too, mostly about what happened when I was last in his company. She's told me little about my ancestry. She said they were keen for my father to be a key figure in my life growing up, but it was too tough for him to be around me. I've been told he blamed me for the loss of his wife. Hardly surprising. They were reportedly happy before she fell pregnant with me. That changed everything, apparently.

I've been sleeping with my mother's book under my pillow for the last three nights, but I haven't found the courage to open it. I don't want her words tarnished by my fresh heartache.

She's often with my father in my dreams, although I've only seen Corinne in pictures they've given me and in video clips of her in interviews. Her happiness shines through as she rubs her bump lovingly. None of the clips are long enough to give me a real sense of what's being discussed, but I've watched them a lot. I've studied them, just like I have those of the Potentials.

I look nothing like her. I'm identical to my father.

Mother Nina filled the void my parents left behind. The thought of not being able to see her ever again, of her not being the first person I see every morning, of never being able to say a proper goodbye or thank her for everything she's done for me, including giving her own life, is crushing.

Despite my early numbness, I have cried solidly since Vivian left my room, allowing me to wallow in Mother Nina's death. My soul feels as black and heavy as the clothes they've allowed me to wear.

I am in mourning.

I've stayed in my bedroom, not caring to venture out. I've just sat here, consumed with guilt and sorrow.

Every time there's been a knock at my door I've momentarily forgotten the terror and expected to see Mother Nina walking in, but now the time has come to end that ridiculous hope and lay her to rest. Vivian has done as she promised and is allowing us to say goodbye in a way we feel shows gratitude and love for Mother Nina.

Minutes ahead of the proceedings starting, I sit out on the Drop, needing a moment or two of quiet reflection before I have to say goodbye. My eyes are fixed on the clouds as I sense Holly move along the walkway behind me and lower herself next to me.

She doesn't say hello. She doesn't try to force conversation or coax out how I'm feeling so that they can psychoanalyze my mental state. She just sits and allows me to be. That's how I know it's her.

Him.

Bram.

I send a mental thank-you to those in charge for allowing me *my* Holly again on what feels like the hardest day of my life so far. I can't look at her, but just having her here is enough.

The silence is comforting. It's what I need. I close my eyes and breathe it in.

"Come on," I croak, a gentle reminder that I've barely spoken over the last few days. "We'd better go in. They'll be waiting." I get to my feet.

I'm hit with heartache as I look toward the building and know that I'm walking in to say goodbye. I take a slow breath, trying to stop the tears from falling as I breathe out and look to the heavens above me.

"I'm here," Holly says, so quietly it's as though I've imagined it.

Swallowing the lump in my throat, I nod. I appreciate the gesture.

With my next breath out, I manage to place one foot in front of the other and lead us back through the upper garden zone, just as the rest of the Mothers start to gather. Like Holly and me, they're all in black and look somber, yet somehow they smile and we exchange hugs. We're unified in our loss and grief.

We're not waiting long before Mother Tabia steps forward. Her graying black hair has been pinned into her usual low bun, yet the air of superiority seems to have left her. Today she's mourning like the rest of us.

As usual after a Mother's death, she cradles a white ceramic pot. There is no body. Instead the pot holds a few of the Mother's favorite possessions. Items that brought her joy while she was here, usually photos or jewelry, little keepsakes from a former life sealed into an urn, symbolizing the woman she was.

"A few days ago a terribly unjust thing happened in the worst way imaginable," Mother Tabia says, taking charge while protectively pulling the pot closer to her chest. "While we may feel that we don't want to move forward, we have to remember that life is ever evolving, ever changing. Nina experienced love and kindness in her previous life, which enabled her to spread her goodness here. We were fortunate to have her walk among us, and must take note of all her attributes . . ."

While she talks I think of our friend and long to be set free from the grief, but I miss her too much.

I shuffle on the spot, shrugging my shoulders and trying to ease the weight bearing down on them.

"I'm going to pass this around," Mother Tabia says, her dark eyes looking down at the container in her hands and raising it a few inches. "I'm sure most of you will echo my own anguish at never having had a chance to say a proper farewell to our Nina. I know that's how Eve feels," she says, looking at me with the saddest of smiles. She's been in to see me regularly over the last three days. She might be the strictest of the Mothers and easily influenced by Vivian, but she's listened to me and tried to coax me out of the darkness. "So, as you find this in your own hands," she continues, "think of how she made you feel. Thank her. Will the love she radiated to shine through us all always." With that, she closes her eyes with a frown, as though she's struggling with her own emotions while communicating with some higher being. I'm still watching her as the faint lines around her eyes soften and smooth. A peaceful expression takes over her dark skin as she grins, white teeth flashing.

She opens her eyes and passes the object to Mother Kadi and then on across the group. I watch as the same acceptance and tranquility befalls them. When it is my turn I almost feel scared to touch the pot, just in case I'm unable to absorb the comfort it's given them. But I take it from Mother Kimberley and pull it to my breast, my arms wrapping around it. I can't remember the last hug Mother Nina and I shared, and the thought saddens me. Was it on the morning of her death? I'm not sure. We spoke of love and her past . . . I wish I'd hugged her more, like I did when I was younger. I wish I'd been more grateful. I wish I'd shown her more often how much she meant to me.

The thoughts of her looking after me fill my heart with gratitude and joy. Not sadness. I was loved. As was she.

A smile of acceptance stretches my lips.

A thank-you.

A goodbye.

I open my eyes and turn to hand the container to the person next to me, but when I open my eyes Holly is looking at the pot regretfully, her brows knitted.

She can't take it.

In that moment I don't feel clever in catching out the system and their trickery. I don't feel smug at the awkwardness created as the Mothers rush in and try to cover up the mistake. I feel sorry for *her*, because she should've been able to put to rest her thoughts of Mother Nina too.

"She'd be glad you came," I tell her, uttering the words like they're some sort of consolation prize while cringing at myself.

She shrugs and nods at the floor, a movement that isn't very Holly. I wish I could give her the same comfort she offers me. Not her, but him. I'm not sure I know where Holly ends and Bram begins. I've spent years trying to figure it out, but meeting him has thrown me. He was so different from Holly in so many ways, yet he was familiar—hardly surprising given the amount of time we've spent together over the years. I do know the person standing beside me and I wish I could console her. Him.

Once Mother Tabia has the pot back in her arms she starts singing, a lullaby Mother Nina used to croon to me when I was younger. Everyone joins in. Even Holly. I asked for this song to be included. It talks of a bird with broken wings being set free. That's how I want to think of her today, learning to fly. It gives me hope and fills me with love.

"Thank you, everyone," Mother Tabia says at the end, indicating with a wave of her hand that we can disperse.

"Where has she gone?" I ask before anyone has had a chance to move.

"To her husband," she replies.

"I thought he was—"

"No," she says firmly, shaking her head, blushing at the

awkward silence that's fallen around us. "He'll be happy to have her back . . ."

I'm happy Mother Nina is back where her heart was. But, not for the first time, I'm seeing the holes in the information I've been given. The lies. I'm sure someone thinks it's for my own good to shield me from a world I know nothing of, but suddenly I'm feeling like an actor in a play: I know my own lines, but everyone else knows theirs and mine and has read the entire play. I want to get my hands on the script and find out what else is being hidden from me. I want to know more about the world my children will be born into and the life we shall lead if I succeed in helping the rebirth. I want to know the truth.

When people slip away to their chores, I wander back toward the Drop, my mind still full of questions.

"What did you think of Mother Nina?" I ask Holly, sensing her a couple of feet behind me. I slow down so she can catch up.

"She was one of the good ones." She sighs.

"She was the closest thing I had to an actual mother," I say, looking across to gauge her reaction.

"I understand that." She nods, her lips pursed.

"Do you?" I ask, looking from her mouth to his familiar eyes. I stare into them as hard as I can, willing the shape to melt away so I can see his true form. "What are your parents like? Tell me about them."

"My mom is a seamstress and my dad a teacher," she says, her voice monotonous at the repetition of the same story. "They were quite surprised when they—"

"I don't want that answer," I stop her, frustrated at the continued lie. "That's not what I asked. What are *your* parents like? Yours."

Her head snaps around to mine, and she answers without skipping a beat. "I had to leave my mom when I was little. My father is . . . controlling. Our relationship is difficult." The hurt on her face lets me know she's telling the truth, not sticking to the rules or the script she's been fed.

"I wish I had that."

"Seriously? One row with my dad and you'd change your mind," she scoffs.

"Maybe. Maybe not." I shrug. "You share the same blood; you were made from him, created by him . . . That must count for something."

She looks crestfallen and as if she's about to say more, but as we reach the end of the Drop and return to our sitting positions from earlier, she decides against it.

"Parents love with no agenda or judgment. I wish I had been born in different times. Then mine might still be with me," I say, sharing thoughts I've never expressed before—a hankering for a love I've never known.

The sound of music from the speakers inside tells me it's dinnertime.

"Already?" I mutter, annoyed that I can't sit here longer.

Holly gives a little laugh and I realize the joke is on me. It's dinnertime because they want this conversation to end. Of course they're listening.

"Want to come for dinner?" I ask cheekily, glancing at her as I bring my shoulders up in an inviting manner. For all the years Holly has been my best friend, I've never seen her eat. It didn't take me long to understand that her absence from meals meant she was unable to consume food like I can.

"I have to get back . . ."

"Time for me to go," I say.

"Yes."

"And for you to leave."

"For now." She smiles, making no effort to leave the spot in which she's sitting.

"What happens if I don't go? I'm not particularly hungry anyway," I say.

"I'll be back, Eve," she says.

"Yes . . . ," I say, hoping beyond hope that she will. "Thanks for being with me today," I add, getting to my feet.

"Of course," she says, her eyes blinking slowly as she gives a sad smile.

"I couldn't have done it without you. Actually, I could've . . ."

"Thanks." She laughs.

". . . but I'm glad I didn't have to." I laugh too.

"I understand." She doesn't look offended. "You don't need me."

"Perhaps not, but I like having you around," I admit, my voice lowering. "You're not like the others."

"Thanks," she mutters, a smile on her perfect lips.

I turn and leave as heat crosses my cheeks. I'm blushing. I pick up my Rubik's Cube from the bowl that's been placed beyond the glass doors for my belongings, then head for dinner, all the while trying to ignore the fluttering in my tummy.

16

BRAM

THE DOME FADES IN MY VISOR.

"And you're clear," Hartman mutters in my earpiece. I sense a slight wobble in his voice, and the line opens again as though he's about to say something else, but I don't hear what it is.

My head is yanked back violently, the visor ripped from my face. The blue glow from the scanners inside illuminates the hard, creased face of my attacker.

"Dr. Wells!" Hartman shouts as his silhouette leaps over his control desk in my peripheral vision and bounds across the studio toward me and my father.

He won't make it in time.

The visor comes crashing toward my face faster than I can react. The state-of-the-art technology smashes into the side of my head, showering me with glass. The projectors inside malfunction with the impact and throw shards of light around the room.

The studio walls shine brightly with the sunset I witnessed with Eve just moments ago, but as my dad's fist reloads for a second round, the deep reds on the horizon don't seem so hopeful anymore.

I hit the floor. It's still warm from the motors that have been running underneath. I look up to see Hartman failing to hold my father back.

As his fist approaches for the final time I'm comforted by Eve's image projected across the ceiling. She's there to help me through.

I close my eyes.

It's dark. I race to keep up with the man I barely know who has taken me away from my life. Too scared to cry. Not in front of my father.

"You're lucky to have a father in your life," my mother's husky voice whispers in my mind, helping to calm me.

The Velcro straps on my shoes are unstuck, soaked in the floodwater lapping at the walkway as we approach the mountain ahead. A flash of lightning electrifies the clouds and I suddenly realize it isn't a mountain: it's a building. Three enormous letters above the entrance come into view as the lowest layer of thin cloud disperses in a gust of wind.

EPO.

"Do only as I tell you," my father says as a beam of light scans his eyes and a set of heavy glass doors slides open, letting us into a cavernous entrance hall.

"Good morning, Dr. Wells," a young woman says from behind the desk.

I pause at the sight of her. She's like nothing I've ever seen before.

"Daddy, her face is smooth," I say, admiring her perfect complexion.

"That's enough now. No talking," my father says.

"But, Daddy, why is she—"

"Enough," my father snaps.

I keep silent, but I watch the woman with complete fascination. She stares at a computer screen from behind her desk, her fingers typing something on the keyboard. That's when I notice that her fingers aren't pressing any keys. They graze the tops of the square letter pads but apply no pressure.

"Miss Silva is expecting you. You are cleared to ascend to the summit once you are through security. You too, young man." She flashes me a smile and I see a small smudge of her red lipstick on her teeth. "How old are you?" she asks kindly.

"I am four," I reply proudly. She smiles.

"Thank you, Stephanie," my father says. "How do you like your new job?"

"Very much, Dr. Wells. Thank you again," she replies with the same smile. She's young. Younger than my mother. I've never seen any woman like her before.

My father walks away. I pick up my suitcase again and scramble after him.

Security checks everything in my case. Every toy. Every book. Once we're through, we board an elevator and begin our ascent.

"Ouch!" I complain as my ears pop.

"Don't worry, I doubt you'll be coming and going from here very often," my father says, noticing my discomfort.

"Daddy, the lady. Why was she different?" I ask.

My father smiles. It's not an expression I've seen on his face many times before.

"Different how?" he asks, seeming genuinely interested in me for the first time today.

I take a moment to think how best to describe it. "She's pretty," I say.

My father chuckles. "Indeed. Very pretty for a dead woman," he says.

"Dead?" I ask, not understanding.

"Yes. Stephanie, the real Stephanie, is dead. The person you just met was not real, just a projection of reality." He smiles.

I don't understand what he's saying.

The elevator doors open and I step into my new home for the first time, but one question pops into my mind: Did I just talk to a ghost?

When I open my eyes I'm blinded by an intense white light.

It's cold and my body itches under whatever material is pulled over me.

"Shhh. I've nearly finished, my dear," a soft voice says kindly from somewhere behind the light. "Must have been quite a malfunction."

"Malfunction?" I ask. The voice is female, so I'm not on one of the medical floors. I can only be in the Dome.

"Yes, the report says that the equipment malfunctioned in the studio during shutdown. Don't worry if you can't remember. It's quite normal for some memory loss after a head injury," the Mother explains. I can't work out who she is: her face is hidden behind the light she's working with.

"So that's the spin he's put on this little *accident*, is it?" I chuckle.

"He?" the Mother asks.

"Dr. Wells. My father."

"Well, I'm afraid I don't have any more information about

the accident to give you, young man, but whatever happened, you need to rest," she orders as she finishes the final stitch on my forehead. She switches off the blinding circular light and I finally catch a glimpse of the fine wrinkles that decorate her face.

"Mother Kadi," I say, sitting up slightly so I can look at her properly. Her marble-like eyes have a watery shimmer, reflecting the room. It's a magical quality, almost enchanting. Her thinning skin radiates experience and knowledge as her lips curl into a motherly smile. Her face is a story, each wrinkle a sentence written into her skin over time, beckoning you to read it, to study it.

"I thought I told you to rest," she says.

"I will. I was just wondering why I'm here and not on one of the medical floors below." I sound casual.

"I'm afraid I don't have the answer to that question either. When Miss Silva gives us an order, we simply obey," she says calmly, walking toward the door, followed by two other women I hadn't seen in the shadows. Mothers Tabia and Kimberley. Even unconscious, beaten half to death, a man is not trusted to be alone with a woman. Especially not in the Dome. Not after the Potential Number Two disaster.

"Rest. Miss Silva will be in to see you in a few moments," Mother Kadi says as she leaves the room. The door hisses shut and the lock clicks, sealing me inside. She places her hand on the glass and I catch her eye as the glass begins to frost. Just before its transparency fades completely she gives me a subtle, comforting wink. I'm not sure what it means, but it fills me with warmth as my head hits the pillow. I'm trying not to think about what Miss Silva's visit might entail.

• • •

I'm standing on the Drop, dangling my feet over the edge as I look down at the distant city below. My shoes swing back and forth as I watch hundreds of workers study each pixel on the screens, cleaning and replacing them in preparation for Eve's first day in the Dome.

As my foot swings back it catches on the bottom of the metallic ledge, and my shoe slips from my small foot, falling into the world below.

Suddenly it stops, hovering in midair just a few meters below the Drop, caught in a seemingly invisible force field.

The workers are too busy to notice. I turn to see my father and Vivian speaking at the other end of the walkway—arguing, it seems, from my father's flushed cheeks.

I look back down at my floating shoe. I think I can get it. I climb over the railings that surround the Drop and stand on the polished metal, but my sock slips and I fall. Although I'm aware of the illusion, my body still reacts as though I'm plummeting to my death. It's an awful sensation and I let out a small yelp.

I hit the screens hard and the ones I'm lying on flicker under my weight. I look up. No one has noticed. The team of lab-coated men obsessively polishing the screens are too preoccupied with their task. I stand and take a step. Then another. I'm walking across the fake sky, each step feeling unnatural as my feet shatter the illusion they are building for Eve. I reach down and pick up my lost shoe.

"Bram!" a distant voice calls. I look around and see no one.

"Bram!" it calls again as I slip on my shoe. The voice seems familiar.

"Bram!" Vivian screams, or is it my father? Perhaps both. I look up and they have seen me. The game is up. I'm in trouble now.

"BRAM!"

I sit up in shock.

"Bram!" Vivian Silva is standing at the foot of the bed. "Bad dream?" she asks as I try to calm my breathing.

"Yeah, one of those that feel real, when you don't remember falling asleep," I explain.

"Those are my favorite," she replies, running her fingers across the metal bed frame. "Those dreams are the only escape from this reality sometimes." She looks troubled. I've not seen her like this before; it doesn't suit her.

"Your father is a complicated man." She changes the subject abruptly, not looking me in the eye.

I've known Miss Silva since I was a kid, when she first employed my father and we moved to the Tower, but I don't see her much now. Of course, she's a busy woman. Being responsible for halting the extinction of the human race has made her the most powerful person on the planet. Governments obey her, royalty bow to her, religious figures fear her. Getting a meeting with her is near-impossible, so spending quality time with me is hardly at the top of her list of priorities. It means I don't know her like I used to, but I can still sense when something's not quite right.

"I know he does things sometimes that are—"

"Crazy." I interrupted her, which I've never done before. I don't think many people interrupt her.

"—out of line," she continues calmly. "Sometimes his

actions are uncalled for, his temper uncontrollable, and the way he treats you can be unacceptable. But he's trying his best to deal with the pressure we all face. Unfortunately, as his son, you get the physical fallout of that pressure."

"Yeah, and I've got the scars to prove it," I say, pointing to the bandage covering my forehead.

Vivian looks away, as though she's almost ashamed to see me like this.

"You know your father better than anyone, Bram. He likes to control things, for life to be planned and predictable. When events don't go smoothly, when life isn't the way he planned it, he finds it difficult to deal with. Particularly when that involves you, Bram." She swipes her hand and audio starts playing. It's Holly's voice. *My* voice, as Eve hears it.

"My father is . . . controlling. Our relationship is difficult."

Vivian swipes again and it stops.

I bow my head in shame. Not only did I break protocol, but I criticized my father openly for everyone watching to hear.

"I imagine those words would be difficult to take from your son," Vivian suggests. "They are also potentially extremely damaging for Eve."

"I know. I'm sorry," I say honestly. "It won't happen again."

"It won't. It mustn't," Vivian commands, suddenly seeming more like the woman I know. "This is a warning, Bram. Not from your father, from me. I won't play games with you. I won't hit you. But if you break protocol again there will be serious repercussions for you and for Hartman. Is that clear?"

"Yes, Miss Silva," I say like a naughty schoolboy in front of the headmistress.

"Once you have recovered you will be escorted back to your

dorm and today's event will not be discussed with anyone." She walks toward the door, which swishes open automatically.

"Rest, my boy," she says as she disappears into the Dome. The frosted-glass door closes and locks behind her. She's never spoken to me like that before. Years of running this place have made her cold, but I guess even the thickest ice has cracks.

17

EVE

MY STEP IS LIGHTER, YET MORE DETERMINED, ON THE STAIRS leading up to my room after dinner. For days I've had this heaviness hanging over me, but sending Mother Nina off today and being able to thank her has left me less encumbered with guilt and sadness. Hope begins to regrow.

The questions that have formed over the last few days invigorate me into moving forward. As does my Holly. I've become increasingly aware of how much I value that friendship and enjoy being with her. The knowledge that she is Bram hasn't drifted far from my mind, so I want to start figuring out what is going on in this building.

It's because I'm feeling like this that I go to my bed and reach beneath my pillow.

I pull out my mother's notebook, my fingertips stroking the front cover. Opening the page, I reread the first entry, then turn to the next.

I've been here before. Not with a girl, but with a boy.
Seven boys, in fact. I'm sad to say that each of your

brothers died in utero. I birthed them all and wept while I held their frail bodies in my arms before they were taken from me. I was so heartbroken. The grief overwhelmed me. I'd failed at being a mother even though I never got to do the things that mothers should, like changing diapers, worrying over when to give solid food, or hearing my children tell me they loved me. Instead I got nothing but dispiriting loss.

Our dream of having children began to appear impossible, even though no one could tell your father and me what was happening and why we were having to say goodbye to those tiny souls so prematurely. We gave up hope. We couldn't risk the same thing happening again and again. My body was considered useless, so my doctor and the team at the hospital wrote me off, like an old car with a faulty engine. We said we were happy not to try again, to leave it there. I couldn't face another goodbye. I couldn't face another midwife giving me "that look" at yet another routine scan. I couldn't bear to go through another fruitless labor. I felt weak, unhappy, and empty. I had to let go of that dream.

It wasn't easy, but once the decision was made I felt relieved not to be consumed with longing. Your father and I fell deeper in love, something I'd never thought possible. He loved me in spite of my flaws and failings. He loved ME. We've been happy. Really, so very, very happy.

A month ago I went to the doctor. I was constantly bloated, my breasts were hurting, I was having regular mood swings and was often a little nauseous. A lot of my girlfriends have been going through "the change," so I'd been putting it all down to that, but I was worried it was something more and wanted to know for certain.

I laughed so hard when the doctor handed me a pregnancy test—your dad said he heard me from the waiting room. I dutifully peed and headed back to the doctor without waiting for the result. I even handed it to her with an air of "This is ridiculous." I didn't expect her to say "Yes, just as I thought" and send me off to be scanned, but that was exactly what happened.

In that moment I felt fearful and anxious as I collected your father and went to the specialist. Pregnant again. I cried. Your father did too. We were in shock. Then, within seconds, we were laughing in each other's arms, unable to believe this had happened when we hadn't planned it. It felt like a gift.

I held my breath as the technician glided her ultrasound stick over my skin while looking at the screen in front of her. I know I was preparing myself for the worst, because that was what I knew from past experience—all hope and joy eradicated when she muttered the inevitable "I'm sorry."

But the stick kept moving and she kept clicking away at the keypad, locking in numbers and measurements.

The gasp was almost comical. "I'll be right back," she said, all fingers and thumbs, the stick wobbling out of her hand and landing on the floor. Your father and I *looked at each other in confusion. It didn't feel like she was about to tell me my baby had died. It felt special. And it was. Five minutes later four other members of the staff entered the room and watched the technician repeat the scan.*

"See?" she said, looking up at them.

They all turned to me and your father. Their expressions were priceless. Honestly, I'll never forget those gaping jaws.

Eventually Vivian stepped forward and introduced herself, then said something along the lines of "Rather remarkably, Mrs. Warren, you're expecting a girl!"

Your dad nearly fainted on the spot, but I just cried. Let's blame the hormones. Instead of sending us home, they asked us to stay in for a few days so I could be monitored properly. Given my history and the fact I'm having a geriatric pregnancy (geri-bloody-atric), I said yes without the slightest hesitation. That was a month ago and I haven't left since. They haven't forced me. In fact, it was me who said I wouldn't mind having regular scans and being taken care of. Plus it's gone crazy outside. Your dad tried to go home one day to grab some things, but there were floods of people downstairs wanting to talk to him, all asking questions about me and you. The world's gone nuts. I think we're happy here. It's safe, and Vivian's been a great help in dealing with everything so that we don't have to.

So here we are. It's my eighth pregnancy. I've been here before, but this time it feels completely different.

It is completely different.

I can't believe I'm six months pregnant with a girl.
I hope this is the start of things changing out there so
that you can have a happy and fulfilled future.
    I love you so much already and am doing all I
possibly can to get you here safely.

                                        Love, your Mama xxx

It's a story I've heard before, but it's so much better reading
my mom's account of it. It's heartbreaking yet funny. I wonder
if this is how she'd have shared the account every birthday if she
were still here. Would she still go on about not having a clue
she was expecting me and make me laugh by reenacting the
sonographer's shocked reaction? And would she bridge the gap
between Vivian and me? Mom seemed to have been glad of her
support, even welcomed it. She didn't seem bogged down with
the pressure of what was expected of her. Instead she sounded
like a mother excitedly awaiting the birth of her baby. Another
baby she would never watch growing up, as she had dreamed
of doing.

I close the book.

That's enough for now.

18

BRAM

I'M FEELING BETTER, BUT I'M STILL SIGNED OFF FROM PILOTING Holly. The last three days I've spent inside that small room in some obscure corner of the Dome have felt more like imprisonment than recovery. I guess it was a prison. I was sent there to keep me silent, to protect my father. Sending me down to medical would have raised too many suspicions. The Mothers were the safest option. It broke protocol, but they don't ask questions.

I'm pleased to be back in the dorm, back with Hartman.

"Dude, it sucked. They've not let me leave the dorm," he explains. "For *three days*!" He notices my lack of sympathy.

I point to the small red mark on my forehead from my father's beating, which is now little more than some barely noticeable scar tissue, thanks to Mother Kadi's expert sewing. Of course, if I'd been sent to medical there'd be no trace of anything, thanks to the technology they have access to, but I've never been shy of scars. I run my rough fingers over the pale, bumpy skin on the back of my left hand.

· · ·

I'm ten years old and my father lashes down on my knuckles. My tears don't stop him.

"You must never speak about yourself to Eve," he growls through his clenched teeth. "You are not Bram when you are with her. You are not my son when you are with her."

You are not my son.

You are not my son.

I'm back in our dorm, rubbing my hand. Eve's not the only one with a physical reminder of her father.

"Jeez, he hit you hard this time, Bram," Hartman says, lowering his voice.

"They all hurt the same." I shrug.

A slip of paper slides under the thin gap beneath our door.

Hartman and I look at each other. An assignment? Are we allowed to get back to work at last?

"Briefing, tonight, nineteen hundred hours," Hartman says, reading the single line of typed instructions from the paper. He looks at me and smiles. "I guess we're back!"

The briefing room is alive with the usual whispered excitement that follows any unforeseen event in the Tower. That Hartman and I have been mysteriously absent for three days has not gone unnoticed.

"Hey, Bram, I read the transcript from your last session," Jackson calls over the noise. "Playing pretty close to the line, aren't you?"

I don't give him the satisfaction of an answer.

"What line is that?" Hartman replies.

Great, here we go.

"Getting into discussions about her parents. *Your* parents. It's all a little *real* for my liking," Jackson says while digging chunks of his dinner from his teeth with a toothpick.

"Well, who gives a shit about *your* liking, Jackson?" Hartman fans the flames.

"Be careful, is all I'm saying," Jackson warns, not bothering to look at us.

"You care about us now, Jackson?" Hartman asks sarcastically.

"Look, I don't know where you two have been hiding for the past few days, but I imagine it has something to do with what was said in the last session. No one gets away with breaking protocol so blatantly without punishment. Rumor has it that you've been holed up in some ward for psychiatric treatment, Bram. That true? Getting things off your chest about your *difficult relationship?*" Jackson mocks.

"And where did those rumors start?" my father says, entering the room behind us. The squad members shuffle in their seats awkwardly, instantly becoming more alert and professional in his presence.

My heart sinks at the sight of him. It's the first time I've seen him since, and I realize I'm touching my head. I snatch my hand away and shake off the memory.

"There's too much at stake to waste energy on rumors and lies. This is not the academy. You are not children. You are young men at the epicenter of the most important moment in the history of our species, and your personal issues are of zero importance in comparison to the challenge we face. Now suck it up and let's get to work," my father commands.

I can't help but feel that his words were meant for me alone. *Suck it up and let's get to work.* That was his apology.

"Potential Number Three," he begins, wasting no time as he flashes up an image of a young man we've not seen before. "Although *Potential* is no longer appropriate, as it's absolutely necessary that this partnership is successful."

My father talks us through Potential Number Three's family history, his genetics, his political value, his fertility, his beliefs and morals. "He has been vetted, cross-checked, analyzed, trained, and briefed down to the most detailed level. He is, if it were at all possible, the most perfect match for Eve we have found to date."

"On paper," I interrupt.

A few heads turn slightly and shoot me awkward looks.

"Do you have something to add, Bram?" my father asks.

The room falls silent.

"Well, it's just that . . ." Suddenly I feel unsure of the words flowing from my mouth. ". . . that it's not about his intelligence or genetics. That's not what relationships are based on."

"Go on." My dad nods.

"So it doesn't matter if we fill Eve's head with how perfectly *meant to be* this or that one is. She's a young woman with a mind and a heart of her own."

Jackson forces a laugh, which I try my best to ignore.

"She can't be controlled like that. After what happened last time, you can't just shove her into a room with one of these guys and expect them to play happy families," I finish.

"Thank you, Bram," my father says calmly. "That's why we won't be asking them to do that. It is no longer an option."

The squad listens intently. Seems that everyone is as eager as I am to find out what the new plan is.

"Things are going to take a more scientific approach from

now on. Eve is required to have no emotional relationship with Potential Number Three. She doesn't even need to meet him if she doesn't wish to. We simply need her cooperation, her compliance, and the procedure will be simple and painless. If it's successful she could be pregnant next month, which is the time frame we are currently working toward." My father has finished, standing in front of images showing various statistics and figures about Potential Number Three's impressive genetic compatibility with Eve.

We take a moment to absorb the new plan. The approach we need to adopt to persuade Eve to comply with it.

"Pregnant within a month and she's not even required to meet him?" I call out. "Is that the way our future begins? Are those the foundations humanity is to rebuild on?"

I feel the stares of my fellow pilots, obviously not sharing my discomfort with this new arrangement.

"Any future is better than none at all," my father says, looking deep into my eyes.

"Is it?" I reply.

19

EVE

"IT SOUNDS SO SCIENTIFIC AND COLD," I MOAN, TURNING TO Holly, who's been lying across the sofa in my room, listening to me vent ever since I left Vivian's office in a rage ten minutes ago.

It's fair to say the encounters haven't been my main focus over the last week, which is odd for me, seeing as I've been working toward them for as long as I can remember. Instead I've been preoccupied with thoughts of my parents, Mother Nina, Bram, Holly, Michael, and dealing with the unanswered questions in my mind while trying to understand what is going on. It seems "what is going on" is the successful pairing of me and Potential Number Three, even though we've never met.

As Potentials One and Two have been discounted—I have no idea what they've done with Diego's body and don't care—I'm stuck with the last option on their shortlist. I wasn't too shocked by that piece of information, as it seems the obvious thing for them to decide when they're eager to get things moving. I've been told I don't have to meet Potential Number Three at all. There'd be no roomful of people standing around as we spoke for the first time, no smoke-and-mirrors tactics to vet him. The vital parts of us would come together in a laboratory, the embryos placed later in my womb to incubate and grow.

I remember Vivian coming to my room two years ago and telling me what would happen after the initial meetings with the Potentials. I'd pick my favorite and would then be permitted to meet him as often as I liked. At the right time, when my body was ready, the Revival would occur. When she revealed what his body would do to mine, I was terrified. "We'll be there with you," she said in an attempt to console me, although the thought of the Mothers bearing witness to that act didn't comfort me.

Since then plans for the Revival have become more elaborate and detailed, with a week-long ceremony to mark the first stage of the rebirth. During this time I'd come to see the importance and necessity of the deed. No longer am I so bashful at the thought.

After all Vivian's preparation, I was surprised to hear her altered plans. Scrapping the ceremony and opting for a scientific route is a dramatic move and vastly different from how I was created.

"There'll be fewer variables this way. Less chance of human error," she said when it was clear I didn't understand why things were changing. "It's your decision, of course."

"Mine?" I practically choked.

I didn't fail to notice the pleasure on her face.

Now Holly remains tight-lipped. I know exactly what she's doing. She's letting me get it all out so she can sweep in and rationalize everything for me once I'm done with my frantic thoughts. She knows there's no point in interrupting me when I'm like this, as I won't listen, and I know she must have had a fair idea of what was going to happen in Vivian's room before I did—so she's been ready for this reaction. Expecting it, even. It's no coincidence that I've been told about the new procedure on the same day that *my* Holly has returned after a few days off. It's all a part of their plan.

I've missed her.

Him.

I know they've been punishing me by keeping him away and leaving me with the other two for company. It's Vivian's way of reminding me that she's in charge of who comes in and out of the Dome and what goes on here. Mother Nina's death is no excuse for challenging behavior, not when we've been hit by a major security issue and they've had to rethink plans that have been years in the making. Vivian is signaling that I have to respect the boundaries they've laid out for me, not be so ungrateful or cheeky. And I was incredibly cheeky.

Asking about the person behind their technology was certainly bold of me. Brazen, even. Going on to admit how much I liked his company was plain foolish on a variety of levels. It was the first time I've actually admitted out loud that I know Holly isn't a real person—although they can't think I'm that dumb, surely. I'm the first and only girl born in fifty years. Who is Holly meant to be if they want me to believe she's real? Not that I've ever cared that she isn't. It's never mattered. Like I've said before, I've always been glad of the company. But now I know that a large part of her is *very* real. Right now I'm acutely aware that Bram is controlling her and that the only way I get to continue having contact with him is through her.

I feel disloyal having reached that realization, as though I'm using Holly to get closer to him, but that's not true. I've purposely not asked for him to join me here and tried my hardest not to schedule extra trips to the Drop in the hope of seeing him. I've allowed them to control when he's with me. I've managed not to ask after my Holly or point out that things aren't running according to our normal schedules. I've resisted temptation, which hasn't been the easiest thing to do when I'm starting to see through the cracks.

I think of my mother and wonder whether I'm wrong to doubt the life they've built for me when she was so willing to be here. She put her faith in them and trusted Vivian. She must've had good cause to. Plus, I can't ignore the fact they're allowing me to make a decision about my future. A decision that'll affect all of us . . .

But then I think of Michael and how he didn't try to spoil me, of Mother Nina and her husband, and of Bram and Holly, and wonder whether I've ever really made a decision or had a true thought, when the facts I've been given have been tampered with. My reality has holes in it. I need to start poking around so that I can see things a little more clearly.

So, when it comes to making this decision about Potential Number Three and dismissing the ceremony, I'm dubious as to whether or not it's all a trick. Whether they're trying to coax me into agreeing to something for their own benefit or whether it's genuinely up to me.

If the decision truly were my own, regardless of all the other thoughts littering my brain, I still wouldn't be sure of what I wanted. The encounters have lost all their appeal. I don't know if I'm open to going through another after two truly horrific experiences.

Perhaps letting science do its thing would make things

easier. Perhaps I should allow them to extract and reposition my eggs, once they've been fertilized by Potential Number Three's winning sperm. It simply doesn't seem as special as the Revival ceremony I've been preparing for.

"It all seems so sudden," I say, my hands working on the Rubik's Cube in the hope that it'll ease the frustration and anxiety I'm currently feeling.

"Eve." She sighs, her fingers twiddling the ends of her hair.

"We're not talking about meeting a Potential, just about being fast-tracked through and partnered up due to a series of failures. Whether I meet him or not, I could be pregnant within weeks. I don't know if I'm ready," I whisper, turning to her with my hand over my heart, my face anxiously screwed up.

"It's overwhelming," she notes calmly, barely moving.

"Yes." I've continued reading my mom's words, and it's become blindingly obvious how prepared she was to have me. Things haven't happened for me as I always thought they would, so I don't feel that way. I'm like a little girl still. Not like a mother at all.

"The outcome and desired results are still the same as before, Eve. That's not changed," Holly says, closing her eyes. "They're just looking at new ways of achieving the prolonged existence of our race without putting the only hope we have of survival in danger."

"The *prolonged existence of our race*? Have you heard yourself? You're talking about a baby. *My* baby!" I say, forgetting for a second that this is my Holly.

Mom seems so jolly and upbeat in her letters. She doesn't seem bogged down by pressure or as though she's struggling to cope with the world expecting her to deliver its savior. She sounds like a happy mom excited to meet her daughter. Our outlook is so different, and it pains me that the one woman who could have shared some of my anxieties can't hear them.

"You won't be forced into the same awful position as last time," Holly says, sitting up while offering an apologetic look. "They don't want the same mistakes to be made."

"I should think not," I grumble.

"They want you to be comfortable."

"Yeah, right."

"They do," she says, and adds softly, "*I* do."

My heart does a little dance. Part of me knows I should be wary. This Holly could still be a part of their plan. But I can't stop the way she makes me feel. I've always loved being around her, but now that I know Bram is saying these words, I can't help imagining him here with me, supporting me and caring for me.

"So, do you want to meet him?" she asks, breaking into my thoughts as she takes a deep breath in and reclines once more.

"I don't know. Is there any real need for a conversation between him and me?" I frown, the weight of the decision slamming down on me and my emotions. "Does it matter if I like him? And by *like him* I mean simply find him agreeable—I'm not holding out hope for much more than that, given who they've previously paired me with. I mean, who was in charge of vetting them? Did they just pick names out of a hat?"

Holly throws her head back and laughs. It's not the cute little giggle I'm accustomed to. It's bigger. Bolder. It has to be more *him*.

I like it.

"I need some air," I huff, putting down the Rubik's Cube

and stalking out of the door, arms swinging rigid at my sides. I can't bear my room any longer. Here I'm trapped in my whirl-wind of thoughts. "Come on," I call behind me. Whether or not she's here to give me guidance, I don't want her to leave me just yet. Not when she's been gone for so long.

"Coming," she calls, jumping to attention and trailing my heels as we follow the path to our usual spot.

My bedroom, the dining room, the classroom, the Drop—that's all I ever see, other than a cold examination room and the occasional trip to my spot outside. It's my routine and it's all I know. It's all they've allowed me to see. Over the years I've felt trepidation over what will take place in these few weeks and this first year, but now that it's arrived, my anxiety runs in a way I've never expected. I don't want my greater understanding of the world to come after I fall pregnant. I don't want to feel I've got only half of the picture when providing the world with my offspring. I don't want knowledge and understanding to come too late.

"There's no rush to decide," Holly says as she lowers her-self with no regard for the Drop below us. Today she's wearing the most girly outfit I've ever seen her in—baby-pink jeans, a cerise skintight top with tassels, and silver-glitter jelly wedges. Someone is trying to erase the fact that she's a he, but all I can think of is that Bram is underneath, wearing his Lycra bodysuit, dictating her every move.

"What do you think I should do?" I ask, the pleading whine in my voice making me shudder. I want her opinion.

"I can't answer that."

"But you always do," I say, shocked, as I turn to her.

"No, I don't." She frowns.

"Seriously? You can be quite persuasive," I squeal. "I'm sure you've talked me into numerous things over the years."

"Eve!"

"Are you going to deny it?" I challenge.

She's looking a little hurt and uncomfortable. "I never make you do anything you don't want to, Eve . . . Do I?"

"No. I guess not," I say, not wanting to offend her and wishing I could nudge her shoulder affectionately to check in with her that she's okay. "But you always have an opinion to share."

"This is different. It has to be your decision," she says, her face not losing its frown. "Your choice. It's your body. I . . . can't imagine what it would be like to do either."

"What—science or intercourse?" I blush. Not because it's the choice I'm faced with, but because I'm speaking about the Revival with *my* Holly.

Once more the sight of his face and sweaty muscular body stirs in my memory. I don't think I'd find the decision so difficult if I were talking about *him*. Although maybe the fact that I'm so disappointed it's not him should help me reach my verdict. I know I have a duty to the world, but I can't be forced into having feelings for someone. If I meet Potential Number Three and there's nothing, I'll be crushed. If I really dislike him, I'll be devastated.

In my silence Holly reaches behind her. When she brings her hand back to her lap she's holding a Rubik's Cube—identical to the one I just left in my room.

"Where'd you get that from?" I ask, glancing behind me and wondering how long it'll be before Vivian comes marching along to reprimand me and drag me back to my room, or whether they'll decide simply to switch Bram off.

"It's fine. I've cleared it. It's mine."

"Oh!" I understand: there's no way she'd be holding mine. Hers is like her: here but not.

Holly laughs—just as loudly and freely as before.

I love that laugh.

"I figured it would help to clear your mind. This place in the clouds, your silly little gadget . . . it'll help."

Despite myself I feel the corners of my mouth twitch into a smile and my own frown easing away.

"You can't touch it, though," she warns, her voice stern while her eyes twinkle. She's pleased with herself for thinking this one up.

"Oh?" I reply, my breath catching in my throat.

"You just have to tell me what to do," she explains, licking her lips and looking at the cube with an intense glare, as though she's entirely focused on the task ahead. "You know I've always been terrible at these."

"Now you might actually complete one," I tease.

"I've done it before, remember?" she says, the pitch of her voice raising an octave in protest.

"Only because you painstakingly removed all the stickers and cheated." I laugh, feeling my body tilt toward hers.

"I got what I wanted, though, didn't I? Sometimes a little cheating is good for the soul."

"It made you feel good?" I ask, finding this response surprising.

"It did until you sussed it out and made me confess to being a cheat. You even told the Mothers on me," she adds, pretending to be wounded.

"You'd roughed up the edges of the stickers. I could see exactly what you'd done, so of course I knew." I recall the look on her innocent face when I called her out on it all those years ago, then watched Mother Tabia give her a stern talking-to. "Imagine how good you'd feel if you did it properly."

"Are you forgetting it's just a toy?" she asks, her eyebrow raised.

"You'll get a real sense of achievement."

"Let's test your theory," she says, holding the colorful object in front of us.

"Fine." I smile, my eyes absorbing the pattern of colors while my brain works out the best way to start. "Put your right hand on the top section and rotate it just once to the left . . ."

Holly misunderstands my instruction and turns the top two-thirds of the cube rather than just the upper layer.

"No!" I shriek, stifling a laugh at how my insides churned with anxiety at her mistake—perhaps she's right and I do need to remember that it's just a toy. "Go back to where we started."

She does as I ask.

"Right," I say, looping my arm through hers so that my right hand hovers above hers. I curl my fingers as though the cube is in my own hands and repeat the instruction, showing her what to do. "Now turn the cube around so that the yellow of this side is at the bottom and . . ." I demonstrate.

She understands and turns. "That's three yellows in a row!" she yelps, delighted with herself.

"You really did cheat if you think that's an achievement." I giggle, sweeping my hair away from my face and over the opposite shoulder from where Holly is sitting.

Her eyes snatch a glimpse of my newly exposed neck and I notice her lips give the smallest pout in response before she focuses back on the cube.

My body tingles at this new level of intimacy and craves more.

I tentatively feed my arm through hers again so that we can continue as before, but this time I don't say a word. I just instruct with my hands.

She mirrors them perfectly, taking note of exactly how my hands rotate, turn, and manipulate before doing the same with her own.

A silence might've fallen between us, but something entirely new is being communicated.

I feel her.

I know that's absurd, but I do. With our arms interlinked and our bodies sitting closer than usual, we're sharing a new energy.

I'm aware of her every breath working its way in and out of her body, each and every muscle as she mimics my movements, and that she is just as aware of the change as I am. It's not in my imagination. It's real. I know she feels it too. It's titillating, tantalizing, and it stirs an inexplicable hunger inside me.

I want her.

I don't need words to define the thoughts being shared, not when my insides are flipping with excitement at the tingling sensation of her body next to mine.

"We've done it," she says quietly, holding the completed puzzle in her hands, neither of us engaged in the game any longer.

We remain in silence.

My thoughts are focused on the heat passing down the right side of my body. It's real. The feelings that are being stirred are here and alive, and I won't have anyone tell me different.

Time passes. It could be seconds, or it could be hours—I've no idea.

"I should go." She taps the top of the cube, then gets to her feet. She starts to say something else but stops herself. Instead she turns on the heels of her jelly wedges and heads indoors.

"I've made a decision," I call, looking at the clouds beyond my feet. "I'll go for science."

I don't need to turn to know that she's gone.

20

EVE

I STAY SITTING ON THE DROP FOR SOME TIME, TRYING TO CALM down and make sure my cheeks aren't still pink from our encounter.

Encounter . . .

An unusual giddiness has risen within me—a warm, fuzzy excitement. I've needed time to digest it, to enjoy it, but also to quash it until I can dwell on its inevitable disappointing outcome. Which I'm hoping to delay for as long as possible. I have to choose science because I couldn't handle meeting Potential Number Three and not feeling that. Whatever *that* was.

While sitting here I focus on the perfection in front of me. It's a sight I try never to take for granted. Living here, seeing the earth in all its beauty, spurs me on. The greens of the land I occasionally glimpse in the distance, the blues of the sky. It's all so inviting. It fills me with love for Mother Nature, even though she's revealed her flaws—or perhaps she's exercising her strength to warn us of the magnitude of her power. She's in charge, that's for sure. Try as we may, we cannot bend her laws. Not if she doesn't want us to. Is it wrong that I'm starting to take solace from that?

A bell tells me it's time for the afternoon's session to start. Gardening. Holly doesn't join me for this: sometimes reality and illusion just aren't compatible. A lesson that's all about respecting the earth, nurturing life, and seeing it thrive at the touch of your fingertips could be ironic with Holly in attendance. I don't mind her absence, as it's a class I get lost in anyway. I always find any manual task highly therapeutic. I need that today, right now. And the last thing I need is one of the other Hollys.

Mother Kimberley is waiting for me when I arrive at my garden plot across the Dome. Elsewhere the Mothers grow all the fruit and vegetables we eat at each meal, but this patch is just for me. It's filled with flowers: roses, daffodils, lavender, clematis, delphiniums, and poppies—to name just a few. I pick up my shears and snip off dead blooms and yellowing leaves.

"Are you well?" asks Mother Kimberley, her rounded frame pulling out two brown folding chairs from my shed and taking a seat. She looks as she normally does in her navy gardening pants, cream cotton blouse, and trainers, with her short red hair curling around her ears, but there's a weariness behind her glistening blue eyes, which usually sparkle with happiness. And there's tightness in her lips, which are usually smiling. She looks shattered. I've forgotten the toll recent events must be taking on the Mothers too. It'll be a long time before things feel normal again. If they ever do.

I let out an exaggerated sigh.

She nods in response, sympathy on her rosy face as she purses her lips in a straight line. "I heard."

"I don't want to even look at another Potential, so how could

159

I let one touch me?" I ask, removing the rosebuds that have failed to bloom and shriveled on the bush, thereby directing more energy into those that show more promise. I'm learning to grow life.

"You don't know how you'll feel about this one until you're in his company," Mother Kimberley advises, her tone all-knowing. I usually enjoy it when the Mothers share some knowledge from their experiences before the current structure was formed, although I'm not sure they always understand what it's like to be me.

"I don't think I'm going to be in his company," I say bluntly.

"Oh."

I watch her face drop as she understands what I've said and feel a pang of guilt.

"That's a shame."

"You think so?" I ask, picking up an empty bucket and disposing of the bits I've been hacking off.

"Any children you deliver will be partly made of him," Mother Kimberley says firmly, her neck straightening a little as she tries to remain diplomatic. I doubt she'll tell me I'm wrong—it's not in her nature—but I'm expecting her to share her thoughts on the subject.

"Does that matter?" I ask.

"Does it matter to you that half of you came from your father? That you only exist because of him?" she asks slowly, her head tilting to one side. "Do you ever find yourself wondering if you're like him in any way?"

I'm rarely asked such a direct question about him. He features in my thoughts, but they focus mostly on my mother.

I don't reply because not only is there truth in what she's

said, but also she knows the answers to each of her loaded questions.

"Wouldn't your child feel the same?"

"Maybe," I mumble.

My life has been so geared toward meeting the Potentials and finding my perfect match that I've hardly thought beyond the act of procreation at the Revival. Until very recently I hadn't really thought about life with a child. A baby. *My* baby. Surely the most significant part in all this is bringing life into the world. It was for my mother. She had plans for me, for us. She'd thought through our lives together.

I wonder what kind of mother I'll be and whether I'll even be allowed to raise my children, if I'm lucky enough to have any. They may be taken from me, raised by another group of Mothers, and given their own Holly to grow up with. The thought of them going through that fills me with dread.

What would happen if I bore a boy? Would we just keep going until another girl was born? That's why they're starting me so young, surely—to get the most out of me while they can.

"I'm old enough to remember a time before you." Mother Kimberley sniffs. She leans forward in her chair, rubbing her hands together while she rests her elbows on her knees. "The tests. The hormone treatments. The poking and prodding. All of it to no avail. They were sure the fault lay somewhere with us women and needed to find out what it was. Eventually we were considered worthless. That was, until your mother and father."

I stop pruning and look up at her, letting her know she's got my full attention now.

"Your mother was a very special woman."

"Did you know her?" I ask, my interest piqued. Now that I'm starting to understand the woman who carried me for nine months, I want to hear everything there is to know about her.

"Not personally," she admits with a touch of sadness.

My heart drops with disappointment.

She glances around us to ensure no one is in earshot, then continues, her voice low and gravelly, quite different from the delicate sound I'm used to hearing from her. "But one of the things that made her special to us women wasn't that she fell pregnant with a girl but that she had done so away from a laboratory. Whatever your mother and father shared was more efficient than a bunch of men and women in white coats telling us our bodies were useless."

"She *was* tested, the same as everyone else." I've read about it in her own letters, her thoughts of failings echoing Mother Kimberley's. "She was one of you."

"Yes, she was told she was of no use and was sent home to your father . . . so the story goes," she adds, with a noncommittal shrug that suggests I'm not the only one to have my suspicions about what we're told. I realize it's not just me being kept in the dark.

"That's true." I nod. "My mother wrote about it."

"Yes." A smile appears on her face but doesn't quite reach her eyes. I wonder if it's for my benefit or theirs. "I just wonder if the power of attraction and emotion should be so quickly overlooked, Eve. Science has failed us before."

"I'm sure it's advanced since then. What else have they been doing all this time?" I ask.

Mother Kimberley shakes her head. She thinks I've not listened, that her words have gone in one ear and straight out the other, but she's wrong. I've heard them and they've made me stand even firmer in my decision.

Science has failed before.

Maybe it'll fail now.

Secretly, that's what I'm hoping for, because being responsible for bringing another human, my child or not, into this world doesn't feel like the right thing to do. And maybe, just maybe, their experimental meddling was Mother Nature's reason for attempting to kill us off in the first place.

21

BRAM

I CAN'T SLEEP.

No surprises there, I guess, although tonight is different. Usually it's my brain that keeps me awake, thinking about the missions, the future, and Eve (of course). During the day a river of thoughts is held at bay behind a dam inside my head, but each night it bursts and the river drowns any chance I had of sleep.

But tonight it's not my mind that's keeping me awake. It's a feeling, a physical feeling, that somewhere in the core of my body something is leaping around. I suppose they call this "butterflies," although that seems to paint a far gentler mental image than what I'm experiencing. Mine are trapped hummingbirds, flapping tirelessly to and fro, their wings relentlessly strumming the strings of my emotions as I lie in my bunk.

A small *pop* breaks the silence and I roll over to see Hartman sitting in the glow of his reading light at his desk in the far corner of the dorm.

"It's called bubble gum," he says, sensing my eyes on him.

"Huh?" I reply.

He purses his lips, and a blue bubble starts to appear. It grows and pops, splattering over his nose.

"It's vintage!" he says, throwing a small, shiny rectangular piece of paper to me. "Try it."

"Jeez, it smells sweet," I say, folding back the silver foil and sniffing the blue strip of gum inside.

"Don't waste it. That stuff ain't cheap!"

"Thanks," I say, avoiding having to try it by subtly slipping it into the chest pocket of my jumpsuit.

"You've not stopped rubbing your fingers together for the past thirty minutes," he says, and I'm suddenly aware that I've been massaging the spot where Eve was touching me earlier, remembering the sensation that my kinetic gloves were creating on my fingers, that *she* was creating as she guided my hands around that cube.

"You know you pushed it to the line again today, dude," Hartman says, and I can't help but feel he's finding this subject difficult to approach. "You do realize that I could tell what was going on, both of you playing along that you were intent on completing the Rubik's Cube—which, by the way, was obviously a totally romantic gesture on your part."

Okay, maybe it's not so difficult for him to approach it.

"We both know she can solve that thing in no more than twenty moves. I know you can too. I've sat here watching you twiddle it around, slept through the constant clicking when you were figuring it out years ago. But today she repeatedly made mistakes. Purposely directing you to make wrong turns, allowing your time on the Drop to last that little bit longer."

I don't say anything. What can I say? He's totally right.

"Look, if I can see it, then you can bet your next set of

stitches that your dad can too, and if by some freaky miracle he can't, then Miss Silva certainly can." He waits for me to fill the silence, but I've got nothing to say.

"You've got to be careful. Sometimes I wish they didn't heal you up so good. Then you'd have the scars to remind you of what happens when you break the rules here. Your dad may not punish you publicly, but he sure as hell makes you pay for it, dude." He sighs.

"Today was the longest Eve and I've had physical contact," I say, staring up at the underside of Hartman's bunk. "I know it's forbidden."

"Exactly! Think how many pilots have lost their jobs, or worse, for that exact reason. Lucas, Kook, that other guy with the weird nose."

"Saunders?"

"Yeah, all of them slowly falling in love with her, then pushing the boundaries of their missions. It's a criminal offense, Bram! Anything that could potentially put her at risk, that's a prison sentence, dude," Hartman warns me. "Don't think I can't see what's going on with you two."

He knows me too well. He knows her too. Plus he's right. It's beyond stupid. I used to laugh at those pilots who came here, swore their oath to the EPO, and then, *wham,* fell in love with Eve within the first few months on the job. Saunders, Lucas, Kook . . . Idiots. I've grown up with her and managed to remain professional. Always kept my intentions, my motivations clear. Why this change? Why now? Where have these feelings come from? Am I jealous of the Potentials? Maybe. Has this love been born out of the fear of losing Eve now that she's being called upon to fulfill her destiny?

Did I just use the word *love?*

Maybe I've always loved her.

"Hello?" her innocent voice calls. "What's your name?"

"I'm Holly," I reply, staring at Eve's incredible face through the prototype visor my father has just finished. Her big blue eyes are trying to figure me out, as though they're staring into my mind even though we aren't even in the same room.

"Who are you really?" she says. So smart.

I feel the nervous energy from the grown-ups surrounding me, even though I can't see them beyond the visor on my face.

"Cut it off," I hear Vivian whisper to my father, followed by a rustle of his shirt as he moves to end this session.

"I'm a kid," I tell Eve quickly. My father pauses. "Just like you."

Eve looks at me. My insides flutter. "I'm Eve," she says, trying to suppress a smile.

I sense the glances around the room.

"Can we be friends?" I say the line as I was instructed to before the session began.

"Maybe," she teases.

I sigh.

"What?" Hartman asks.

"Do you think . . ." I stop myself asking the question.

"What?"

I look at him. I can trust him. More than anyone.

". . . that she feels it too?"

He rolls his eyes, then lets his head hit the table. "Oh, my God, Bram. I can't believe you said that. I mean, I know you two have been getting closer—I can see that, anyone can see that—but seriously, dude, this is Eve. The person you're talking about, the girl you're asking me if I think she's *feeling* things for you, is *Eve*. The. Savior. Of. Humanity. E. V. E."

I shouldn't have opened my mouth.

"I mean, I *thought* that was how you were feeling, but I never *really* thought it, you know what I mean? I never thought you'd be dumb enough to act on those feelings. To let it start affecting our missions."

"Okay, okay, forget I said anything!"

"Oh, believe me, I will! I'm going to erase this whole conversation from my memory, then empty the trash," he says, while pretending to tip the contents of his brain into the bin next to his desk. "I'm going for a shower. Actually, no, you are."

"What?" I ask as he points to the bathroom in our dorm.

"You, shower, now. You need to cool off. Wash off this craziness and come out with a clear head. I want the old Bram back, professional Bram, top-of-the-leaderboards Bram. Not this lovesick Romeo zombie that's going to get us both locked up for the rest of our lives. Shower, now," he orders.

I reluctantly peel myself from the bed and walk to the shower with my tail between my legs.

Well, that didn't go so well, Bram, did it, you complete dumbass?

The shower is cold but I welcome it. I need it. It's refreshing and instantly clears my mind. The only problem is that it clears away the last fifteen-minute lecture from Hartman, and now all I'm left with is a fresh flutter of hummingbirds as the cold water reinvigorates them.

The thing is, he may know Eve, but he doesn't know her like

I do. This isn't just in my head. Things have changed since she saw my face. She knows what I look like now, the face behind Holly. When she sees Holly, does she see her or me? More importantly, whose face does she want to see?

I step out of the shower. The water stops automatically and the soft buzz begins of the recycling process that cleans the water and pumps it back into the system. I look at my face in the mirror. My deep brown eyes study themselves, searching for something. An answer? A sign? *Jesus Christ, Bram, pull yourself together.*

I know I pushed the boundaries today, I can't deny that. The rules are black and white: Holly must not initiate physical contact with Eve. Simple as that. But when it comes to Eve initiating physical contact with Holly? That is a gray area. Today was a totally gray mission.

I guess I went fishing with the cube and Eve took the bait. I can't promise I won't go fishing again.

I dry myself and head back to my bunk.

"Better?" Hartman calls.

"Much better, thanks," I reply. "Look, let's just forget what I said earlier, okay?"

"Forget what?" he says, not bothering to look up from whatever he's reading.

I climb onto my bed with my hummingbirds, place my hands together, and get back to staring at the bunk above, thinking of what will happen next time I see Eve.

22

EVE

THEY MIGHT HAVE CREATED THIS PRETTY DOME FOR ME TO grow up in, but the laboratories of my early years have never been far away. They followed me here. Specially built stark-white clinical rooms for me to visit twice a month for scans and blood tests. It's so routine and monotonous that I'm usually unfazed by having to recline in a hospital chair and splay my legs in stirrups so they can get to work.

Today is different.

I'm nervous. I'm tense.

Usually I'm here so they can observe any changes in my body. They practically held a party when I first started ovulating. Today the room feels even more cold and barren now that a serious task is at hand.

"Hold your knee up into your side," Dr. Rankin says without looking at me as she adjusts her prodding stick, causing me to wince at the sensation. I've had the same doctor my entire life, but there is no personal relationship between us, no niceties, even though she's seen more of me than almost anyone else. I am a scientific puzzle to her, nothing more.

I wonder what would happen if I successfully had girls and this doctor were to die—she must be in her seventies at least, judging by the multiple folds in the skin around her hazel eyes and the S-shaped curve of her spine. Her white coat hangs loosely over her skinny frame, and her walk has turned into a shuffle since I've been seeing her. She's not aging particularly well. At some point she will perish like the rest of them. Will my female children be studied like this, exposed to a man? My body constricts at the thought.

"Keep still," Dr. Rankin barks, her large nostrils flaring angrily.

"Sorry," I mumble.

"Thoughts?" Vivian asks over me. She has been standing silently in the corner for the last few minutes. She doesn't usually bother coming, but today is different. She didn't seem surprised when I told her I was choosing not to meet Potential Number Three—in fact, it was the first time I've seen something resembling relief flit across her stony features.

"We're early, but I should be able to retract in a week or so. We'll need to monitor closely until then," Dr. Rankin replies, squinting at the screen in front of her through her thick-rimmed glasses.

Retraction is nothing new. They probably have a freezer drawer somewhere full of my unfertilized eggs, but this time my eggs are being taken on a different journey. Rather than being stilled and preserved, they will be encouraged to live and flourish—to help me fulfill my destiny.

"How many will there be?" Vivian asks, walking around so that she has a clear view of the screen.

I never get to see what's on it. I'm never shown my insides—

although I doubt I'd understand what I was looking at, even if they pivoted the screen in my direction.

"I'd predict only one or two this cycle," Dr. Rankin replies, the tip of her index finger tapping twice on the image before them. "They're a good healthy size, though. Exactly what we want."

"Great." Vivian's eyes are glued to them.

"There'll be more next month if things don't work out this cycle."

"They will," Vivian declares, with the forward tilt of her head that I know means she's demanding her desired outcome. She doesn't want to think about plan B.

"I can only do so much. There are still some variables, as we know," Dr. Rankin reminds her.

"Well, limit them."

The two women look at each other, and for a split second it seems they're about to clash. Then Dr. Rankin nods multiple times, conceding to the one in charge.

"I'll need a fresh sample from the donor," Dr. Rankin tells Vivian as she taps at the screen.

"Fine."

"Daily," she adds authoritatively.

"Fine." She forces the word out in a growl. I can practically hear her teeth grind at being given orders to follow. "Koa is already here," she adds.

I decided not to look at Potential Number Three's file, but now I have a name: Koa. I wonder what his background is and where he's come from, what heritage he'll be passing on along with his aesthetics.

The donor. That is what I've demoted the possible father of the future to: some swimmers in a cup.

The rod is moved and I yelp.

"Honestly," Dr. Rankin hisses before turning back to Vivian. "We'll fertilize both and pick the one with the stronger grading. If both are outstanding I'd advise against implanting them together at this time."

"We can discuss that if it occurs." Vivian clearly disagrees with the medical advice.

"It's early days and I advise we take things slowly. There is the risk of it being too much of a strain on her body. Given the medical history of her mother—"

"Doctor!" Vivian spits. "Know your position."

Dr. Rankin is stunned into silence, her cheeks burning a bright red. She doesn't utter another sound as she peels off her examination gloves and leaves the room.

Vivian gives the screen one last hard stare and then, without a glance in my direction, follows her out of the open door.

I breathe a sigh of relief that it's over, taking a second or two to stop my crying, then freeing my legs from the stirrups. I sit up on the bed and take a moment to still my racing heart.

23

EVE

"YOU SEEM DISTRACTED," SHE OBSERVES WHILE WE PUT ON OUR shoes at the end of another dance class. I needed that physical activity. I've been transported from my worries and freed as my body bent, twirled, and kicked, spinning unwanted thoughts from my head at great speed. Now that we've stopped, it's time to interact as the anguish elbows its way back in.

I've avoided talking to Holly the whole session, but this one is never shrugged off without a struggle. She's persistent, and not in an endearing way. I don't trust Know-it-all Holly.

"Do I?" I frown at the floor, letting her know I'm not in the mood for her today.

"Anything on your mind?" she asks, pushing me further. I understand that she's meant to seem caring and concerned, but instead she sounds false.

"There's plenty on my mind," I snap.

"Care to share?"

"No."

"I bet you would if we were out on the Drop."

"What do you mean?" I ask, looking up at her pinched face.

I never see the beauty in this one, even though she's the same aesthetically as the others. She makes Holly ugly, which is no easy feat.

"Nothing," she says, a little startled at being pulled up on her comment.

"Right." I feel my back prickle in self-defense.

"It's just you seem to open up more there."

"Must be the view," I retort, leaving the room and slamming the door behind me.

I shower off the day and throw on a loose-fitting black floor-length summer dress. I leave my hair to dry naturally, letting it hang over my shoulders, then head barefooted to the Drop.

I ache to see her.

It irks me that the special connection with my Holly has been noted, but something within me doesn't care. We're currently counting down to a life-altering change that is beyond my control and will imprison me more inescapably than ever.

This is it.

The last bit of time for me.

The end of my so-called youth.

"What took you so long?" I ask a few minutes later. I feel as if I've been sitting on my own for hours, even though I know it could only have been a few minutes.

As I ask the question, I suddenly feel a pang of fear that it's not her. It is, and my smile grows in a way it never has before, surprising me. That cements what I already know.

"Nothing." She shrugs, giving a subtle frown.

"What are you wearing?"

She looks down and her jaw drops at the sight of her frilly pink lace gown. It's awful.

"Just a casual number." She laughs, breezily arching her back against the metal pole frame of the Drop and stretching out her arms in a dramatic pose.

"It suits you."

"You think?" she asks, a cheeky glint in her eye that causes another smile to form on my lips.

"I'll have to see if they do something similar in my size," I say through muffled giggles. "You've always been such a fashion icon to me. Vivian would be so pleased that I'm following your lead."

"I'm sure she would."

I enjoy the easy laughter that descends upon us.

"So how was it?" she asks, draping her arms over a railing and looking out at the view. "As horrendous as I imagine?"

"It was fine," I lie. "Crazy to think a small part of me is going to be meeting him in some science lab downstairs soon."

"And that something so tiny has the potential to have such a huge impact on the world," she says, not looking at me.

"That too," I say, but the thought of what will take place the next couple of times I'm in that room is making me feel uneasy. It's what I've chosen, but that doesn't mean I want it to happen. It was simply the lesser of two evils.

"Did it hurt?" she asks quietly, catching my eye before bashfully looking at the clouds below.

Her question surprises me, mostly because of the genuine anguish on her face, as though any pain I might have felt would affect her too somehow.

I shake my head, giving a noncommittal smile that I know she'll see through.

"Sorry," she says, trying to gather the endless material of her dress behind her knees so that she can sit next to me. There's so much that it's not an easy maneuver. If it weren't for the current topic of conversation I'd find her struggles hilarious.

"It's not your fault," I say, tearing my eyes away from her to look ahead. "It's the world we live in. The life I was born into. I should be used to it."

"Yeah . . . ," she says. She opens her mouth to say more but stops. She blows out a lungful of air.

"And I was used to it," I say thoughtfully, letting my mind wander. "There was a proper plan before and I knew what lay ahead of me. I didn't expect this series of events."

"No one could've predicted it."

"I guess not."

We sit in silence for a few moments. A comfortable one, but it's a rarity for us nonetheless.

"Do you ever wonder what it would be like to live in a different time?"

"Like when?" she asks, moving her weight backward so that she's resting on her elbows and looking at the sky above. I copy her.

"I don't know." I sigh. "The 1960s, when they danced all the time?" I suggest the first era that pops into my head. I think it was a happier time in our history.

"I bet they didn't really."

"Are you saying my history lessons are founded on lies?"

"N-no!" she stammers.

I laugh. "Or maybe the seventeenth century, when I could've been a grand thespian on the stage, spouting Shakespeare in a melodramatic voice," I say, swinging my arms around.

"Young boys played girl roles back then. You'd have had no chance." She giggles with me.

I can't help but turn my head so that I can take in her perfectly sloped upturned nose and pink heart-shaped lips—a boy playing a girl. Imagine that.

"What is it that makes you wonder about those times?" She coughs, her laughter dying. Sitting up, she scratches her ankle, as though it's not the conversation that's made her move.

"I just bet it was simpler." My eye is drawn to a little black dot far away in the clouds above. I watch it flicker and hover.

"They all had their troubles," she says, turning to me and gesturing for me to sit up.

"And I'm just not told of them?" I ask, seeing the raised scar on my wrist as I push myself into a sitting position.

"You know more than me," she states, which is probably true, as she doesn't come to those classes with me. I've no idea what Bram knows about our history or if what I know is even true. We joke, but they could've rewritten the whole lot to brainwash me into their way of thinking. There may be huge chunks of our past that I know nothing about because they've decided they aren't right for me, and I wouldn't have a clue.

My mom trusted Vivian and the team around her. She'd suffered loss after loss and suddenly a powerful figure was taking care of her, saying they'd do everything in their power to bring her daughter safely into the world. Of course she trusted them. Of course she listened to their advice and did all they asked of her. She trusted their knowledge. She must've felt she had no other choice.

I've lived under their knowledge for sixteen years, and although I might not have my mom's experience of life out there, the manipulation in here has fogged my vision for long enough.

It's time things changed. It's time to break down that wall and see through the cracks.

"I wonder what it was like back then to fall freely and unequivocally in love," I say, my voice shaking. I know where I want this to lead. "To follow your heart's desire, to do exactly as it directs and not hold back."

"Every generation had rules, Eve," she comments, adding flippantly, "except the 1960s—then they seemed to do whatever the hell they liked."

"So I've heard," I say, although I can't recall anything particularly interesting about that decade. "I wonder what it was like for my mother and father. To find love."

"Love?" she asks, her voice soft as the energy around us shifts, becoming charged once more.

"Yeah . . . To find each other in a sea of thousands," I add, forcing myself to continue—because I want to. I want to say these things to him. "Don't you ever feel a grief over that? A loss for what should have been? We should've had that right. Love can't be contained. But they've contained us."

"I . . . ," he flounders. I've caught him off guard. Him. She is only he to me now. I've become more aware of it in every conversation we've shared, in every thought I have of us when we're not together. I barely see Holly anymore. I just see those dark brown eyes. I see Bram.

"Do you want to know the one thing I'm sad about?" I ask, my insides flipping.

"What?" he croaks.

"That I'll never find out what it's like to be kissed. Properly kissed. By someone I love." That sentence takes my breath away.

Now that I've said it I have to wait for him to grasp what I'm yearning for him to do. I keep my eyes low and almost closed as I turn my face in his direction. My lips prickle at the thought of what's to come and how desperately I want it to happen. A huge part of me is scared he'll just disappear before we get the chance. But it can't be rushed.

Ever so slowly I'm aware of his face behind hers moving toward mine. The world stops turning. I hold my breath as I lean over, my face edging closer to my best friend. My Holly, dressed in a ridiculous pink outfit yet looking as beautiful as ever. My lips become fuller.

I close my eyes to see only him in my mind. "Kiss me," I whisper.

Then I feel him.

24

BRAM

CONNECTION LOST.

The words blind me as they illuminate the inside of my visor.

"What happened?" I blast, holding my thumb and little finger together to speak directly to Hartman, in case Eve can still hear me.

Eve. Our lips touched for the briefest moment, my first kiss with a female, her first kiss ever, and it was over almost before it had begun.

"Hartman? What's happening? Are we disconnected?" I ask, growing more frustrated at losing the moment. Eve chose me. I know she wasn't kissing Holly. It was me she was reaching out to, the real me.

I slip off my visor, half expecting to have it ripped from my hands and smashed around my head again. Instead I'm greeted with a far more concerning sight.

"Miss Silva," I say, dipping my head in respect as her unmistakable silhouette catches my eye while my vision adjusts to the darkness of the room. I've never seen her in the studio before. Something moves in my peripheral vision. I take a quick glance and see Hartman being escorted by security out through the door and into the locker room.

"That's mine. It's got, er, sensitive data on it," he cries as the guard rips his drive from the terminal and drops it into a black plastic bag.

"I think we need to have a talk, Bram, don't you?" Vivian says calmly, hands behind her back, her cold face catching the dimmed lights of the studio.

Hartman is shoved out of the room and the door hisses shut. It's just me and Vivian now.

I'm suddenly cold and very aware of how exposed I feel, wearing nothing but a Lycra bodysuit in front of her.

She says nothing but instead lets my brain do the work for her. The silence is intimidating. She emits power so effortlessly that I'm defeated already.

"Hartman had nothing to do with that. It was all me," I say.

"That may be so, but you are a team, and the actions of one impact on the other. He could have asked you to stop. He could have made us aware if he was troubled by your recent behavior."

"You mean report me?" I ask.

"Precisely. He is the only one of your team not to have done so." She pauses to let those words sink in.

The entire squad has reported me? Have I been that reckless? Have my actions been so obviously selfish? Have I actually put in jeopardy what we're trying to achieve? The future of humanity? My heart is beating almost as fast as it was a few moments ago, when my lips were millimeters away from Eve's.

Almost.

"You're suspended, Bram," Vivian says. "You and Hartman."

"No, you can't. Not now. We're so close. This is what we've been working toward our entire lives. She needs me right now," I beg, realizing I won't be able to see Eve. I'll never get that moment back.

"Have you forgotten your place?" Vivian says calmly, almost as though she revels in my panic. "Eve doesn't need *you*. Eve does not need Bram Wells. Eve needs Holly." She corrects my obvious blunder. "Eve will get her scheduled time with Holly as she always does, except the person behind the eyes will not be you until you have proven to us that you are once again up to the standard we require of our pilots."

I can't look at her. There's so much history between us. I've grown up here. I've stood in front of her as a boy, being given my orders for what she wanted me to get Eve to do. Now I'm eighteen, a man, but I feel like that little boy again.

"You're to take a week to retrain yourself. To get your head back into shape. We need you, Bram, now more than ever, but I cannot allow you to be with Eve until you remember why we're all here. We need you, but you're still replaceable." Vivian stares at me and I bow my head to let her know that I've heard her words, that I have absorbed and understood them.

She turns to leave and waits for the door to slide open. Before she goes she glances back at me.

"Oh, and, Bram, it's not just your career on the line. If you don't get back into shape you'll be escorted from the Tower and off base for good. Out into the world down there. You *and* Hartman. Don't forget that."

"You *idiot!*" I scream at myself as I punch the locker. I pull my fist out of the dent that has formed around my knuckles and thrust it back in, making the dent twice as deep. "What were you thinking, you complete moron?"

I slam my head into the sheet metal and hold it there, trying to calm the raging thoughts in my brain.

"Yeah, exactly. What *were* you thinking?" Hartman interrupts my moment of self-punishment as he enters the locker room carrying the black bin liner containing his hard drive.

"I'm so sorry, man. I just got carried away. She leaned in for the kiss and I . . ."

"Okay, okay, I get it," he says, and I can't help but notice his concerned frown. "Dude, are you all right?" He places his hard drive on the bench and approaches me. It's only as watery droplets frame my vision and blur the edges of the room that I realize I'm crying.

"Yeah. Yeah. I'm fine." I laugh it off, wiping away the tears before they fall. "It's just a bit overwhelming, all this."

"I know it's hard for you, Bram. You've grown up with Eve. You've spent your whole life working toward what's about to happen in the next few weeks, and it's natural that you're going to feel more emotional about it than the rest of us." Hartman tries his best to console me. If he weren't so off the mark it would probably have had some impact.

Sure, everything he's saying is correct. It *is* more emotional for me than the others. I've been here from the start and we're approaching the moment we've all been working so hard for. But the truth is, I don't think I'm upset about that. As I search my brain, the thing that keeps coming back to me is that somehow I have to finish that kiss.

25

EVE

THE KISS. *THE* KISS. THE *KISS*.

I sit there with my eyes closed for what feels like hours. Every little hair is standing on end. My whole body feels alive, wanted, and wanton. Heat gathers at the spot where our lips met, then disperses, touching every inch of me, even my toes.

I breathe into it, loving the silent buzz that surrounds us, numbing any rational thought that might be urging me to stop. I won't. I don't want to hear it. Not now.

Nothing else matters.

Just.

That.

Kiss.

When I feel him leaving, when I know they've taken him from me, I stay there, kissing the air, still able to feel the energy we've created, thanks to the burning sensation on my lips.

My body is relaxed, and I'm the happiest and most content I've felt in ages. Possibly ever.

Who'd have thought one of the Hollys could make me feel like this? Perhaps I should feel foolish for not having spotted the potential spark between us sooner.

Potential spark.

Potential.

Could Bram be a Potential? Would they allow it?

The butterflies swirling in my tummy tell me it has to be a possibility. I don't know why I didn't think of it sooner. Whatever hoops they made Connor, Diego, and Koa run through to get into that meeting room, whatever tests they completed, whatever special DNA they carry to have made it as a Potential, can't be compared to the natural chemistry between Bram and me. It's the same as what happened with my mother and father. Like them, what we share is real. It's magical. And they allowed me to make a decision about the last meeting with a Potential. That must mean my own opinions and desires have some weight finally—so they'll listen.

Suddenly my mouth curls into the biggest grin my face has ever cracked and a giggle spills out of me, forcing me to cover my mouth with both hands as the laughter grows. The cold metal of the Drop is beneath me as my back collapses against the floor.

I was blind before to the oppression and control, even if that's not the intention of those who lovingly care for me, like the Mothers. I've always known the direction my life is heading, my purpose, but as I look at the blue skies above me I am hit by an overwhelming sense of hope. For once the future holds something special for me. I finally care about it and the life I may be able to live that would fill me with happiness.

I wonder how they could change the current arrangements to accommodate Bram and whether there would be a proper meeting, like I had with Connor and Diego. It would be awkward with everyone surrounding us, and I know I wasn't keen on having one with Koa, but this is different. I know Bram to some extent, and he certainly knows me. This meeting wouldn't be for us to confirm what we already know about our connection, but to highlight the strength of our feelings to them, so that they couldn't dispute them. They would have to support us.

I don't see how they couldn't.

Minutes and hours pass while I dream, wondering what the next stages might be. I even think of our wedding. They probably don't happen very often now, with the numbers dwindling outside, but it would give the people a surge of hope that the old life is returning for future generations.

Then there are the living arrangements to think about. I wonder if he'd move up here into the Dome with me. It would make sense for my life partner to be at my side, not living out there with everyone else. How wonderful it would be to wake up in the morning and have another person sleeping next to me. A constant companion, not just someone they send in to see me when they're after something.

Most importantly, I think about our children. I wonder what they would look like. Would they have his dark brown eyes or my bright blue ones? My curly brown hair or something more like his? Would their faces be square, or round like mine?

I'm lost in the possibilities that lie ahead. Each question leads to another, and before I know it, the sun is nearing the horizon. Darkness is seeping in to engulf the Drop.

It's only when I notice day turning into night that I realize something isn't quite right. No one has been sent in Holly's place—not another Holly, not a Mother, not even Vivian. I've been allowed out here alone. It's possible that the incident has caused commotion among the Hollys, but even if that were so, no Mother has been sent to usher me inside, and Vivian hasn't been out to reprimand me for earlier and banish me to my room.

There's been nothing.

I've just been left here to dream. They've allowed me to spend longer than ever before out on the Drop on my own. And not just by a few minutes, but by hours.

A small part of me wants to believe that it's because they witnessed what Bram and I did and are busy hatching new plans that involve us both. But a larger part of me is worried it means something more sinister.

A chill creeps over my shoulders and I shiver. Slowly I bring my feet up from their dangling position and pull my knees protectively into my chest. Suddenly I don't feel so free and light. With my heart full of apprehension, I stand and start back along the walkway into the Dome.

Wandering through the garden zones, which are usually scattered with a few of the Mothers tending the plants, I pass no one.

I am alone.

Moving on to the cafeteria, where I usually have my evening meal, there is nothing and no one. No food, no people. Nothing.

As a last resort I find myself walking to the last place I ever want to go: Vivian's room. Knocking on her closed door, I'm greeted by nothing. There is no answer. She's either not there or ignoring me. Either way, I'm surrounded by nothing but an eerie silence.

This is how I am being punished.

I bow my head.

Loneliness speaks louder than any words of discouragement or disappointment. It hurts more too. Words of annoyance or disbelief I could have shrugged off, but the desolation they've left me with is deflating and cruel. Why would they let me fall so far from such a high?

I fear I already know the answer. It's to remind me that without them I am completely alone.

26

EVE

I DON'T SLEEP MUCH. INSTEAD THE EVENTS OF THE DAY PLAY over and over in my mind. A moment of total bliss followed by the crushing despair of knowing I'm being punished for experiencing a forbidden joy.

However naive, I still hold on to the hope that they'll see sense in my thinking. After all, we'd be working with Mother Nature, not fighting against her. Likewise, they'd have my full cooperation and I'd be happy, not acting like the sulky teenager they've turned me into with their bullying.

Even though there's so much to think about, I must have drifted into sleep at some point during the night, because when I wake up it's morning and the sun is shining through my window as usual. For a nanosecond I find myself wondering whether everything has returned to normal. Perhaps they've decided they've made their point and that I needn't continue my exile. Maybe they even want to talk through my ideas.

I soon realize I'm wrong.

Silence fills my ears, and my bedroom door remains closed, no Mother sent in with my breakfast or to get me ready for the day.

Nothing.

My stomach grumbles. After missing dinner last night, I'm hungry. It's quite an alien sensation for me.

I wait a few minutes to be sure no one's coming, but when my door fails to open I decide to get myself ready. It's a ridiculous notion, my having to rely on the Mothers for everything anyway. It's not as though they can do it for the rest of my life.

I walk into my bathroom and undress myself. While I'm removing my nightdress I catch a glimpse of my naked flesh in the mirror. I stop and walk toward it. I rarely get a chance to look at myself in this way. There's always someone watching, eager to move me along and get me ready for the day ahead, but now that they're not here, I have the freedom to study myself.

My eyes trace the pertness of my lopsided breasts, my small waist, and the curve of my hips—all covered with smooth pale skin. Is this what a woman's body is supposed to look like? Having nothing to compare it to, I find myself wondering if it would be pleasing for others to look at. Does it matter? Yes, because of Bram. I want him to see me like this and enjoy what he sees.

The thought fills me with an unexpected sadness.

The fact that I'm standing here alone does not bode well for my dreams. I choke back my tears as I go into the shower. The only place I can cry without being seen.

27

BRAM

SO, DAY ONE OF MY SUSPENSION SUCKED. I KILLED TIME MAINLY by pacing the dorm, cursing the situation, trying not to think of Eve but mostly failing. I was glad to get into bed and looked forward to sleep giving my mind a rest. Sleep that appeared briefly, then disappeared.

I've been awake now for three hours and twenty-two minutes. I guess day two of my suspension has begun. Day two of pacing the slick floors of our small room. Not that I can't leave and kill time in other areas of this vast, city-sized building, but without any idea of what's happening up in the Dome, without knowing when I'll see Eve again, I've lost my purpose.

Hartman is still sleeping. He's taking it well, considering none of it is his fault, but I feel stabs of guilt deep in my gut when I think of how I've risked our futures. His snoring is reassuring, though, even comforting. I roll over and peep out from my bunk up at his and see a few wisps of curly brown hair poking out, flapping in the breeze of his breath. Despite all that's happening, he can still sleep so soundly.

We are of the lucky elite who live their lives behind the protective walls of this tower. We're not equipped for life out there anymore, and if we were to lose this . . . I can't even think about it. What am I doing, playing with his life like this?

I've had enough of rolling around in my sweat-soaked sheets. I pull them off and slide quietly out of my bunk. I slip on my casuals, still emblazoned with the EPO logo, still uniform but comfortable. If I can find anything to be happy about today, it's that I don't have to wear the compulsory navy-blue jumpsuit and boots.

I walk barefoot to my glass desk, which illuminates as I sit. The paper notes and heaps of files glow from underneath as the system recognizes my face and the holo-screen projects my welcome image, a photograph of a tree.

I've always loved this photo. I don't know who took it or where the tree is. I reach out and run my hand across the projected leaves and remember the first time I saw it as a boy in my father's office.

"Are you lonely?" I ask.

"No!" he snaps. "Holly would not say that."

He pulls the visor from his face and rubs his eyes.

Then something catches my attention. Something shimmering on his desk to my right. My mother's silver cross on its broken chain. It lies among his files and pieces of broken circuit board, like some strange souvenir of his past.

"Let's try this again," he mutters, not looking at me as he slips the glowing visor back on his face.

I don't think. The second his eyes are covered I reach out and take back the small cross, not for its connection with any god but for its connection with my mother.

As the chain slips across the table into my hands the movement awakens my father's holo-display.

"When you're ready . . . Holly!" he barks, waiting for me to begin the rehearsal for Holly's new assignment, but I can't take my eyes off his desk, which is now alive in incredible greens and yellows as this tree of light floats over his work.

I've never seen any real trees, not in Central. Its streets were flooded and the ground was way below the waterline when I was born. There was no green, just concrete and clouds. Gray.

I begin muttering Holly's lines, while my father studies the image of Holly, tweaking her programming with magical waves of his gloved hands in the air.

I reach out to his holo-display and clone the file. The tree is mine.

It's been my holo–home screen ever since. There for me to look at, to study whenever I please, both as a reminder of the world we destroyed and a promise of what could be again. This giant plant towering triumphantly over a grand brick building in the distance, the natural claiming victory over the man-made. The sun glistens on the leaves in a way I've never seen. It's real. Not like the sun in the Dome.

I've still never seen a real tree. The ones in the Dome don't count—they've been fiddled with, artificially grown to what we consider perfection, but all I see are mutations of their far superior relations. Mother Nature is always one step ahead when it comes to beauty. She's quite the artist.

I place the files on the floor, clearing space on the desk in front of me. Something falls out. A photo. Potential Number Three—Koa. I slip it back inside the cardboard folder it came from. I'm not ready for that yet.

I wave my hand through the tree's leaves, the glowing greens flowing around my fingers, like we're connected.

"Morning," Hartman croaks behind me.

"Hey," I reply, pulling my hand from the screen.

"Coffee?" he asks.

"Absolutely." It's exactly what I need right now. One of the perks of living in the Tower: they grow coffee here.

"Can you believe this stuff just used to grow out there?" Hartman says as he loads a coffee pill into the machine. "Totally extinct in the wild now. Shame. No coffee! What the hell do they drink out there?"

He takes a deep breath and revels in the strong aroma. "Aaaah, God bless science." He makes a cross with his hands, mimicking the religious symbol for the Father, Son, and Holy Spirit. I chuckle at the lack of a female presence in the ancient gesture to which so many still cling.

"What's funny?" Hartman asks.

"Coffee," I reply. He returns a confused frown.

"A powerful plant that Mother Nature took from us, yet we still have it, locked away in this place for our own satisfaction. We study it, experiment on it, consume it, and try to reproduce as much of it as we can for future generations." He still looks confused. "Remind you of anyone?"

"The floods came and we built an ark, dude. Welcome aboard," Hartman says, rolling his eyes at me and handing me a cup.

My nostrils flare in anticipation of the caffeine I'm about to consume as its scent wafts my way. Okay, maybe those mutated trees aren't so bad after all. "I love coffee." I sigh.

"Yeah, it's worth not getting kicked out of this place just for this stuff," Hartman says, knocking his shatterproof mug against mine. "Cheers!"

"Cheers."

We sip and stay silent, savoring the coffee, our unspoken words making us both smile. We've been through a lot together.

The room is suddenly engulfed in a deep red light, and a screaming siren pierces my eardrums.

Fire.

"Shit! Is this a drill?" Hartman shouts over the alarm.

"I didn't see one on the schedule," I lie. I've not even glanced at it.

"That's not the fire siren. Listen," he says, putting his finger on his lips. We hear the muffled announcement from outside our door.

"This is an emergency evacuation. Please follow your hosts to your designated evacuation point." It is Vivian's prerecorded voice.

"Shit!" he says, panicked. "Let's go."

I follow his lead, sliding my heavy boots onto bare feet. Our door slides open as we approach it and we are suddenly consumed by chaos. Hundreds of men are moving down the corridor toward us, guided by holographic hosts. The appearance of their virtual femininity has no effect among the EPO employees: we're all used to seeing these representations of a young female form. We interact with them as we would with any other employee. At least, that's the idea, but with an emergency evac in the cards, there's more to be concerned about than EPO protocol for holograms.

"What the hell?" Hartman says, staring at the commotion as the first EPO employee gives in to the crush and pushes forward.

"This is not good," I say as the first men step through the holograms, breaking the illusion. Others follow through the light, and the holo-hosts step aside in defeat, still speaking their preprogrammed emergency script.

"Slowly follow the strip lighting to your assigned evacuation point. Do not push. Do not run," they mutter while the men who share our floor scramble toward the exit chutes.

"I guess we'd better get going," I shout.

Hartman and I step out into the flowing river of bodies, trying not to be swept away in the current. Our assigned evacuation point is not the same as theirs. Unfortunately.

The Tower's summit is over four thousand meters tall at the pole of the Dome—that's two and a half miles high. We're currently pushing through the human crush on our dorm level as we head to our designated escape route.

"Slowly!" commands one of the holo-officers as a couple of people are trampled along the corridor behind us, the red emergency lighting adding to the panic.

"God, I hope this is just a drill," Hartman bellows. "I do not feel like taking the Leap of Faith today."

When the Tower was built they had to invent safety features that could get its occupants out and down to ground level if necessary. They tried everything: parachutes, inflatables, small unpiloted aircraft. Eventually two external methods of escape were selected.

The first and safest are the chutes. Long tubes that drop down the side of the building at an almost vertical angle. The idea is to climb in, close your eyes, and enjoy the ride while you plummet to what you pray is safety as you hit the air cushions at ground level. However, only one person can use a chute at a time. It takes approximately fifty seconds to ride the chute from the upper levels to the bottom. A full evacuation of the building using this method alone would take days.

The second means of escape is the one we're currently running toward. It's what we call the Leap of Faith, and you have to be trained to use it, so only a small percentage of the Tower's staff are allowed to go near it. Unfortunately, pilots are in that small percentage.

"Is this a drill?" Locke calls from behind us as we push through a side door leading us away from the crowds heading toward the chutes.

"Dunno," Hartman replies as we pick up speed.

"If it isn't a drill you're gonna freeze your nuts off in those shorts," Locke says, referring to my casuals. He has a point.

Hartman leads us into the evacuation corridor. It's already lined with a hundred or so Tower personnel. All male. The women who work and live in here have separate internal evacuation methods, far safer than ours, for obvious reasons.

"Fall in at the back," Ketch commands from the far end of the long circular hall. We do as he says. My heart is pounding. A slight breeze weaves through the fine hairs on my legs. Cold air. *Real* air. Somewhere up ahead a hatch has been opened.

"You feel that?" I ask.

"Cold air? Yeah," Locke replies.

"Is this for real? Are we actually doing this?" Hartman asks the guys ahead of us, who must be one of the engineer crews, judging by their stained coveralls and filthy hands.

"Not sure, but we've never known them to open a hatch during a drill before," the nearest replies, concern mixed with excitement on his face. People love a bit of drama in here.

A female voice cuts through our nerves. "Please walk calmly and quietly."

"Holy shit," the filthy engineer replies as a young woman comes into view ahead. The unexpected sight of her perfection takes his breath away. She eyes the line, making sure everyone is conforming to protocol. Her black hair is tied back in a tight ponytail. She's focused, strong.

"She's just another hologram, you idiot," Locke tells the openmouthed man. "She's not real. They must have put her here to calm us down."

"Actually, she's a Projectant," I correct him.

"A what?" Locke says, taking a closer look.

"She's not programmed. She's a real thinking mind," I say. The difference between holograms and Projectants is subtle, especially at a casual encounter like this, but I remember the program well enough to recognize one. It's the imperfections that give them away. The nervous tremor of a lip, the slight twitch in an eye; they're as close to being real as you can get, but, like humans, no one is perfect. This one's little finger won't keep still, causing her to grip her hands behind her back to retain her aura of authority: a hologram would never do that. This alone gives her away, if only to me.

"Out onto the walkway. Single file," she says as she marches along the line of men with an air of authority that Vivian Silva would have been proud of.

"Gentlemen, you look like you've seen a ghost. Shall we focus on the task at hand? I'd hate for any of you to fall to your deaths today." She smirks. Her words sober the men up as she walks back down the line and out through the open hatch.

"Follow me onto the walkway, please, and remember to

pick up an Oxynate as you exit," she says calmly, holding up a small nasal device as her projection steps out of sight, causing gossipy whispers to erupt among the crowd.

"Walkway? Shit," I hiss at Hartman. "What's going on? Has something happened in the Dome?" My heart stops. If this isn't a drill, if this is a real evac, what's happened? Where's Eve? Who's with her?

"Don't stop, you idiot!" A gruff bald man shoves me from behind and I'm thrust farther into the tunnel. "We want to see the hologram."

"She's a Projecta—okay, okay," I say, getting shoved along the tunnel.

There are holograms at work throughout the Tower, even out in Central. Programmed organized particles of light that perform menial, nonphysical tasks, glorified computer programs. The more advanced tasks were offered to the remnants of my father's abandoned Projectant Program. Overseeing the emergency evacuation procedure is obviously too unpredictable to leave to a preprogrammed hologram. It requires a thinking mind. Even if it is an uploaded one.

We creep along the wall toward the opening, toward the outside. My head is spinning. Why am I here? I should be with Eve right now. I would have been with her, as Holly, if I hadn't been such a dumbass. I should be calming her, comforting her, protecting her, like I did before.

Blinding light hits my eyes and stings my retinas. The air in my lungs is freezing and takes my breath away, like I've jumped into an icy pool.

We're outside.

"Don't forget one of these," Hartman hisses, shoving a small piece of plastic into my hands. I quickly insert the Oxynate into my nose—a small, strawlike tube in each nostril—and feel the cool stream of oxygen begin to flow.

"Breathe slow. These things don't last long," Hartman explains. "They hold just enough oxygen to get you out and down."

"What happens if my Oxy-thing runs out?" Jackson yells from somewhere up ahead.

"Irreversible brain damage," the Projectant replies coolly.

"You probably wouldn't notice much difference, Jackson," Hartman calls.

"Keep moving, gentlemen," the Projectant instructs.

My eyes adjust and my heart is wrenched to the bottom of my stomach as the sight before me registers with my brain. We're standing on a two-foot-wide walkway with nothing below us but two and a half miles of air. This isn't like being out on the Drop. This is real. Shit-scary real.

Many people are on their knees, trembling their way along. More than one person is vomiting at the thought of what we're about to do.

My fingers are stiff as I move along the walkway behind Hartman.

"Slow down!" I whisper. "I'm a bit light-headed."

"Keep up. We do this together," he says.

"Gentlemen," the Projectant calls as she passes us in the opposite direction. My stomach turns as she steps dangerously close to the edge. "Thank you for your cooperation. I now leave you in the capable hands of Ketch, who will guide you through your escape route."

We keep moving until we find our spots. Each of us has a small yellow box with our name printed in black letters, bolted to the walkway.

"Listen up." Ketch's voice echoes over the wind, blasting

through sound projectors suspended underneath multiple EPO drones that are hovering a few meters away from us. I've counted at least twelve in the glances I've taken. Looking out at them makes my heart miss a beat.

"Inside your allocated box you will find your Gauntlet. Please remove it and put it on," his voice booms, and we all obey.

I fumble over the lock. Twice.

"Let me," Hartman says, carefully nudging me out of the way.

"Watch it!" I clutch at the railing and drop to my knees, breathless, hearing low laughs around me. The air is thinner up here, and there's hardly enough oxygen to satisfy my lungs, even with this thing in my nose. This, combined with the dizzying sight that falls away beneath me, sets my head spinning.

Not everyone shares my dislike of heights.

"Here, get up, you're making a scene," Hartman says as he stands over me, offering me my Gauntlet from the box.

I take the equipment and he helps me stand, but I notice something behind him. It's the Dome. I saw it from the outside when I was young, before we moved onto the base permanently, but not for many years and never from this angle.

"Pretty amazing, right?" Jackson says, noticing what I'm staring at. I hadn't realized he was so close to us out here.

"Yeah," I agree.

"I mean, it's a pretty elaborate prison cell, but still amazing," he adds. He always adds.

We're standing at the base of the southern hemisphere of Eve's Dome. It protrudes from the Tower above us, creating its own horizon. I reach up to touch its outer skin, but suddenly the entire surface of the Dome rotates. A gust of wind blows over us, and everyone on the walkway clings to the railings. The Dome's sensors saw the gust coming and adjusted for it before we felt it.

"Gauntlets on, gentlemen," Ketch commands. Then there is the sound of metallic clicks and rusty motors warming up. I place my hand inside the bullet-shaped metallic glove, and its base automatically tightens around my wrist, more like a hand-cuff than a bracelet. The inner glove is rubberized and has a tight squeeze to stop my hand from slipping out.

"Sir, these things must be over ten years old. How do we know they'll still work?" a faceless voice cries over the noise of drone propellers and the wind.

"That's why we're here today," Ketch replies. There is a pause as the entire group, myself included, takes a look over the edge of the platform we're standing on at the clouds below.

"Calm down. You'll be relieved to hear that this is a drill," Ketch says, obviously picking up on the vibes from every single one of us standing two and a half miles above the earth.

I've never experienced a release of energy like the one that follows those words. A few people are sick again.

"We're testing these today so that should an occasion present itself where you are required to take the Leap of Faith, as I believe you call it, we can all rest assured that even if your faith fails you, your equipment will not. Now, if you'd all be so kind as to place your arms out over the edge and ensure you're standing at least a meter apart. Good. When you're ready you may follow the instructions printed on the side of your Gauntlet and activate the blades."

I stand immediately and hold out my arm. I want this over with as fast as possible so I can get the hell off this ledge. I've read how to activate these things a hundred times or more. When you hate heights as much as I do, you make sure you know how to get down in an emergency.

I shield my eyes with my free hand and twist the handlebar inside the Gauntlet as if I were revving the throttle of a motorbike. As it rotates I feel a vibration, then some sort of release. The sensation of real moving parts feels dated compared to the technology we use daily in the Tower.

There is a loud swish, like a sword being unsheathed, as three fiberglass rotor blades shoot out from the side of my metallic glove, along with a cloud of rust-colored dust.

That's not comforting.

"If your device releases three blades it's cleared for the Leap and will be reset back in your box. If your device releases fewer, well, you can thank your lucky butt that this is just a drill. Your Gauntlet will be replaced with a newer model," Ketch explains.

I look at the corroded rust bucket wrapped around my upper arm that just got cleared for use and thank my lucky butt that today is just a drill.

28

EVE

IT'S BEEN HOURS AND NO ONE HAS COME FOR ME. I'VE TRIED MY door several times, but it's remained locked. They cannot come in here. I cannot go out.

I'm being segregated, kept in isolation. Imprisoned.

It's crushing. I know they want to break me so that I succumb to their will and curb my own desires.

I'm foolish for having any hope for a future with Bram.

While I'm experiencing a growing fear of what's to come, my enforced hunger is causing my emotions to fluctuate. I'm becoming increasingly irritated at my lack of control over my own destiny and angry at their unwillingness to listen.

I sit, wait, and think.

Don't they know they should never leave me to think?

I must have fallen asleep, because suddenly I wake up to sunshine pouring into my room and the click of my door unlocking. It should fill me with joy that I'm being freed from these four walls, but it doesn't. Instead I feel my jaw clench and my nostrils flare.

They've left me alone for over twenty-four hours and it's my turn to play them at their own game, asserting my own authority.

"Morning," Mother Kadi sings as she wanders in. It's as if I haven't just been released from isolation.

I catch sight of the tray in her tiny hands as the smell of cooked food wafts over to me.

"Brown-sugar porridge. I made it myself," she proudly tells me when I fail to turn over and sit up so that she can put the tray on my lap.

My mouth waters. I know how tasty her cooking is. I bet they've been talking about what to bring me first. The Mothers know all my likes and dislikes. Part of me wants to consider this offering a thoughtful gesture. A bigger part doesn't.

Of course, I feel for the Mothers. I know they were following orders yesterday. I know it must have been awful for them to see me punished in that way, but happily or not, they went along with it and betrayed my love for them.

I always want to believe that their role with me is far more personal than their simply fulfilling the requirements of their bosses—after all, they are the closest I have to a real mother. But mothers don't abandon their children. They fight for them. Perhaps the Mothers are closer to *them* than they are to me. Not knowing who I can trust means I have to stand my ground against them all. And that includes darling Mother Kadi, with her inked skin, whose cheerful demeanor usually fills me with such joy. Today I'm dead to it.

"Eve?" she coos softly.

I don't reply. I just stare at the blue skies outside.

"I've got your vitamins too . . ." Her voice is wobbling and she sniffs.

I hear her suck air into her lungs and wonder if she's getting tearful. A lump forms in my throat. I try to listen harder to see if she's okay, although I don't contemplate turning over and doing as she asks.

"I'm going to leave it here." Her voice is firmer and stronger now and I hear the tray being placed on my bedside table. "I'll be back in a few minutes for your shower," she says, leaning across me and adjusting the sheet so that it covers my shoulders. Under the fabric I feel her hand reach down and give my arm a tight squeeze. Quickly, she turns and walks away.

It dawns on me that she genuinely cares and that the brief contact was her only way of communicating with me because we are being watched.

Of course we are.

It's not me against them; it's *us* against them. Whether that's just me and Mother Kadi or me and all the Mothers, I'm not sure. But it's comforting to know I'm not on my own in my feelings. The unity steels my nerve.

I won't be eating that tray of food and I won't be conversing as normal. Not today. Maybe not even tomorrow. I'm going to become mute. More than that, I want the Mothers to know I'm not sweeping my treatment under the carpet. I need them to see me and know that I'm not a meek young girl with no claim to her own life. If I have to starve myself to death to hammer the point home, then that's what I'll do. Although I doubt things will go that far. They'll let me have Bram. They will.

Fired up, I climb out of bed in the clothes I threw on yesterday and walk straight to my first lesson. Dirty clothes, unwashed body, and bare feet—if this is the only way I can rebel, so be it.

29

BRAM

HARTMAN HAS PERSUADED ME TO EAT IN THE MESS HALL.

"It'll be good for you to show your face," he says as we walk. "They'll only be making shit up about you if you don't."

They make shit up about me anyway, so that's not a compelling reason to sit through dinner with Jackson. The real reason I'm going along with this new, more sociable approach is that since they've restricted my access to her daily reports, it's the only way I can get information about Eve.

"Well, look who's decided to grace us with his presence," Jackson announces as we walk into the mess hall, a decent-sized room with high ceilings and a long buffet counter that hasn't been filled yet. For some reason they painted the walls green: light green at the top and a dark green border. It's meant to be calming, but it gives off more of a medical vibe, which I've always felt makes the food taste worse. That's why I eat in the dorm most days.

"Jackson, gentlemen." I nod at everyone as we take our seats at the end of the bench. "Today was interesting," I say, trying to take part in conversation from the get-go.

"I'd totally have jumped if they wanted someone to test it," Jackson claims, stabbing a butter knife into the table in the gaps between his fingers. Something he's obviously not very good at, judging by the spatter of thin scars on his hands.

"Would you have jumped before or after you threw up over the side?" Locke jokes, and Jackson flushes, then shoots him a death stare.

"On a serious note, did you hear that more than half the Gauntlets failed?" Watts asks, pushing up the frames of his black glasses that constantly slip down his greasy nose.

"More than half?" Hartman asks in disbelief.

"Yup. At least half of us on that ledge would have taken a giant Leap of Faith to our very abrupt deaths, had yesterday been a real evac." Watts uses his hand to demonstrate, slamming it down on the table. "Splat!"

"Damn shame they didn't get you to jump after all, Jackson," I joke.

It gets a good laugh.

"Why don't they just replace all of them?" Jackson asks, ignoring my jibe.

It's a good question.

"The chances of there being a catastrophic emergency that requires us to leap from this building with those ridiculous things is about one in eleven million. When you think about the resources it takes to replace every Gauntlet and maintain them, you can see why it's not a priority at the moment," Watts explains. He's always been good at keeping up with the politics involved in running this place, plus he loves a statistic. "Then again, they thought the *Titanic* was unsinkable."

"The what?" Jackson asks.

"Never mind," Watts replies, rolling his eyes.

"Hey, what about that Projectable thingy they had down there? Ain't seen one of them out and about before." Jackson is still fiddling with the butter knife.

No one replies. Then I notice all eyes are on me.

"There aren't that many, from what I remember my dad saying. When the program was abandoned, there were a lot of debates about what to do with them," I say.

"Debates?" Watts asks.

"Yeah, well, they are conscious minds, after all. Is it ethical to just switch them off?" I ask, not expecting an answer. Squad H thinks about it for a moment.

"So what happened?" Kramer says.

"They stopped creating them and dispersed the existing Projectants among the population."

"Jesus! There are more of them out there?" asks Kramer, fascinated.

"This is typical EPO bullshit. Shoulda just turned the things off. Soft bastards."

"But they think they're alive, right?" Kramer says, totally getting it.

"As far as I know." I shrug.

The green walls fade and the realiTV monitors that line them flicker to life. They blast an advertisement into the mess hall. Ads like this are displayed throughout the Tower. Whatever the EPO wants us to see, whatever it's trying to push on us, is repeated throughout the day at regular intervals on all public realiTV monitors, not just here but throughout the entire city.

You are the last women of our species, a mature female voice says, over a beautiful setting sun. Her voice never fails to make the men fall silent.

Your bodies are the most valuable asset we have for the future of the human race. Locked away inside your body could be the answer to a new generation of young women, but technology hasn't developed the key . . . yet.

If only we could freeze time.

The sun sets.

Well, now we can.

The screens plaster the same image multiple times across every wall of the mess hall and on the thousands of screens up and down the Tower. A clean, white, high-tech room full of silver tubes.

Your body can be frozen, perfectly preserved as it is, here inside the Tower until technology finds the answer. When we do, you will be revived, revitalized, re-energized, and we will be equipped to start this new future, mothering the daughters we deserve.

"Can't be many left to freeze," Jackson interrupts.

"Shhh!" Kramer throws a spoon at him to shut him up.

We all watch the screens. Reflective cryo-tanks, all with their lids sealed, housing the bodies of frozen women, their hearts beating inside at a rate of one BPM—Beat Per Month. Time not so much frozen as drastically slowed down.

One tank at the end sits open, inviting. It beckons the viewer to step inside, through the billowing dry ice.

Should your time come before you've decided to freeze your remaining years, we can still preserve your valuable body and use it to shape our future once technology catches up with our ambition.

You don't have to be the last women on earth. Visit your nearest EPO cryo-clinic today.

The screens become translucent again, returning the room to its green glory.

"You think Eve has any idea her mom's lying in a freezer a few floors below her?" Jackson asks as he stands and heads to the now-full buffet.

"Oh, yeah, of course, like she knows that one-third of her best friend Holly's personality is a complete tool," Kramer jokes.

"Crazy to think she's so oblivious to all this," Locke adds.

"I'm not sure she's as oblivious as she lets everyone believe." I can't help but get involved in this conversation.

The Cold Storage levels below us take up the majority of the Tower's square footage. They are full of preserved women, frozen in time, saving their bodies for the future, in the hope that one day they'll be thawed into a new world where science has solved this devastating puzzle.

"You ever been down there?" Jackson asks.

"Cold Storage? No, why?" I ask.

"Just wondered." He sniggers, shoving some bread into his mouth.

Locke elbows him in the ribs as we line up to get food.

"What have you been doing in Cold Storage?" Hartman asks. I'm not sure any of us really wants to know the answer.

"I should report you for that," Kramer warns.

"Yeah, go ahead, and maybe I'll tell Dr. Wells what you and Holly do after hours in the studio," Jackson calmly replies.

Kramer goes bright red, opens his mouth to say something, closes it again, and sits at the table, defeated.

"I guess we've all got our guilty pleasures in here. We're all men when it comes down to it. Same programming." Jackson grabs his balls with one hand while carrying his plate of meat in the other. "Right, Bram?"

Everyone falls silent and looks at me, waiting for my response. Obviously they know what happened with me and Eve.

"So who is on duty today?" I ask, not taking Jackson's bait. "How is she?"

Silence.

They take quick glances at each other and avoid making eye contact with me.

"What?" I ask.

"Look, man, I hate to be the bearer of bad news—" Watts says with an awkward smile.

"We've been given direct orders not to discuss with you anything that happens in the Dome," Jackson interrupts, delivering the punch line. I can't help but notice the slightest twitch of a smile at the edge of his mouth. "It's for Eve's safety."

My blood boils. Hartman places his hand on my arm and I realize I'm clenching my fist.

Jackson stares at me, begging me to do it.

I breathe deeply. I'm in enough trouble as it is at the moment. Jackson knows it. I relax and smile. I take a bite of my bread.

"You know, you gotta control that temper of yours, Bram," Jackson says through his mouthful of food. "You're a real loose cannon, one minute all smiles, the next you wanna throw that fist around. Unpredictable. You know who else was like that? Eve's dad, and look what they did with him!"

Hartman joins in the conversation. "Eve's dad was a lunatic. He got what was coming."

"You believe all that?" Watts deals in.

Silence falls on the group as the squad shoots him a look. Words can be dangerous in a world where the walls have ears.

Jackson breaks the moment. "There's more to all that than we'll ever know. Only those at the top are in on it."

"What's that supposed to mean?" I ask, noticing the little look Jackson gave me when he said it.

"Nothing," he replies.

"No, go on, *those at the top.* You mean my father?" I ask, defensive of him for the first time ever. It's a strange sensation.

"Yeah, I guess. Never really thought about it like that." Jackson shrugs. "Maybe *you* know too." He laughs.

I take a moment to absorb what he's suggesting. "Is that what you all think?" I ask the team. "That I'm part of some sort of grand conspiracy that ripped Eve away from her family?"

My so-called friends look around at each other and unconvincingly shake their heads.

"No, man, we know you're one of us," Locke says, but I detect a hint of uncertainty in them all. Like they've thought it, even if they don't believe it.

"I'm going to finish eating in the dorm," I say to Hartman, leaving him to conspire with the others.

30

BRAM

I WALK FOR A WHILE. MY BODY MOVES THROUGH THE SEEMINGLY infinite corridors of the Tower while my thoughts navigate the complex corridors of my mind. So many dead ends, so many un-answered questions. Eve's mother and the conspiracies around her death, most of which were born from the interviews Eve's father gave in the weeks that followed, when he was cut off from Eve, before he tried to kidnap her.

They murdered her.

My mind recalls his voice from one of the many interviews he gave. Distraught and desperate. A man who'd just witnessed the death of his wife. A man half responsible for creating the most famous person on the planet. Father to the most impor-tant human ever to live.

Enough to drive him insane?

Maybe.

I pass two EPO employees, both technicians, judging by their navy-blue uniforms.

"Sir." They salute.

I nod. I hate the rank system here. The graying men are

probably three times my age, and yet, because of my job, they are made to salute me, take orders from me even, if that's what I wish.

I've always felt that life experience, age, miles on the clock, stand for some sort of rank, deserve some authority. Not in here, it seems.

As my thoughts settle I realize I've walked past the entrance to the wing that holds our dorm. I've reached the nearest elevator to our living quarters. The metallic ball swishes elegantly upward past our floor behind vacuum-sealed glass doors, its light reflecting on the polished black floor.

Without thinking, I wave my hand over the sensor to call one to stop. It arrives within five seconds, which still amazes me: there are one thousand floors in this place.

The doors slide open silently and I step inside the round pod. As I enter, a small beam of light fires into my eyes, scanning my retinas.

"Good evening, Mr. Wells," the automated voice greets me. I can't stand being called that.

"Mr. Wells is my father's name. I'm Bram. Just Bram," I instruct, and the system understands. I have to instruct it like this every day, as the EPO refuses to reprogram it to recognize me by my first name, like everyone else does. Damn regulations.

"Very well, Just Bram. Where do you require me to take you?" the voice asks, which I think is its attempt at a joke. I found it funny when I was ten. Eight years later? The joke's worn off.

"CS, twenty-four," I say. Cold Storage.

The beam of light fires again: the system is double-checking my security clearance.

I wait. The elevator has not moved since I stepped inside.

"Of course, Just Bram. On our way. Would you like to listen to some music on the journey?" the voice asks.

"No thanks," I say, declining the optional entertainment we're offered when riding alone in an elevator.

We descend. My eardrums throb with the rapid change in altitude. Through the transparent walls of my carriage I see floor after floor of the Tower shoot by, each level occupied by enough personnel to fill a town. All male, of course.

Men working in kitchens.

Men working in engineering.

Men working in the research laboratories.

There is a female sanctuary in the Tower, the upper level. The Dome. The Mothers are safe there, protected. It's an honor for them to live there. I'm headed to the only other place women are permitted within these walls—Cold Storage.

They're either confined to the Dome, passively keeping up appearances for Eve, or frozen in the basement. If Mother Nature is observing us, it's no wonder she won't provide us with any more women.

"CS, twenty-four, Just Bram," the elevator announces as we slow to a stop and the doors hiss open. Cold air floods the elevator. It's refreshing. I breathe in its artifice, savoring the taste of whatever chemicals they pump around here to keep it sterile.

I step into the dimly lit lobby.

"Hello, young man." A familiar face smiles at me through the dark.

"Good evening, Stephanie," I say, stepping toward the reception desk for Cold Storage.

"It's been a while," she says, flashing me those perfect teeth smudged with the tiniest speck of red lipstick.

"Busy times. Lots happening these days," I reply.

"There's always time for your mother, young man," she teases, speaking to me as if I'm still the same boy who walked through the doors to the EPO all those years ago. A lot has changed. Not just for me but for her too.

"Actually, don't log me in yet." I reach out to stop her fingers typing and she instantly snatches her hands away before we touch.

"Sorry, I . . ."

"No, it's okay." She smiles. "It's just, no one touches us."

I nod and she places her hands back.

"I'll give you five minutes before I log you in, but only because you're a good boy who doesn't forget his mama, okay?"

"Thanks, Stephanie." I smile, and she nods for me to carry on.

It must be tough for her down here. Hidden away where no one remembers her. No one questions her existence. I stare down the empty halls ahead of me and wonder what a Projectant would do down here all day. This place doesn't get many visitors.

It suddenly occurs to me that she must be down here too. Stephanie. The *real* Stephanie. Her frozen body suspended in eternal sleep while her mind lives a hundred feet away, sitting behind a cold desk. Some afterlife!

I pass a man walking in the opposite direction. He hides his teary eyes from me as I catch a glimpse at his security uniform beneath his long coat. He doesn't even glance in my direction, not that it would matter if he saw me. I'm cleared to be down here. Pilots have free run of the Tower for the most part. There are exceptions, of course. We can't just waltz into the Dome, for obvious reasons, and Miss Silva's quarters are by invitation only.

I turn right into the blue hallway and run my fingers along the insulated walls. A thin layer of ice collects under my nail, leaving tracks behind, like scooping up ice cream from a tub.

My feet feel the chill more with each step. The temperature penetrates even my heavy boots. I zip my jumpsuit to the top. I'm not appropriately dressed for this spontaneous visit, but I'm here now.

As I pass the first doors on my left, marked by semitransparent strips of plastic hanging from the ceiling, I take a glance into the deserted hall. They used to laugh at cryonics pioneers, dismissing it as nothing more than science fiction. That was until it became a necessity. All these millions of women reaching the end of their lives without creating a new generation of females to replace them. Cremating them, burying them: such wasteful practices. Something had to be done.

I push my head inside the first chamber. A graveyard of the future. I try to estimate how many women lie silently inside the seemingly infinite rows of vertical silver tubes in front of me. It's impossible to tell.

This floor is reserved for deceased women. Women who were frozen after being declared physically dead, in the hope that their cells can be revived at some point in the future and, more importantly, used.

There are other levels for the brave women who volunteer themselves for the process pre-death. The odds of their bodies being more useful in the future are dramatically increased. The downside is obvious, though.

I continue along the hallway. As I turn the corner to my

right, another figure is walking toward me, a young man wiping his eyes. I've seen him down here before. Slim build, around my age, blond hair poking out of the baseball cap he's wearing backward.

We don't say anything as we pass each other. His eyes are puffy and his cheeks blotched from crying. This place might look like a science lab, but there is something spiritual about the atmosphere. Peaceful, even. Like a cemetery—except here the visitors pray that this is not their friend's or family member's final resting place.

As I reach the entrance I'm heading for, I turn back. The young man has gone. I'm alone.

I step through the plastic and shiver as the temperature drops even lower, making the hallway seem warm in comparison. It takes my breath away as my lungs fill with the frozen air. I can feel goose bumps appearing down my arms underneath my uniform.

The lights are kept low to prevent them emitting heat. If science does discover the key to ending the drought of females, this place holds the future, and it has to be well maintained.

My feet do the work without my head having to instruct them. I might not have admitted it to Jackson, but I've wandered this path so many times since I was a boy. More often then than now, back when I needed answers, when I required comforting.

Three blocks down I take a right, and count fourteen tanks in. I stop as I reach the fifteenth chrome cylinder. I take a breath and place my hand on the smooth metal. I look left and right to make sure I'm alone before crouching and running my fingers along the bottom of the tank. Suddenly my fingers find the small piece of tape, exactly where I left it. I peel it back, allowing the thing it's concealing to fall into my hand.

I stand up and hold my palm to the light so I can see the tarnished silver chain and the small cross attached to it. I sigh and rest my head on the tank.

"Hi, Mom."

I swipe my hand over the sensor and call for the elevator. I've been down here for thirty minutes and the cold is starting to make my bones ache. My mind is busy. A few moments with my mother is usually enough to calm me, but there's so much happening right now that even she couldn't help. The knowledge that Eve is unaware of all of this, yet it all revolves around her, weighs heavily on my shoulders. She deserves to know the truth.

The truth.

What is the truth? Who knows what really happened to her parents? Vivian and the EPO aren't murderers, but if something more *did* happen, then my team is right about one thing: my father would know about it.

The elevator swishes into place and the doors slide open, but from farther down the hall a loud clang echoes around the corner, passes the elevator, then disappears behind me.

I've never heard such commotion in these peaceful levels before.

I ditch the elevator and head in the direction the noise came from, my boots clomping on the surface hidden below the layer of dry ice.

"For God's sake, man, you can't do anything right!" a deep, gruff voice barks in a whisper from inside the hall ahead of me as I approach the plastic screening.

I peer through and, ahead, see two men with headlamps operating some sort of machine. On it sits a large cryo-tank with a small dent in its outer surface, distorting the reflection.

"Who's there?" the other man calls, noticing my head popping through the sheets.

I step inside. The men drop their tools and salute me the moment they see the badge on my uniform.

"Sorry, sir. We didn't realize we weren't alone down here," the gruff one says, obviously nervous at my presence.

As one of only six pilots who have direct contact with Eve, I have a certain amount of fame within this place. My badge proudly displays the emblem of the Dome, and the large letter *H* informs any observers that I am one of the elite. It never fails to cause a reaction among the lower levels.

"It's okay. At ease," I say. "What are you doing?"

"Got a fresh one," Gruff chirps, nodding at the cryo-tank on their machine. "Just installing her."

With all the high-tech science that surrounds me, I'm amazed that the installation of preserved humans is left to the likes of these two. "I see. And are you concerned about the damage?" I ask, pointing to the fist-sized dent.

"Nah, these things are practically bombproof. That little thing isn't doing her no harm." His skinny colleague chortles. "She had worse bumps out there at any rate. She'll be happy to be in here."

"How do you mean?" I ask, intrigued by his comment.

"The old birds, they haven't got nothing out there. These tubs are the only ticket inside this Tower. It's why they all sign up so willingly," he explains. "There aren't no jobs for them upstairs," he says, flicking his finger at the Dome on my uniform.

"So, unless they come in one of these, them gates outside remain closed."

"I see." I nod. "Well, continue with a little more care, if you don't mind. It's the future inside these tanks."

"Yes, sir," Skinny says, and they start hoisting the tank onto the red lifting machine once again. I walk away, occasionally glancing back as they slot the silver tube into position, connecting the hoses that regulate its internal temperature.

I return to the elevator and step inside the next that arrives.

"Where to, Mr. Wells?" it asks me again.

I roll my eyes at hearing my father's name, but it triggers an idea. I place a hand on my chest, feeling my mother's cross hanging beneath my jumpsuit. Something stopped me placing it back below her tank this time. I needed her with me.

"Dr. Wells's office," I say.

Retina scan.

"Would you require any music for—"

"No."

The doors close and the elevator ascends.

223

31

EVE

I'VE BEEN SITTING BEHIND OPEN BOOKS, STARING INTO THE AIR in front of my face for hours. Not reading. Not writing. Sometimes not even listening. I've been present and absent at the same time. English, French, Spanish, and biology: it's all gone by in a hazy blur of nothing.

At lunchtime I sit in the middle of my garden plot and do nothing but pretend I can see the flowers bloom and flourish before my eyes, my mind speeding up their lengthy process of development. Mother Kimberley comes to offer me food—a sandwich, I think—but I decline. I say "decline," but really I just ignore her while my eyes remain fixed on the tightly closed bud of a rose. She soon sighs heavily and leaves me to it.

Sitting in mathematics with Mother Juliet and I-concur Holly, I haven't a clue what puzzle they're trying to solve, their voices nothing more than buzzing to my ears. Even if I wanted to, I'd be unable to make out the words they're exchanging or give them any meaning. They wash over me. They are unimportant and futile, given the turn my life has taken lately. I don't understand why they want me to learn all this nonsense anyway, or where they expect me to put Pythagoras's theorem to practical use.

I've always known there was a plan for my life, a scheduled set of events to be followed to ensure the desired outcome, but ever since that plan came into action with Potential Number One, Connor, my life has started to unravel more than I could ever have feared or predicted. I feel as if everything I ever knew will never be the same again, or that everything I thought I knew I never did.

A large part of that stemmed from the death of Mother Nina, but recent events have forced things to spiral even further away from my past beliefs and ideals. I don't feel like the girl I was the day I turned sixteen, or when I met Connor. I don't even feel like the girl who helplessly watched her friend be murdered or who kissed her virtual lover.

I'm starting to discover who I really am or what I could be. I've always thought of myself becoming good enough to fulfill their version of who I should be, but now I don't know if their opinions really matter.

In my empowered mental state, I sit thinking about many things. At some point I linger on the wonder of that kiss and how my first experience of a true connection was literally unplugged. It doesn't surprise me that I have returned to thinking of Holly and how much I miss Bram. That relationship was one of many catalysts that have spurred my change in drive.

I wonder what he's doing and if he's thinking about me at all. My every fiber tells me he is. He must be. I can't be imagining the spark between us. It's beyond anything I could've fabricated.

I haven't found myself thinking of food, not in the same way as I did before. I don't think of the fruit salad I'd like to eat or the milkshake I'd like to slurp. Now I think of how my body feels, after almost two full foodless days. I'm getting used to the hollow sensation in my stomach. I'd even say I like it. It shows I'm taking control of my body and moving their claim to it from their grasp. That I can make myself so light-headed and weak shows I have power over it, and I like that feeling.

"I'm talking to you, Eve. Look at me."

Her harsh voice snaps my focus back into the room. I'm not sure when she arrived to tower over me, but her presence has caused Mother Juliet to cower in the corner of the room and I-concur Holly to disappear. I do hope they let her leave through the door—otherwise they're being really slack on this whole technology-versus-reality thing.

Slowly I trail my eyes up Vivian's crease-free white blouse and force myself to look her square in the eye.

I'm not scared, my inner voice yells at her. *I'm not scared of you.*

Her eyes widen expectantly, as though she's heard my head's whisperings and is daring me to voice them, to cave from my chosen stance of deadly silence.

I squint at her in an uncharacteristically challenging manner, telling her I'm not going to budge, that I'm prepared to stay mute, despondent, and wither away. That their one chance of survival is on the verge of collapse.

"Are you done?" she asks in a belittling tone, the sort I'm used to hearing from her. "You've had your fun. Now it's time to move on and stop sulking."

My unblinking eyes just stay on her.

"What is it you want?"

A silence lingers. I know she's asking me this question so that I show weakness—not just for her own pride but for the sake of everyone else. For them to turn me into a starved mute is one thing, but it says something quite different to anyone watching if I'm acting of my own accord. I imagine my reluctance to submit doesn't send out the image of hope they need me for.

She needs me to talk. Two days ago I wanted to. I wanted to ask her about Bram and figure out a way we could go about making him my Potential, my one. But her actions have shown me the answer to that. They do not care about me or my happiness. Their only wish is for me to comply with their orders and beliefs.

"Do you really think we care if you don't talk?" she asks, as though she's reading my mind. "We don't. But you must give your body what it needs. That is not optional."

Suddenly I'm looking down on me, rather than being me. The sight of Vivian leaning over my frame in such a threatening manner causes a smile to bubble onto my face. The very fact she needs to use these intimidating tactics to suppress me shows I have more power than I thought. Her words, her physicality—they're all empty threats. After all, what can she really do to me now?

I raise an eyebrow at her.

"Oh, really?" She laughs, her face tightening in surprise before her arms reach up and beckon toward the classroom door. "Mothers."

Mothers Tabia, Kimberley, and Kadi walk in sheepishly, looking down at whatever is in their hands. None looks happy. They seem apprehensive and miserable.

"Either you eat or I'll instruct the Mothers to place this tube down your throat and force-feed you, like a goose."

"You wouldn't," I find myself saying, despite my desire to remain quiet. I can't believe she'd be so barbaric.

My confidence dissipates as quickly as it formed.

"Wouldn't I?" she asks, her face cold and stern. "Of course, I could just inject sufficient vitamins to keep you alive. I think you've forgotten how clever we are here," she adds menacingly, not even flinching as Mother Kadi drops the tray and equipment on the floor with a bang and scrabbles on her knees to collect it.

"You don't have to eat to stay alive, Eve," Vivian snarls. "In reality you can keep starving yourself for as long as you like. But—and this is a firm but—it goes deeper than that. How many times are you going to defy me? How many times are you going to step out of line and cause a minor blip in our plans? Because that's all they are. Minor blips."

She pauses, giving me time to reply.

I don't.

"If you will not cooperate, lessons will have to be taught," she threatens.

"There has to be another way," mutters Mother Tabia, who is clearly distressed.

"She means no harm," Mother Kimberley pleads into her hands, unable to watch.

"She's just young," adds Mother Kadi, once she's finally back on her feet.

"Silence," Vivian barks, irritated that those beneath her are questioning her methods.

"We mean no disrespect, Miss Silva," squeaks Mother Tabia. All three stand a little straighter and bow their heads to her.

Vivian looks at them, then back at me. "I will give you one last chance to eat," she says coolly. "Or these ladies will force a banquet of nutrients into your gullet and do so repeatedly until you cooperate. Understand?"

I'm aware of a sob escaping one of the Mothers.

"And don't think they won't. If any of them refuses to follow my orders, I'll be forced to evict her from the building." Her low, venomous tone leaves us in no doubt of her serious intent. It's a warning to us all. "I'm not here to make friends, Eve. I'd be happy to have you tied to a bed and force-fed for the rest of time. At least then I wouldn't have to put up with this rebellious, selfish nonsense."

I lower my eyes to my lap and note how tightly my hands are clenching each other, helping me keep my nerve.

"Very soon we'll be at the point of retraction, a step closer to achieving our race's survival. Play your part, Eve. Do. Your. Duty." Her voice is slow and punchy, but barely above a growl. It's scarier than when she shouts at me. It's more calculated and manipulative, more than empty threats.

My body curls and shrinks as her words keep coming.

"The public is on your side, but fail to deliver and that'll quickly change. You gave them hope once, but they will act in the most vulgar and crude ways if what they live and fight for is taken away. I'd hate them to learn it was your selfish actions that caused humanity's demise. They wouldn't think so much of their precious Eve if they heard she was uncooperative and not looking after herself. And if you're not doing as we ask, you're of no use to us here. We'd continue looking at other alternatives and send you out there. Alone." Something outside must catch her attention as she looks over her shoulder and listens before turning back to me and continuing. "But I'm sure it won't come to that. I've raised you to have more sense."

She inhales a lungful of air as though wanting to say more, but instead she walks out of the classroom door.

I breathe a sigh of relief and feel my head spin. The last thing I'm aware of is Mother Kimberley wailing before the world goes black and I fall onto the cold tiles of the floor beneath me.

32

BRAM

"HE'S UNAVAILABLE." MY FATHER'S ASSISTANT, WOO, SAYS WHILE picking her pristine holographic teeth with her holographic thumbnail, barely looking at me from her perch behind the solid steel desk.

"Tell him it's me and that it's important," I say, not in any mood to be messed with. I've never understood why my father programmed such a difficult assistant.

Woo looks at me through her small gray eyes with resentment, like I'm an ant at a picnic. Perhaps she's just programmed to dislike me. "Look, Bram, he's busy and said he doesn't want to be disturbed. Okay?" she says, as if I'm still that ten-year-old kid wanting my father to fix my broken toy airplane. One of the downsides of growing up in the same place, surrounded by the same people, is that to some I'm still just the boss's kid. Even to holograms, it seems.

"Now, I've got important work to be getting on with." Her eyes return to whatever trash she's programmed to simulate reading.

"Tell him I've been down with Mom," I say, and instantly

Woo's face changes. She sighs. I knew that'd get her attention. Dad hates me visiting Mom. He knows it's where I go when my mind is troubled, when I have questions. Funny how the dead sometimes have more answers than the living. Tonight, though, I'm hoping that's not the case.

Woo stares at me with her not-impressed/could-really-do-without-this resting face.

I've had enough of waiting.

I walk toward the door to my father's office. It's not protected by the same technology as the rest of the building. He creates the most advanced technological systems, but he prefers to be surrounded with things that remind him of his past, of the world he came from. The steel desk is the last metallic surface I see as I head down the oak-clad corridor toward his office.

As I get closer I can see light through the frosted glass coming from inside and his silhouette waving his arms in the air.

"Bram!" Woo calls, her hologram glitching slightly as she tries to keep up with me. "Dr. Wells!"

I open the door without knocking.

My father whips around to face me from beside his leather-bound desk, but he can't see me through the visor on his head. A pilot's visor.

He rips it off and, for a brief moment, I catch a glimpse of the display inside. I recognize it instantly. The Dome.

"Bram? What are you doing here?" He's obviously flustered.

"Sorry, Dad," I say as Woo arrives at the doorway, appearing out of breath.

"Dr. Wells, he pushed past. I couldn't—"

"It's okay, Woo," my father says, holding up his hands to calm her. "You can leave us."

Woo shoots me the filthiest look, then disappears back down the hall.

"Come in and close the door," my father tells me.

I do as he says, and while my back is turned, I hear the elastic snap of him removing his kinetic gloves. "I've been testing some software updates to the system. I think you're going to like them," he says, pointing to the visor lying on his desk.

"Sounds exciting," I say, not sounding in the least bit excited as my mind races forward, assessing the best way to get the answers I need from him.

"That is, if you return from this suspension, of course. How are you coping? What's it been—two days now?" he asks, packing the visor into a titanium case.

"Fine," I lie, not wanting to give him the satisfaction.

"Really?" The foam lining squeaks as he slides the visor snugly inside. The sound makes me shudder. "That's disappointing. I was hoping it would be a lesson to you, son."

Son. The way he emphasizes the word makes it seem forced. Like he's so not used to saying it.

"A lesson?" I ask.

"Yes, a lesson in discipline. A lesson in restraint. For too long you've walked the line, and your name, *my* name, has kept you here when so many others would have lost a whole lot more than their jobs," he spits, not making eye contact with me.

"That's the only reason I'm here, is it? Because of *your* name? Not because I'm the best-performing pilot the EPO has ever employed, or the longest-serving, most dedicated member of the squad? The one Eve trusts more than anyone else?" I bite back, my heart beginning to race.

"Eve trusts you, that's true, but you have abused that trust, like other foolish young men before you." Carefully and precisely, he closes the lid of the visor case and locks it with his thumbprint.

"Well, I guess that's something we all have in common in this place," I snap. He doesn't say anything, but his face dares me to continue the thought. "We've all abused her trust. Everyone in this place, from the guards at level zero through to Vivian in the penthouse. Eve lives up there in the 'perfect' world Vivian invented for her, a world that you helped create, completely oblivious to reality."

"Guilty as charged," he says, holding up his hands, mocking surrender. "But tell me, son"—he moves to the window and flicks his wrist—"would this inspire you to save humanity?"

The outside storm bursts to life on the screen. Rain pounds the side of the Tower as a bolt of lightning illuminates the pollution clouds, bathing the room in a deep, eerie purple.

"Would you want to save a race that has done everything but completely destroy the planet sustaining it?" he asks, and there's fire in his eyes that I've not seen since we first came here. When Vivian plucked him from the gutter and gave him purpose, gave him power.

"If that would be her choice, then it's one we surely deserve. What gave us the right to decide for her?" I ask slowly and calmly.

"My God, boy, you're beginning to sound like one of them." He seems truly disgusted by my question as he points to the faint silhouette of the city's cloudscrapers in the distance.

There is silence. The atmosphere is thick. I can sense his

frustration with me building, like the storm. The signals he's projecting are hateful. My father can't even look at me.

"How is she?" I ask.

"You're not permitted to know that while you're on suspension," he replies.

"Oh, come on, Dad. Is she okay?" I ask again.

He closes his eyes and sighs, letting his shoulders sink underneath his crisp, deep red shirt. "I think it's time you returned to your dorm and studied," he says bluntly.

"Sending me to my room? I'm not a kid anymore."

He pauses. I sense his irritation at my persistence, but I hold my ground. I'm not going anywhere.

"What did you come here for?" he asks, obviously wanting to get rid of me.

"I need some answers."

The room is quiet and my father is still. I see lightning striking the city, reflected in the lenses of my father's glasses as he stares outside. Magnified and warped. That's how he views the world. .

"Answers?" he asks.

I nod.

"Answers require questions," he says.

"Corinne Warren," I say slowly. That name is never spoken here, not unless it's whispered behind closed doors. It feels strange forming her name with my lips.

My father's eyebrow twitches. The wrinkles at the corners of his eyes deepen as he squints, obliterating the freckles and moles that surround them. "A name is not a question," he says.

"No, but that name raises so many I'm not sure where to

begin," I reply. "I've heard so many stories about Eve's mother, so many theories, and if any of them were true . . ."

"Yes?" My father fills my silence.

"Then surely you must know about it."

I say it.

Just like that.

He moves nothing but his eyes. They lock with mine. He stares with an uncomfortable intensity that urges me to look away. I don't.

"What stories are you referring to?" he asks.

"You know what I'm talking about. Don't play ignorant with me, Dad."

He studies me as he would a chessboard, carefully plotting three moves ahead and never giving away his plan.

I don't break the silence: it's his move.

"I'm assuming you're referring to the rumors around Corinne's death. Rumors concocted by a mentally ill, emotionally unstable man." He sounds like he's reading some sort of press release. He's been media-trained to perfection.

I nod.

"Tell me, who speaks about these *stories* in here?" he asks.

I pause. He's trying to distract me with this question, pretending he wants to discover the source of my knowledge while he prepares his true attack.

"Everyone," I say simply, shrugging it off like it's no big deal.

"I see, and everyone assumes that because you are my son you must know something. That you must be *in on it*?" he says, almost smiling.

"Something like that, yeah."

Why is he laughing? Am I losing the game he's playing, or is this a bluff?

"Funny, isn't it, how people assume the importance of a relationship? How much stature you are bestowed because I chose to bless you with my name." He places the tips of his fingers together, his index fingers grazing his lips as they curl into a smile. "The truth, Bram, is that you were spared due to simple necessity."

My turn to use silence to dare him to continue.

"When your mother joined the millions to fail to produce a female, you were to be disposed of along with the count-less other boys that this planet had no room to accommo-date."

His words cut more than I expect them to. More than I think even he realizes. Did my mother agree to that?

"I had no objections. It was nothing unusual. But your mother had other plans." He slips comfortably into his chair and crosses his legs casually. He's enjoying this. "She hid you. Kept you secret from me until you were past the age when anyone respectable would . . . deal with you."

My heart pounds at this new information about my exis-tence. It aches at the thought of my mother fighting for me to live.

"Of course, I was totally wrong."

Did he just say that?

"I thought you were just another male to join the endless list of *missing boys,* or whatever they call them these days. It was so obvious, but I failed to see your potential. Until *she* came along."

"Eve," I say.

"No." He laughs. "Miss Silva."

He stands abruptly, becoming more animated as he remi-nisces. "She pulled me from the depths of that hellhole and saw the potential in my work. She had the resources to allow my imagination to run wild." He moves to the window. "Of course, I never wanted to bring you here."

If the window wasn't just a realiTV screen, I'd be tempted to push him through it.

"Vivian needed a young female companion for Eve, and my ideas were the answer. That was when the pilot technology was conceived, and I just so happened to have the perfect guinea pig for my innovations."

"Guinea pig?" I repeat, the words catching in my throat.

"I think we both know that I'm not a model father. Even by today's abysmal standards," he says.

"Is that an excuse or an apology?" I ask.

"Neither. It is simply the truth."

"And what is *simply the truth* about Eve's mother and father? Were they model parents?"

"Unfortunately, I assume they would have been, yes," he snaps.

"Unfortunately? Was that a problem? Were parents never part of the plan for Eve?"

"Corinne and Ernie were too much of a risk. Their presence in her life made the future unpredictable. Vivian could not accept unpredictability—" He stops himself. His cheeks are red and a vein in his forehead pulses with his breath.

I'm silent.

He's silent.

My heart is pumping so hard I swear I can see the zipper of my uniform jumping. I have to give myself a moment to absorb the information he just delivered. To figure out what this means.

"Vivian *did* do something to Corinne." The words tumble out of my mouth—I'm speaking more to myself than to him.

His eyes slide up carefully, like they're slicing me in two.

The rumors are true.

My father knows.

33

BRAM

HIS BREATHING REMAINS SHORT. HIS EYES ARE FIXED ON MINE and his body is rooted to the spot, but inside his brain he is frantic. Passion made him weak. He has made a wrong move.

"So it's true?" I whisper, at first with disbelief. "Something more *did* happen . . ." As I speak, I realize how obvious it is. "And you knew about it. You've always known."

I head for the door, but a firm grip restrains my wrist. I look down to see my father's pale hand grasping it.

"Son," he growls.

I snatch my arm away and move around the distressed-leather chair, putting it between us.

"Let me explain. You're confused and your emotions are clouding your judgment," he says.

"No, *Father.* I'm thinking clearly. Perhaps for the first time in my life I'm seeing things as they really are."

"And how's that? What are you seeing?" he asks.

"I see that it's not just Eve you're keeping under this cloud of illusion. It's all of us. It's everyone in this place. We're all being fed lie upon lie, and the real kick in the teeth is that it's all to keep *this* lie alive," I say, spreading my arms wide in realization at the real purpose of this place. My head is sprinting. "It's a perfect system. Completely screwed up, but perfect."

My father has backed away. He's listening to me, watching me as my mind opens to the reality of the world I'm living in.

"So where is he?" I ask.

"He?"

"Eve's father. Where is he now?"

"Oh, he's somewhere safe. Somewhere he can't hurt Eve."

"Stop lying!" I scream. "I know now, Dad. I know the truth."

"I see," he says, leaning on his desk. "But *if* you were right, *if* the rumors were true, *if* the EPO purposely eliminated Eve's parents from her future, how come you're the only one to work it out? How come there haven't been others?"

"Oh, there are others," I say as I walk to his realiTV monitor. "There are hundreds of thousands, maybe millions, of others who worked it out long before me. Who've been screaming it, marching against it, protesting it for years." I point out at the flooded city, hidden by pollution. "I never thought I'd say this, but the damn Freevers were right."

"Then why hasn't anyone in here done anything about it? Why haven't we been stopped?" he asks, and I notice that small, malicious smile twitch back onto his face.

My heart starts pounding.

"People *have* worked it out. They've been figuring it out for years. But whenever someone gets too close to the truth they—"

Suddenly, red emergency lighting engulfs the room, and the piercing screech of a siren vibrates inside my skull.

I see shattered glass on the floor by my father's feet. Glass from the emergency alarm. My dad has pulled the security alarm on me.

In the pulsing red light, I catch a flash in the reflection of my father's glasses as his head whips up from the top drawer of his vintage desk. Something glistens in the light. It's heavy in his hands as he raises the long barrel in my direction.

I dive behind the chair as he pulls the trigger of the antique weapon. The explosion blasts a hole twice as big as my head in the leather.

My body slides across the polished hardwood floor and I'm stopped only by the wall.

"I should have done this the second you were born." He pulls the trigger again. The wood at my feet splinters into a thousand shards. His inexperienced aim and the age of the gun are the only reasons I'm not plastered all over the wall.

"Dr. Wells?" Woo calls from the other side of the door.

I take advantage of the distraction and bolt toward it. My father doesn't hesitate. He wants me dead. I'm too dangerous now. I know too much.

He shoots.

The glass shatters, revealing Woo's cowering figure. I leap through the now-empty frame and don't look back.

Woo freezes on the spot, paralyzed with her programmed fear in the center of the hallway. I hurtle through her as though she's nothing but air, disturbing the flow of light as I sprint down the corridor as fast as my boots will carry me. I don't stop to see where the next shot lands, but the shower of wood splinters and chippings suggests that it was the wall to my right.

My feet feel the smooth poured concrete under them as I land after hurdling the steel desk, the lights making everything red, then pitch black.

Red.

Black.

Red.

Black.

Ketch.

His squad exits the elevator, armed and ready.

"Arrest him!" my father calls as he rounds the corner, his gun nowhere to be seen. "He is a traitor and a liar and not to be trusted. He is now to be considered a threat to Eve's safety. You have my orders to arrest him using any methods necessary."

I look Ketch in the eye. I can see his confusion.

"Bram," he says. "Let's calm this down, shall we?"

I may know these guys, but my father owns them. From now on they cannot be trusted. I can't assume they'll go easy on me. Their eyes have not been opened yet. They are still part of the lie. This is what they are trained for.

"You don't have to do this, Ketch," I say, keeping my eyes on all five members of his security force as they reposition themselves to get the advantage over me. "Don't trust him, guys. We've all been lied to."

"He has been brainwashed. Do not listen to a word he is saying. Arrest him at once," my father demands, standing behind the steel desk.

"You know the drill now, Bram," Krutz, second in command, says as he approaches me. "Take my hand and we won't have a problem."

He reaches out to me, spreading his gloved fingers wide. His fingertips glow blue and emit a soft, steam-like haze. A Pacify Glove: designed to induce a peaceful, unconscious state in whoever takes the hand of the wearer. The action of taking someone's hand symbolizes compliance, surrender, when all options have been exhausted and there's nowhere left to run.

"Bram?" He steps a little closer. Spreading his fingers wider.

Tiny blue dots appear on my chest in my peripheral vision. I sense more than see them. The alternative way to use the Pacify Glove: half a million volts pulse through the subject's chest and into the heart. Not quite as peaceful as the first option, but far more common.

"Don't make me do this, Bram. I like you, man," he says as the squad edges a little closer. They create a semicircle in front of me, blocking my path to the elevator. The route to my father's office sits to my right, a dead end—literally. Behind me, a solid wall, unimaginably thick, acts like the sixth member of Ketch's team, boxing me in.

I scan my surroundings, searching every surface, every object. I feel adrenaline rip through my veins as my body switches to fight-or-flight mode. Fighting is not an option. Flight?

My back hits the wall as I take the last step away from them.

My heart stops.

As they continue approaching I slide my hand discreetly behind my back and feel along the cold panel. It's smooth, nothing there as I run my hand along, but then . . .

It's here! I feel it.

An emergency-exit chute.

I don't have to see it to know exactly what my fingers are touching. A small glass box with a red handle inside. Above it there is writing: *Pull to activate chute. Emergency use only.* They line the walls of every floor at regular intervals, my father's office being no exception. Thank God for health and safety regulations.

The blue beams of laser light on my chest burn hotter as the team looms closer.

I don't waste another second.

I pound the glass with my fist, open my mouth, and pull the handle as hard as I can.

I feel the air freeze instantly as the seal to the chute entrance cracks open. The difference in air pressure blows the wall panel out and sucks it down the chute. The squad members drop to their knees, grabbing at their ears with their hands, their eardrums having burst the second I opened a hole in the side of the building. Opening your mouth allows the pressure to disperse. Simple but effective.

Their pain buys me a few seconds. I use them to glance at my father, who is scrambling back to his feet behind the desk, fear, anger, and pain on his face.

Our eyes meet, and in that moment he knows I'll come back.

I'll come back for Eve.

I lean backward and let the air take me through the chute, over the edge of the building, and down toward the world below. The world outside the Tower.

The real world.

34

EVE

WHEN I REGAIN CONSCIOUSNESS THE MOTHERS ARE LOOKING around the room frantically. At first I think it's because I passed out, but the speed with which Mother Tabia yanks at my arm and gets me to my feet tells me it's something else. Slowly I become aware of the sirens blasting from the speakers in the hallway, calling us all into action as they alert us to some unknown danger.

"What's going on?" I whisper, feeling frail, weak, and fearful.

"We need to get you to safety," says Mother Kadi, widening her eyes at Mother Tabia as though confirming a plan. Then she gestures for us to follow her. Mother Tabia's and Mother Kimberley's arms loop mine protectively, taking most of my weight as we exit the room. We run down the corridor and through the garden zones. Several other Mothers join us, each one looking as perplexed as I feel. They gather around us, with me in the center of the group, their eyes darting around the space as though they're seeking out any hazards. The way they sidestep obstacles and squeeze through gaps belies the fact that they're all well into their sixties and beyond. Right now they're able and determined.

I try to question those around me so that I can understand what's happened, where we're going, or what we're running from, but there's no answer. They don't even look at me. Everyone is focused on getting where we need to be.

To my surprise they lead me toward my bedroom. Once we've all clambered up my spiral staircase, the glass door is shut behind us. We hear the lock slam into place as the thick panel frosts over, separating us from the rest of the Dome.

The women around me, all of whom are out of breath, sigh with relief. I've never seen any of them move so fast.

"What's going on?" I repeat with more determination than before.

Mother Kimberley turns to me with troubled eyes. "I've no idea," she whispers, apprehension in her voice.

I catch Mother Kadi's eye. Perhaps she can offer some clarity. But she looks at Mother Tabia.

"No sitting down, come on," Mother Tabia calls to Mother Caroline, who's perched on the side of my sofa. I feel for her as she hurls herself back to her feet. At ninety-six, she is the oldest Mother here. That doesn't usually hold her back, but she's not normally sprinting through the building.

I turn to see Mother Tabia muttering nervously to herself while her trembling hands reach out and swipe a handful of books from the shelf onto the floor. She places her wrinkled hand on the white wall, which suddenly glows. The edges of the shelf unit hiss as the whole thing swings forward, and I realize that it is a door, not simply a place to store my few possessions.

"What? How? . . . When?" I'm asking the backs of the women's heads as everyone makes their way toward the newly exposed doorway and along a narrow corridor lined with steel.

We walk for a hundred meters or so before Mother Tabia

pushes open another door and we enter a room. The brightly lit space is filled with a few dilapidated sofas, several bunk beds, a shelving unit containing books and ancient board games, a little kitchen area, and a bathroom. As far as I can tell there are no windows or exits, apart from the door we've walked through. There is a black telephone and a shimmering screen on the wall, showing nothing but three letters, EPO, rotating continuously.

"A safe room?" The surprise in my voice doesn't come from there being one. I've been in many over the years, usually with Holly to keep me company. These little areas are dotted all around the Dome, but I've never been aware of one branching off the room I've slept in for more than a decade and thought I knew like the back of my hand. Understandably, I feel a little duped and cheated. I haven't been lied to, but they have kept it a secret from me until now.

The phone rings, causing the Mothers to fall silent, knowing this call will offer us some answers.

"Mother Tabia speaking," she says after picking up the receiver, in a voice that seems perkier and more pleasing than her own. I watch as she listens intently to the person at the other end of the line while her fingers grip the cable. She sighs. She frowns. She bites her lip and nods. Her eyes glance up at mine, then down to the floor. "Of course. We'll stay here until we know more. Thank you."

As soon as she's hung up, the rest of the Mothers ask all the questions I'm wondering.

"What has happened?"

"Are we in danger?"

"Where are we?"

"How long will we be in here for?"

"Who was on the phone?"

"Calm down, calm down," Mother Tabia says, waving her hands to shush us. "It was Ketch. There's been a situation downstairs."

"What sort of situation?" asks Mother Kimberley.

"I'm not sure."

"Well, what did he say?" demands Mother Caroline impatiently, her hands rubbing her hips.

Mother Tabia glances at me and they fall silent.

Ah. They have decided this matter is not for my ears.

"What's happened?" I ask, aware that my voice is louder than I mean it to be.

"Everything is fine. This is only a precaution," Mother Tabia says calmly.

"A precaution from what?"

"I'm not sure."

"Then what was said on the phone?" I'm letting her know that I'm not going to leave the matter until I'm told more.

"Someone has threatened our security," she reveals, pressing the palms of her hands together, as though in prayer.

All the Mothers start talking at once, asking more questions or muttering their concerns to themselves.

"Now, now," Mother Tabia calls over them. "We're safe here, so let's not panic until we know more. For now let's just sit tight. We won't be in here long, I'm sure."

"I'll pop the kettle on," Mother Kimberley says decisively, scuttling off into the kitchen area while the other Mothers congregate in groups to continue speculating—some just standing in the middle of the room, others getting comfortable on the red sofas lining the walls. As awful as it is, I take some comfort from the fact that I'm not the only one being kept in the dark.

"You should have a lie-down," says Mother Kadi, her hand gripping my elbow as she leads me toward a lower bunk bed.

"I don't want to," I moan.

"Well, you will," she says, handing me my Rubik's Cube, which she must've picked up from my room. I place it on the bed next to me. I'm glad she brought it, but I'm not about to tell her that. "And you're going to eat something too."

The firmness in her voice stops me from answering back.

I crouch on the bunk as asked and almost feel relieved as my tired body melts into the mattress. I am beaten, both mentally and physically. I'm exhausted.

Satisfied that I've listened to her, Mother Kadi pats my shoulder before turning away. I watch her exchange a few words with each of the others, eventually reaching the mini kitchen area, where she rummages through the cupboards and starts pulling out tins, each one hitting the countertop with a loud clank that makes my head throb.

I rub my temples, wondering how my life could've flipped so dramatically in the last forty-eight hours.

While Mother Kadi dollops food onto a plate, Mother Tabia approaches and stands beside her. As they have their backs to me, I can't make out what's being said, but their hushed tones make it all the more intriguing. The conversation goes back and forth, Mother Kadi nodding in agreement. Apparently satisfied, Mother Tabia busies herself with sorting through the books while Mother Kadi snatches up some cutlery and the plate, then heads over to me.

I shuffle backward, making space so that she can perch on the side of my bed. She puts the plate beside me and offers me the knife and fork. Even though I'm not hungry, I sit up and put a spoonful of cold baked beans into my mouth and chew. My tummy growls. I shovel in spoonful after spoonful until I clear the plate. I instantly feel heavy and sick.

"Thank you," Mother Kadi whispers, her hand resting on my wrist before she picks up the Rubik's Cube by my pillow and plays with it—treating it like a ball.

As I look at her I remember Vivian's threat to evict her and the others. But if the outside world is as pleasant as they've made me think it is, then what would be the issue? To live out there, to have that little stream to sit beside would be a blessing. That's why I'm here, surely: to ensure that future generations get to enjoy that beauty.

Vivian spoke of the world outside in much the same way that she told me of the guards all those years ago: that I had to hide myself and avoid eye contact with them so that I didn't get *spoiled*.

And Mother Nina admitted that women stopped going to bars. I don't think she would've lied to me about such a thing. In a time of no hope, I can almost understand things changing to protect the last generations of women. But that was before I was born. Before I gave them the opportunity to ensure that our race survived.

If the public really is looking to me for hope, surely they wouldn't hurt me. And if that is so, why do I need Vivian to dictate things? Surely there's a way for all of this to happen naturally.

I'm sure that, just as Vivian said, the world outside contains cruel and barbaric people, but others may be full of compassion. Living up here in confinement means I have no way of knowing.

"Feeling better?" Mother Kadi asks.

I nod and smile. "What's happened?" I ask, keeping my voice low in the hope that she'll confide in me.

"Eve . . ." She sighs, putting my toy back beside me as she realizes that the main reason I've complied with her requests is to gain information.

"I want to know why we're in here."

"There was an incident," she mutters, glancing at the other Mothers, who're talking among themselves.

"Keep going," I whisper, picking up my Rubik's Cube as though we aren't even talking to each other.

"Your friend."

Bram.

"Did anything happen?"

"Your friend has left," she says.

I run the words over in my head and try to make sense of them, wondering if they've kicked him out or whether he's fled, because surely he would've stayed if that were an option.

"Gone where?" I ask slowly, still twisting the toy in my hands as my brain churns through possibilities and panics at the thought of life without him. "Is he okay?"

"I don't know."

"What happened?" I sit up so that I can hear her more clearly.

"I've not been told exactly, but there was a concern that you might be the target of an attack."

"He'd never hurt me," I say, feeling the blood drain from

my face at the thought of someone I care about so much possibly being capable of such a thing.

"Eve. Not all people are good," she says.

"I know that." I frown, annoyed that she considers me so gullible and naive. I encounter the wrath of Vivian on a daily basis, and I witnessed the murder of the kindest woman I've ever known: of course there are bad souls, but I'm certain Bram is not one of them.

"Do you?" she says, her voice calm and kind as she pulls her fingers through my ponytail. "Sometimes I wonder if they've done you a disservice by allowing you to remain so sheltered here."

"I'm not sheltered." My jaw tenses.

She opens her mouth to say more but stops herself.

"I know there are bad people in the world," I tell her adamantly. "He's not one of them. He's nothing like Diego."

"Maybe not, but there are also people who think they're good but can't distinguish whether their actions work for good or evil. Their views are wonky, their trust misplaced."

"How do you know yours aren't?"

She gives me a stern look as she takes a long, slow breath.

"I made a pledge to protect you, as has every woman in this room," she says. "We love you as though you were one of our own children."

"Did you have any other children?" I ask.

"I miscarried several times—all girls—but birthed eight boys," she says, her tone unwavering.

"And where are they now?"

The wooden beads around her neck bash together as she shrugs. "I made a choice when I came here. You. You were my choice."

"But your boys?"

Her expression is unabashed.

"So they made you disown your own flesh and blood?"

"It's not that simple or heartless. We want a future for our children." She sniffs, looking around the room before bowing her head into her chest. "We believe in you, Eve, so we have given you our all."

"At such a cost?" I ask, hearing the pain in my own voice.

I've always been drawn to Mother Kadi. There's something about her that's enchantingly unique. She seems full of wisdom and a certain worldliness. Perhaps it's the colorful beads, or the age-blurred tattoos that tell of a cultured life before she came here. She's petite, but she's fearlessly strong in spirit. I don't understand how such a woman could walk away from her family for someone she didn't know. It doesn't make sense to me.

"That's not for you to worry about," she says, getting up and ending the conversation. Before she leaves me she turns and places her mouth against my ear: "For what it's worth, I don't think he'd hurt you either. But they don't want him near you."

I watch as she straightens up and takes my plate to the sink, then accepts a cup of tea from Mother Kimberley.

Closing my eyes, I pretend to sleep, but all I can focus on is a tightening sensation in my chest and an overwhelming feeling of loss.

He's really left me.

35

BRAM

I'M FALLING HEADFIRST, UPSIDE DOWN ALONG A SLIM CARBON-fiber tube. Emergency strip lighting flashes past, blinding me.

I try to glance back up the chute. Has anyone followed me? It's impossible to move my head due to the g-force holding me against the wall as the chute rounds out, following the contours of the exterior of the mountain-shaped Tower. My body slows from terminal velocity to a slightly more comfortable speed.

I can move again. Just. The forces from the fall are diminishing as I approach flood level. I need to move fast. I need to think fast. Ketch's team will be making their way to wherever this chute ends. I won't have long.

I lift my head and peer along the miles of tube I'm leaving behind. I never thought I'd be using one of these things. I'd rather this than a Gauntlet, though.

Something hits me. A freezing-cold force slams into the top of my head, shooting down my neck and back like lightning. I want to scream with pain, but my breath is taken away from me as the icy temperature engulfs my entire body.

The next panel of emergency lighting flashes by in a burst of yellow, and I see that the chute is half full of water. This is not normal.

This is not good.

My whole body burns as I submerge in the liquid, my descent slowing rapidly. There's no going back: this chute is a one-way trip with only one exit. Like the Gauntlets, not all chutes on the Tower were operational after today's drill. Some were declared unsafe and scheduled for maintenance. I guess this is why.

The water is up to my chest as I continue sliding downward. My ears submerge and I feel my body slowing even more. My heart pounds. How far is the exit? How long can I hold my breath? Is this tube big enough to swim in? I'm about to find out all those answers.

It happens fast. The chute drops again, winding around the Tower, and I'm totally submerged. Completely upside down. My body slows as I sink into the water.

I pull my arms up and try to swim, but my elbows hit the walls of the tube. I can just about kick my legs to give me some forward motion. It'll have to be enough. It's all I've got.

I open my eyes and the pain is intense. Excruciating. It feels like the fluid inside them wants to freeze.

I kick. I know my body is using oxygen fast, but I'm not going to die without a fight.

I use my fingers to grip the walls, assisting my restricted legs by pulling myself downward along the tube, clawing chunks of ice out of my way.

I can hear my heartbeat. It practically echoes around my head, like a drummer inside my skull. It gets faster. Faster. Booming down the tube ahead of me.

I must go down. It's against every instinct: when you're submerged in water you want to go up, but if I turn back I'll never get out. They'll leave me to rot in here. I must keep moving. There are only two options for me now: either I make it out, or I die trying.

Suddenly I see it.

The chute straightens in front of me, leveling off from vertical to horizontal in a tight bend, at the end of which is another panel of yellow lights, this one circled by green.

Green is good.

Green is my exit!

My heart pounds at the sight, and adrenaline pumps through my veins. I accidentally release some air. Bubbles float away, like tiny life rafts escaping.

I can make it. I must make it. I kick my water-filled boots as hard as I can, smashing the side of the tube with each blow. The sound booms along the chute ahead of me, almost showing me my path to safety, like sonar.

I grab at the walls and try to slide myself along faster, but my fingers slip on the ice that has formed on them. I feel my pulse throbbing in my neck as my body aches for oxygen.

As I stare at the beautiful green exit lights illuminating the murky ice water, the edges of my vision begin to darken and blur. I claw at the walls, digging my fingernails into the frozen lining inside the chute. Suddenly everything is glistening, sparkling, as though the water is full of diamonds, or the sort of microscopic life that inhabits deep oceans and emits its own light.

It's beautiful, losing consciousness. Peaceful.

A block of ice smashes into my head. It burns, but it knocks a moment of sense into me. I can see the shape of the exit hatch a few feet out of reach, but my legs aren't cooperating. My body is shutting down, trying to protect itself from the cold. My fingers are useless too.

I'm drifting like a dead satellite, lost in space.

The green is overpowering. The hatch is close. So very close. I blink and feel ice crystals crack and float away from my eyeballs. There is a small red square of lights in the center of the circular door in front of me, illuminating a metallic lever. I try to stretch out my arms. They obey, but in slow motion. The lights dim, the color fades. Now it's just white light on a gray door.

My fingers graze the metal. It sends tingles up my arm. I wiggle my fingers but can't get a grip—it's just a few millimeters out of reach. The remaining air in my lungs is burning my throat, desperate for me to release it and replace it with clean, fresh oxygen.

This is the end. My dying moments. My mind is racing now, thoughts traveling at light speed, flashing images into the forefront of whatever remains of my consciousness.

My father.

My mother.

Hartman.

Eve.

The Dome.

A Rubik's Cube.

Eve.

Dangling my feet off the Drop.

Eve.

Eve.

Eve . . .

Whatever energy reserves my body was holding release into every muscle. Warmth swells inside me. My vision goes black, but then her face appears as I stretch for the last time. My fingers grip the handle, and as the air explodes from my mouth in a rush of bubbles, I pull hard and lose consciousness.

36

BRAM

MY LUNGS BURN. I'VE NEVER BEEN ABLE TO FEEL THEM BEFORE, and now I wish I couldn't. I float across a small courtyard, flowing with the ice water that escaped with me from the chute. I have no energy to fight the current.

It's dark—black, even—or maybe my vision hasn't returned. I'm pretty sure I blacked out. Last thing I remember I was underwater, reaching for a handle.

I come to a halt lying faceup, floating in a foot of water. With every breath of fresh oxygen come equal parts relief and agony. My vision is still blurry and colorless, but I can make out the enormity of the EPO Tower standing over me. I've not seen it from this angle since I was a boy. When you make it inside the Tower, you don't leave unless you have to. Unless they make you.

I blink and take some deep, burning breaths, putting the pain to one side and enjoying the oxygen soaring around my body. As the color in my vision begins to return, so does my hearing. The silence is replaced by a high-pitched, constant ringing. It hurts, but before I can shake it off it is replaced by something else, something deeper, with rhythm, something repetitive.

Voices. Chanting voices.

I gather my strength. There's no time to recover completely. I settle my breathing as best I can, but I must get to my feet. I must work out where the hell I am and get as far away from here as possible. Ketch will be on his way down right now, and I've no doubt surveillance drones will drop through the cloud base at any second to locate me.

I hurl myself onto my side and force myself to my knees as something hooks under my armpits and hoists me into the air, like a doll.

"It's one of *them*!" a gruff voice booms. As he yanks hard on my soaked uniform, I see the outline of a surging crowd. I get my first distorted look at who he's speaking to, who the chanting voices belong to.

Freevers.

The raging crowd of protesters seems to multiply, and the men in my immediate range hoist me above their heads, cheering, shouting, passing me around, parading me. I swing a punch and hit air. I swing again and get laughs in return. Fists pound my ribs from below—one connects with my stomach, knocking the wind out of me.

"EPO scum!"

"Criminal!"

"Free Eve! Free Eve!"

"Kill him!"

"Free Eve!"

The men's voices chant all around me. I'm completely at their mercy. All at once the hands that are lifting me into the air are gripping me, pulling at my clothes, tugging me in different directions. Hands are everywhere, stretching my limbs, ripping at my skin. I've been fed to the lions. No, I fed myself to them.

Suddenly the hands around my wet boot slip and I see the filthy man stumble to the ground. Mid-fifties, judging by the wrinkles in his skin.

Wrinkles? My vision's returned!

I swing my free leg around, driving the steel toecap of my boot hard into the jaw of the muscular Freever pulling at my other leg. Teeth fly through the air, and in the sudden commotion caused by my attack, I know I have a window of opportunity. This is my only chance. I must fight.

My legs are free, and I don't hesitate to use them. I wrap them around a young Freever's head—he's around my age, but twice my size. As the crowd tries to pull me away, I use their momentum to bring him forward, driving him facefirst into the water. The bigger they are, the harder they fall.

The crowd surrounding me loses its collective balance and falls back, releasing its grip on me. My body hits the water, but I'm back on my feet in a split second, fists ready for whoever gets up first.

The surrounding men stand slowly and I see their faces up close for the first time. This isn't like watching them on realiTV monitors, zooming in from my dorm as they protest outside. This is real. I can smell their matted beards, their sweat-soaked clothes. I can see the passion in their bloodshot eyes, their hate for me and everything I represent. No, everything I used to represent.

As I stare back at the ten or so men who front the hundred-strong crowd, I see the Tower behind them. Its sleek metal frame, its impenetrable concrete walls. It is ugly, inside and out. Impressive, but ugly. Here in front of me, for the first time, I'm seeing something real. Men who stand for something they believe in, something I'm only just starting to understand. The truth.

"Wait," I say, holding up my hands. "I'm not what you think I am. I'm not one of them."

I point to the Tower looming over all of us. Suddenly I see the damage on my chute. Water is pouring out of holes from an explosion. I'm lucky I made it.

"Your uniform says you are," a gritty voice grumbles back at me.

I look down at my jumpsuit. My name badge and the mission patches sewn onto my chest and arms give me away.

"I know what this looks like, but it's not what you think. I'm not one of them anymore." I try to sound genuine, which is always harder when you're actually being honest.

"Don't listen to this shit-stain. He's like every one of those bastards keeping her locked up in there," the heavy younger Freever says.

"Wait, look!" one of the oldest says through his gray, soggy beard. His deep brown, heavily scarred face glares menacingly across the flooded courtyard at my uniform. "Look at his patch . . . He's a pilot."

Whispers and gasps ripple back into the crowd and they fall silent around me. I stay quiet. My heart races.

"Is it true?" the gritty voice asks, his hard black eyes piercing into my own. "You've met Eve?"

Do I tell them? Would they even believe me? Can I trust them?

I nod, and as my mouth opens, something falls from the sky above, dropping through the purple clouds, buzzing like wasps from hell. Drones.

"Run!" the man orders. "Retreat!"

It's like someone has dropped a bomb of chaos on the protesters. A human stampede erupts in my direction as the sleek black craft scan the hundreds of faces, dropping Fear Gas canisters on particular areas once they've established I'm not there.

I get body-slammed to the ground. My head slips below the surface of the water, where the booted feet of Freevers stomp any serenity to death.

Suddenly I'm pulled up. I can breathe again.

"If you're a pilot, you're coming with us." The scarred man's breath stinks as he spits his words at me, an inch from my face.

I look into his eyes. "Get me as far away from here as you can, and I swear I'll help you get what you want."

He looks back up to the Tower with a smirk. "You know how many of you 'insiders' have said that? How many times we've paid for knowledge, put our trust in men of your kind, and got nowhere?"

"You've never had anyone like me before." I grab his arm. "I promise you that."

He takes in my words. Then he nods, drops of water falling from his matted gray hair, a few wild dreadlocks whipping around as he stands to command his team. "Let's go," he orders. His men reach down into the water, pull out homemade riot shields, and lift them over their heads. As we hunch together beneath them and march out through a hole blown into the perimeter fence, I steal a final look up through a gap in our protection at the Tower, and although I can't see the Dome through the clouds, I stare in its direction and make her a promise.

I'm coming back for you.

37

BRAM

THE WIND PUSHES MY CHEEKS BACK AS WE SPEED THROUGH what were once the streets of this enormous city, in what I heard one of the Freevers call a pod. It's a homemade boat, its curved-glass bottom allowing us to sail silently and speedily away. The makeshift engine strapped to the back is pretty impressive for tech they've botched together out of whatever they could find or steal.

"When we get closer, blindfold the pilot," I hear the scarred man bark. I assume he's their leader. The younger, larger one nods and picks up a length of black material.

"Two more of 'em coming in!" cries a Freever from the pod sailing to our left, as it weaves between the rooftops of two sunken buildings.

The seven men in my pod look in the direction he's pointing, as do I, and see the two remaining drones following us. I'd watched the Freevers take down five in our escape through the perimeter wall, so these two shouldn't be a problem.

"Down 'em," the leader orders.

The pod beside us immediately slows and falls back. It pulls up next to a flat rooftop that sits a meter above flood level. Two men climb up, silhouetted in the light emitted by the enormous Tower in the distance. Although we're a few miles clear of the perimeter, the Tower doesn't seem any smaller. In fact, against these sunken relics of Central's ancient landmarks, it seems even more colossal.

Two rockets blast into the sky, illuminating the floodwater as they explode like violent fireworks. Instead of pretty little sparks twinkling like starlight, sharp lightning bolts zap in every direction, electrifying anything they connect with: clouds, buildings, water—drones.

Both drones fizz and fry in the bolts, then drop out of the sky, making huge waves that rock our pod as they hit the water.

"Salvage!" the scarred man calls. The two men drop back into their pod, head to the crash site and begin pulling the smoking drones out of the water. So that's how they get their tech. Smart.

The scarred man nods and our pod picks up speed, throwing cold, salty water into my face. I swallow a mouthful and cough it back out. The men laugh, but I don't mind: it's refreshing to feel something real. If my life weren't in some serious danger right now, I might even be enjoying myself.

The buildings get taller as we head into the heart of Central, once called London, following the sunken streets below us, where the roots of these buildings now lie untouched at the bottom of this ever-growing ocean.

Light from our pod streaks down into the watery ghost world below. My heart leaps as I see a face staring up from near street level, but it's nothing more than a statue reaching up at us as if begging to be rescued. We turn a corner, floating above a wider sunken street, and I see more statues observing us from the depths, as if our presence is interrupting their peaceful sleep.

I've seen photos of these statues, of when they stood gracefully in this glorious city, before the storms claimed it. Just like every other city, or so we're told.

I remind myself that I used to live out here, and as I take in the sights the city once had to offer, I can't believe people still do.

"Enjoying the view, are ya?" the fat one says, kneeing me in the back.

"Just reminiscing, that's all," I say. "I lived here once."

"Really?" He whips the black material around my head and yanks me backward, slamming me onto the glass floor of the pod. "Welcome home."

I hear him spit and feel it land on my face. I crawl back to the side of the pod, irritated that I can't see anything through the blindfold.

Our boat makes multiple turns for the next ten minutes. I try to trace its movement in my mind. I've looked down on these streets from the Tower for most of my life and can recall them, like reading a map. If my senses are correct, I think we're about to enter the area where the gaps between the rooftops widen, where the spires and towers of wrecked buildings don't meet, where the old river used to wind through them, like a snake.

Wind rushes over my face and I sense more space around us. I'm right. We're sailing down the old Thames route.

There is a click, and even though I thought I couldn't see, everything somehow gets darker. The lights of the pod have been switched off. We're sailing in darkness now.

"Dock them both and we'll take the dinghy across," the scarred man orders. No one replies, but I sense their compliance as our pod turns to the right and crosses the river.

We slow, and through the gauze of my blindfold, I see light shining from somewhere outside our boat.

"How many souls?" a young voice calls from alongside us.

"All accounted for, plus one," someone beside me replies.

"Who the hell is *he*?"

"Pilot."

There's a silence and I sense people staring at me.

"Say that again? I thought you said you'd picked up a pilot."

Someone grabs my arm and makes me stand. I feel his flashlight beam blast on my chest, lighting up my mission patches.

"Not here, you idiots," the leader barks. "Get him to Ben, and then you kids can gossip all you want."

"Yes, Frost. I mean, sir. Sorry, sir," the young voice stutters.

Our pod hits something metallic and I lurch forward as the entire boat is hoisted out of the water. We come to a complete stop. No motion at all.

In the slight pause in our journey my head fills with questions. Where are we going? Have we arrived? Can I escape? Who is Ben?

Suddenly I'm lifted from the curved glass deck, and my stomach hits my throat as I fall.

The water pierces my skin as I sink into it, the cold gripping my bones, like the icy hands of the Grim Reaper pulling me down. They've thrown me overboard. I splash with my arms and feel the cold grip me tighter. Suddenly they pull me up and out of the water.

I flop into a dinghy, still blindfolded. Voices laugh and argue around me as I cough up salt water into the boat.

"Jesus, if you're gonna spew, do it over the side," a new voice, with a hint of the north, says, as a nudge with his foot shows me where the side of the rubber boat is.

I haul myself up onto it and feel the vessel speed off. I take the opportunity to adjust my blindfold minutely, giving me the thinnest sliver of a view down the crack between my cheek and the material.

As we cross to the other side of the river, I see the glass pod we traveled in resting in its dock, suspended in a giant circular metal frame, half of which is submerged beneath the water. Freevers making good use of Central's history.

Resourceful bunch!

As the small boat bounces across the open stretch of water, I tilt my head to see where we're headed and realize I know where we're going. I know exactly who Ben is.

38

EVE

HOURS PASS, WITH US WOMEN COOPED UP IN THE SAFE ROOM, wondering what's going on outside as we putter around aimlessly. There's no way out: they've locked us in.

Drinks are poured, more food is eaten, card games are played and naps taken—all while we wait for the phone to ring so that we can know more of the incident that has disrupted our daily routine and removed Bram.

I lie on the bed, monotonously playing with my Rubik's Cube while my head becomes a little less giddy, thanks to the food I've been eating. I wonder what Bram could possibly have done to spark such a panic. The realization that they haven't sent a Holly to me keeps playing on my mind. I shouldn't be surprised, given that it was one of the Holly team who caused the lockdown, but the significance of my being put into a room that I didn't even know about is telling. If I didn't know about it, I can only assume the Hollys didn't either. And that must be what they want—to put me somewhere he can't find me. The thought sends a chill up my spine and makes me shudder. I don't want to think of us no longer being allowed that connection, or of him not being here. He's been the sparkle in my day for as long as I can remember.

I wonder what could possibly have happened. It's been two days since we had our moment on the Drop, and I don't believe it's taken this long for him to be reprimanded.

He cared too much to leave me. I know he did. I don't believe he would just have left without saying anything, without giving me an inkling that he was thinking about it. But I'd been pushing him more and more with each visit to show me himself. Maybe they deemed him too much of a risk. Or maybe he found out something and threatened to tell me. Perhaps they wanted him to do something he was uncomfortable with and Vivian sacrificed him as an example of what happens if you don't obey orders. Or maybe he'd had enough of life up here and just felt like getting out.

Even I don't believe that, but the possibilities are endless, and unless someone is willing to give me answers, I guess I'll never know the truth.

This is how my time has been spent: I've been worrying about Bram and dreaming of all the things I don't know about life in the Tower and the world outside, and how I can find out what's being kept from me.

A trio of musical notes sounds loudly, causing the women around me to hush their conversations and focus on the screen as it flickers from its usual logo to Vivian's face.

I move to the other side of the bed to get a better view. She looks as stern, cold, and unperturbed as usual, her eyes squinting through the screen as though she can see each and every one of us. Maybe she can. I've no doubt they've got cameras on us here too. She sits there, as still as stone, waiting to ensure she has our full attention.

It looks as though she's linking in from her office, although I doubt she'd have remained in there with all of us herded into this little bunker. I imagine the thought of being here with us was too much. I've no doubt her office is just as protected as this room and more practical: she can still control everyone from there. And we all know how much she loves control. She's an important woman, after all. I'm sure anyone of such stature has enemies regardless of their behavior, but as she's heartless, I'm sure she's more hated than anyone else. But maybe I'm wrong: it was the people who put her in that position of power. I think back to the Vivian I used to know and the woman my mother talks about in her letters. It's hard to believe they're the person I'm watching on the screen now. They're worlds apart.

This Vivian is so driven, determined, and focused she's forgotten how to be human. How can such a woman be in charge of mending the human race?

"Hello, ladies." She sighs, acting exhausted while slowly tilting her head to one side, as though she's trying to empathize with us cramped in here while she's still out there. "We trust you're comfortable. Well done for getting in there so quickly and without panicking—we'd never drilled for this scenario, but you coped with utter professionalism. Thank you," she says, bowing her head slowly. I look around and see many of the women nodding and smiling, finding joy in her praise, but I don't buy it. I don't think it's genuine, either her words or their reaction to them.

"Now," Vivian continues, "I know you'll all be wondering what's going on, but it's for your own security that we keep certain matters classified. They do not concern you up there, as we've ensured you're safe, as is Eve. That is all that matters, and that alone must always be at the forefront of your minds.

Rest assured, we are dealing with the situation, and things will be back to normal soon. The intolerable problem will be eliminated promptly. Thank you for your cooperation."

Vivian's face fades back into the logo as the same trio of notes rings out to let us know the message is over. We have learned nothing of the situation downstairs. The low grumbling that follows tells me some of the Mothers feel as I do, that they're frustrated at being kept in the dark and cooped up in this room.

I wonder if any are worried about Bram. He's one of their own, a friend in the Tower whom they've worked with regularly. They've grown to know him through Holly. I wonder if they're afraid of him and glad to be in here, or feeling betrayed. Or, like me, just scared for him and what might happen if he's caught.

I saw what they did to Diego when he threatened my life. So although my heart is heavy at the thought of never seeing Bram again, I'd rather he escaped unharmed.

As a tear drops onto my cheek, I slide under my duvet so that the Mothers can't see me. I bury myself and close my eyes, willing the thoughts and fears looping through my brain to stop.

Seconds later a hand lands on my arm and I feel someone lean over me, then plant a kiss on my cheek.

"Please don't cry, little one," Mother Kimberley's voice whispers with a quiver. "I'm so sorry we left you, Eve. We were wrong. We're here *for* you. We're yours." Her cheek rests on mine for a few seconds longer. Then she leaves me on my own once more.

They're scared, I realize.

At least when Vivian threatens me I know she can't do anything to me. Yes, she can take away my possessions, my food, and lock me in my room. She said I'm a "small cog," but I know I'm a vital one. Without this little cog, Vivian's infrastructure would fall apart and she knows it.

The Mothers, however, are in a more precarious position. I know Vivian wouldn't think twice about making an example of one. If I'm a "small cog," then I can't imagine what she calls them when I'm not around.

I think of my mother feeling like a failure after losing her sons, and of the many others who felt worthless because their natural ability to procreate no longer existed. Women haven't had an easy ride. Those in charge have been working so mindlessly on the rebirth, fighting to bring a new generation of women into the world, they've forgotten to look after the ones who are here. They've been enslaved to Vivian, and I'm not sure she deserves that control any longer.

39

BRAM

"IT'S FROST," THE SCARRED MAN CALLS AS I HEAR HIM PULL alongside us in a separate boat. From the chugging engine, I'm assuming it's another inflatable dinghy. "Open up."

Frost. I make a mental note of his name.

I scrunch up my face to widen the gap between my cheek and the itchy blindfold. A thick wooden door opens in what was once a glorious glass clock, its enormous hands now hanging limp, a reminder of a time gone by. This face, which once looked down on a city, now has its chin in the water, gazing up at the new era of cloudscrapers that ignore it.

"Take the pilot to the Deep," Frost barks, and Fatty kicks me to my feet. I've yet to hear his real name, but if he kicks me again, Fatty might stick.

I play blind, not giving away my few millimeters of sight as I scramble out of the boat and into the clockface.

The air inside is thick and stale. Still, it's nice being out of the chill. As I'm nudged forward I sense harsh white light on the lower half of my face. The kind that gives you a head-ache if you're in it for too long. Peering down, I see steps that descend into dark water, which ripples with the soundtrack of drips falling from every surface. Somehow they've contained a portion of this tower, separated it from the flood so that the water level within is a few stories lower than that of the river outside.

"Down," Fatty orders, and pushes me in the back. I start walking down the steps, guiding myself with the freezing metal rail beside me. It gets warmer with each step and I come to a stop when my feet splash in the water. It's as far as I can go.

"Where now?" I ask.

"Quiet. You'll speak when spoken to." He leans over me and I see his chubby, wet arm reach to the wall on my left. I tilt my head and see a switch. He flicks it, and a red light flashes on.

The decaying stone steps rumble under my feet. The water around us begins to bubble.

"Step back," barks Fatty, tugging at my soggy uniform, pulling me toward the wall.

I twist and contort my face to see through the slit: something is rising up through the water from below. Blue lights illuminate the deep hole in the center of the building's iron frame. As the lights approach the surface, the water hisses and splashes. A large iron sphere breaks the surface next to us, and the switch on the wall flashes green.

"Surface!" Fatty shouts, using a hook to secure the iron ball floating next to us. I hear the deep boom of metal knocking on metal and the screech of something turning.

"Evening, Chubs." A new voice greets Fatty from inside the now-open iron submersible. *Chubs.* I was pretty close.

"Got an extra passenger tonight," Chubs says as he pushes me toward the ball.

"Watch your head," the voice says, and I instantly like him more than Chubs.

I duck as I lift my feet off the stone staircase and into the ball. I feel a hand around my arm guide me inside. The ball dips and lurches.

"Jesus, Chubs," the new guy says as we grab the side to steady us while Chubs climbs into the craft. "Okay, all aboard? Door closed and locked." I hear clanks and screeches as the ball is prepared. "Clear to dive?" he asks.

"Clear," a crackly voice replies through some sort of on-board speaker.

The iron ball bounces up and down, and bubbles knock on the curved walls around us.

"I think we can take this off now," the kind voice says, and unwraps my blindfold. My eyes adjust instantly to the dim yellow light and I can't believe what they see.

"Saunders!" I say, recognizing his crooked nose and long face.

"Bram?" Saunders greets me with a hug. "I don't believe it!"

"Neither do I! What the hell are you doing here? I thought you were arrested!" I say, baffled as to how this ex-pilot has found his way down here.

"I was! Arrested, sentenced, imprisoned, escaped!" he says proudly.

"Rescued," Chubs says.

"Well, yeah, technically these guys broke me out, but we certainly wouldn't have got away if it weren't for me. It helps having retinas registered on the door systems." He winks and taps his large nose.

"So, what? You're a Freever now?" I ask with a slight laugh.

"Ha, yeah, I guess I am. Well, once your dad decided I was a hazard to Eve, and Miss Silva put me behind bars, it kinda changed the way I saw things. I suddenly realized that Eve might not have bars but she was locked up in that place the same as me. Once these guys got me, they showed me things I never knew, Bram. You don't know what the EPO is, what it's doing to this place."

"To Central?" I ask.

"Central? The whole world, more like! This rabble down here, they don't look like much compared to life in that tower, but this is real. It's honest. I had to help them," Saunders explains. "Wait! What the hell are we talking about me for? What are you, the Wonderful Wizard's son, doing blindfolded by this numbnuts?"

"Wait a sec, you're Dr. Isaac Wells's son?" Chubs asks. "Wait till Frost hears this!" He rubs his fat hands together.

Our descending vehicle comes to a sudden halt, and a muffled ringing from outside announces our arrival.

"Saved by the bell!" Saunders says. "You can tell me all about it later. Welcome to the Deep!"

Someone twists the hatch open from the outside and I feel the hot, thick air rush inside the small iron craft.

I wait for Chubs to climb out, then Saunders and I follow. We step through the small sealed chamber into an adjoining room, then descend another flight of stairs. The walls are lined with a thick layer of rubbery fabric, spattered with drops of condensation. We fall out into a long, dark corridor, lit dimly by sparsely positioned LED lights.

"This way," Chubs grunts, and trundles down the corridor. We hit a dead end, and Chubs lifts part of the waterproof lining to reveal a door. It's old, part of the original building, and the wood is chipping away, rotting from the damp. As we step through and into what appears to have been a waiting area, I hear voices in conversation from the room beyond.

"Good luck," Chubs says with a cocky smirk as we step into a mighty chamber. The ceiling towers over us, and the original beams keep it in place, now lined with the same waterproof material and reinforced with steel to hold under the pressure of the water outside. The place feels like a makeshift army headquarters. Rows of tables are arranged lengthways down a narrow strip of floor in the center of the room, tiered rows of benches looking toward them.

The walls are thick and sealed. Dozens of Freevers already surround the tables and fill the rows of seats, and more are pouring in from the far end of the room and above us, spilling out onto a mezzanine level. Not just men but women too, far more than I've seen in one place inside the EPO Tower. They fall into the chamber, talking excitedly to each other, to the men. I'm instantly reminded of the Mothers in the Dome, except the Freever women aren't dressed in any uniform designed to disguise their femininity. There is no separation, no segregation. These are powerful women among powerful men, and the energy here is electric. Contagious. I watch as one soaking-wet Freever I recognize from outside the Tower is greeted by a woman. They kiss and embrace as the crowd welcomes the team home. Judging by the streaks of gray in her hair, she's older than he is. The women are older than most of the men.

My eyes dart away from the couple to the flickering lights of the electronics wired up on the tables. Their setup is impressive. Far more advanced than anyone in the EPO knows.

Holo-displays project stolen classified images of Eve into the air. Maps and blueprints of the Tower line the tables, covered with scribbles and pins.

We walk through a gap in the tables as the Freevers stare at me, all studying my uniform. The room is noisy, with deep voices bouncing off the high ceiling.

"All right, cool it, fellas, cool it." Frost's booming voice calms the room as he steps through the rabble to a table in the heart of the chamber. The men and women surround him.

"So, before we start breaking down tonight's events, I want to address the matter I'm sure you're all talking about: our new guest." Frost reaches a hand in my direction. Heads turn.

"You blindfold all your guests?" I ask, projecting a confidence I'm not sure actually exists.

"When they wear that uniform we do," Frost replies, nodding at my navy jumpsuit emblazoned with EPO mission patches. "So, let's hear some more about you. Bram, is it?" He reads my name badge.

"He's Dr. Wells's son," Chubs blurts.

There is an eerie stillness, like someone pressing pause on life.

"Is this true?" Frost asks, brushing his damp gray dreadlocks over his shoulder, his dark eyes looking into mine, trying to read me.

I nod.

"Well, it seems the catch of the day is turning out to be quite the trophy."

"It's easier catching a fish that wants to escape the river," I reply.

"Bullshit," Chubs says, with a slight lisp from where I kicked a couple of his teeth out earlier. "No one wants to leave that place willingly, especially not the doctor's son, not from what I've heard about you. You've got it pretty cushy up there. He's got spy written all over him."

Eyes are glaring at me from every direction. I feel the suspicion, the nervousness, the hate. Beads of sweat form instantly and drip down from my forehead to my eyebrows.

"Please, enlighten us as to why you were escaping. Got yourself into trouble?" Frost asks, his poker face not giving away his judgment on me yet.

"I've spent my whole life inside that place. The Tower—it's like living life wearing a blindfold. I guess I was just ready to open my eyes," I say.

"And I'm assuming your father wasn't best pleased with your awakening?" Frost asks.

"That's one way of putting it," I reply. "Another way would be that he tried to kill me, failed, then set his security force after me. I escaped. A few minutes later I was being ripped apart by your men, and now I'm here."

"It's been quite an eventful evening for you, then," says Frost, combing his beard with his fingers.

The benches surrounding us are silent with apprehension as the Freevers await Frost's orders.

"Do you know who we are? What we stand for? What our mission is?" Frost asks, taking a seat at the head of the long table.

I nod. "You want to free Eve."

The room rumbles with laughter.

Frost holds up his hand and silence falls. "Yes, that is part of what we wish to achieve, but only a small part. This isn't just about freeing your precious prisoner." He gestures to the army-like battle plans around us. "It's about justice."

"Justice?" I ask.

"Yes. Justice for Eve, justice for us, and justice for the millions of people living under the rule of the EPO and every like-minded organization on what's left of this planet. Destroying them is justice, removing the unelected powers before their grip tightens even more on the precious little that is left of this planet while hiding behind their unwilling human shield, using her to disguise their true objective."

"True objective? What true objective?" I ask.

Frost gets comfortable in his seat and starts playing with a small replica of the Tower in his solid, grubby fingers. "How do you become the most powerful organization on the planet? More powerful than governments, than royalty, than armies, even than God? By controlling the most important person on the planet. Eve. They only care about Eve because she brings them unlimited power. Take Eve out of the equation and what do they have?" He topples the model onto its side. "Once we take Eve, once we destroy the EPO, we will bring back order. The first step is reclaiming Eve."

"Reclaiming her?" I ask.

"Yes. She is the savior of humanity. It's time that humanity took her back, and with your help, we now stand the best chance we have ever had."

40

BRAM

CHUBS, MY NEWLY APPOINTED CHAPERONE, SHOWS ME TO A room where I can rest. It's small and damp, but the moment my head touches the boarded floor, I feel a strange, alien sensation drift over me.

Sleep.

I'm woken by fists thudding on the temporary door. "Breakfast," Chubs says through a mouthful of something. I stand and put my jumpsuit back on. It's relatively dry now, but I guess nothing ever gets truly dry down here, judging by the smell of damp.

I open the door and follow him down the narrow hallway. Low-watt bulbs throw a warm orange light over the walls, which are made from every kind of material you could imagine: wood, metal, plastic, whatever they could scrape from other buildings, I guess. Every so often a hole in this inner layer reveals a shiny waterproof surface behind, with drops of water running down it.

I start to wonder how deep we are and how much water surrounds us. How many gallons are pressing in on these walls and this ceiling? The thought makes my chest tighten.

"Breakfast ain't great down here. There's plenty of it, though, so eat as much as you can handle. You look like you need a good meal," Chubs says.

It's the kindest he's been to me, so I hold back the obvious reply. "Thanks."

"Food's better up in Central, but too many eyes up there. Can't get away with all this," he says, pointing through a door-way to another large room, like the one we stood in the day before. In this one the tables are laden with guns and ammunition, body armor, and weapons of varied levels of technology.

"Why not? Doesn't everyone feel the same as you?" I ask.

"Oh, sure, 'course they do! We all despise the EPO. I mean, just look at the state of this place."

"And that's the EPO's fault?" I ask.

Chubs chuckles. "Mate, you haven't got a clue, have you?" he says. "'Course it's the bleedin' EPO's fault. Who do you think cuts off our power generators to fuel the Tower in high storms? Who manipulates the water flow to ensure that the city floods before the Tower ever would? We're just bloodsucking leeches to the EPO."

"So if everyone feels the same, why hide down here?"

"It's *them* we hide from, the EPO, not our kind in Central. It's *your* folk and the patrols they send out," Chubs explains. "Once a day we get scanners over Central, searching for any rebel activity. That's how we ended up here. The iron keeps the scanners out—can't get through it."

"I see," I say, genuinely amazed by their setup and that the EPO scans this place daily. I never knew that happened. I guess there's a lot I don't know about the company I work for.

Worked for.

"Plus, everyone built on top of these sunken buildings. They don't expect anyone to be down here, inside 'em. They think they're all flooded. We're pretty safe."

We enter their dining hall, where I'm served a plate of some sort of brown vegetation.

"Homegrown goodness, that." Saunders slaps me on the back as he sits next to me with his own plateful. "Floodweed, comes from right here on the riverbed. Full of nutrients!"

"Tastes like shit, though!" the chef calls from the open kitchen, comically holding his nose while stirring a boiling pan.

"Not much grows out here anymore, so we make the most of what we can get. When we excavated this place and flushed the water out, we found tons of this stuff growing. It's a Freever secret. We don't share it with Central—not enough to go around."

I put a forkful into my mouth and instantly regret it. I gag. Cough. Spit.

The Freevers around me crack up laughing.

"You get used to it. Like everything in this place," says Saunders.

"You like it down here?" I ask, having managed to swallow a little.

"Well, I guess you have to look at the alternatives. I could have carried on working for the EPO, pretending I didn't care about the way they were treating the planet, the way they were controlling Eve. I could have refused to go with this bunch of misfits when they broke me out of my cell at the Tower, and stayed there to serve my sentence, or I could live down here with people who share my beliefs and are willing to fight for them. So, yeah, I guess out of those options this is the one I like best."

After breakfast I'm shown around. It's too much to take in in one go. So many rooms. Rooms off other rooms. Small ones made into private sleeping quarters, large halls with bunk beds from one end to the other, kitchens, medical facilities, an armory. They have everything they could ever need to be completely self-sufficient.

There's enough going on in my mind to keep me busy after they escort me to my room and leave me. It seems that I'm not trusted to wander around unaccompanied yet.

I reach out and run my hand down one of the planks of wet wood that is nailed to the walls. A small piece splinters into my finger, sending a jolt of pain through my hand.

"I'd get that washed out if I were you," Frost says from my doorway.

"Sorry, I didn't realize you were there," I say as I stand up.

"No, no, sit," he says as he enters the tiny space and sits down next to me. "Splinters are painful little buggers, considering how small they are."

I stare at the tiny piece of brown wood protruding from my finger and watch my skin swell and flare around it as my body tries to reject it.

"It only takes one tiny piece like that to strike the skin at the right time, at the right place, and it can break the surface, penetrate your body's defenses. If you don't eliminate the splinter it will become infected, and if the infection is aggressive and spreads, you could lose your hand or your arm, all due to that seemingly insignificant splinter."

As I pull it out with my teeth and suck the drop of blood away from the top of my finger, I notice Frost smiling through his gray beard.

"What?" I ask.

"I think you might just be the splinter we've been waiting for," he says, dropping a file onto the floor beside me. A single photograph slips out and my heart stops.

It's grainy, but the image is clear enough for me to recognize it instantly. It's a shot from one of the Dome's surveillance cameras of Eve and Holly, and I know immediately that it was me piloting her.

It's a photo of our first kiss.

41

BRAM

I HOLD THE PRINTOUT CLOSER TO MY EYES, TAKING IN EVERY detail, trying to recall the feeling, the exhilaration of that moment. Holly's lips, *my* lips, touching Eve's for that briefest of seconds, and in that moment I knew what I was feeling wasn't one-sided. The way she leaned in, the way her hands touched me. She wanted me too.

My breath catches as I remember the sensation of her body against mine, the microscopic motors of my kinetic suit replicating her curves and the warmth of her skin against the artificial breeze of the Drop.

Frost clears his throat and brings me back from above the clouds to the room buried beneath the flooded city.

"How the hell did you get this?" I ask. "This is beyond classified. Not even we pilots have access to this sort of footage." My mind is ticking, trying to piece together the puzzle. It's the most watched location ever to have existed on the planet, but the footage is, understandably, heavily guarded.

"Let's just say that we have friends in high places." Frost smiles beneath his wiry beard.

"But that makes no sense! Someone on the inside secretly working with the Freevers? Who would risk that?" I ask, searching my memory for any clues as to who their inside man could be. "Getting to work with this sort of access takes years, trust . . ."

"It takes sacrifice," Frost interrupts, with a more serious tone.

"Sacrifice?" I ask.

Frost nods. "Leaving their life behind, saying goodbye to their family, the people they love." Frost's voice wavers, as if he's been caught off guard by his emotions.

He sees me notice and coughs it away.

"Dedicating themselves to the cause. Fighting for their belief, for what's right," he grunts.

"Leaving behind *this* for the Tower? Who wouldn't volunteer for that job?" I say, looking at a trickle of floodwater seeping in through cracks.

Frost snatches the photograph out of my hands. "If this place doesn't live up to your standards, I'm sure a return trip to the Tower wouldn't be too difficult to arrange. They've got scanners doing flybys every thirty minutes at surface level, and you're welcome to head up to see your old pals," Frost says as he stands and fills the doorway, ready to leave.

"No, wait!" I stop him. "I can't go back." I nod at the photo in his hand and he looks at it for a few moments.

"Yeah, well, I guess this isn't really in your job description," he says, pointing his grubby finger at our touching lips. "The boss's kid falls for the savior girl, just like every other hot-blooded male in that place, brain down in your pants."

"It wasn't like that," I snap.

"Oh, let me guess, it's *different* with you two. She really has *feelings* for you," he says mockingly, making me feel like a stupid kid. From him, it sounds completely ridiculous.

"Oh, please, do you know how many boys like you we've broken out of that place for that exact reason? Okay, maybe not as highly qualified as you, but still, since the second she was born, it became every male on planet Earth's fantasy to have her fall madly in love with him. Every one of these guys down here thought the same as you. Half of 'em still do, no doubt. You don't really think I recruited this many men, or built this sort of place, because they want to *do the right thing*?" He laughs. "Nope. It's because each and every one of them, even if they don't admit it to themselves, feels like he has a chance of being THE ONE man that THE ONE girl falls crazy in love with." He shoves the photo back into my hands. "Or at the very least getting a little of this action, you lucky bastard."

"Does everyone down here know about it?" I ask, wondering how the Freevers will judge just another Tower kid who fell for Eve.

"Not yet. We have our own levels of classification down here. This came directly from our source to me."

I sigh. That's one positive.

"But they'll all find out soon enough," he adds. "Your *relationship*, or whatever you want to call it, could have some use."

"Use?" I ask. "You want to use me?"

"Everyone down here has a use, kid. If they didn't, they wouldn't still be here," he says.

"You don't know Eve like I know her, or like she knows me," I call after him as he exits my room and disappears into the dark corridor of his headquarters.

I know what I'm saying sounds crazy—it *is* crazy, completely nuts. This is what every idiot snob thinks when they first start at the Tower. Statistically it's the reason 99 percent of men sign up to work there, why there are no job vacancies ever. Once you get a job at the Tower, you don't leave until you retire. Or die . . . Or fall crazy in love with Eve, almost get yourself killed by security during your escape, and run away with a bunch of Freevers. *Jesus, Bram, what the hell is happening?*

I drop my head into my hands, trying to clear my racing mind. There's a knock on the door.

"Can I come in?" Saunders asks through the crack.

"Sure," I reply, not even trying to hide my gloom.

"Damn, mate, you okay?" he asks, taking a seat on the floor next to me.

"I just had a visit from Frost," I explain.

"Oh, I see. Well, he's a tough bastard, but underneath all that beard there's a good man, you know. He's genuine. Not like most of the mindless half-wits down here. What did he say?"

I hand him the photo. If everyone's going to find out, he might as well be the first. He recognizes the Dome as fast as I did. When you're a pilot, that place is your home.

His jaw drops. He studies the shiny surface of the photo, turning it in the light to see the detail. "You actually kissed her?" he whispers.

"No," I reply. "She kissed me."

Silence.

"Well, you mean she kissed Holly," he says smugly, as if trying to find a hole in my story.

"No. She kissed *me* . . ."

"You mean she knew it was you?"

I nod.

"But . . ."

"We met." I hit him with this bombshell and he stares at me, openmouthed. "Just briefly, but it was enough. She recognized me somehow. My eyes, I guess."

"So they just let you back in with her? Miss Silva allowed it?" he asks, trying to process the impossible photograph in his hands.

"No, they didn't know what was happening. Well, they sort of did. They just underestimated Eve. They underestimated us."

"Us . . . *us*?" Disbelief pours from Saunders's face, perhaps with a little jealousy too. "Did you actually just refer to you and Eve as *us*? Bram and Eve . . . Breve!" he jokes.

I roll my eyes.

"This is pretty immense, though."

"I know." I take the photo back from him and place it in the pocket of my jumpsuit.

"So what's your plan? Thought you'd get out and run away with this circus, did you?" asks Saunders.

"I had no choice. My time there is over. I can't be part of that lie. I need to find the truth, and it's definitely not inside the Tower."

"What truth?"

I take a breath to prepare myself. I already know that what I'm about to say will sound crazy.

"I'm going to find Ernie Warren."

Saunders pauses. "Why?" he asks.

"I have to know the truth. I can't hear any more lies from my father or the EPO, and I can't trust anyone else yet. All I know is that this goes back to Eve's parents. If anyone has answers, it's him."

As the words leave my mouth I see Saunders's lips curl into a smile. "What is it?" I ask.

"You're going to fit right in here." He laughs. "We've been looking for him for years."

My heart sinks. "And you've not found him?"

Saunders shakes his head. "Nope. Too many loose ends. The list of places he could be is endless. Rumor is that they drugged him up so good that even *he* doesn't know who he is anymore, and the people looking after him don't know who he is. How do you find someone who doesn't even know who they are themselves?" Saunders shrugs.

"What do the Freevers want with Eve's dad?" I ask, my question creating a bemused expression on Saunders's face.

"Are you kidding? This is Eve's dad we're talking about. This is the guy who single-handedly took on the EPO when the rest of Central was too scared to step even an inch out of line. He made the first crack in the wall of the EPO and we've been chipping away at it ever since."

"Ernie, the first Freever."

"The original." Saunders salutes. "If we ever actually managed to get our soggy hands on Eve, if we ever managed to prize her from the EPO's clenched fist, do you really think she'd want to hear a word any of *us* had to say?"

I don't know if he expects a reply. I don't give him one.

"Of course not. But she might just listen to the people who reunite her with her father. Then we might have a chance."

"So he's your Eve bait?" I ask, half in jest, half deadly serious.

"Bingo." Saunders winks. "We just gotta catch the guy first. Welcome to the search party, my friend."

42

EVE

A LOUD BANG STARTLES ME AWAKE. FOR A SECOND I THINK someone is breaking into our safe room, and my stomach flips with fear. I wonder whether it's friend or foe beyond the thick metal. But no force is used. Instead the heavy door that's sealed us in unlocks with a clunk, swinging gently forward a few inches, then comes to a natural stop.

My surrounding community of women inhale an audible breath as we sit and watch, waiting for someone to leap out from behind the door. Seconds pass.

The phone blares, making us all jump. I put my hand on my chest and can feel my heart thumping.

While Mother Tabia hurries to the phone, Mother Kadi moves to sit next to me on the bed. Her body remains facing the threatening door, as though she's ready to protect me. The thought warms me, even though we both know I have age and fitness on my side.

"Mother Tabia," she says, picking up the phone and listening with a look of deep concentration.

Within seconds she places the receiver back in its cradle and nods to us all with a sigh of relief. "We can go," she breathes.

"But what about—"

"Not now," Mother Tabia warns a Mother in one of the upper bunks.

I know she was going to ask what has happened to Bram to make him no longer a threat. I start to wonder if he's escaped or whether the worst has happened. Not knowing is unbearable.

They *will* tell me more. They have to. I can't be expected to bend to their will while getting nothing in return.

Mother Tabia goes to the door, pulling it wide. Even though we've been told there's no danger lurking behind it, I'm still shocked and relieved to see no one on the other side to greet us.

We're free to return to our normal lives, as if we haven't been cooped up here with no real explanation why.

The women around me chatter as they make the beds we've been lying on, wash the dishes, and sweep the floor, reverting it to the state we found it in.

I get to my feet and head for the door, but before I walk through it I stop and look back, taking in the sight of the women who've looked after me my whole life. The women who've cared for me, clothed me, taught me how to double-pirouette or speak Mandarin badly, and shown me what it is to be a compassionate human. They've already sacrificed so much in the employ of a woman who doesn't care for them at all. They are nothing to her, but they are so much to me. I owe who I am to them, and I don't want to be blind like her.

"You've not gone unnoticed. I see all you do," I say, my voice rising above their chatter until I've got their full attention. "Whatever it was that brought you here to be with me, I want you to know I'm grateful it did. There is so much I've yet to learn, but one thing I'm sure of is how I feel about each of you. I've recently been doubting the sort of mother I'm going to be, but if I follow the example of the women who raised me, I know I'll be a good one. A mother who is willing to sacrifice herself and do all she can to protect and provide for her children. Thank you."

"Thank you," Mother Kadi says with a big smile.

"I wouldn't have had it any other way," chips in Mother Kimberley.

"Nor me," croaks Mother Caroline. "It's been the best years of my life, and I've had a long one."

"Steady on." I laugh.

"It's true," shouts someone from the back of the room, but before I can identify her, the other women are adding their own words of encouragement or joy at being here with me.

It's a strange feeling to have such love expressed to me, but I welcome it. I need it.

I look to Mother Tabia, the only one to stay silent. For a second I think she's going to say something crushing, but instead she smiles.

It's enough.

As I walk back to my room and straight into my bathroom, I feel empowered. I meant what I said to them: they've given me so much and I'll always be grateful, but the future is mine to write. Suddenly the responsibility of being the one to prolong the existence of humanity doesn't seem so daunting, not when I have the Mothers' support.

I stay there, looking at my reflection in the mirror and noticing the fire behind my eyes. This could be a fleeting moment of buoyancy, but I embrace it.

Before long I hear the door close in my bedroom and become aware of the silence that is left behind. I'm alone.

I walk out of the bathroom and take a breath, then go

straight for my mother's book of letters. Its pages have become well thumbed in the short while I've had it. I don't think she'd have minded that, though. Her words have brought me closer to her, even if they've not helped me answer any of the questions I've unearthed.

As I flick through the pages to read my favorite passage once more—the one in which she lists all the things she's looking forward to us doing when I arrive in the world—my eyes are drawn to something new, a page I've not seen before.

Darling girl,

I fear I'm losing you before you even arrive. Your father thinks I'm being foolish, but I think my maternal intuition has seeped in early. They're creating a safe place for you. A tower where you can spend your days in a loving environment and know nothing but good. This makes me happy. I want you to see the good that life has to offer—because already the promise of your arrival has brought about so much change—but their scope is so vast, their plan so complex and intricate, I fear my love won't be enough to keep you with me. They can offer you so much, even a garden to call your own, so that you never have to leave.

Vivian is still being incredibly sweet and supportive, so maybe I'm panicking over nothing. It's not hard to see I'm buckling under the pressure here. There's so much to take in and prepare for.

I've always wanted to be a mother, but being the

mother to the first girl born in fifty years has added
so much strain. I feel judged already, with people
wondering whether I'm going to do right by you and
for them. I could just be being paranoid, of course.
Pregnancy hormones will do that to a woman—be
warned!

I know how loved you are and can see you will
have the best life ever lived. But, my little one, what if
I'm not enough? They'll take you. They'll take you and
bring you up their way so that you will become who
they want you to be.

There I go again.

You are loved. You are yours. Not mine, not theirs.
Remember that.

Love, your Mama xxx

I read the note a few times to be absolutely certain of its authenticity. Of course I am. These are my mother's words, intended for me to read. Although they've been stripped out of the book I was given, which was evidently an altered version of my mother's reality, manipulated to keep me on their chosen path. To let me think this is what she wanted for me. But like me, she had serious doubts. I only wish she hadn't doubted herself so much. I know she would've been a fantastic mother to me.

Glancing back at her words, I wonder who snuck this between the pages I've come to know so well. It wasn't in there earlier, so it must have happened before we were ushered into the safe room, or while we were there, or when we came out and I was in my bathroom. Whichever, someone has decided to make the most of the commotion downstairs and sneak this to me. I wonder how many more entries were edited out or stripped of my mother's intention.

I look out of the window in my room at the beauty of the garden zone below, the Tower they built for me and brought me up in, because my mother wasn't around to do things her way. If only Vivian hadn't lost the ability to connect with me like she used to.

A thought occurs to me.

Surely not.

Could it all be a lie?

I need to find out now, before it's too late.

43

BRAM

I SWALLOW A MOUTHFUL OF FLOODWEED. IT COMES STRAIGHT back up, but I force it down again. I'm trying not to show any sign of weakness.

"Looks like you're getting used to it." Chubs laughs, noticing my wince while slurping his third helping.

I take my empty tin, rinse it in the large iron bowl they call a sink, and place it with the rest of the pile, ready for the next meal. It's not home, but I'm starting to see how things work down here. Everyone has their place.

Frost is their leader, a man as harsh as the world he lives in. Saunders, ex-EPO, has knowledge that is invaluable. Chubs, Johnny, Nix, and many more names I'm yet to commit to memory, make up Frost's army, the Freevers.

I take a moment to scan the room, watching the ten or so Freevers eat, whispering secrets, sharing information. Eve's name is audible every few seconds and catches my ear, like someone calling my own name.

"Bram?" A woman's voice startles me.

"Yeah, sorry . . . Helena, isn't it? I was just . . ."

"Daydreaming? Don't blame you. Any chance you get to be somewhere other than this is worth slipping away for," she says, tapping the side of her creased, freckled head.

She lifts the toughened plastic container that's overflowing with at least a hundred used tins and mugs. I see the veins in her arms pulse as she relocates it to the other side of the room they're using as a kitchen. She's physically strong for someone in her early seventies.

"Ain't you ever seen a woman lift?" she jokes, flexing her biceps before leaving the room.

I follow her out, heading back to what has become my room for the foreseeable future.

As I navigate the seemingly endless corridors, avoiding the drips of floodwater falling from the ceiling at each intersection, I realize I've taken a wrong turn.

"Hello?" I call. My voice is dead in the heavy air.

Shit. This is all I need. Such a noob.

"Hey?" a small voice says.

I turn on the spot to find a head poking out of a doorway about ten meters ahead of me. "Oh, it's *you*! The pilot!" he says, lifting the tinted goggles from his eyes.

"Hi, Johnny." My heart sinks. He's the youngest person in the Deep, one of the youngest on the planet even. My guess is that he's around fourteen, and he's not left me alone since I arrived, like some sort of Eve fanboy, obsessed with hearing every bit of info, every detail on Eve, Holly, and my father's inventions.

"You lost?" he asks.

No use hiding it, and it's better bumping into Johnny than Frost! I nod.

"Come in—you can help me, actually." His head suddenly disappears inside the room, and the door stays open as he waits for me to follow.

I sigh and walk in.

My eyes narrow and I raise my hand to shield them from the light as I enter.

"Oh, sorry!" he mumbles. "Here, use these!"

He shoves at me a pair of tinted goggles, like the ones he's wearing, and I place them over my eyes before the light melts my retinas.

"Better?" he asks.

I nod as the light is blocked and I can finally see where I am.

My heart stops. Standing there in front of me . . .

"Eve?" I whisper, ripping off the goggles.

"Put them back on!" Johnny shouts as I'm blinded again by the intense white light.

I snap them over my head and blink. Eve reappears. It's her, standing in the center of the room, staring at the wall.

"She's not real, you idiot. I thought you of all people would be able to spot a hologram when you see one."

Suddenly I see the light-throws from the holo-projectors rigged up to the corners of the room.

"B-but how are you doing this?" I stutter, more at seeing the perfection of Eve's face again than anything else.

"Don't you recognize your own father's invention?" Johnny says, picking up the illuminated keypad from the floor.

He types a few things in and Eve suddenly turns to me.

"Hello, Bram. I've missed you." She winks.

"Stop," I say, placing my hand over Johnny's to stop him from typing.

"Okay, okay."

I step to the corner of the room and take a close look at the small projectors blasting Eve's image into Johnny's damp room in the Deep. I read *Wells Innovations* embossed on the side of the matte-black outer casing. "How did you get this?" I ask.

He turns to me. "These? Oh, they're everywhere in Central, just standard holo-projectors."

I stare back at him and wait. That's a lie, and he knows I know it is. Of course there are holo-projectors inside and outside every building in Central—there have been for years, installed as part of my father's Projectant Program with the intention of using them to allow Projectants to walk freely among society. When his program was scrapped the projectors remained, taking on a new role throwing advertisements and EPO propaganda into the streets, projecting the latest-model boats and floating homes onto the river.

But these are not standard holo-projectors.

"Okay." Johnny smiles. "I knew you'd spot it."

He's referring to the small letter *H* embossed after *Wells Innovations*.

Holly.

"Those are my projectors," I say. "They're only used in one place."

"The Dome." Johnny raises his eyebrows.

"How did you . . ."

"Some good men gave their lives to get these," he says, his expression suddenly changing.

"Oh, I'm sorry." I place my hand on his shoulder.

"Nah, it's okay. It's what we sign up for." He shrugs. "I just gotta get this damn thing to work."

I glance at Eve, now standing as though she's in a moment of deep thought. Then I glance around Johnny's room. Wires, circuit boards, screens, computers, keyboards. His role down here is pretty obvious.

"What the hell are you planning to use this for anyway?" I ask, trying to choose from the endless possibilities.

"Well, that's classified." He smirks. "But between you and me, let's just say that if Eve ever made it outside that place, a decoy might not be the worst idea in the world." He winks.

I nod, lifting my goggles slightly and squinting at the mess of light splashing around the small room. "Well, she's far from perfect at the moment." I chuckle.

"You think you could help?" He can't contain the hopeful grin on his face. "If anyone's going to be able to get this working, it's you!"

Of all the definitive moments in the last few days, of all the life-changing decisions I've made, this feels top of the list. The ultimate betrayal of my father. My heart leaps at the idea of helping the Freevers to use his own tech against him. "Yeah, I'll help," I say, taking a seat on the floor next to him. "But I warn you: I'm not my father."

"From what I hear, that's probably a good thing," Johnny says. "But you must have learned a thing or two from working with him all these years."

"With?" I chuckle. "No one works *with* Dr. Wells. You work *for* him."

"Jeez, and I thought I had it bad," Johnny replies.

"What do you mean?" I ask, not understanding his remark.

"Frost. Dad. My dad!" Johnny explains.

"Frost is your father?" I say, maybe a little too shocked.

305

"Yeah. The apple fell a long way from that tree, all right!" He laughs. "Much to Dad's disappointment."

I spend the next few hours sharing my limited knowledge of holography with Johnny. He laps up every word, fills in the blanks. By the time we remove our goggles, the blinding lights have been tamed, the exposure corrected, the focus calibrated—and standing before us is a perfect replication of Eve.

Johnny sighs at her beauty.

"You should see the real thing," I reply.

"With you on our side, maybe I will." He smiles.

He might just be right.

44

BRAM

"RISE AND SHINE, YOUNG BRAM," SHE RASPS THROUGH THE THIN crack of my door.

My tired mind takes a few moments to remember her name. "Morning, Helena." I yawn.

"Actually, it's afternoon," she replies, stepping in and handing me a tin mug.

The hours pass quicker in the Deep. Sunlight barely breaks the storm clouds, let alone reaches the catacombs of this Freever hive far below the rivers of Central.

"It's impossible to tell when day ends and night begins down here," I say, sipping the water, using my lips to filter the few petals they add for flavor.

"Day, night, it doesn't matter here, my boy. Someone's always awake and someone's always asleep," she says, rapping her fist on the wall dividing me from the next room, where Chubs is undoubtedly still snoozing.

"I'm up!" his muffled voice moans.

I like Helena. She's made my time in the Deep a little easier, her quick mind and sharp tongue putting me in my place, and others too. They all respect her here.

"On your feet then, Tower Boy. Frost doesn't like to be kept waiting," she says, watching me as I stand and pull my damp jumpsuit up over my naked torso.

"Getting a good look?" I tease.

"Cheeky bugger! I'm old enough to be your grandmother," she jokes, picking up my mug, finishing my water, and disappearing into the hall.

I drop to the floor and start my new ritual of a hundred push-ups. Being down here makes you feel unfit, out of shape. I can't afford to be either of those. I feel the oxygen flooding my muscles and the adrenaline waking my senses. I need to be alert if I'm being summoned by Frost.

One. Two. Three. Four . . . Frost, Chubs, Helena, Saunders . . . I start listing the names, trying to remember the new family I've fallen into. Quite literally, in some cases. There are entire families living down here. Fathers, mothers, and sons, all united in the fight to free Eve from the clutches of the EPO.

"Bram?" Johnny whispers through my door.

"Come in," I grunt as I push up. The door opens and in he comes, his goggles dangling around his neck.

"Hi, erm . . . It's Frost. He's sent me to get you."

"Jeez, must be fairly urgent. Helena's only just left."

Johnny widens his eyes.

"It's about me and Eve, right?" I ask, already guessing.

He nods. "Did you actually *kiss*?" He runs his hands through his hair in excited anticipation of my reply.

"Yes and no. It's complicated," I say, standing up and squeezing past him through the door.

"So, like, your lips actually . . . I can't even . . . How did you . . ."

"Okay, chill, Johnny, chill. There's a lot more to it," I say, trying to speed up our walk. I already hear the crowd in the main chamber, the largest one. It's where they hold all their meetings.

I turn the corner and Helena's figure fills the open doorway. "Good luck," she whispers, giving me a little pat on my butt as Johnny and I pass her to enter the lion's den.

She follows us as we walk into the long, dimly lit hall, every head turning in our direction.

The room falls silent.

All eyes are on me.

Now I see why. A small old-fashioned projector sits on the central table, casting its light toward the largest wall. The beam is interrupted by a jet of fine mist, pouring from a pipe in the ceiling. The projection on the mist acts like a makeshift hologram, showing everyone in the room the photograph sitting on top of the projector. The photo of the kiss. Our kiss.

The reaction is mixed. Some of the Freevers spit on the ground at my feet. Others laugh and give me congratulatory nudges in jest. I see the scattering of women gather around Helena. She continues to walk behind me as she hears whisper after whisper. I glance back for some reassurance as she waves them away like annoying flies buzzing around her head, and nods for me to keep moving.

"Calm yourselves, please." Frost calls the rabble to order. "Obviously, you've seen we have breaking news fresh from the Dome about our guest of honor and newest recruit, Mr. Bram Wells."

The room half applauds. I don't know how to react. This is weird. Awkward. I stare at the floor, trying not to make eye contact with anyone around me. I sense the trust I've been trying to build hanging by a thread.

As I do my best not to look at anyone, I find myself facing a scattering of photographs on the long table in front of me while Frost addresses the crowd.

"Leaked EPO images," Helena whispers from behind, sensing my interest.

"What are you looking for?" I mutter back, our voices lost under the constant Freever babble.

"Ernie Warren," she replies. Eve's father.

I raise my eyebrows in response, looking at the haystack of images for a needle that might not even exist. I scan the photographs, from dilapidated cloudscrapers to family photos of EPO personnel outside their homes. How have the Freevers gotten their hands on these?

Suddenly something catches my eye.

A small speck of color on the corner of a photograph sticks out from underneath the pile. I recognize the deep green of the few leaves visible at this edge of the picture.

While the noisy room surrounding me is preoccupied with Frost's speech, I lean forward casually and subtly slip the photo out so I can see the whole thing. My heart is racing as I stare at the photo, the one I've had as the home screen of my holo-display since I was a boy: the large, beautiful tree.

Suddenly an impossible thought streaks across my mind, like a news flash. Why else would my dad have had that exact photo in his office all those years ago?

This place *has* to be significant.

I run my hands across the photo, as if my fingers are touching the leaves, and I stop them at the bottom, at the thing that has been staring me in the face my whole life.

This isn't a photo of a tree at all. It's a photo of the building behind it. My youthful mind was blinded by nature's beauty, disguising the small brick building in the background. It's been there all this time, sitting at the end of a gravel driveway, sheltered from the sun by the gracious tree.

My father is not a sentimental man. He has no family portraits or photos of his past. Everything has a purpose; everything has a use. My father would only have had this photo for a specific reason, and if he was in on some cover-up, if he was part of Ernie's disappearance . . .

My brain is spinning.

I suddenly realize that I know more than any of the men in the room. I know where Eve's father is.

"So, Mr. Wells," says Frost.

"It's just Bram."

"Very well, Bram."

"And I'm not down here to join you," I say to them all as I stare into Frost's eyes. My heart pounds. I've not thought any of this through, but somehow I know it's right.

"Oh, really?" Frost says, digging his dirty fingers into the arm of his chair.

"I'm here to lead you."

45

EVE

"EVE." I HEAR MY NAME WHILE A HAND GENTLY SHAKES ME awake.

"Hmm." I stir, feeling groggy. My head seems heavy as I lift it. Mother Kadi is gazing down at me with a concerned look on her face.

"We need to go to the doctor. For retraction," she adds with a sad smile.

It comforts me.

That face.

That compassion for the situation I'm in purely because I was born.

I've barely slept. I felt so energized last night that I simply couldn't sleep. The black of night seemed to go on forever as I watched it linger from my sofa. I must've dozed off at some point and my body aches because I didn't get into bed.

"Come on. Let's get you ready," Mother Kadi says softly.

"Will you stay with me?" I ask. "Retraction is nothing new, I know that. But this is different. This time I'm saying goodbye to my eggs, knowing they may find their way back to me."

"And that's a good thing," she says encouragingly.

"Obviously." I decide not to add that the thought of them gluing those fertilized eggs into me makes me feel physically sick.

"I can stay." Mother Kadi extends a hand for me to take. She helps me to my feet and follows me through to the bathroom. While I'm undressing she turns on the shower, checking the temperature, then picks up the dirty clothes I've been wearing and puts them into the laundry bin. I didn't shower last night. When we first left the safe room I was intending to, but those plans vanished once I found my mother's note.

I walk into the shower, closing my eyes as the hot water hammers at my body, waking me fully. I keep my eyes closed as Mother Kadi applies shampoo to my hair while sitting on the ledge above me, massaging it into my scalp. She rinses it, then smooths on the conditioner.

She is about to climb down and leave me to wash it out myself, but I sense her hovering next to me, as though she's waiting for something.

I open my eyes as she reaches out to cradle my cheek.

"You're stronger than you know, Eve," she whispers. "And your mother was too. Trust your instincts. Follow them."

My eyes squint at her through the water running over my face.

She glances at the shower, then at one of the microphones hanging above us. It can't hear us over the noise of running water, and we can't be seen, thanks to the steam on the glass. Not if we're careful. Yet before I have a chance to say or ask anything in return, she's gone to fetch a towel from the heated rack. The moment is gone.

I search her face when I get out of the shower, but there is nothing to read. It's as though I imagined the exchange.

46

BRAM

ONCE THE LAUGHTER DIES DOWN, THE FREEVERS LOOK AT ME with the strangest mixture of expressions—some confused, others angry—but Frost's face is unreadable. He keeps his cards close to his chest.

He raises a hand and the whispers hush. "Lead us?" he says calmly. "Where exactly are *you* planning to lead us, Bram?"

I pick up the photograph from the table and walk through the crowd to where the projector sits. I slip the photo of our first kiss off the light plate and replace it with this photo.

The projected tree fills the center of the room, and the men step back out of its light.

"I'm leading a rescue mission for Ernie Warren, here." I point to the brick building sitting in the tree's shade. There are murmurs and whispers from every Freever in the room as they stare at the photograph before them. I glimpse Helena's long gray hair and see her still batting off the whisperers around her, asking her opinion. She tilts her head, waiting to hear more from me.

"And what makes you think this is the place?" calls a thin

voice from the back. "Of all the hundreds of thousands of locations where he could be, of all the possible photographs on the table, you just happen across the one photo of his whereabouts?"

The rabble immediately erupt, firing more questions in my direction. Frost remains a silent observer of the chaos.

"Listen." I calm them with my hands, but it's not enough to silence them. I step up onto a bench at the table, raising myself so I can see the whole room and they can see me. "Listen to me. You've been searching for years, with no luck. Yes, I know it sounds hard to believe that I would walk in here and pick up this photo, but it's even crazier for me to find it here." The room of damp people quiets as they pause for a moment to listen. "Or maybe it's not crazy. Maybe it's meant to be. Maybe I was meant to be here, to find this photograph, because I know one thing for sure: there isn't anyone else in the world who would know that this is the place. Not anyone on your side anyway. You've only known me a short time, but you're just going to have to trust me. It's too important for you not to. I've spent nearly my entire life up there, inside that Tower, working to keep their lie alive. Staring into Eve's eyes, delivering their messages, getting Eve to cooperate with their demands, and she would do it for me every time. Why?" I hold up the photo of our kiss. "Because Eve trusts me, more than she trusts anyone else, and that's why you should too. That's why you have to, for Eve."

I have the room's attention. Helena raises her eyebrows, impressed, I think, with my speech.

"This is where Eve's father is. I know it. I've looked at this photo more than any other image and only just realized what it is."

"What are you going to do with him when you find him?" asks Chubs.

"Are you out of your mind? He's not going to be there. He's dead," calls one of the older men of the group, starting a series of exchanges about my spontaneous plan to lead them on a search for Eve's long-lost father.

"What if he's lying? What if he is just another EPO spy?" cries another of the more mature men.

"What if he isn't?" Helena says, her raspy voice demanding that people listen. "What if he's right?"

The heads in the room turn to her, but her powerful gaze is fixed on me. "This kid could be everything we've ever wanted."

There is a silence as they absorb her words.

"If we're ever going to have a shot at finding him, surely it's with Bram," Saunders adds clumsily.

"How can we trust him? What if he's just luring us into a trap?"

The noise erupts again, reaching an unbearable volume. Frost stands up, his arms raised. Silence falls over the room and I realize he owns these people. It's not them I need to convince; it's him.

He turns to me and looks me in the eye, and I can see the cogs of his mind working.

"Look," I say to him, "I want to get Eve out of that place as much as all of you do, but I've got to know the truth, and Ernie is the key. I know it. If he's still alive, this is where we can find him."

"Okay, Bram," says Frost.

Silence. Stunned silence.

"Okay?" I reply.

"Let's do this your way. You call the shots. You wanna lead this bunch, they're all yours."

The room twitches silently. I can feel the discomfort his decision causes. "For real?" I ask.

"For Eve," he replies. I nod in agreement and reach out to shake his hand.

"For Eve!" the room shouts in unison, some voices more reluctantly than others.

Frost takes a seat and ties his thick dreadlocks behind his head. "So, Bram, what's the plan?"

The pods are loaded with supplies, mainly weapons. We leave through the broken glass of Ben as weak sunlight turns the pollution clouds from thick purple to heavy gray.

"You sure you know what you're doing?" Saunders asks, stepping into the pod I'm waiting in.

"No," I say honestly. "But if there's a chance I'm right, we've got to take it, yes?" Before he has a chance to reply, Frost steps into the pod behind us.

"Ready when you are, Captain," he says. He pulls the hood of his deep green waterproof jacket over his matted locks and awaits my orders.

We've planned for this as best we can. It was Helena who realized it might be a sanctuary, meaning that it's kept well hidden. Protected. But that information at least narrowed the search. If Eve's father is there, it's a clever move from the EPO, hiding a man in a place no men are allowed to go to. Smart. The kind of thing my father would have thought of.

Whether this place is still standing is another question. The most recent charts of that area are all BE, pre-flood. It could be in ruins now, but my gut says differently. All that's left is to go and find out, to see if I'm right or if I'm leading Frost's rebels on a wild-goose chase.

"I know that not all of you are comfortable with this mission, but I thank you for your commitment to me," I say, sounding far too rehearsed.

"It's Eve we're committed to, dumbass," says a young blond Freever from the second of the three pods we're taking out. I see Chubs elbow him in the ribs to shut him up.

"He's right. It's Eve we're all committed to. Let's go and find her father." I nod at Saunders and he eases the throttle forward. We cruise out onto the open river, where I see the city alive for the first time.

I can't believe how busy it is. So different from the night I arrived. There are large boats, almost ships, moored to the rooftops of sunken buildings. Men walking along gangplanks suspended hundreds of feet over the water, bridging the gap between building and boat.

"Pretty amazing how fast they built these," Saunders says, noticing my eyes gazing up at Central.

I'd forgotten what this place was like. Vast structures attached to the old buildings, like sitting on the shoulders of a drowning man, soaring toward the sky. Square buildings that tower over the rivers flowing between them. These new cloud-scrapers weren't designed to look nice, just to withstand the storms and provide homes so life could go on.

And life did go on, surprisingly normally, considering what happened. I take in the sights and smells all around as we sail north, over Regent's Lake. Men out here look happy. I see men chatting, kissing; men drinking coffee simulants, reading the news on their holo-players on their way to work as they tread the weather-beaten pathways of this place.

No women, of course: it's not safe enough for the few who remain to leave the female-only communities. I guess the women of the Deep are living outside the EPO law. Another reason to stay hidden.

"Everything sits about ten feet above the current waterline, allowing for the flood level to rise, which it will," Saunders tells me, shaking his head. "They might have stopped dropping bombs, but the oceans didn't stop rising."

Our pod is rocked by the wake of a larger ship cruising past us in the opposite direction.

"I'd keep your head low if I were you, kid," Frost radios over the intercom from his pod, and as the ship passes us I see why. On the side of its black hull the words *Cold Storage* are printed in large white letters. A blue light flashes on top, signaling other boats to clear out of its way. Armed guards pace the top deck, wearing the EPO's security uniform under the same black body armor as Ketch's men.

"Deliveries for the Tower?" I ask, and Saunders nods. A cold vapor pours from the back, like a heavy steam that sits on the surface of the water. I watch the huge ship sail in the direction of my old home and wonder how many women it's carrying, all headed toward their prestigious place in the depths of the Tower, beside my mother.

I instinctively reach for the silver cross around my neck.

As the EPO ship disappears between buildings, I follow the farthest structure upward. I strain my neck and see the enormous realiTV screens strapped to the sides, my father's tech. I can't escape him: it's like he's looking down on me wherever I go.

"They used to pump out constant updates on Eve," Frost's deep voice says over the intercom. "Everyone watched—we'd all gather out here for the latest news, to see how *the savior* was getting on, what she was doing from one day to the next. It gave everyone hope. Made us remember what we were living for. That we had a planet to protect for our kids."

As we sail out over the open stretch of water I look back at the city skyline, every building covered from top to bottom with screens. "Who wouldn't want a glimpse of the girl who was going to save humanity from extinction?" Frost says.

"I knew they showed people what was happening, but not that it was like this," I say. "It's like some reality show."

"Are you kidding? Your girlfriend was the biggest realiTV star on the planet once," Saunders jokes.

"Once?" I ask.

"Yeah, until they decided we weren't important anymore, that it was better keeping secret what goes on up there," Frost explains. "They shut down the live streams from the Dome, just gave us momentary glimpses of Eve when it suited them. Mostly doctored footage and faked images. We all knew they weren't real from the moment they started."

Suddenly the screens flicker to life. Three huge letters illuminate the fine mist that hangs in the air like fog: *EoM.*

"EoM?" I ask.

"Eve of Man," Saunders explains. "That's what they've branded her. They want us to think she's *our* Eve."

"We just get this propaganda shit now, that's all. Whatever the EPO want us to see, whatever they think is going to keep us all in line," Frost tells me from his pod, sailing along to my left. "It's about keeping the powerful, powerful; and the rest of us, well, who cares? Eve's just their poster girl. We'd pull the screens down if they weren't protected."

"Protected?" I ask.

"Yeah. They're all solar panels. Those screens feed us lies and give us energy. They power the whole city. Can't live without 'em, so we gotta put up with this crap," Saunders says.

"Pretty clever." It would have been another of my father's genius ideas. It's got him written all over it.

"Here we go," says Saunders, pointing to the video that begins to play across the surface of every building around us.

Eve picks flowers in her garden inside the Dome. Cut to Eve exercising, sweat dripping from her chin. Then she gracefully pliés at the barre in her ballet shoes. Now she's drinking green juice.

A deep voiceover booms out, echoing across the lake.

"Eve is working hard, preparing for the future, for your future. She is your savior. She is Eve of Man."

Eve stands on the Drop alone, looking out at the sunset.

"This is all old footage," I tell Saunders.

"Yeah, we know," he says. "They recut these things all the time, flip the images around, change the camera angles, anything to make it seem new and fresh. We rarely get any current glimpses of her."

The three large letters, *EoM,* glare out at us one last time before the screen fades to black.

I turn away and look ahead to where the open stretch of water narrows. I hear that deep voice echo in my mind and can't help but wonder if I'm prepared for the future. I guess I'm about to find out.

47

EVE

"SHE'S STAYING WITH ME," I SAY FIRMLY AS I ENTER THE CLINICAL examination room with Mother Kadi at my side. My chaperoning Mother is usually sent away, told she isn't needed within these walls, but today Mother Kadi *is* needed. By me. I need her comfort. Her kindness. Her compassion. Her presence.

Vivian's eyes dart between us as though she's trying to work out if I'm up to something, but she seems to dismiss the idea with an exasperated sigh. "Very well. Glad you're feeling up to speaking, Eve." She smirks. "I see you've been eating too. Good, good."

Ignoring her jibes, I stand by the metal chair in the corner of the room, stripping off my clothes. Then Mother Kadi helps me into the garment laid out for me, a blue hospital gown.

I thought about saying something before this process took place. I debated whether or not to go to Vivian and tell her I'd changed my mind and didn't want it to happen in this way, but I know that would give her the upper hand and an inkling of what's going on in my head. I'd have to give reasons, and I didn't want that. I didn't want to tell her that I'm doubtful of what they've given me as a reality. I have to be sure of the truth first.

It's the same reason I've not spoken to her about Bram and Holly. Anyway, I'm not sure how much it matters now that he's gone. She wouldn't let him be my Potential. I'm certain that if I asked she'd refuse and mock me because I've fallen for him. She'd resort to belittling our love as a childish crush. I know what we have is far more than that. I'd have loved Bram and Holly regardless of their form. Part of me would be happy to keep things as they have been, with us out on the Drop forevermore; that's how much she—he—has affected me. But I know that could never happen.

I climb onto the table next to Dr. Rankin, who's already standing there with the rod in her latex-gloved hand, eager to get to work. I take a breath to calm my insides as they tense at the sight. This will be even more unpleasant if I don't relax my muscles. I shuffle to get myself comfortable, the synthetic fabric rustling underneath me.

"Legs up," she instructs, not looking at my face, her focus purely on the task ahead as she lowers my knees into the usual position.

I close my eyes as she stands between my legs and lifts the material protecting my modesty, starting the examination. The coldness of the rod as it enters makes my brain shudder. When she angles it in different directions and tugs at my insides, I want to vomit. I clench my jaw to stop the bile from rising.

"We've lost one," Dr. Rankin murmurs a few moments later, holding the stick in one position, then firmly guiding it in another.

"What?" Vivian marches over to the screen. I'm not sure

whether she's angry with me for having lost it or Dr. Rankin for failing to collect it.

"We still have the other," Dr. Rankin says, with a little more joy in her voice than usual. "Although if we'd left it any later, we'd have lost that one too. I said for her to come in every day."

"We had a situation and her safety was more important," Vivian states, not bothering to look away from the screen in front of her as she greedily eyes my one egg that's ripe and ready for the picking.

Dr. Rankin doesn't respond, but I hear the clanking of equipment next to me, letting me know she's about to go on to the next stage.

"Is this how it used to work?" I ask suddenly, to no one in particular.

"Pardon?" asks Dr. Rankin, after a brief pause.

"For women before me?"

A stillness settles over the room. I can only imagine they're wondering how to respond. I used to ask a barrage of inappropriate questions when I was younger, not knowing they were so. Then I asked questions because I *knew* they were inappropriate. But now? Now I just want to know what I'm saving by bringing more life into the world.

"The procedure was similar," replies Dr. Rankin, her tone indifferent.

"So you all know what it feels like to be sitting here. To be laid bare and exposed. To feel like you're nothing more than a piece of meat," I say, waiting to be stopped as I look at them all. I'm so used to Vivian shooting me down it's become a habit to push her until I'm reprimanded. I'm surprised she hasn't scolded me on this occasion, although as Dr. Rankin is still going about her business, I doubt Vivian cares too much about what comes out of my mouth. She's not even looking at me.

"I've experienced this many times. I know what you're going through," Mother Kadi replies tenderly, her hands wiping down the sides of her black dress, highlighting the curve of her hips. "But it'll be over soon, Eve."

"How many times?" I ask, my tone more forceful and direct with her than usual.

"I . . ." She struggles, looking from me to Vivian.

"How many times did they put your legs in stirrups and strip you of your dignity?" I ask.

"You asked for it to be done in this way, Eve," Vivian cuts in, her voice calm, as though she's talking to a child. "Koa is still here if you'd like me to bring him in. I'm sure he'd enjoy that very much."

"Once you were pregnant, when you birthed your boys," I continue to Mother Kadi, ignoring Vivian, "how long did they wait for you to recover before you were forced back onto a table like this?"

Mother Kadi's eyes widen imploringly, begging me to stop.

I want to carry on, but a burning sensation from my lower body makes me yelp in pain.

I stop.

Squeezing my eyes shut, I feel my chest deflate as a single tear rolls down my cheek. This is no different from what I usually experience. It's no more painful. It's nothing new. But it is. Because I know that if this is successful, it's just the start. It's not a case of fertilizing my egg and leaving me with a child to bring up. It's going to be a never-ending cycle. It'll be repeated until I'm no longer of use to them.

"I just want to know what to expect," I say through gritted teeth. "What my life is going to be like."

"You've had your life, Eve. We've given you everything: entertainment, education, a friend. Just look at this place, this world we've made for you. Now it's time for you to give back. You do your duty. You bear us a future of girls, and you'll live your life doing much the same as before."

"And what kind of future will *they* have?"

"Best not to concern yourself with that," Vivian quips, her eyes rolling with annoyance. "You need to play your part in Destiny's game first."

Destiny. I repeat the word in my head a few times. Destiny. What is my destiny? Is it my destiny to be treated like a breeding bitch for everyone else's benefit? Or is the fact that Bram found me and that we shared such a strong connection, despite being separated by a man-made illusion, part of it? Perhaps Mother Nature will toy with us again and stop us humans from making the same mistakes. From intervening in her plans for us.

Mistakes.

I've always known I'm lumbered with a huge responsibility, but the thinking behind any decisions surrounding my mission has never been mine. It's never been about me. But what if Mother Nature chose for me to be laden with this duty for a reason? What if Bram and I were meant to meet? What if this is all about free will and the beauty of human nature? The power of instinct.

Mistakes.

I've always wanted this course of treatment to fail, but what if it succeeds? Will I have failed in my destiny?

Mistakes.

I can't stop thinking about my children and the lives they will lead. More than that, I wonder what my parents would think if they could see me now. Would they have wanted this life for me? Would they have chosen it?

Mistakes.

I know my mom would be mortified to see me like this, just as I will be to see any daughters of mine lying on this bed in years to come.

"I said you can go," Vivian barks at me, bringing my focus back into the room. "We'll call for you when you're needed again."

The procedure is over. Dr. Rankin has already gone, taking my egg to be fertilized, to start the process of life. Even before it's put back inside me, that little being has started its own journey to becoming a real person.

Mistakes.

It's time to test the world they've made for me.

48

BRAM

WE SAIL AWAY FROM CENTRAL. TRAVEL IS SLOW AS WE AVOID areas patrolled by the EPO, which means staying out of sight as much as we can. It was easier where the buildings were tall and the river and canals between them were busy. Out here, these pods stand out. We don't want any attention.

As the buildings become less frequent, sections of sloppy mud break the surface, with an occasional patch of dull green sprouting. The heads of the twelve men who make up our team are turned toward the grassy mounds: they're staring at this rare sight.

"Tree!" Chubs calls, waving at the barely visible leaves just poking through the mist ahead.

"Not far," Frost says. There's no need to use the intercom as our engines are near silent now that we're sailing so slowly and so close together.

As the pollution mist clears, more trees appear ahead of us, stepping out of the fog like the ghosts of a time we left behind, a time we destroyed.

A great barricade emerges ahead, stretching as far as I can see on either side.

"It's the boundary," grunts Frost. "This is as far as the EPO want you to come."

As the mist clears I see those three letters again—EPO, surrounded by warnings. Radiation. Explosives. Toxic waste. You name it, the sign is there, plastered all over the rusted metal barricade.

"Inviting," Chubs jokes.

"Is it safe?" Saunders asks.

We stare at the fog beyond the border, tinged with a slight green hue.

"Looks safe enough for trees," I reply.

"'Course it's bloody safe." Frost laughs. "This is all smoke and mirrors, kid. The EPO trying to keep us in one place, where they can watch us."

"Move on." I signal and our pods press forward, floating through the large gaps between the partially submerged barricade.

The farther we go, the more we feel Mother Nature reaching out to us. Only the tops of the taller trees are visible at the moment, their highest branches piercing the surface, like arms stretching up to a sun that barely shines, a few dull green leaves fluttering from them. Mother Nature is tough.

Through the floodwater beneath us I see a sunken street, the red tiles of rooftops, the black paint of streetlights. Farther down there's a bench, now wrapped in reeds and plant life.

"The water's pretty clear here," I say to Saunders.

"Fewer people, less pollution," he explains, and I nod as a school of fish swims underneath our pods, still visible through the glass floor.

I take a breath of air. Real air. It hasn't been filtered or tampered with. It isn't full of pesticides and chemicals to sterilize it. Just simple, natural air. It feels wonderful and cold in my lungs.

Suddenly our pod jolts and I'm thrown forward, just managing to stop my face from smashing against the front handrail. I stand and see everyone else recovering.

"We've hit land," I call as I catch sight of the watery earth pressed up against the glass pod beneath my feet. "We can walk from here."

We jump into the knee-deep water, our boots and waterproof flood suits keeping out the wet but not the cold. It's uncomfortable but not unbearable. We group together in the bow of the leading pod, where Johnny, the most eager member of my new team, is reading a handheld GPS unit.

"How old is that thing?" I ask.

"Older than any of us, but it's reliable and can't be traced by the drones," Johnny says through the strands of hair covering his face, not taking his eyes off the old-fashioned touchscreen display. "We're about a mile from where that photo was taken, if the building still exists."

"It's right there on the map," says Chubs, pointing at it, clearly visible in the bird's-eye view on Johnny's GPS.

"Yeah, but these maps are BE, about forty years old, dumbass. Look, there's no floodwater," he says.

"All right, all right, let's keep our heads together. We don't know exactly what we're walking into here," I say to them, taking the GPS from Johnny.

"Sorry, sir," he says nervously.

"It's okay," I reassure him. I wish he'd stayed in the Deep—his youth and his keenness to impress me aren't helpful. "Let's move in single file. I'll lead," I say, and set off toward the little red blip on the GPS monitor.

As we walk, the ground under our feet rises and falls, the depth of the water varying from ankle- to waist-deep. The closer we get, the more trees rise before us. Before we know it we're walking along an old man-made path. It's like nothing any of us has ever seen before.

The men walk silently, taking it all in, everything seeming calm.

I kick something hard floating in the water. I turn it over with my foot.

"It's a signpost." Saunders passes it down the line following us.

"'Grim's Ditch,'" I read aloud. "This is the place. We're here."

I look ahead and see a break in the trees off the path to the right. As we approach, my heart is pounding.

"There it is," I whisper. A gentle wind is blowing through the deep green leaves of the tree I've stared at for years. Now that I'm here it's even more beautiful, despite the surrounding conditions: the gray skies and the foot of water it now stands in. It's still as elegant and graceful as I could ever have hoped it would be.

I step closer, remove my glove, and touch its rough, damp bark. The Freevers group around me and admire it too. No one can deny the majesty of a tree, especially one that has survived these conditions, stood its ground against everything humans have thrown at it. It makes me think of Eve.

"We're not alone," Chubs says, noticing a figure standing in the doorway of the brick building, about twenty meters away from us. "It's a woman."

The men scramble to get a clearer view.

"Calm yourselves," Frost orders, fierce and authoritative. He shoots me a look.

Helena was right. It's a sanctuary.

"You are not permitted to be here," she calls to us across the flooded pathway. She is concealed beneath a long gown, and her gray hair is cut short. "You must leave at once."

Frost looks at me. "Well . . . Captain?" he says quietly. "You wanted to lead us."

I take a step toward the frail woman.

"I warn you, this is a sanctuary. We are legally protected."

"Miss, I apologize for turning up like this. I know it's against protocol, but we're soldiers from the EPO."

She stares at me. Her watery blue eyes twitch from my face to my rain gear to the gun hanging over my shoulder.

I slowly pull it off and she instantly raises a shotgun concealed beneath her robes.

The men behind me raise their weapons at her.

"Whoa!" I cry, turning my back on the old woman, raising my arms at the Freevers. "Weapons down. Now!"

They hesitate, their eyes flicking from their target to Frost.

"You heard him, men. Weapons down," Frost says. "Apologies . . . *sir.*" He flashes my arm a subtle look and I understand instantly what our next move is.

"Let's start again. I am Captain Bram Wells, a senior officer at the Extinction Prevention Organization." I start taking small steps toward the old woman, her wrinkles becoming more defined the closer I get. I turn my weapon around and offer it to her. "We're here to collect something that belongs to us."

She pauses, gun still aimed at my chest. Her eyes search mine deeply, searching for truth.

I slowly unzip my heavy waterproof jacket, not losing eye contact with her. I open it and reveal the name badge on my EPO jumpsuit.

She takes a moment to read it and think. "Wells?" she asks. I nod.

"As in Dr. Isaac?" she says.

My heart skips. She knows my father. We're in the right place.

"My father," I explain, and I see her shoulders rise as she takes a deep breath, then releases it.

"You scared the hell out of us, showing up unannounced. There's a schedule for visits for a reason, you know. I could have blown your head off, young man," she says as she lowers her gun.

"I'm sorry this is unscheduled. It's something of an emergency. We need to see him. Is he here?" I ask, and she turns to look at me suspiciously.

"Is he here? Of course he's here. Where else is he going to be?" she asks, but before I can answer, she speaks again: "Well, I don't know why they always send so many of you. You know the protocol here, two men at a time. Leave your weapons at the door." She turns and steps inside the house.

I look at Frost and beckon him over with a nod. He takes off his gun and hands it to Saunders, then comes across to me.

"So far so good," I whisper.

"Keep your wits about you, kid. If he's really here, this place is going to be watched by more than an old lady with a shotgun," he replies as we step over a wall of sandbags and follow her into the sanctuary.

49

EVE

WE STAND IN SILENCE FOR A FEW MOMENTS, ONCE THE DOCTOR and Vivian have left. I need time to process how I'm feeling. I close my legs, my hospital gown rustling as I slip off the table, and find myself clutching Mother Kadi's shoulder.

Her dainty arms are crossed over her body, but her hand finds mine and pats it gently.

"Well done," she whispers sympathetically, her eyes telling me she understands how I feel after such an invasive procedure. I'm glad that's the case, but she doesn't know what's going on in my head. Yes, I feel violated, but the fire that was already lit within me is roaring now. The flames flicker and burst, telling me it's time.

I turn to make my way back to my safe haven of a bedroom, but before I can leave, my eye is caught by something.

"I want a shower," I say to Mother Kadi.

"Of course. Let's go back to your room." She's gathering the clothes I discarded earlier.

"No. Here will do," I tell her, walking to the shower in the corner.

Before she can advise me not to, I yank off my gown, tossing it to the side in my hatred for everything it represents. It drops to the floor in a crumpled heap.

"Wash my hair," I say, glancing back at her confused face. I open the glass door to the shower and twist on the water. My body tingles as I walk under the jet and feel the hot water running over my skin.

She's with me in seconds, her fingers running through my hair and massaging my scalp.

"Where are the labs?" I whisper, loud enough for only her to hear, while being careful not to look directly at her.

"Sorry," I hear her mumble, having been caught off guard. We're not in my room now. Perhaps she doesn't feel quite so safe revealing things she shouldn't, but I need to know now—while I can potentially act on my findings.

"The doctor, where would she have gone? This level?" I hiss.

All I hear for a few seconds is the water splashing in the cubicle.

I'm about to ask again when I hear her soft reply: "Outside. Turn right. Third door on the left."

"And my spot by the stream?" I ask, looking up at her.

Mother Kadi's eyes widen, not in a way that tells me she's surprised I'm asking the question, but rather that I'm asking at this particular moment.

"I need to be sure it's not another lie," I tell her.

"Level eight hundred. All of it," she says quickly.

My jaw clenches as I look away from her. It's not even near ground level. "How can I get there?"

"The elevator."

"There's no chance of that," I say dismissively.

"This place was built for you," she hisses. "Just say the number."

I think I must've misheard her, but her tone fills me with confidence.

"But, Eve, they'll come after you. They'll—"

"Let them," I say firmly, trying to work out the best course of action.

"Let me come with you."

"No. Absolutely not," I say, looking up at her earnest face.

She lowers her head sadly in agreement and I bow mine in return. She doesn't need to be more involved than I've already made her.

She washes the suds out of my hair. I'm grateful for her speed. I need to act fast and I know she understands.

Once I'm out of the shower, Mother Kadi wraps me in a white towel and I feel her squeezing my arms tightly as she dries me. I'm not sure whether it's offered as encouragement or a warning, but I'm hoping it's the former.

My legs shake as I step into my panties, then the khaki dress she holds out for me. I try to move quickly, but without making it look like I'm rushing; someone could be watching. I can't be seen to act frantically or out of character. I don't want to raise suspicion or attract attention any sooner than necessary.

I swoop my wet hair into a topknot while Mother Kadi helps me with my knee-high black boots.

"Did I leave my necklace in the shower?" I ask her.

"What necklace?" she asks, looking suitably confused. I rarely wear jewelry.

"Will you have a look for me? It's the one with my birthstone on it," I say, my hand going to my chest as though it's a treasured possession.

She doesn't even frown as she goes along with what I've asked.

As soon as she steps into the cubicle I shut it after her, pulling a unit of medical equipment across to block her exit.

"Eve," she whispers, her open palm resting against the glass between us, her eyes wide and shiny.

"Sorry," I mumble, then turn and head for the door. It's not that I don't trust her, but it's the only way I can be sure they won't think she's in on it.

I catch sight of myself in the reflection of the mirrored wall and see the determination on my face. I don't know how the panic I'm experiencing isn't displayed there, because my insides are churning at the thought of what I want to achieve in the next couple of minutes. Seeing the look on my face spurs me on.

I'm stronger than I know.

I can do this.

I turn the handle and open the door. My heart is in my mouth as I step out into what has become the unknown, expecting to see someone waiting there or a crowd of security guards stopping me from going any farther. Instead there is nothing but the sterile blue corridor I walked along earlier.

I turn right and pass the third door on the left, where I now know the lab is. I have to do something else first.

I go straight to the elevator. It's already waiting when I get to it, but when I step inside and a robotic voice asks where to, I say words I've never said before.

"Level eight hundred. My garden," I hear myself say.

"As you wish, Eve."

The doors close and my heart spins at the realization that we are traveling downward. It doesn't swell like it usually does when I'm on the way to my little spot outside. Instead it tightens in trepidation of what I'll find there.

The journey takes a couple of minutes, as long as it usually does when I'm permitted to "go outside," but the only journeys I have to compare it with are those to the encounters and for examinations, both of which must take place far closer to where they keep me, because they take just a few seconds.

The elevator slows to a stop and the doors open on what should be the collection bay. It's pitch black and I notice I'm not hit by a wave of fresh chilly air as usual. Instead there's nothing. No change in the atmosphere at all.

I know there's no turning back, so I force myself to take a few steps out of the elevator. As I do so, light ripples across the space in front of me, showing me the collection bay, but not as I know it. The lighting is harsher and not as inviting.

The usual black car is waiting in front of me, its door open and ready, but without Ketch beside it, like he was the last time I was here.

I close the door I usually get into and walk around to the driver's seat. I've never driven before, or watched anyone else do it, but as I climb in and look at the space around me, I realize it isn't going to be a problem. A button has the word *ON* engraved into the dark metal. I press it, knowing I don't have long. The car roars into life. The only other gadgets I can see are a black leather wheel directly in front of me and two pedals at my feet. I press one and nothing happens, but when I place my foot on the other, the vehicle flies forward and wobbles, thanks to my hands grabbing the wheel, which I can see will steer me where I want to go. I take my foot off the floor and notice the car begin to slow. I press the other pedal and come to an abrupt stop.

Okay, I think. *This is okay. Go, stop, steer. That's all you've got to remember.*

As I take a breath, I spot shadows in the little mirror slightly above me, which is angled so that I can see behind. Someone's coming. With that knowledge I place my foot on the go pedal and propel myself far from them, my hands gripping the steering wheel in an effort to keep control. I don't know where I'm going, but straight and away seems good.

Within seconds I'm out of the collection bay. There's nothing but dull gray concrete all around me. I keep going.

Then I notice lines that have been painted on the floor in bright yellow. It's hard not to laugh. I always knew when we were close to my little garden, and I knew the whole route we took to get there. My body memorized every bump and turn that meant I was getting closer to my little haven. They must've known that.

Poor little gullible Eve.

In the distance I can see a clump of green and notice that the end of the maze on the floor will eventually lead me there. I decide not to go by their usual pointless route and take a shortcut.

It's only when I see the height of the trees that I observe the height of the ceiling above me. The space is gargantuan. There's a clear break in the man-made forest for me to drive through, and it isn't long before the path becomes uneven, causing the car to jitter. I put my foot slowly on the brake—so that I'm not in danger of veering off the track, but still moving.

And then I see it, the place where the car usually stops before I step out of my padded cell to take in the natural beauty.

I want to slow down, to get out and take in the falsehood of the piece of outside they gave me to fulfill my inquisitive mind. I want to rip apart the leaves and see what they're made of. I want to hunt for the pump that engineers my perfect stream, and the lights overhead that make it all seem so magical when it's nothing but a fabrication. This is what I want to do, but I can't. My hands are so tightly on the wheel, my foot so clamped to the floor.

"Stop, Eve. Stop now." Vivian's voice is so loud that I think she's in the car with me.

I gasp but keep my eyes ahead of me and focus on my steering. I know she isn't here, but her voice is being played in the human-made, heartless void of level 800.

I'd thought this place was special, but it was just another part of their trap to keep me here, unquestioning, so that I live my life as they've always wanted me to.

It's another form of manipulation. Another lie. At least I always knew Holly was a figment of someone's imagination. This trickery seems far crueler.

I don't know what is real anymore.

Do they really want me to become a brainless dummy so they can do as they like without me wanting things for myself? Would it make life easier for all of us?

I push my foot down harder and accelerate.

The car growls in response, pushing me back in my seat.

"You are breaching national security. We will be forced to take drastic measures if you do not come to an immediate stop, Eve," Vivian barks.

"Go for it," I snarl. It's not like I can actually go anywhere.

A bump from behind causes my chest to bash against the steering wheel. With my concentration gone, the car gains a mind of its own. I struggle to regain control. Another hit from behind causes it to spin to the left. The fake shrubbery gets under its nose and propels me upward.

For a brief second I fly.

Then I flip.

I see the tree ahead moving closer and closer in slow motion. We collide. I hear a bang, a crack, and a thump as my head makes contact with something hard.

The glass around me shatters.

There is no smell of jasmine. No sound of birds singing or the stream cascading through the meadow.

"Eve!" she shouts.

Just her.

50

BRAM

"IT'S OKAY, LADIES. IT'S JUST THE EPO SPRINGING ANOTHER NOT-so-routine visit on our guest," the old lady calls up the stairs to where a dozen or so equally wrinkled faces look down on us.

I smile at them, but no one smiles back. Some turn away in disgust and I hear sobs from a room above us.

"Don't mind them. They never take too kindly to the men the EPO sends to check on Mr. Warren."

The woman's words fill my veins with fire.

He is here.

We have found him.

Now we just have to keep our cover and get him out of this place.

"Would you gentlemen care for a drink?" she asks.

"No thanks, Miss . . . ?"

"It's Mrs. Sutcliffe. But you can call me Anne," she tells Frost, with a twinkle in her eye. She might be old, but there's a feisty youthfulness about her.

"We'd just like to see Ernie and get out of your way as fast as we can," I tell her.

"Very well. He's downstairs. I'll leave you to it. The door is open." She gestures to where the stairs wrap around on themselves and disappear into a basement.

Frost and I look at each other. *The door is open?* I take the lead and walk down to the lower floor.

The sight that greets us takes my breath away. It's a vast open space, with long wooden floors that stretch the entire length of the building. The brick walls are lit by soft bulbs, giving warmth to what is essentially a cellar. At the far end of the room two windows look out at a beach, where transparent waves crash against the white sand. Suddenly it vanishes and a lush rain forest stands in its place. Sunlight pierces the deep greens, and the ultra-realistic views on these screens help to create the illusion that this isn't just a basement with no windows and one door.

As we step into the room I see a worn leather sofa with deep depressions in the cushions. A table is piled high with paperwork and littered with mugs half-full of cigarette butts. A small single bed stands across the room, near a toilet and a bath. A man is shaving in the mirror by the washbasin.

"Gentlemen," Ernie says as he shaves the fine gray hair around his upper lip.

"Mr. Warren," I begin.

"Mr. Warren? It's been a while since anyone's called me that. You must be new. Shall we get this over with?" He washes the shaving cream from his chin and pulls a white vest over his wrinkled body.

I'm not sure what I was expecting to find, but it definitely wasn't this man. After all the stories, all the rumors surrounding the dangerous, mentally unstable individual who had to be confined and sedated, this one standing before us, taking a seat in his well-worn spot on the couch, seems . . . normal.

He sits back and holds out his wrist to us.

Frost and I look blankly at each other.

"Well? Quick as you like, chaps. Arthritis doesn't make this too comfortable, you know," Ernie says.

After a second or two he relaxes his arm and looks at us. "Are you going to check this damn thing or not?" he says, pointing to a small scarred patch of skin on the side of his wrist.

"I'm sorry, Mr. Warren, but today isn't going to be like our normal visits," I say.

"Oh? Why's that, boy? My goodness, how old are you? Do they really let kids come and do this now?" he asks, talking to himself more than to us.

"We're leaving," Frost says. "And you're coming with us."

Ernie is dead still. He looks up at Frost and then at me. His eyes drop to the EPO patch on my chest. "Leaving?" he asks.

"Yes, right now. We have a lot to explain, but not here," I say.

"Where are we going?" the old man says, sounding concerned. "We had a deal! I've not tried to escape again. I've not left this room. I've done everything you've told me. Is it Eve? Is she all right?" He grabs my arms, worry written on his tired face. I glance around the room and see photos of Eve on every surface. Newspaper articles, magazines, pencil drawings—every bit of table space, every spare chair, is covered with them. My heart aches for him, the man who lost his daughter.

"Eve is fine," I say, placing a hand on his shoulder to calm him. "We just need to move you somewhere safer. Grab anything vital that you need and let's go."

"So, you're going to take this out, then?" Ernie says, pointing to the scar on his wrist again.

"Take what out?" I ask.

Ernie stares at us. His wrinkles rearrange themselves and I can almost hear the questions inside his head.

"You're not from the EPO, are you?" he says slowly, his veiny hand trembling slightly.

I feel Frost look at me. There's no time to muck around. "No, we're not," I say. "We've come for you, and then we're going to free your daughter."

The old man takes a moment to absorb what I've said, then slumps back into the sofa, cupping his hands over his face.

"No, no, no," he says through his fingers. "They'll already be on their way."

"Who will?" Frost barks.

"*Them!* The EPO! What—did you think they just locked me away down here and forgot about me? They're watching us right now. All of us!"

He raises a bony finger to a patch of ceiling directly over our heads. Frost and I look up to see a 360-degree camera staring down at us, still and cold, its small red light blinking with each subtle movement we make.

"Shit," says Frost. "We've not got long."

"We need to leave right now," I tell Ernie.

"You're not listening to a word I'm saying. I can't leave. Not unless they remove this thing in my arm," Ernie says, waving it at us.

"What's in your arm?" I ask.

"It's an explosive, isn't it?" Frost says.

"More than that. It's the trigger," Ernie tells us.

"The trigger for what?"

"For the rest of the explosives," Anne says from the stairs behind us. I turn and come face to face with the barrel of her shotgun again.

"What explosives?" I ask.

"This building is not what you think it is," Anne replies

simply as she tightens her grip on the weapon to steady her aim. "If he leaves that door—*boom*. He kills us all. He's the trigger, and this whole house is the bomb. They figured it was the only way to stop him from trying to escape."

"This isn't a sanctuary—it's a prison," Frost barks.

My blood boils. How could they keep him here like this? How could they put these poor women through such torture? "Why don't you all leave? Together?" I ask.

"And go where? They'd find us. We'd all be killed," Anne replies.

"Can't we cut it out?" Frost says, studying Ernie's scarred arm.

"Not unless you know how to disarm it. It has sensors on it. It knows if you cut it out, and it'll set them all off," Ernie says.

"We need Johnny," I tell Frost, but suddenly the ceiling above us is vibrating. Dust falls through the cracks, and the threatening hum of arriving airships rumbles down the stairs.

"They're here," Ernie says.

Muffled gunshots ring out from above, and the sound of men shouting is just audible over the noise of an airship hovering somewhere above.

"I can't let you take him. You'll kill us all," Anne says again, looping her finger around the trigger of her weapon.

"We need to get out of here fast," Frost says.

"I didn't come all this way to leave him behind now!" I shout over the sound of bullets hitting the bricks of the house above.

"You can't take me! People have tried and failed so many times. They all have the same fate, boy, and you're too young for that yet," Ernie says with a worn kindness in his voice. The voice of someone with no fight left. "Get out now."

"He's right, Bram," Frost says to me. "We've got to leave him."

"No!" I shout back. "I'm not leaving him here." I stare Frost in the eye, his heavy body towering over me. "If we leave now they'll move him and we'll never find him again."

Frost's eyes don't leave mine. He's trying to read me, trying to see how far I'll go for this man, for Eve. I don't budge.

"There is one way to do it," Ernie says, interrupting our stare-off.

"Ernie, no," Anne whispers sharply.

He shrugs away her plea and points to Frost's boot. "I don't suppose either of you has a knife?" he asks.

"They're unarmed," Anne replies, but Frost is already reaching inside the lip of his heavy boot and unsheathing a small machete.

"Do it quick and don't feel bad. I'm tougher than I look. Tried doing it myself years ago, but they caught—"

Ernie doesn't get the chance to finish the sentence before Frost raises the blade over his head.

"Wait!" Anne calls, dropping her gun and reaching out toward Frost, but her old legs can't get there fast enough. He swipes in one swift, heavy movement, cleanly slicing off the old man's arm from the elbow down.

I jump to Ernie's side, pulling off my belt and strapping it tight around his upper arm. The scarred patch containing the trigger sits, lifeless, on the floor at his feet.

"Shit, Frost," I say, my words barely coming out through the shock of what he just did.

Frost bends down and carefully picks up Ernie's lower arm. He pulls off his own belt and ties it impossibly tightly around the end as blood seeps out of it.

Anne covers her mouth with trembling hands, trying to process what is happening.

"Gotta keep this warm," Frost growls as he rips a wool blanket from the chair opposite us and neatly wraps it around Ernie's amputated wrist. He walks toward the far wall, near the sink, and places the arm on the towel rail. "Don't turn the heating off."

51

BRAM

WE PULL ERNIE UP THE STAIRS, KEEPING HIS BLOODY STUMP raised. As we enter the landing, the front door bursts open and our Freevers fill the hall, followed by a shower of bullets across the front of the house.

We duck for cover. The women's screams pierce my ears worse than the bullets do.

"What the hell happened?" Saunders asks, rushing over to help lift the old man.

"I'll explain later. We've got to get him out of here now."

We hoist Ernie up and move through the rooms to the back of the house.

"They've landed!" Chubs cries as he takes aim through a broken window at the front of the house and fires.

"There has to be another way out," I say to Saunders.

"Th-that way," Ernie's weak voice stutters as he motions to a corridor off to our left.

"Let's go! Follow me!" I call to the men behind me as they begin returning fire through the windows and doorway at the front of the house. "Frost, we need to leave now!"

A scatter of shrapnel shakes the house, like an earth-quake.

The flash blinds us momentarily, and the high-pitched tone drowns out all other sound. As my sight returns, I glance around to check Ernie. My heart stops at the sight.

"Man down!" Chubs cries.

Frost is kneeling over a bloodied body.

It's not Ernie.

"It's Johnny," Saunders cries, looking back too.

Johnny's lifeless body lies on the wooden floor.

Frost gently places his large palm on his forehead and I see tears pour from his eyes and disappear into his beard.

"It's his son," Saunders whispers, the words catching in his throat.

"I know," I croak back. Barely.

I can hardly watch.

Johnny.

This is my fault. I brought them here.

My heart aches for him. For them both. But in that moment of sadness, among all the mayhem, I'm suddenly overcome with a strange admiration. Like I'm witnessing some beautiful event. Tragic, of course, but beautiful. Seeing the love of a father for his son at its most extreme, pouring out of him in a flood of tears, his voice screaming at the sky. To feel this kind of love is something I'll never know.

Frost stands, picking up his and Johnny's guns before marching to the door.

"No! Frost!" I cry, handing Ernie's weight to Saunders. I run toward him as fast as I can but don't get to him before he steps out onto the front porch and opens fire. Between the flashes from his gun, I see the approaching EPO squad scramble for cover.

Frost's vengeful rampage takes down one, two, three men. Then I see him. Ketch.

He sees me too. Our eyes meet before an explosion between us sends mud and water flying twenty feet into the air.

Frost shields his eyes and I use the distraction to grab the hood of his jacket and yank him back inside. Chubs comes to my side and helps drag Frost's large frame into the house as he fights against us.

"You're no good to Eve if you're dead," I shout at him. "You'll have your chance to avenge Johnny, just not here. Not today."

Frost relaxes his fight against us and releases a final tear for his son. He looks me in the eye and nods.

"Let's go!" I call, and the men fall back from the windows and make their way down the corridor to the back of the house.

"Someone's got to stay and give covering fire or they'll catch us," Chubs says, releasing a few rounds from his heavy gun through the front door before closing it.

"You go. I'll catch up with you," Frost says, taking Chubs's gun as well and heading to take his place at the window.

"No, Frost, we need you," I say, grabbing his arm.

"I'll catch up," he growls, pushing me away with a strength I've never felt before.

I have no choice but to obey. There's no time to argue. I scramble to my feet and head to Ernie's side, sharing the old man's weight with Saunders.

"He's not looking great, Bram," Saunders says.

"Hang in there, old man. For Eve," I whisper.

"For Eve," he says softly back—and I know he's going to make it.

"Wait!" a frail woman's voice cries out to us, and Anne comes up the stairs. She's nothing like the strong woman who held us at gunpoint a few moments ago. "You can't leave us. They'll kill us all," she pleads.

"They're coming. You need to get Ernie out of here now," Frost barks. "Take the women with you."

Anne looks from Frost to me.

"It's either come with us or take your chances with the EPO," I tell her.

She dashes for the stairs, calling for the other women.

"Get out of here now," Frost orders, then ducks as a spatter of bullets slices through the front of the house. He quickly returns fire. "I can handle these idiots, but more will be on the way. If you don't go now you won't get out alive."

I turn my back on Frost and help Saunders to carry Ernie. We head down the hallway, followed by Anne and, at a glance, five other terrified women scrambling behind her.

We follow Anne's screamed directions through the hallways of the manor house. After dragging Ernie's weight for a few minutes to the soundtrack of gunfire and grenade blasts, we hear the noise suddenly stop.

The silence is almost worse than gunfire.

"What do we do?" Saunders asks.

"We keep moving," I say. We follow in the footsteps of our remaining men as we find our exit through a conservatory, onto a grand patio, and into the gardens.

"You're out!" Saunders whispers to Ernie, who, despite the pain, manages a rebellious smirk.

"I've been waiting thirteen years for this," he mutters.

"We're not clear yet," I say, picking up the pace as we head to the bushes at the back of the garden.

Suddenly gunfire rattles the windows of the hallway we just escaped from.

We all turn.

"Frost?" I whisper.

"Are they inside?" Ernie asks. "Th-the EPO?"

"I've got to go back," I tell Saunders. "I've got to help Frost." I'm interrupted by the sound of gun blasts. Shadowy figures emerge from the hallway.

With each flash of gunfire, their blast-proof helmets and riot shields light up.

"They're coming!" I cry. "Get to the trees!" Anne and her rabble of terrified women scramble past us, deeper into the garden.

A gunshot suddenly cuts through the air. It's closer than before.

"Is that Frost?" Saunders asks, looking at a large figure hurtling past the windows of the long hallway, silhouetted in the gun flashes that chase him.

"We need to run," I say. I pick up Ernie's shivering body and move away from the house as fast as I can, Saunders helping me with him. "RUN!" I bellow, and the team of Freevers and the scared women don't wait around.

We fall back into the trees, the grass under our feet transforming into ankle-deep water.

I look back to see Frost barreling through the glass of the conservatory. I catch sight of the crazed look in his eyes as he frantically unwraps a woolen blanket.

My heart catches in my throat as I realize what he's done. What's about to happen.

Bullets connect with Frost's back, but it's already too late. He pulls Ernie's severed arm from the blanket. As he stumbles across the threshold of the house and steps into the garden, the glass around him shatters. More bullets and pulses from Ketch's squad catch up with him.

"FROST!" the Freevers cry.

"He's not going to make it!" Chubs yells from behind.

"He never planned to," I whisper as Frost launches the bloody limb away from the house. It hurtles through the chilled air, the device implanted inside it flashing red under the cold skin.

It doesn't even reach the ground before I feel the heat. Intense warmth hits my face, like an oven door opening. Then the brilliant glow of orange-red, like the sun emerging from behind a cloud, followed by blinding white and a burning sensation on my face, neck, hands, any exposed skin. I shield my eyes and try to place as much of my body as I can in front of Ernie to protect him as the entire building behind Frost's tumbling silhouette breaks apart and explodes in a great fireball, engulfing Frost and incinerating everyone inside.

I scramble to my feet as the flames settle and the thick black cloud ascends to join the gray sky above. My body aches, but not as much as my heart. Aching for Frost, for Johnny, for Ketch and the men I used to see at the Tower. How many were caught in the blast? Are there any survivors?

I step forward, instinctively wanting to search the inferno for anyone in need, when a hand grips my leg.

"Ernie!" I whisper, helping the old man up.

"We need to go—now," Saunders growls. I look at the frail figure of Eve's father. He's my responsibility now. I'm in too deep.

I hoist Ernie up with Saunders's help and turn away from the smoldering wreck where the house once stood. There is no turning back now.

52

EVE

BEEP, BEEP, BEEP. THE SOUND IS SO MONOTONOUS I FIND MY brain beeping along with it. Beep, beep, beep. Beep.

I try to move but wince in pain.

"It's okay, Eve," I hear Mother Kimberley say, a quiver in her friendly voice. "You're all right."

I don't feel it. There are wires around my chest, tubes under my nose, a clamp on my finger, all monitoring me and bleeping out my stats.

"Up her meds," Vivian orders sternly.

"Yes," murmurs Dr. Rankin.

I let go.

I pry open one eye and feel a searing pain shoot through my head at the bright white sight before me. I'm not in my room.

"Where am I?" I ask, hoping someone approachable is with me.

"Downstairs. You're being taken care of," says Mother Tabia, all sternness and authority gone from her voice as she mothers me.

"Why? What's wrong with me?" I ask feebly.

"Shush now. There was an accident. You—"

"Enough. Out," Vivian's voice orders.

I close my eyes and try to sleep again, attempting to ignore the tightness in my chest.

My breathing is calmer. My body feels better. My mind seems less foggy. This time when I open my eyes, I do so without too much of a fuss. I'm able to take in what's around me, a hostile examination room. At least I'm no longer hooked up to all that monitoring equipment.

"That was quite a little adventure you had."

Vivian is at the end of my bed, as composed as ever in a gray pantsuit, yet I vividly remember her screaming my name—the horror and fear, the desperation.

"What happened?" I ask, crinkling my forehead into a confused frown. "Why am I here?"

"You tried to escape."

"I did? Why?"

"You panicked," she states, her voice measured as she looks me up and down.

"About what?"

"Retraction."

"Really?"

"It would seem so."

"Where did I go?" I ask as glimpses of the collection bay, the car, those trees, and me flying toward one flash through my mind, along with all the lies and deceit.

"Not far enough that the public saw, don't worry," she says, with a look that tells me she feels sorry for me. Not in a way that reveals she's suddenly full of compassion, but rather that she thinks I'm pathetic. "Your little secret will stay here, within the safety of the building. We can't have them thinking you were about to abort mission and abandon them all."

"No. I'd never do that." I shake my head, wondering if she really believes I was running away.

"Quite."

"How long have I—"

"Just over twenty-four hours," she interrupts, looking at her watch.

"Oh." I hadn't realized I'd lost a day. I hadn't intended this to happen. All I'd needed was to confirm what I already thought I knew, before heading back here. Although any other way and I'd be upstairs in my room. This is better. "Where's Mother Kadi?"

"Poor Mother Kadi." Vivian sighs, feigning distress and shaking her head regretfully. I have a sinking feeling that I've put her in harm's way and that Vivian has evicted her, or worse. "You treated her terribly."

"*I* did?" I ask, confused.

"Yes. Barricaded her in the shower, apparently."

"I didn't want her stopping me," I confirm.

Unimpressed, Vivian just stares at me, her eyes full of contempt. "Sleep, Eve. Rest. I'll be back later," she says, looking at the door. Clearly she's needed elsewhere. "Now close your eyes."

I do as she says, relieved to hear she's leaving.

"Where's Vivian?" says Mother Kimberley seconds later as she pops her red head around the door and looks about.

"She just left."

"Must've missed her. Good," she says, sounding relieved as

she walks in. Her rosy cheeks are full and round as she stops and stares at me, her hands clasped to her chest. "How are you?"

"Fine."

She comes to my bedside and grabs my hand, stroking it. "Are you? You really had us worried, going off like that."

"I'm sorry."

"Don't be," she shushes me, giving my hand a firm squeeze.

"Can you do me a favor?" I ask.

"Yes, of course."

"Grab me something nicer to wear? I can't stand this gown. It reminds me of . . ." I stop and take a breath. "I just think I'd feel better in something else."

"Oh, little love. I won't be long."

As soon as the click of the door lets me know she's gone, I sit up slowly. My head spins, but I close my eyes to steady myself. My body feels painfully bruised, but I don't have time to acknowledge the state I'm in. I'm just thankful for the medication.

I go to the door and turn the handle as quietly as possible. Peeping around, I see Mother Kimberley heading to the elevators, but otherwise the corridor is empty. I'm glad I'm on the same corridor as usual. I know where I am.

My bare feet step out and I'm at the door within fifty meters or so. It's locked, although that shouldn't be too much of a surprise, given that they're creating a human life in there, possibly the new savior of humanity who'll lap up this lie like I have.

The thought is chilling.

I bash the vast metal door as hard as I can, the force against my muscles and bones making me cry out in agony.

The chrome handle lowers with a squeak before the door is opened and a face appears.

"Eve?" Dr. Rankin frowns, looking me in the eye—a rarity for her. "Can I get you something?"

The phone behind her starts ringing. Her face turns toward the sound while her jaw slackens, a question forming.

No time, I realize.

I barge through, accidentally knocking her over and wincing when her hip hits the corner of a low cupboard and she yelps.

My first thought is to go to her, to check I've not hurt her too badly, but then my eye is drawn into the room in front of me and my body tenses in horror. It's big, cold, barren, and sterile, with row upon row of science equipment and technical apparatus spread across each table. What causes my jaw to stiffen and my stomach to convulse, though, is the sight of test tubes, jars, and larger glass containers, all filled with liquid. Its subtle green hue casts eerie streaks of light on the cold floor. But it's what occupies the jars that I can't pull my eyes from—the results of their experiments, floating lifelessly inside. Through the tears that form in my eyes, I read one of the labels stuck to the side of the glass. It is dated—twice.

My heart pauses as I realize what these two dates are, what they mean. They leave me in no doubt that at some point these creations lived. Lungs would have filled, hearts would have beaten, yet now they are no more than tortured souls looking out through the glass preserving them and their brothers.

I want to speak to Dr. Rankin in the hope of gaining some answers, but I can't focus when I'm surrounded by this failure of human life and the extent to which they've meddled, their work seemingly spanning decades.

This isn't trusting Mother Nature or the gods. It's experimental science—science that's repeatedly gone wrong.

"What are you doing here?" I demand breathlessly, turning to face Dr. Rankin, who has been taking in my reaction. With my focus now on her, she backs away from me, rubbing her hip and shaking her head in a defiant silence.

"Tell me!"

"We've been doing all we can to prolong life, Eve. You know that," she says, her jaw clenching as she tries to regain her calm.

"With me. You've been doing that with me," I state, thinking of how many times they've scraped out my insides and stuck needles into me.

"Well, yes."

"What are these?" I demand, pointing at the jars and test tubes. "Science has failed us before. Decades were spent testing, screening, and manipulating to no avail. You got it wrong time and time again. Haven't you learned?"

"We need you to have a girl," she says curtly. "We've been learning how to rule out the variables."

"How?"

"Pardon?"

"How have you been doing that?"

She glances around the room.

"Creating and killing," I say, agog.

"Be thankful you're not part of the experiment."

"But I already am, aren't I? 'Bone of my bones and flesh of my flesh . . . ,'" I quote, edging closer to her as the contempt inside me builds.

She doesn't deny my assumption.

"There was never going to be a Revival ceremony, was there?" I say, the words making sense as I hear them. "It was always planned to be this way."

"I shouldn't . . . I can't . . ."

Another lie.

Before I can stop her, she reaches for the insistent phone and puts it to her ear. "She's here," she hisses. "Come quickly."

With no time to think, I simply act. I grab hold of a metal fire extinguisher and start by whacking the locks on the door several times, breaking their mechanisms and hopefully buying myself a few moments more. Then I start swiping the tables clear of their contents. The glass containers tumble and smash, the metal equipment clanks, the wood snaps and splinters—all of it falling to the floor with a deafening noise, filling me with conviction and rage, propelling me to the next workstation on the route of my destruction. I want it all gone. They can't be allowed to play God—to pick and choose which experiment gets to live and which to die.

My body moves like it's not my own, my burning muscles becoming more frantic by the second. My mind focuses on the initial reason for my being here: my retrieved egg. I think of it in this laboratory of horror and let out a cry of fury. It could be anywhere within these walls, so everything becomes a target.

Fighting blind, I decide I won't stop until there's nothing left to smash and destroy, so that none of it can be used in this way again.

Clearly worried that her team of helpers isn't coming quickly enough, Dr. Rankin tries to take control of the situation. Her arms wrap around my chest while she attempts to pull me back from a workstation I'm obliterating. I manage to shake her off, pushing her to the floor again with a thump.

I leave her and move on, lifting the red metal weapon above

my head to swing it into a row of test tubes and Bunsen burners, but Dr. Rankin tries again.

Her hand reaches out and grabs my ankle. I struggle to get away from her tight grip. I look around me. I see all the equipment and experiments waiting to be demolished, and I groan in frustration. I shake my foot manically, feeling her hold loosen. Somehow managing to pull it free, I hear her cry of horror as I run across the room.

I fly around creating chaos, screaming as I go. Sweat drips off my back as I sweep, smash, hit, and throw every object within my reach. Running around the room like a human hurricane, I ache to destroy everything in my sight. At first I had hoped to find the parts of my soul they'd extracted from me, but now, with adrenaline pumping through me, I'm charged with a fire and hatred I've never let free before. I feel alive, I feel wicked, and I feel driven. A powerful force from within shows me I'm far more physically capable than I could have imagined. It leads me on. It goads me. These lives they've created and destroyed, these experiments they've conjured and failed at, are all the result of their barbarism. I want it all gone. I don't want them to be able to create perfect little boys only to dispose of them because they're surplus to requirements. I don't want to be a part of their lie.

The banging at the door reminds me I don't have long to act. They'll be in here soon to drag me back upstairs to carry on living the life they've planned for me. I was never their creation, and it angers me that they've had such a say in the way I live my life.

I break anything I can get my hands on—not just for me, but for any child being brought, wanted or not, into their care.

53

BRAM

WE SAIL HOME IN SILENCE. THERE WERE NO BODIES TO RECOVER. No possessions to bring back with us. Frost and Johnny are gone.

All that remained was a pile of rubble where the grand house once stood. Ernie's disguised prison is no more.

As we weave slowly through the shallows of the outer city, the medics go to work on Ernie.

"He'll make it," a voice says over the intercom. I slide to the back of the boat and pick up the microphone.

"Good. How are the women?" I ask, staring across at the pod sailing a few feet behind ours.

No reply.

"Hello? Can you hear me?" I ask.

"Yes, sir," the voice replies, and I see the young Freever turn to me from the same position in the pod behind. His words echo in my mind. *Sir.* That term they used to address Frost is now aimed at me. His voice cuts through the thought: "The women won't let us check them, sir."

I stand to look at the pod carrying our newest passengers. Anne and the five other women are huddled together, trembling with so much fear that it's visible even over the vibrations of our pods on the water.

"We'll do what we can, though, sir. They seem physically unhurt."

"Thanks . . . What's your name?"

"Grobbs, sir."

"Thanks, Grobbs, and I'm Bram, not sir," I tell him, and hang up.

My head pounds with a million thoughts fighting for my attention. First Eve, always Eve. Then Ernie, but now that I know he's going to make it, that thought quiets. What to do with the terrified women we've acquired? How to break the news of Frost's death to the rest of his team, *my* team? Then my mind lands back on Eve, and I hold her image there as we enter the heavier traffic of the river and the fog thickens.

Our arrival plays on my mind as I walk into the heart of the base, deep below the surface. The two women who required sedation for the descent into the Deep are carried through the wooden halls. Chubs and Grobbs escort the others.

"We'll take these two straight to the medical bay with Ernie," Grobbs tells me. "Follow the old signs to Peers Court and you'll find us."

It was a hard decision to sedate them, but onlookers had begun to notice their screams across the river as they resisted our efforts to get them through the entrance in the face of the old clock. The sound of women's voices doesn't go unnoticed out here. I had to make the call.

Once those two were carried carefully into the iron elevator, the others followed reluctantly.

Saunders and I enter the main chamber and I feel the eyes follow us as we walk beneath the overhanging balcony and between the green benches to the large oak desk. The projector still sits on the table in front of me, like a ghost of times past.

I clear my throat and the Freevers gather around. I hear Ernie's muted groans echo through the corridors.

"Saunders, I want you to make sure that no one has access to Ernie. Let the old man recover," I whisper. He nods and immediately heads back the way we came.

Suddenly I feel alone in this room of strangers. Strangers awaiting news.

"What the hell is going on?" a voice calls.

"Where's Frost?" asks another.

"Why are there more women here? This ain't a sanctuary," someone else chips in.

I hold out my arms and they fall silent, as they would have done for Frost, and I suddenly feel the weight of his responsibility on my shoulders. I look around the room at the thirty or forty pairs of eyes staring expectantly at me. More men enter on the balcony above.

I take a breath. "Frost is dead," I tell them, short and sharp, although the words sound so strange that it's almost as if I didn't say them. "Johnny too." Straight to the point, and to the hearts of the men in front of me.

I hear cries and sobs from the crowd. "Frost sacrificed himself for us, for Ernie."

"No, he didn't," someone calls.

The crowd parts and I see Helena. A tear forms in her eye and slowly drops onto her cheek, following the wrinkles like a river.

"I'm sorry?" I say.

"He didn't sacrifice himself for you or for Ernie," she chokes out. She turns her head and I follow her gaze to the far wall, then up above the balcony. Behind the dim hanging lights suspended over our heads, carved deep into the ancient wood of the ceiling beams, two words stare down at us all: *FOR EVE*.

"For Eve," I say in agreement.

"For Eve," the room repeats.

"He died so that we could escape, so that we could continue the fight." I pause. "No, so that we could *finish* the fight," I correct myself, and feel the shifting of feet as my words connect with the people hanging on them.

"We have Eve's father. If we're going to get Eve out, he is going to play a vital part. The world needs to know his story. Eve needs to know the truth. Our priority now is his safety. I want a complete lockdown on this place. No one comes in or out of the Deep without me knowing about it first." As I speak, I realize that this is the first command I've given the group that I've elected myself to lead.

No one questions it. They look at me, ready for my next command.

"We are also welcoming six new female recruits. I want a section of this place made secure and comfortable for them as they adjust to life down here. Helena . . ."

She wipes the tears away.

". . . perhaps you can take care of that."

She nods.

"So what now?" All heads turn toward the balcony and the man behind the thick glasses who is calling down. "You think you're our leader?"

The heads of the men snap back to me.

I take a moment. "I didn't know Frost well, not like you knew him, but he was a good man. Good enough for all of you. Good enough that you would give up your lives, commit them to him, to this place, to fighting for what you believe in," I say, pacing a little behind the desk. When my foot hits a little step, I stand on it, using the height to help project my voice to every listening pair of ears in the room. "I never meant for Eve and me to fall in love, but she needed me and I was there. Frost didn't want to die, but we needed him and he was there. Right now, you are the only people who have a shot at getting Eve out of that place. You need a leader and I'm here."

"He's right," Chubs calls, entering at the back of the long hall. "He's bloody right. I didn't want this EPO boy anywhere near the Deep when we first dragged his soggy arse out of the water. But he's the only one who can get us to Eve."

"And you trust him?" asks the man with the glasses.

"Frost did," Chubs replies.

"And look what that did to Frost," Glasses snaps.

"Exactly," Chubs calls back. "He gave his life for him. He stayed behind so that this stranger could see it through. I was there. I saw it with my own eyes. We've worked for so long, for so many years, and it all comes down to right here and now. This is the best chance we've ever had at freeing her, at liberating our savior. I'm with you, Bram," he finishes, and the heads turn back to me.

I nod in thanks to him and look out at the crowd to see if anyone has anything to add.

Silence.

"I won't let Eve down and I won't let you down either," I tell them all, and it's true. I feel their passion, and the same passion is pumping through my veins. In that moment I feel I've found a place where I belong.

"So what happens now?" Chubs breaks the silence.

"What happens next will change everything," I reply.

54

EVE

I'M SO CONSUMED WITH THE URGE TO DESTROY THAT I DON'T realize others have managed to enter the room until their hands are on me, stripping me of my makeshift weapon. A guard pushes me to the floor and pins me down, my cheek resting on the cold tiles. There's no time for rules, barriers, and boundaries— I need to be contained and stopped. Clearly, by whatever means necessary. The protocols we've all been living by since my birth are slipping away thick and fast.

"Get off me!" I yell, trying to free my arms while kicking my legs. "You can't do this."

"I've been told to," a low voice I recognize mutters.

Michael.

My mind quickly flashes back—Potential Number Two, the meeting, Diego, Mother Nina, the elevator, feeling threatened, the fear, the hug, then Bram's punch. It seems like a lifetime ago now.

"Calm down or you'll make this worse for yourself. Please, Eve," he begs, his voice just a hissed whisper as his breath warms my ear.

He releases a little of the weight he has on me so that I can turn over and take in his concerned expression but still remain beneath him.

I start to wonder why he has been given the task of man-handling me, but quickly realize there's no way the Mothers could have tackled me to the floor. I recognize only a few of the other faces as part of my usual team, and that makes me feel uneasy.

"Where's Ketch? I want to speak to him. He needs to know what they're doing here," I demand, trying to wriggle free. Surely none of them could've known about the experiments that have been taking place in this room, and as these men are here to protect me, there must be a way for them to help prevent further experiments—especially if parts of me are being used to conduct them.

Michael gives an audible sigh at my reluctance to comply with his request to calm down. "He's had to go out," he says, frowning as he looks around the room and takes in the mess I've made.

"Out?" I repeat, unable to hide my surprise. "Out where?"

"I don't know." He shrugs, his eyes wandering to the bloody masses on the floor.

"My head of security has left the building and I'm not allowed to know where he's gone?" I push for clarification.

"He's on an assignment, something important," he says through gritted teeth, pulling his gaze away from what he's just seen.

"More important than keeping me safe in here?" I challenge.

"You're under no threat."

"You think?" I ask in a high-pitched squeak.

He opens his mouth to speak, but nothing comes out. His eyes go down to the floor next to us, though I can tell they want to return to the carnage of the laboratory. He, too, needs to make sense of what he's seen.

"Cuff her," the hard, cold voice of Vivian orders as she walks into the room and renders us all silent.

Michael's weight shifts on top of me before he tugs on my wrists and I feel the cold metal clasps shut tightly.

"Up," Vivian commands.

His weight eases off me as he gets to his feet before gently pulling me to mine, turning me so that I'm facing her. She looks at me with disdain. Pure disgust. Her eyes scan me, taking in my bedraggled hair, my torn hospital gown, my face red from exertion and hands sore from grappling—the chaos of destruction turning me into something like a banshee.

"Out," she whispers, her gaze landing at my bare and bloodied feet on the glass-scattered floor.

Michael and I don't move, both of us seemingly waiting for more instructions or scathing remarks.

"Now." Her voice is low, stern, and full of hatred.

Michael takes hold of the chain between my hands and pulls me from my rooted spot, causing me to gasp at the pain from my cut feet.

We walk past Vivian, the doctor, and the others in the security team, out of the room, and toward the elevator.

When the door pings open Michael places me inside but swiftly steps out. I look at his face for some kind of recognition, but his eyes are on the floor between us—clearly eager to get back to formalities.

The doors close, the elevator moves. It takes only a few seconds for them to reopen on my floor.

The floor of the Dome.

My prison of lies.

Mother Tabia rushes toward me as I hobble through the doors.

"Where on earth . . . ?" she hisses as she observes the mess I'm in.

Then she sees the cuffs.

"Oh, dear Lord." She drapes an arm around me and supports some of my weight.

"Did you know?" I whimper, feeling spent.

"Know what?" she asks, looking confused.

"All of it."

"Let's take you to your room," she says, holding me a little tighter to her body. "It'll all be fine."

I wish I could share her optimism.

55

BRAM

"HE'S AWAKE!" SAUNDERS BURSTS THROUGH THE DOOR TO MY small, damp room. Ernie has been sleeping nonstop following the events that got him down here. Losing his arm sent his frail body into shock, and for a while the small medical team here thought we might lose him, but the old man's tough—I'll give him that. He's a fighter.

"Can I see him?" I ask, getting to my feet.

"Of course, if that's what you want," says Saunders. "You give the orders here now, remember?"

I'm still not used to these people looking to me for leadership. Even the ones who resented it at first have fallen into line since I delivered the news.

I still don't know half their names—I'm not sure I've even met all of them yet: new faces appear constantly as I walk the hallways or stand next to me as we line up to collect meal trays. I am, however, becoming more familiar with the doctors and the medical team due to the amount of time I've spent with them. I've been continuously visiting the hospital-like rooms over the last twenty-four hours, first checking on Ernie and then our group of female guests, who are slowly accepting their new surroundings. Anne constantly brings up the fact that I'm not letting them leave the Deep.

"What's the point in freeing us from one prison and throwing us into another?" she snaps.

She's right, but I can't let them go yet. I can't risk the EPO finding this place, finding Ernie.

I'm doing my best to control the situation, to keep things calm and relaxed.

For now, the women are kept in a separate court of this sunken maze, watched closely by Helena.

I follow Saunders from my room and down Ministers' Corridor, stepping over the thick blue piping that pumps the floodwater out of our sealed building. Although the interiors are covered with watertight wall panels and sheets of thick polyethylene, I'm still blown away by glimpses of the building the Freevers have commandeered. Some of the original wooden ceilings and beams poke through, like ghosts of a past life, staring down at us as we walk.

"Mr. Bram," Dr. Oliva greets me with a nod of his balding head. "I'm sure you've heard the good news."

"I have. Can I see him?" I ask.

"Absolutely. In fact, he's been asking for you," Dr. Oliva says, and points to the open door behind him.

I step inside and see the old man sitting up on the bed in the center of the empty room. This is no hospital, but they've done a good job of making the space work for their needs.

"Bram, isn't it?" Ernie says, squinting in my direction. "Sorry, I must have left my glasses behind at the house. Anne, the women, are they . . . ?"

"They're fine," I say, holding out my hand to calm him. "Anne's giving me a hard time for saving their lives, but what can you do?" I joke.

"Ha, I bloody bet she is. They don't get a bunch of men turning up at that place if they aren't after some sort of trouble," says Ernie.

"We weren't after trouble, sir. We wanted you," I tell him.

"Well, if it wasn't trouble you came looking for, you certainly brought it with you. Your friend, Frost, was he . . . ?"

I nod.

"I'm sorry. He seemed like a good man." Ernie peers at the bandage around the end of his elbow, where his arm used to be. "I should have done this myself a long time ago. Coward."

"Sir—"

"Please, it's Ernie."

"Very well. Ernie, you're about as far from cowardly as I can imagine a man to be. What the EPO has done to you is beyond comprehension," I say, taking a seat on the small plastic chair and pulling it along the side of his bed.

"What they did to me is not the issue, my boy," he says.

"You're right. What they're doing to Eve is despicable and—"

"No," he interrupts. "Not Eve either."

I stare at him, confused.

"It's what they're doing to the entire world that's the most alarming thing," Ernie says, with a glint of passion in his Eve-blue eyes. "Eve is just their weapon, their ace to play at any hand dealt against them in their power trip to take over the world. It's not about the future of humanity for them, kid. That's what the rest of the world cares about; so as long as they hold the key to that, as long as they control Eve, they control the world," he says, gazing straight into my eyes. "Governments bow to their will, countries obey their commands, armies take their orders, and just look at the state of this world, at the state of the future they appear to be fighting for! But all they're fighting for is more power. If Eve has girls, what do you think will happen to them?"

I shrug.

"They'll be pincushions for a while, of course, just like Eve when she was a baby. Then the whole process will start all over again. Do you really think any daughters of Eve would ever have any more freedom than their mother?"

I think about that for a moment.

"Of course not," Ernie scoffs. "Their entire lives are already prearranged. Even their Potentials are lined up."

"What?"

"Yeah, those deals have already been made."

"Deals? What deals?" I ask, my mind racing to keep up.

"Powerful men want the blood of powerful men running through the veins of the children of the future, of Eve's children. There's only one person who can make that happen."

"Vivian Silva," I mutter.

Ernie replies with a nod.

"But why would Vivian make those deals? What does she get in return?" I ask.

"Power," Ernie says. "Continuing, unlimited power." I stay silent, hanging on his words. "If Eve does provide us with a future, Vivian has put deals in place that will ensure that the person controlling that future is her."

"So it's not just about saving humanity anymore—it's about controlling it?" I ask.

"I'm afraid, for Vivian Silva, that has been the case for a long time. My darling Corinne and I created Eve, perfect Eve, and Vivian knew from day one that controlling her meant controlling the world."

"How do you know all this?" I ask.

"When you've lived as long as I have, when you've had everything taken from you, you have two options: give up and die, or stick around and fight. I might not have had the luxury of freedom on my side, but people talk, kid. People see things, know things, learn things. Ask the right people the right questions and you get the right answers. There are people in that place, people with loose lips and small brains," he says.

He falls quiet, and I look behind to see if the door is closed. It is.

"Do you mind if I ask you something personal?" I say.

"Of course not, kid. I owe you my freedom. Whatever you need to know, I'm here to help," he says, with a surprisingly youthful quickness for an injured old man on a hospital bed.

"How did you end up in that place? I mean, the rumors that you tried to hurt Eve and that your wife's passing drove you insane . . ."

"Let me tell you something now, my boy. Something you gotta know about me. Eve is my little girl, my everything. I wouldn't pluck a hair from her head if I thought it would hurt her. I know what they said about me, that my mind went, that I was a danger to Eve. That was the hardest part of it all."

"But did you try to kidnap her?" I ask.

"Kidnap? My own daughter?" he asks calmly. "Taking my own baby girl home from the hospital? Is that not every father's right?"

I nod.

The old man seems to shake a little.

"Are you okay?" I ask.

"I witnessed them do the most awful things to my Corinne. She could still be here today. They could have saved her. But they didn't. *She* didn't."

"Miss Silva?" I ask, and he nods as though the thought of her burns in his mind.

"She let my wife die. Out of convenience. With her out of the way it was one less obstacle."

"That just left you," I say.

"Precisely," he says, swallowing the emotion. "I tried to tell people what was happening, what I'd seen with my own eyes, but the harder I tried, the crazier they made me seem. *Eve's crazy father, crackpot Daddy, Danger Dad!* I had it all written about me. I'd had enough. After I lost Corinne, all I had left in the world was Eve, and I wasn't going to leave her in the hands of the people who let her mother die."

"So you broke in to take her?" I ask.

"Broke in? Kid, I walked in," he scoffs.

I take a moment to process this information.

"But all the stories I've read say that you broke into Eve's secure, guarded quarters and took her from her bed," I tell him.

"That's the way they spun it. Truth is, I just walked right in through the front doors, straight to her room, and straight out again. Didn't see anyone else until I was halfway out of the front gates. That was when they brought in a whole squad of their goons. They zapped me with one of their stun-glove thingies. Last thing I remember before my head hit the ground is one of them burning Eve's arm with a Taser. The sound of her screams and the smell of her burning skin have haunted me ever since."

"I don't believe it," I say. "I'm not saying you're a liar, obviously, but it's unbelievable."

"I still can't believe it either," says Ernie.

All these years I've thought of this man as crazy, a risk to Eve's security, rightly sentenced to a life of isolation in a secret location for Eve's protection. Now I see a caring father ripped apart from his daughter by a corporation so powerful that no one could question their actions even if they wanted to.

I try to imagine the old man walking alone into that place, like a damned hiker at the foot of a mountain with stormy weather closing in around him. I wonder what was going through his mind the night he went to take his daughter back, as he stepped across the threshold for the last time, as the beams of light scanned his eyes and granted him access to his doomed future.

"So what's the plan?" the old man asks, interrupting my thoughts.

"The plan is the same plan you had all those years ago. We're going to take back your daughter," I tell him with conviction.

"That's all well and good, but how exactly do you think you'll do it? I'm assuming you're not welcome to waltz up to the front door and ring the bell."

Suddenly my thoughts click into place, like planets aligning. The plan lays itself out before me in flashes, stepping-stones to victory, with huge, treacherous gaps between them.

I stand up sharply, making the old man jump.

"I have an idea." I lock eyes with him. "I know how we're going to get Eve."

56

EVE

BY THE TIME WE'VE MADE IT UP TO MY ROOM, MOTHERS Kimberley and Kadi have joined us, looking wounded as they take in the state of me.

"I'm sorry," I say to each of them, but they shush me.

They have no choice but to cut me out of my hospital gown, wash and dress me with my wrists still clamped together in cuffs. They tend my injured feet, working quickly and in silence, not knowing when Vivian will descend upon us, and each apprehensive of her arrival.

When I'm ready and fully dressed, the room seems eerily quiet, despite the other women being with me. We aren't talking. I'm sure that they, like me, are thinking over my actions and the repercussions they might have. I wasn't expecting to have this time to contemplate what I've done or digest what I've seen. Vivian is reactive. She doesn't sit and plan a response. Or maybe it's more accurate to say she's usually a few steps ahead in any given situation, just waiting for me to act in a way she disapproves of so she can wade in with her matriarchal force.

What will she do with me now? My recent actions must

have hindered whatever plans she's spent years concocting. She's wanted me to be fully dependent on her and the world she's built for me. Having caught her off guard and destroyed years' worth of work, I can't even imagine the depth of the hatred she's feeling for me right now. But hate as she might, her anger toward me is nothing to the revulsion I feel toward her and everything she stands for.

I will not be her accomplice and bring more children into this fabricated world where we have no understanding of what is going on with the species we're meant to be saving.

"You should lie down until she comes. You've had an eventful few days," says Mother Kimberley, going to my bed and pulling back my duvet, giving it a little pat, as though the sound of its softness might tempt me.

"I'm fine," I say, shaking my head while trying to ignore my body's exhaustion. It's as though huge weights are hanging off every part of me.

"You look tired," she pleads, her hands now rubbing the fabric.

"Did you know?" It's a question I have to ask to understand how deep the lies run.

Mother Kimberley sighs guiltily while stealing glances at the other two Mothers, then looks back at me. "Which bit?"

"I see," I say, feeling deflated and foolish.

"We wanted you to be happy," chips in Mother Tabia. "To us it was a beautiful place for you to escape to, away from the Dome."

"But the reason I loved it so much wasn't because it was away from here but because it was real and tangible. It was a link. When I was down there I didn't feel I was being mollycoddled and protected. I felt like I was a part of it. I have never set foot outside this building since the day I stepped into it," I say, hearing how ridiculous it sounds as I say it, and feeling more impassioned. "Yet I'm meant to continue whatever is going on out there. Is that what I want for my children? Is that what we want for the rebirth generation? To be shut off like breeding slaves?"

"No, Eve!" Mother Kimberley exclaims, frantically shaking her head.

"Because what would be the point of any of it if those who are prolonging life aren't given a life of their own?"

"An ironic outlook," notes Mother Kadi, pensive.

"You're overthinking it," mumbles Mother Tabia. "It wasn't meant to be like that. It was to lift your spirits."

"But I didn't need that. You ladies and your love would've been enough for me to believe in what we're trying to save." I look at the three of them, each solemn and somber, and know I'm not the only one who's been misinformed and manipulated. They've already told me they were here "for me," but would they still be here if they knew of the horrors below?

"Did you know there are babies down there?" I say, my mouth talking before my mind decides whether or not I should share what I've seen. I can't hold it in and keep the nightmare to myself. I want them to understand. With no Holly around to confide in, I need to share elsewhere. The Mothers are bound to love and care for me supposedly as a biological mother would. I need to voice the sights in my head.

"Stop," says Mother Kadi, her eyes going to Mother Tabia, who instantly looks worried and pained.

"You must be mistaken," mumbles Mother Kimberley, her

hands hovering between her mouth and her ears, as though I've just blasphemed and she can't bear to hear it. "You are the only living girl who can reproduce now—our last hope."

"Naturally, yes, but they're experimenting. Trying to make girls. No, *failing* to make them."

"Surely not," mutters Mother Tabia, looking at me intently, seeming eager for more but fearful of what I might say. "Why would they do such a thing?"

"Because they've learned nothing from the past," I say matter-of-factly. "They think they know better. I wouldn't be surprised if they set up my encounters for failure so they can carry on doing things as they wish."

"I don't understand," Mother Tabia says quietly. I feel for her. For so long she's been Vivian's accomplice, but it's clear to see she's been just as easily manipulated as the rest of us.

"Being up here, you're just as cut off as I am—of course you are," I say, my voice softer than before. "I've been living with the notion that things are not as they seem for a while, but for Mother Tabia, who's clearly never doubted it, I imagine it's quite a shock to see cracks appearing. She's always believed this was the righteously divine plan. "You have to be. How else would she have managed to get you to leave your families?"

"I came for you," she replies. "I can remember where I was when I first heard about you. My mother was poorly and I'd become her full-time caregiver. She died before you were born. My dad had long since passed away and I had no other family. No siblings, no partner, no children. I was alone and lonely. I felt I'd failed at life, but you were my beacon. I thought your arrival allowed me to play a part in something wonderful."

"It did, Tabia," Mother Kadi says softly, taking her hand as tears spring to Mother Tabia's eyes.

"I'm sorry . . ." She sniffs.

"We should go," Mother Kadi says, taking a breath. "Vivian won't be long and she won't want us here."

The Mothers exchange knowing glances at having to leave me. I want to ask them to stay, but I know they've done more than they should have already, and they all look regretful as they walk toward the door.

"We'll be back," Mother Kadi promises with a sigh, squeezing my hand before she leaves my room. She's fine. We're fine. Or at least she wants us to be. The door closes with a gentle click, yet it leaves a merciless clamp on my heart.

I'm alone again.

Mother Tabia's confession plays on my mind. She was out there and lonely, just like I am in here. I often feel as if I'm waiting, but for what I don't know—to become a mother? To fulfill my destiny of procreating? For someone to come and rescue me from this burden? To be set free and allowed to choose?

I wonder what freedom would look like for me. It's so far away from my grasp that I can't even imagine it.

I look around my room as emptiness engulfs me. How I wish I lived in different times. I'm tired of living in this bubble. Of having nothing for myself other than what they allow me. My Mothers, my friends, my potential lovers—they have all been chosen for me by others. I no longer want to be just another pawn in their game. I want real choices. I want my desires to be taken seriously. I want my children to know their mother did all she could for them. I want them never to experience this imprisonment and manipulation.

It seems cruel that they've allowed me to destroy their intricate plan. Perhaps I'd have been happy living out my days here, thinking I was making a difference and believing whatever lies they fed me.

It dawns on me that even this, my sitting here having to digest everything they've done, may be part of their plan—maybe I'm one big variable they'd rather make more stable. They'd rather I was lifeless, or an unfeeling robot just doing whatever they asked, without question.

I am a very small cog.

In their plan, I am.

If I have to live their lie for the rest of my life, I want them to dull the ache in my heart, to stop this yearning for something that's not available to me.

Numb me.

Fry my brain.

Pickle my body in a jar like the others.

Just stop my having to think and feel when all I'm greeted with is emptiness.

"Come and get me, then," I shout at the air around me, blood rushing to my brain. "Come and punish me. Do your worst. Turn me into one of your monsters and be done with it. Then you can poke and prod me to your heart's content and breed from me as much as you like. I'm done. Do you hear me? I'm done!"

I scream. No words. Just a high-pitched deafening wail. I scream until my lungs shrivel and hurt from lack of air. Then I breathe in and do it again.

I scream.

I scream.

I scream.

I scream.

I scream until my voice cuts out, my throat burns, and my eyes sting.

I scream until my body gives up.

I scream until I've nothing left to give.

I scream.

I remain alone.

57

BRAM

"YOU'VE LOST IT, MATE," CHUBS BELLOWS, HIS VOICE BOUNCING off the high, dripping ceiling.

"Shh! Keep it down, for heaven's sake," Saunders hisses across the large central table. The vast meeting chamber is quiet at this hour. Not that anyone could tell it's five a.m. down here. No light penetrates the watertight seals.

The only people in here now are the team I invited, the only ones I feel I can trust with the plan at this early stage: Saunders, Chubs, and Ernie.

"He's right. It's the only way," Ernie says. He's brightened up since the doctors allowed him to leave the ward to attend the meeting. Mind you, I think I'd have an issue with being confined to one space if I'd lived his life for the last thirteen years.

"But is that even possible? I mean, if it goes wrong you'll die. There has to be another way," Chubs says.

"Trust me, I know the Tower. There's no way in or out of it unless your retinas are registered on the security system, and mine are definitely off that list now," I tell them. "If I get anywhere near those eye scanners, I'll be arrested before I reach the front door."

"Arrested?" Saunders says with a chuckle. "Do you really think that after all this they'll bother sending someone down to arrest you? You're the biggest risk to Eve they've ever had. You'll be dead before you reach the front door, mate!"

"That's why this is the only way. They'll never suspect it," I tell them.

"So let me get this straight. You're going to freeze yourself until you're not alive anymore, hide in one of those tanks, and pray your pal can thaw you on the other side?"

Sounds crazy when you hear it like that.

"And you're sure your friend can revive you? I didn't think that technology was approved yet," Ernie says.

"'Not approved' doesn't mean much in that place," Saunders explains. "They're thawing women from Cold Storage all the time, reviving them, testing the process. Experimenting."

"Then why don't we hear about it?" Chubs asks.

Saunders and I look at each other.

"Why don't you hear about the puppies they tested your rash cream on?" Saunders asks, looking at a dry, flaky patch of skin on Chubs's arm. He covers it quickly, becoming self-conscious. "Because sometimes the results aren't very pretty."

"So what happens to the women they get out of CS?" Chubs asks.

"Thawed, dissected, refrozen, thawed, frozen—you name it, they do it, and no one can stop them," Saunders says, perhaps making it a little more theatrical than I would have done. "Once you donate your body to the EPO it's theirs to do with as they wish. They just don't market it that way."

"Always read the small print!" Chubs jokes.

"So, your friend inside the Tower can get to you and thaw you out before someone else finds you?" Ernie asks.

"Hartman? Yeah, he'll figure it out. He always does," I say, almost believing it. "That's only half the problem, though." I rub my temples to help me think through my headache.

"What's the other half?" Chubs asks.

"Actually letting Hartman know the plan! This is all useless if he has no idea what we need him to do. If I can't get a message to him, he won't even know I'm back inside the Tower. I'll just be there, frozen for eternity, or at least until someone eventually discovers a perfectly preserved male squished up inside one of those tanks and decides to thaw me to find out why," I finish, and they're all quiet.

The riddle plays on everyone's mind.

Ernie breaks the silence: "I'll give him your message."

"You? How?" Saunders asks the old man, who's sitting thoughtfully in the glow of our torchlight.

"I'll walk in there and tell him," Ernie says simply.

No one says a word.

Then Chubs bursts out laughing, his belly wobbling.

The laughter settles a moment later when we all realize the old man is serious.

"Jesus, and I thought Bram was crazy!" Saunders says. "You two were meant for each other."

"They'll shoot you as soon as you set foot on-site. You won't make it inside," Chubs says.

"Yes, I will," Ernie says.

"What makes you so sure?" Saunders asks.

"They went to such desperate lengths to cover up the murder of my wife, then created such an elaborate fiction about me to justify locking me up for all these years, when they could have just killed me then. It's all about perception, creating this facade for the public, showing the world that they were doing what was right for Eve."

"But things have changed now. The world is different," Chubs says. "People don't care as much since they started being so secretive about Eve. Showing us less of the real Eve we used to see and more of their manipulated version."

"He's right," Saunders chips in. "If the public isn't interested, the EPO won't think twice about killing you."

"Then we need to make the public interested. We need to make people care again," I say.

"How?" Chubs asks.

"We need every person in Central at the EPO gates. We need every lens of every camera, every holo-player, pointed at those front gates, just like they were when Eve was born, beamed on those screens around Central, around the world, to witness the return of Eve's father after all these years. Reformed, rehabilitated, ready to see his daughter," I say, staring at my team.

Ernie smiles, despite the tears in his eyes.

"They won't have any choice but to open up and let him inside," Saunders adds excitedly.

"But what about once he's inside?" Chubs asks.

"I'll refuse to talk to anyone but Kartman," Ernie says.

"Hartman!" I correct him.

"Sorry, Hartman. Don't worry, I'll get it right on the night!" He chuckles with the youthful glint of rebellion in his old eyes.

"Yes, but once you're out of sight of the crowds, there's no guarantee they'll cooperate, no guarantee they'll allow you anywhere near Hartman," Saunders says.

"He's right. You'll need to call him out to you," I say.

"What?" Ernie says.

"You need to stand outside the front door, in broad daylight, and say you won't go inside or talk to anyone but Hartman. With the world watching, they won't use physical force on you," I say.

"Say the plan works up to then and Hartman comes out— then what? How can I tell him without telling everyone else watching?" Ernie says.

The four of us fall silent again and mull over this new conundrum.

"I could be dead for all the EPO know," I say, the dust of an idea gathering in my mind. "I could easily have been caught up in the blast at Grim's Ditch."

"True," Saunders says. "They won't assume you're dead, but they'll certainly know it's a possibility."

"So tell them you've come to deliver a message to Hartman in person," I say, suddenly having an idea. "Tell them you won't answer any questions until you've given him the message. Let them think you're delivering news of my death to my best friend."

Ernie smiles and nods. I can see that the thought of his part in this mission is igniting a fire inside him, like he's been waiting to free his daughter his whole life, and this is his shot.

"Assuming they play along and Hartman comes out to greet you, tell him this: *Your dear friend Bram is at peace. He is now with his mother.*"

"Your mother?" Chubs asks.

"She's in CS," I say.

"Are you sure he'll know what that means?" Chubs asks. "I mean, it's not giving him much to go on."

"It's as obvious as we can afford to be," I say.

"What if he doesn't believe me?" Ernie asks.

I think for a moment. Then I feel it, the cool metal hanging around my neck. I slip the silver cross over my head and hand it to Ernie. "Give him this."

"You believe in God?"

"My mother did. It was hers," I explain.

"Well, we need one now more than ever," Ernie says, placing the chain over his head and tucking it safely under his cotton shirt.

"If we can get Ernie's return out there for the public to see, the whole world will be watching. Waiting to see what happens next," Saunders tells me.

"I know," I say.

I know.

58

EVE

"VIVIAN HASN'T BEEN IN," I SAY THE FOLLOWING MORNING when I hear Mother Kadi walk through the door. I'm glad that she's come with a key for the cuffs, which remained on my wrists all night. The skin beneath them is now red and sore, but that has hardly troubled me at all. Instead my mind has been busy batting away the inevitable nightmare visions fighting to invade my head. At first I tried to stop myself from nodding off, sure the horrors would infiltrate my sleep, but they came anyway, bringing with them a night of cold sweats, vomit, and anxiety.

I'm relieved that it's now the start of a new day. A new day feels hopeful somehow, as though it comes with fresh possibilities for new discoveries. I'm still none the wiser on how to move forward after yesterday's revelations, but a new day symbolizes new opportunities to make sense of it all.

I keep telling myself that more will become apparent in time. The world around me is starting to unravel and show its true self. I just need to be open and alert to what I see and hear around me. Once I have more information, I'll be able to formulate a plan somehow.

"She's been busy," Mother Kadi says, seeming distracted as she hands me my cup of tablets before laying the tray by my side, revealing a breakfast of fruit and herbal tea.

While she arranges my clothes for the day, I tip the tablets into my hand and take a closer look at them, thinking of how many I've taken over the years.

Vitamins, as they say, or another lie?

I quickly place them under my pillow before Mother Kadi turns back to me. "Everything okay?" I ask.

"Of course it is, darling!" She smiles, nodding in her usual upbeat manner. Yet I hear the wobble in her voice and see the bottom of her eyes fill with tears. I know she's lying.

She stops and takes a breath. "I'm sorry," she chokes, putting the clothes she's fetched on the bed. "I'll have to ask Mother Tabia to get you ready today. I'm not feeling too well."

"Mother Kadi?" I call as I watch her flee.

I'm meant to be gearing up for implantation, when my altered egg will be returned to me, and my womanly attributes given their first proper test. As I'm not sure if I failed in my mission to destroy that egg, and anything else they hold of me, it's unclear as to whether the previous plan is going ahead. All I know is that if it does, I want Mother Kadi by my side. I know I can trust her.

"Stay with me," I call, my hands reaching out and imploring her, wondering what's changed since yesterday to make her so distant and distracted.

I pull back my bedding and am about to go after her, but as she flings open the door and runs through it, I feel light-headed. I take a deep breath and close my eyes, but the feeling intensifies, my body heavy and uncontrollable. I try to call out to Mother Kadi for help, but nothing happens. I can't seem to open my mouth or shout.

I know I'm exhausted from the previous day's events. Although they've tried to build up my fitness with dance, boxing, and martial arts over the years, yesterday I moved in ways I've never had to before. I overexerted myself too soon after the crash. My body is paying for it now.

Ever so briefly my mind turns to my mother. Her body couldn't keep her and me alive. It failed us. Maybe mine will be the same. Maybe my own future is doomed. Maybe history will, inevitably, repeat itself.

My fingers rest on the rough patch of skin on my wrist, a heavy sadness creeping in at the thought of what might have been.

Wave after wave of wooziness washes over me, nausea building. I close my eyes and take a deep breath, slowly letting the air go, then sucking in a fresh lungful and feeling it disperse around my tired bones.

"Well done."

My eyes snap open. Vivian is standing at the base of my bed, looking at her fingernails, as though I don't warrant her full attention.

"You've really made quite a mess downstairs. A ball of destruction."

"Good," I say defiantly, sitting a little taller against the headboard, forcing my dizzy head to pull itself together while she's in front of me. I don't want her to think of me as weak. Not only that: I don't want her to panic and restrict my life here any further. To be bedbound would be horrendous.

Her eyes flick up to lock with mine, pinching together in a squint of disgust.

"I know all about your lies. I don't want to be any part of it," I declare, an eyebrow edging skyward.

"I know. We heard," she says with a sickly smile, glancing to the corner of the room, where a chrome security camera is staring straight back at us. "It was quite the emotional display you performed last night. All that weeping and sobbing," she mocks, her hands rolling in a circular motion while her face drops to mimic mine. She stops suddenly, her face deadpan. "You shouldn't be putting yourself under so much strain."

"Like you care."

"Eve . . ." She sighs, sounding exasperated, as though I'm being unreasonable in taking offense. "You have to start leading with your head, not your heart."

"Meaning?"

"What we're doing here is for the greater good."

"By playing God?"

"By sacrificing the overpopulated to give a chance to those who can make a difference," she says, cocking her head to the side.

"Girls?"

"Of course."

"And what if I can only produce boys?"

"We've been working on that on your behalf," Vivian shares, as if I'm an accomplice in her plan. "We couldn't have left it to chance. A boy would've been a failure. You wouldn't have wanted that. Everything you saw downstairs was done for you."

My jaw drops in horror. Then I say, "I don't want that. I didn't do any—"

"Your emotional attachment is natural, Eve. But this goes far beyond mothering a child. It's a fight for survival. If we don't manipulate nature, if we don't use the science we've created to its full potential, we've lost our right to be here."

"It's more than a game of win or lose. By doing what you're suggesting, we don't deserve to be here anyway!" I yell, my body becoming hot as I speak. "Mother Nature didn't just turn off her love for us overnight. It's actions like the ones you're committing that turned her against us in the first place. The lack of respect for her . . . magic," I say, searching for the right words, which is not easy when I'm debating with Vivian. "Her ability to give life and love is what has led us all here. We have to show her we care, that we've atoned for whatever monstrosities occurred before."

"An interesting thought." She nods slowly.

"I mean it. We can't just repeat past mistakes," I say, my hand on my chest.

"You're right." Vivian purses her lips but is unable to hide the start of a smile. "Let's see what she does with your 'atoned' and caring heart tomorrow."

"Pardon?" I swallow.

"Implantation?" she whispers flamboyantly, her eyes round with surprise as she mocks me. "You've not forgotten, have you? We've been monitoring the process. The fertilized cells have been multiplying perfectly . . ."

My resolve drops along with every muscle in my face.

Vivian's face twists into a snarl. "That's right. Tomorrow is the special day when you will collect your potential offspring and give her the chance of life. She's already waiting for you, Mother Eve—her cells multiplying, her budding future sparkling with possibility. All she needs now is her kind mother, who recognizes the beauty of life, a girl who finds those who crush any promise of life abhorrent and cruel, to collect her. She's already here, Eve. Congratulations."

I have nothing to offer her in return.

"Enjoy your day exploring the wonders of the Dome," she says, her voice thick with sarcasm. "I'll be waiting for you tomorrow night, with your daughter."

I was wrong. Vivian is, as ever, two steps ahead of me. I'm exactly where she wants me. In just twenty-four hours my fate will be sealed. I will be trapped here forever.

59

BRAM

"TWO TEAMS," I ANNOUNCE TO THE WATCHING CROWD LOOKing down at me from every angle of this grand submerged room. Briefly I become aware of the importance of this moment, of the effect my words will have on the future for all of us. Either way, what we do next will make history.

"But how will we know if the other team is successful?" Helena calls, and I see Anne and the women from the sanctuary standing around her.

"We won't," I reply without hesitation. "We will be working completely in the dark, zero communication. Once I'm in the tank, I won't know if Ernie has succeeded in passing on the message until I'm revived. If he fails, I'll never find out."

"And what if you fail?" another voice calls. "What happens to Ernie?"

"Then I shall face my fate in the Tower alone," Ernie replies as he stands at my side. "I've been an observing prisoner for too long. It's time to play my part."

I look around the room. It's silent. These men and women, these Freevers, have been no more than protesters and rioters for years. Now they are soldiers, an army, and war is imminent.

"Helena, you will lead the Tower team. You're to escort Ernie to the EPO Tower at sunrise. We have leaked messages throughout Central, hinting at something monumental occurring at the Tower today. Expect crowds. This is to be peaceful. This is the epic return of Eve's father. It is not a protest. You are to keep Ernie hidden and protected until he is ready. Then give him space. We want the world to see this. Show the people that even after all these years, the EPO can't destroy the love of a father for his daughter."

There are a few mumbles around the room, people discussing the plan, but no one questions it. Helena nods at me, accepting her mission.

"Cold Team, you're with me. This will be a little tricky. We'll be secretly boarding the morning delivery to the Cold Storage levels of the Tower."

I flick a switch, and the projector splashes an image of the large ship, armed guards pacing the deck. There are whispers around the hall.

"We'll have approximately twenty minutes to board, make our way to their storage level, and, well, the rest is up to the docs here." I nod to Dr. Oliva and his small medical team, who will accompany us onto the ship.

"What happens after that? After Ernie shows up it's going to be mayhem down there. The crowds will be massive!" an older Freever calls down from the balcony.

"Yes, and that's exactly what we want!" I say.

"It'll be hysteria again, like back when my Eve was born," Ernie adds. "The crowds won't leave."

"And neither will we!" Helena cheers, and voices rise in agreement.

"Stay hidden among the crowds. I can't say how long for, but if we succeed, we'll need you out there waiting for us. If I make it out of that place, I won't be alone."

The room is silent. Everyone trying to picture the impossible image of Eve leaving the Tower.

"How will we know?" The old voice speaks again. "How will we know if you've succeeded?"

"Trust me. When the time comes, you'll know."

The meeting comes to an end after hours of intense talks, memorizing river bends, studying the blueprints of the EPO ship, preparing weapons, and loading the equipment we'll need.

I hand a portable holo-player to Chubs, and as my fingers slide over the smooth surface of the projector screen, my mind skips back to Johnny. Poor Johnny. This plan has to succeed for him, for all he did for us, for Eve.

My heart pauses for a moment. Johnny's work.

It gives me an idea.

Leaving Ernie was hard. I could see the emotion in his eyes as he boarded the pod with his new army. These people who look to him as some sort of saint, the man who gave them hope, the father of their beloved Eve. His whole life has been building toward this moment, the moment he would return to the Tower to free his daughter.

But that won't happen unless I succeed in what I'm about to do. What the hell *am* I about to do? This is crazy! I step into the small black dinghy, which is already occupied by Chubs and Saunders.

Helena emerges from the clock and looks down at me with the expression of a woman prepared for battle. She looks more ready for this than anyone else.

I tilt my head and beckon her closer. "Take this," I whisper.

She takes the package from me, trying to work out what is concealed inside the large camouflage shoulder-bag.

"It's heavy," she says in a low voice, her watery eyes scanning mine for clues.

"There's a letter for you inside. Only you."

"Must be a pretty long one. What am I meant to do with it?"

"When you need this, it will be obvious. It's vital that no one knows this part of the plan. Just you and me," I explain.

"Ready?" Chubs interrupts us.

Helena nods.

"Let's get going!" Chubs calls.

The dawn air is cool and brings with it a sense of promise, as if a new era is rising with the sun and only we select few are aware of it.

Dr. Oliva leads the small medical team into an identical dinghy next to ours. We push away from the side of the enormous clockface and drift out onto the open river.

Helena watches us float away, her long gray hair starting to vanish in the mist that forms between us. I see her mouth two words and offer them back in reply.

For Eve.

It's already busy on the water, people sailing to their places of business, trading goods on the waves from boat to boat. It feels surreal to see such normality ahead of what is potentially a historic day. Soon their holo-players and displays will be dominated with news of Ernie—the return of Eve's father. Part of me wishes I could be around to witness it, but I have my own task to focus on now.

"There it is," Saunders announces.

In the distance the shadow of a large black vessel appears through the cloud of murky pollution. It breaks through the smog and pushes up the river.

"Shit, this is scary," Chubs says.

"It's okay," I say in my best fake-calm voice. I can't let him know how much my own nerves are making my insides twist.

"There's a small boarding deck on the rear, starboard side. One guard max, if any," Saunders says. "Leave him to me," he adds as he pumps a red lever on a long rifle-shaped weapon. A high-pitched ring fizzes out as it charges.

I look at him for reassurance and he understands.

"It'll knock him out for a few hours. Nonlethal. He won't remember it. Don't worry," he says.

I nod in thanks. I don't want any unnecessary deaths, or the attention they would bring.

We steer our two tethered dinghies through the traffic, blending in among the countless boats, rafts, and ships. They won't see us coming.

The EPO vessel draws closer. I see the familiar uniform on the armed guards standing on the top deck. It makes my blood boil now, seeing that patch with the Tower embroidered on it beaming out from the guard's chest. Everything it represents is a lie.

"It's time," Saunders says, and gestures to our captain, who steers the dinghy toward the center of the river, weaving through the traffic. The EPO ship pulls alongside us, slowly overtaking our boats and all the other small craft we're hiding among.

From his position at the front of our dinghy, Saunders subtly takes aim, keeping the weapon hidden under his rain gear. As the ship pulls in front of us I see the small docking bay, an opening in the back. I feel our dinghy vibrate under my feet as our captain accelerates to match the speed of the target.

"I don't see anyone," I say, trying not to look too hard at the ship.

"Me neither," replies Saunders.

"We're approaching the bridge," says Chubs.

I take a look around the side of the giant black ship we're tailing and see it. This is our cue. This is our chance. Our only chance.

"Once we're under it we'll have about sixty seconds of darkness to get on board," I say quietly, even though we've gone over all this a hundred times now, more for my benefit than anyone else's.

The bridge, an enormous concrete structure, crosses the river about half a mile ahead. It's one of the few crossing points from one side of the new city to the other now that all the original bridges are rotting at the bottom of this vast river. All water traffic has to pass under it. It's dark and noisy, the perfect place to board.

As the ship enters the darkness under the bridge, the concrete shadow ripples over it like a wave, until we too are under its blanket.

Our engine roars to life and we rapidly gain momentum. I wrap the wet ropes on the side of our dinghy around my wrist and hold on as we bounce blindly over the wake of the EPO ship.

As my eyes adjust to the lack of light, I see Saunders slip a pair of glasses onto his face that subtly illuminate his eyes. He can see in the dark.

Suddenly he dives onto his stomach, leaning out over the front of our dinghy as it rushes toward the opening at the back of the ship.

He rests his head on the silver gun in his hands, and a brilliant blue flash sparks out, lighting up our immediate surroundings like a lightning storm. In the flash I see a body hit the deck of the loading dock of the vessel, bolts of electricity frying his black overalls as he lies motionless.

"Clear!" Saunders shouts over the deafening roar of the ship's engines as our inflatable boat bumps its nose up and onto the open dock.

I nod at Chubs and he follows me as I leap onto the ship.

Once the two of us are on deck, our dinghy falls back, making way for the medical team to board. I crouch and take the pulse of the stunned guard. He's out cold. Alive, but unconscious.

As Dr. Oliva and his two assistants scramble toward the front of their boat, a second blinding flash blasts over our heads. I hear a heavy clang and a sudden thud and see a second body hit the deck. Another guard. I glance out at the river, and Saunders gives me a look that says, *Close one.* I give him a nod of thanks as the medical team climbs on.

I take a breath. We're aboard.

60

BRAM

WE MOVE QUICKLY, THE STOMPING OF OUR BOOTS LOST IN THE noise created by the ship as it slices through the river toward the Tower.

"Two flights down," Chubs says, referring to the three-dimensional map shimmering on his holo-player, our destination highlighted by a flashing red beacon at the bottom of the ship, inside a sealed room within its hull.

The five of us descend in the dim light, the change in temperature noticeable by the visible breath escaping our mouths.

"Not far," I say, seeing the worried expressions of the medical team as Dr. Oliva and his two men hesitantly follow. None of us are soldiers, but especially not the three shivering doctors, who have volunteered to be here. Their lack of combat training and experience is starting to show. "We're going to be fine," I say as I lead them down the dark metallic staircase into the unknown.

We reach the bottom and are confronted by an imposing door that looks like it would be more at home on a military submarine. A large metal wheel seals the room beyond it. A thick glass porthole glows with a cold blue light, but it's impossible to see through the ice crystals that have formed on it.

"This is it," Chubs says.

I reach out and turn the wheel. It's stiff. Frozen. Chubs grabs hold too and we turn it together. It takes all our strength, but eventually ice fragments crack off and fall to the floor as the metal lock twists in our hands. After three turns the wheel stops. We step back and pull out the gun Saunders gave me before we left the Deep. I double-check that its nonlethal lock is on and take aim before giving Chubs the nod. The members of the medical team duck behind me as the thick metal door swings open. If any room on this ship would be guarded, it's this one, where they store their precious cargo.

As a cloud of chilly air escapes it, the cool blue light of Cold Storage hits my face.

I take a moment to scan the room. "Clear," I whisper.

Chubs steps in front, his round figure blocking the doorway as he takes the lead. I can sense his fear growing with each step he takes into the eerie hull of this vast ship. We follow slowly, all of us expecting someone to jump out at any moment.

The room is packed with huge, seven-foot-tall cylinders. Our distorted reflections mimic us in the frosted chrome as we step deep into the hull.

"There are so many!" Chubs whispers as he takes in the sight of what must be at least fifty cryo-tanks, which, they claim, will perfectly preserve the inhabitant's body, peacefully frozen, until the time comes for them to be revived. I'm counting on that claim to be true today.

My heart starts pounding in my chest as if it suddenly realizes the events about to unfold. I can almost hear it over the droning of the engine, trying to make up for the beats it will be missing.

"Okay, Doc. It's over to you now," Chubs says, coming to a halt at the center of the room.

"Let's open one and prep the tank for two people," Dr. Oliva says.

He walks down an aisle between the tanks, his small eyes scanning them through his glasses until he stops at the last tank nearest the wall of the ship. He wipes away the frost with his hand and reads the details of the woman inside it. The steady green light on the side indicates normal conditions within.

"This one will work fine," he says.

"Great. How long do you need?" Chubs asks.

"The cooling process is rapid, almost instantaneous. The tank takes care of that. Prepping the body . . ." Dr. Oliva pauses, realizing this is no ordinary operation. "Ordinarily the patient is deceased or placed in a controlled comatose state before this process begins. It has not been tried on a living, healthy young man such as yourself," he tells me. Again.

"We have no other option," I say, already stripping off my jumpsuit, dropping my clothes onto the floor until I'm standing in a thin set of thermal underwear, designed to rapidly and evenly distribute the cold around my body as it freezes.

As I pace the aisle, failing to keep myself warm, Dr. Oliva's two medical assistants climb the metal rungs of the short ladder connected to the side of the tank and begin unbolting the latches securing the lid. The seal gives a little hiss as the pressure holding it shut releases.

They lift the chunky lid of the cryo-tank, and thick white gas spills out, creeping down the side until it meets the floor, where it disperses in every direction, eventually finding my bare feet.

The two men slide the lid onto the top of the next tank and peer inside.

"Whatever you do, don't touch that liquid," Dr. Oliva warns. "It's minus one hundred ninety degrees. Your blood would freeze instantly."

The men move back from the opening and start climbing down.

"Sir, it's going to be a tight squeeze in there," the first medical assistant says to Dr. Oliva, his young eyes betraying his doubt.

I need to see inside for myself. I push past them and climb up toward the top of the open tank. The icy rungs sting the soles of my feet, but I push aside the pain: it's nothing in comparison to what my entire body is about to experience.

As I reach the top, the last of the cloudy white gas disappears, revealing the liquid that fills the interior. It is crystal clear, like glass, with a subtle tint of blue.

"Chubs, hand me your flashlight," I say, holding out my hand. "I need to see inside."

"You don't need a flashlight," Dr. Oliva says as he walks around to the small box attached to the outside of the tank. He stares at it for a moment, looking for something. He finds it and pushes a button. The inside of the tank illuminates instantly.

The light is white and harsh, and I have to shield my eyes to allow them to adjust. As I peer in through the opening, I feel the light on my face. Staring down, I see that the base of the tank is made up of a flat panel of lights, blasting up at the body inside it. The lifeless woman, floating peacefully.

The doubtful assistant was right. It will be a tight squeeze, but comfort is of no importance on this trip.

"I'll fit," I say to the team.

The woman inside is still. Her features are calm as her body lies in the supercooled liquid. Even her hair seems to float normally, showing no sign that every cell in her body is currently suspended in a deep-frozen state.

"I've never seen inside one of these, only in photographs," I say, almost to myself. My mind flashes to thoughts of my mother and the countless times I've visited her, speaking to her through the thick walls of her tank, wondering what's on the other side. It comforts me seeing the serenity of the woman I'm about to share one with.

"Bram." Chubs interrupts my thoughts. "We've not got long."

I nod. The freezing temperature of the room is already unbearable. Shivering, I slide onto the top of the neighboring tank and sit on the lid.

"Wait," Chubs calls up to me. "How's your pal supposed to find you?"

I glance around at the room full of identical cryo-tanks.

"There'll be even more of these things in the Tower, right?" he asks.

My heart skips suddenly.

"Pass up my jumpsuit," I say, reaching down to Chubs.

He hands my clothes up to me and my trembling fingers search the pockets.

"What are you looking for?" Chubs asks.

"For a sign," I reply. I slip my fingers into the chest pocket and pull out a small strip of silver foil. I unfold it and the sweet smell floods my nostrils.

"What the hell is that?" Dr. Oliva asks.

"It's called bubble gum," I say, throwing the blue strip into my mouth. "It's vintage."

I chew for a few seconds, feeling the strip become soft and sticky in my mouth. I take the gum out and stick it to the side of the open tank. "It's small, but it's better than nothing." I nod to Dr. Oliva, who climbs up after me and places his medical bag next to me on the tank.

I glance at his equipment—three syringes lined up neatly in a row, the silver needles glistening in the cold light.

"This is not going to be comfortable," he tells me.

"Let's get it done," I reply, not wanting to think about the effects the drugs will have on my body.

"You will need immediate medical assistance once you're removed from this liquid. Your friend Hartman, he'll be able to get you to a doctor?" he asks.

I don't have the heart to tell Dr. Oliva the truth, so I just nod.

"Strap this around your arm." He hands me a rubber band, then makes a fist and opens it a few times, showing me what he wants me to do. It takes only a few seconds for my veins to obey, the dark blue lines that carry blood around my body rising under my skin as though telling me they're ready.

"Good," Dr. Oliva says, admiring my arm. He picks up the first syringe. "This first one is just a drip to administer the rest. You can look away."

I don't move my head. I want to see.

He shrugs and plunges the needle into my arm. I feel nothing as it pierces my skin, the cold temperature already numbing my senses. He places a small bandage over the point of entry, holding the needle in place as he attaches a tube to the end.

"Okay. Are you ready?" he asks.

"Yes," I reply without hesitation.

"Once I put this into your body, there's no turning back." He holds the first syringe up to show me.

I nod.

I'm ready.

He attaches it to the tube that plugs directly into my vein.

"This one will begin to slow your heart rate so your body doesn't go into shock when it hits the liquid," he says, and takes a deep breath. I see his thumb twitch nervously over the plunger of the small syringe.

I reach out instantly and press it down for him, slowly administering the contents to my system, relieving him of the responsibility.

"No turning back now," I say as the last of the drug flows down the clear tube and into my vein.

He unscrews the now-empty syringe and attaches the next.

"This one will feel strange," he says. "It's to stop ice forming in your cells."

"Like antifreeze?" I ask.

"Exactly," he replies. "It's nontoxic, but it's not designed to be used on conscious subjects. It will allow your cells to freeze without becoming stiff. It prevents the damage of traditional freezing."

"Clever stuff," I remark.

"Once it's in your system, we must wait three minutes for it to distribute evenly around your body before you enter the tank. If your cells don't contain this drug they will not survive the rapid cooling process."

He slowly pushes down on the syringe and starts a timer on his watch.

Three minutes.

I feel this medical-grade antifreeze flow into my body. It tingles at the spot on my arm where it enters, like cool pins and needles. The tingling spreads up my arm—and suddenly I'm engulfed. It's the strangest sensation I've ever felt. It's as though I'm aware of all the veins in my body. I feel them. All of them. All the thousands of intricate tunnels and pathways winding around my organs, twisting through my limbs. They're all alive, like they've been wired with electricity.

It intensifies. The tingles become stabbing pains. Deep shocks strike every part of my body; invisible fingers with razor-sharp edges tighten around my brain. My body convulses uncontrollably. I fall back onto the top of the closed tank, and through the shakes and twitches, I hear Dr. Oliva call down to his assistants for help.

I black out momentarily. Suddenly three bodies are standing over me.

"Bram," I hear Dr. Oliva calling.

"I'm . . . I'm okay," I say, sitting up. My head spins. My body feels weak.

"Your heart is slowing. You have one minute before you can be submerged in the chamber. Stay calm and breathe through the pain. Your body still needs oxygen," Dr. Oliva instructs.

Another wave of stabbing washes through me.

"Sedative," I hear Dr. Oliva request. "This will calm your seizures," he tells me as he sticks a needle into my neck.

The alarm sounds on his wristwatch.

"It's time," he says.

My body is limp. My vision blurs. I cannot stand.

The three men hook their arms under mine and hoist me upright.

Below, at the base of the tank, I see a large, hazy figure.

"Chubs," I shout, but only a mumbled whisper escapes.

The men wobble with my deadweight as they carefully lift me over the open tank.

"We must lower him swiftly," Dr. Oliva's voice instructs, while straining to hold me steady, along with his two colleagues.

"Chubs . . . ," I call again as my head flops forward. I don't have the strength to lift it.

The men hold me over the liquid nitrogen. My feet dangle a few inches. I can't feel them now. I can't feel anything. My mind is escaping as I face my fate, the tank beneath me. The floating woman.

"On my count," Dr. Oliva calls. "Three, two, one . . ."

As I fall into the tank, the world fades. I feel no cold. The supercooled liquid freezes every cell in my body, but the chemicals Dr. Oliva put in my blood prevent them from turning to ice. For the briefest of moments, a fraction of a second, I'm engulfed in the most excruciating pain I've ever experienced. This fleeting moment of unbearable suffering ends abruptly with the sound of Chubs's worried voice echoing around the hull as he cries out to me: "For Eve."

61

EVE

MY EYES OPEN TO THE MOST BEAUTIFUL SUNRISE I'VE EVER seen. Purples, pinks, oranges, and blues fill the window in front of me, all bleeding into each other to paint the perfect picture of harmony. As I lie here, looking at its splendor, it would be easy to forget my own reservations about the day ahead and what's to come. To believe that Mother Nature is trying to will me on. Why else would she shower us with her artistry and grace today and every day for as long as I can remember? She's luring us in, constantly winning us over, telling us we need to prolong our existence with her on this earth.

The heavy block that's sitting in my stomach says otherwise. It fills me with a sense of foreboding and doom—my life is about to be crushed, controlled, and discarded, my dreams tossed aside for others' gain, but not for the benefit of my children. Instead I'll be starting a chain of women who'll all be treated in this way. Giving life for no life to be lived. Producing another little cog.

I'd rather have woken up to see nothing at all. A sea of black would have been my own preference on this pitiful day.

Mother Kadi walks in.

Pills.

Breakfast.

The same old routine, yet this time it feels very different.

As Mother Kadi straightens the sheets around me I hear a thump on the floor. She bends down and picks up my mother's book. It's been living under my pillow, so I must have moved it while I was asleep.

I take it from her and rest it on my lap as I look at the garden outside my bedroom window. It's not as beautiful as it once was, so I turn away and look down at the object in my hands instead—a book that's filled with my mother's hopes for me to live a life of love and freedom. Words she wrote for me. She could never have known her life would end so abruptly, that she'd be taken from me within minutes of our meeting, but in this book she'd written words of love, encouragement, and support. When it's in my hands, it's as though she's with me.

I flip through it, absorbing snippets, until a lump forms in my throat.

I've failed her. I'm nowhere near the girl she thought I'd be.

My fingertips find the extra page, added in secret. One line stands out to me.

You are loved. You are yours. Not mine, not theirs. Remember that.

I wish I knew how to make that a reality, because right now it feels like everything I am is theirs.

62

BRAM

I CAN HEAR.

It's the first thing I'm aware of.

I hear the humming of a machine. The beeping of a heart monitor. The hissing of fresh oxygen being pumped into the room. It's all so piercing and harsh.

I can't feel my body.

Suddenly my sense of smell returns, as if someone's flicked a switch. Scents punch me in the face and overwhelm my foggy mind: sterilized equipment, washed linen, even glass. Everything seems to have a distinct smell. These scents grouped together create a picture in my mind, one that I recognize instantly.

The Tower.

My mind races, firing so many questions. Why am I here? What's happened? Where's Eve?

Eve.

I remember.

The Freevers. Ernie. The cryo-tank.

Has it worked?

I'm inside the Tower.

I try to open my eyes, but they're not ready yet. My eyelids remain closed.

If I can smell, I must be breathing. I try to focus my thoughts on the steady flow of air, in and out of my mouth. After a few moments I notice the repetitive rise and fall of my chest as it rubs against the sheet covering me.

A sudden blast of noise explodes in my ears as the door to whatever place I'm in slides open. I hear it click shut again and lock.

I try to speak.

Nothing.

I try to move.

Nothing.

Complete paralysis.

I hear footsteps. Someone checks the heart monitor, then slumps into a seat at my side, a button or zip on their clothing scuffing the plastic of the chair. Just relying on my hearing makes it all so sharp and vivid.

Then I hear his breath. A sigh.

"Hartman . . ." The breathy sound escapes my mouth without my needing to think, fueled by a wave of adrenaline at the thought of the plan working, the thought of freeing Eve.

"Bram!" Hartman whispers excitedly. "You're awake? Can you hear me?"

"Ern . . . ie?" I muster just enough strength to mutter his name before the black world turns blacker and I'm gone again.

I sit bolt upright.

My throat burns. I can't breathe. I gasp for air. Lashing out, reaching for nothing, I roll off the bed and hit the floor hard. It illuminates as it connects with my skin and glows a soft blue.

I can see.

"Bram!" Hartman scrambles to my side. "Breathe!"

I clutch at my throat as my body cries out for oxygen. Hartman reaches over me and pulls out a red tube. He snaps the lid off, revealing a needle, and he doesn't hesitate to stab it into my neck.

The chemicals react instantly and my throat widens. Oxygen, sweet oxygen, floods my lungs and I slip away to nothing.

"Bram?" Hartman says softly. I feel his warm hand on the skin of my right arm. "Bram?"

I open my eyes and see my room. Our old room, the one we shared before I escaped this place.

"Hartman," I sigh, and my cheeks ache with a smile. It's the first time one of those has appeared on this face in a long time. "Where is Ernie?" I ask.

"He's okay. You can't get to him, though. They have him now," Hartman says, his round, unshaved face the most welcome sight I've ever seen.

"Eve?" I ask.

He pauses.

"What is it?" I ask, forcing my sore muscles to sit up.

"Whoa, slow down. You're not ready to move yet. Your body has to adjust," he tells me.

"What about Eve? How is she?" I ask.

"She's okay. There were a few . . . incidents while you were away," Hartman says, removing his thick glasses and pretending to clean them so he doesn't have to make eye contact with me.

"Incidents?" I ask.

"She's fine for now, but not for long," Hartman says, looking at my heartbeat on the monitor. "Today's the day," he says.

I stare at him, wanting more information.

"They're planning the procedure for later today. Early evening," he explains.

My mind suddenly pieces the puzzle together. She's ready to try carrying a baby. As this thought enters my head, I realize that this baby wouldn't be hers. It wouldn't even be its biological father's. It's *their* baby, the EPO's.

What if it's a girl? What if there are complications when Eve gives birth, eliminating her chances of conceiving again? Would she become disposable, like her own mother?

"Then we don't have much time," I say, swinging my legs around and placing my feet on the dorm floor. "Who else knows I'm here?" I ask.

"Mother Kadi," says Hartman.

"Mother Kadi?" I'm confused.

"Yes. She reached out to me once news of Ernie's return found its way upstairs. It seems that you share some friends," he says.

Frost!

My heart sinks as Frost's words echo in my head: *We have friends in high places.* And I realize the sacrifice he referred to. Mother Kadi was his informant. His wife.

"Frost . . . didn't make it," I tell Hartman.

He gives a knowing nod. "She already suspects that. She's not had contact from anyone in days and knew something had happened. She's a good woman. Tough. Strong. She's ready for your instruction. We all are."

"*All?*" I ask.

"When you left here, people began spreading rumors about why you were a wanted man, why you were so dangerous, and not everyone saw it the way the EPO sold it to them. People in here like you, Bram. People want to help."

My mind aches with this news.

"People don't want to be lied to anymore, Bram. They just need to know the truth. They're waiting for you to show them."

I reach out a hand and place it on his shoulder. "This won't be easy," I say.

"Of course not! It's you!" he replies with a smile, and for a brief moment I'm pleased to be back.

"So what's the plan? You do have one, right? Because I sure as hell didn't go through all of this for nothing." Hartman nods to the medical equipment that has transformed our dorm into a small hospital.

"How are you getting away with this? Has no one questioned it?" I ask, finding it hard to fathom how keeping me a secret is even remotely possible.

"Trust me, since Eve started destroying the place and Ernie turned up, things have been different here," Hartman says, shoving his glasses up on his nose. "Plus, I've hacked the sensors in here so they only show one person's heat signal."

"I knew I could count on you," I say.

"Although having Eve's father return and demand to speak with *only* me did put me under some scrutiny. It's not been a walk in the park by any means," Hartman says, and my mind snaps back to Ernie.

"Where is he?" I ask.

"Last I heard they were holding him on the lower levels," Hartman says. "As far away from Eve as possible."

"Smart," I say.

"Obviously they don't want her knowing about his return. The pilots have all been strictly briefed on the new codes of conduct should Eve mention him." Hartman rolls his eyes.

"So there's no way to get to him?" I ask, my stomach pulling at the guilt of sending the old man in here on his own.

Hartman shakes his head.

"How long have I been out?" I ask.

"Awhile . . ." He shrugs and scrunches his shaggy, unwashed curly hair. I give him a look. "Hey, it took me most of the day just to find the damn cryo-tank you'd hijacked. Oh, and by the way, you owe me a pack of bubble gum. I told you not to waste it. That stuff is vintage!"

I roll my eyes at him.

"It wasn't easy spending so much time down there unnoticed, let alone retrieving your frozen butt and getting back up here without anyone asking questions!"

Suddenly the floor shudders.

I look to Hartman, who seems not to react. Like this is normal.

It happens again, the vibration causing the screen of my heart monitor to flicker.

I stand up, but my legs wobble and fail me. Hartman grips my arm and helps me back to my feet.

"The window," I say, pointing to the realiTV displays.

The screens flicker on as we approach, showing, as always, the gray clouds. I swipe my hand until it shows the outside world in infrared. Suddenly the windows light up in vibrant reds. Below us swims a sea of hot people, crowding around the base of the Tower.

"They've been out there since Ernie showed up. The numbers just keep growing," Hartman says as we stare out at the enormous crowds surrounding us. I zoom in and see people cheering and chanting. Some hold photos of Eve or huge banners with Ernie's face on them. Others wave painted signs in the air.

Free Eve.

EPO—Let Eve Go!

Free the truth.

"The world is watching," Hartman tells me.

"Then we'd better give them something to see," I say. "Where's Mother Kadi?"

63

BRAM

MOTHER KADI ARRIVES AT OUR DOOR, HER NERVES VISIBLE through the small opening in her veil that reveals her eyes. Mothers are allowed on our level at their own risk, but it's a rare sight.

"Good evening, Mr. Hartman," she says calmly and casually as she steps inside. No one is in the corridor. Hartman locked the doors and elevators briefly to allow this secret visit.

"Kadi," I say as I step out of the shadowy corner of the room.

She freezes, staring at me. I know she's reading my expression, trying to get confirmation of her suspicions about her husband and son.

"I'm so sorry," I say, not wanting her to suffer any suspense.

She doesn't cry. She doesn't move. She swallows hard and bows her head.

"Frost and Johnny were strong men. They sacrificed themselves for us," I say.

"For Eve," Mother Kadi corrects me.

"For Eve," I agree. I'll get the hang of that eventually.

"Then we must not let their sacrifice be for nothing," Mother Kadi says, her voice indicating that she's ready to hear the plan.

"We don't have much time," I say. "I need you to give something to Eve." I scan the room. "A message."

I hold out my hand to show her and she smiles.

"And what do I tell her?" Mother Kadi asks.

"Nothing. Eve will know how to read it."

"But I thought the plan would be to get her out, to free her. You *are* here to rescue her, aren't you?" Mother Kadi asks.

"No. Eve doesn't need saving. She needs to free herself. She needs to see. I'm just going to open her eyes. She'll do the rest," I tell her, and she takes the object from me and hides it under her gown.

"And once I give this to her?"

"Just be ready. You must hide yourself. It will be dangerous. I don't want anyone getting hurt," I say.

Her old eyes twinkle at the thought of the events about to unfold. I see the same fire of rebellion in her that I saw in Frost. I bet they once made a formidable team.

"If this is all you require of me, I'll return to the Dome," she says. "I'll be delivering Eve's dinner tonight before she's transferred to the hospital level."

"Then make sure she gets that message before they come for her," Hartman says as he walks her back to the door, checking his monitor first to ensure that the hallway is empty. He nods and she leaves. Before the door closes, she turns back to me.

"For Eve," she says.

"For Frost and Johnny," I reply.

Tears swell in her eyes. Then she turns and disappears into the hallway.

. . .

"Are you sure you want to do this?" I ask.

"There's no other way," Hartman replies without looking at me, his focus set on the suit he's squeezing himself into. "I don't know how you wear these things."

I can't help but laugh at seeing him suit up. Lycra does nothing for him.

"Nice," I say, giving him a thumbs-up as he slips the kinetic gloves over his swollen fingers.

"Don't even start," he says.

It seems strange, him gearing up to pilot Holly. Unnatural. But I know he can do it. I trust him.

"And you're sure you can log in to the Dome from here?" I ask.

"Come on, it's me you're talking about," he says confidently, readjusting his glasses as they slip down his nose on the beads of sweat. "Walk in the park!"

"But if they trace the signal . . ."

"You just make sure you get Eve out of there. Don't worry about me. She's more important than all of us," he says, and I nod.

I pull the needle from my arm that has been removing the antifreeze drugs and replenishing my blood. I rip the pads monitoring my heartbeat from my chest and drop them to the floor. I'm ready. I have to be. I slip into one of my old jumpsuits and find a pair of my boots, still waiting in their usual spot as though nothing has changed.

But everything has changed.

This will be the last time I set foot in this room.

"I've programmed you a window when the security systems will cycle through their test settings. It means they'll power down momentarily," Hartman says, waving his hands furiously over the holo-display at his desk, zooming in and out of the schematics of the Tower. "Momentarily!" he repeats. "You won't have long to get there."

"How long?" I ask.

He pauses, scrunching his hair nervously as he thinks.

"Hartman, how long?"

"Thirty," he replies.

"Minutes?" I ask.

"Seconds," he says, looking back at me.

I stare at the projection illuminating his face, my route shown by a thin yellow line that zigzags through the corridors, service stairways, and emergency exits.

A small beep interrupts my doubts.

"It's time," Hartman says, the alarm indicating ten minutes until Eve receives her dinner. He looks at me. "This is it," he says, his magnified eyes looking out at me.

I can't think about the possibility of not seeing him again. Or what fate lies ahead of him if he's discovered.

He stands and we embrace.

Friends.

Partners.

Brothers.

"Thanks," I say. That word isn't enough, but it's all I have.

"Go!" he says, and pushes me toward the door. I hear the emotion in his voice. "Don't screw this up!"

I laugh. "You know me," I say.

"Exactly," he replies.

I stand at the sealed door of our dorm and take a breath.

"Ready?" Hartman calls.

I look over my shoulder at him.

"Thirty seconds. Don't stop," he says. He taps his finger on the display, and our door swishes open. I hear the clicks of the cameras powering down in the hallway outside.

"*Go!*" he cries.

I run.

64

EVE

"LET'S GET YOU DRESSED, THEN GIVE YOU SOME SUPPER." Mother Kadi fusses as we walk out of the bathroom.

"No," I tell her. My stomach has been in knots all day. The very thought of food makes me feel nauseous.

"It'll do you good to have a nice meal," she says in an irritatingly upbeat manner before retrieving clothes she's already laid out on the bed for me and handing over my white cotton underwear.

I can remember the first day they gave me a bra to try on. It was almost a ceremony. Mother Nina brought in a measuring tape and differing sizes of the same white design, while a select few of the Mothers joined us, all taking pride in the way my body was changing. The little girl they had raised was slowly turning into a woman. For them that day was full of hope and promise. To me it was just another item of clothing, a restrictive one I was relieved to take off at the end of each day.

"Pants?" I question with a croak, confused at the sight of the charcoal item she's holding out for me.

"You'll be in your gown when you go over to see the doctor,

but you may as well be comfortable until then," she reasons, shaking them at me.

"True." I take them from her and put them on. My fingers fumble while I try to fasten them, alerting me to the tremor in my hands that I hadn't realized was there.

"Here," Mother Kadi says softly. She does up the button, then the zipper. Her hands rest on my hips, as though she's trying to steady me.

"Thanks." I sigh.

She picks up a light gray T-shirt, which she gathers together and eases over my head.

While I sit on my bed, my mind spacing out over what's to come, she puts on my black socks and trainers. "Put this on too. It's cold in here tonight," she says as she guides my arms into a black hoodie and zips up the front.

The warmth engulfs me like a much-needed hug. But I don't want the comfort of a piece of clothing. I need a human to give me that physical support. It's such a natural instinct, such a simple desire. I want something real.

Impulsively I jump forward, catching Mother Kadi off guard. Crouching, I bury myself in her chest, my arms cradling her bony little frame.

"Bless you, child," she whispers, her hand sweeping the stray hairs from my face, her eyes looking deep into my own. She kisses my forehead and rests her warm cheek against mine, her hand holding me there.

"If only Mother Nina was here too," I say into her softness.

"She loved you very much, Eve."

"Thank you for being there when I've needed you," I say, taking her in. I've always been fond of Mother Kadi—she's an intriguing little thing, with the wisest eyes I've ever seen, but we've only grown closer in the last few weeks since we were robbed of Mother Nina.

"My role with you is not over yet, Eve," she says, pulling my cheek back to hers, as though she's soaking me up—an action that makes me question her words. If things were going to stay the same after tonight's procedure, I'm not sure she'd be talking to me like this.

We stand there for a moment or two, knowing that in less than an hour the connection between us will be different, our lives altered—even though we're unsure of the specifics, just certain of change.

"Sit down, Eve," she whispers, gesturing toward my desk as she pulls away from me.

"I'm really not hungry," I moan as bile rises in my throat.

"You will eat," she says sternly, her forehead wrinkling into a frown.

Not wanting to argue, I do as she asks and sit at the table, ready to move my food around the plate so that it looks like I've at least tried to obey.

I shuffle in my seat as the tray is placed before me. Yet when Mother Kadi lifts the silver cover, I barely look in the direction of my food. Because there is another object on the tray. A Rubik's Cube. And I can tell instantly that it's not mine. Because this one has been tampered with. Around the squares of color I see little crinkles of white: the stickers have been pried off and repositioned.

I blink at it.

I've only ever seen a Rubik's Cube look like this once before, but it wasn't real. It never actually existed. Right?

My heart stops as my brain tries to comprehend what's in my hands. This is Bram's. Peeling back the stickers and repositioning them was the only way he could ever complete the puzzle. I'd spent ages perfecting my technique and learning to master the cube, but Bram never had. He'd found his method worked far better, and his Holly would always tell me so with the biggest grin.

I force myself to swallow the smile that is dying to spread across my face while I rotate the object in my hands, enjoying something of his having such weight. I wonder if this was the actual object used in their trickery, or one that's been created for me to hold right now. I'm unsure what to think. All I can focus on is that it's real. It's no longer just an illusion. His reality is now mine. My body tingles at the thought of him being near, even though I know there's no chance of that, but this is a bridge, and I make the most of the gap between us seeming that little bit smaller.

I hold the cube. Rotating it, rubbing it, my fingers tracing every groove and crack that's felt his touch, longing for something of his to rub off on me, wanting to be brought closer.

While I'm playing with it and inspecting every minute detail, as though this toy is alien to me and nothing like my own—because it's been in *his* hands and feels different—my fingernail sweeps under the dog-eared fold of a shiny red square.

I leave it there, remembering a conversation I once had with Holly: *Sometimes you've got to peel the stickers off the cube,* she told me.

My hand pauses. I want to believe something could be there, waiting for me . . . Slowly I peel back the red square. I stop breathing as I read two words: *Throw me!*

I peel back the green sticker next to it, just to be sure, and again read, *Throw me!* The blue says, *Throw me!* and the yellow: *Throw me!*

Throw me!

Throw me!

Throw me!

"Let's go for a walk, Eve."

My head whips up at the sound of the familiar voice they've not let me hear for so long.

I've missed her . . .

I'm startled by who's before me. This is not the Holly I love. This isn't *any* Holly I know.

I look toward Mother Kadi for a sign that this isn't another of Vivian's tricks, but I quickly realize she's busied herself in my wardrobe, turning a blind eye to whatever is going on, even though I'm in no doubt that she's part of it. I'm dressed in the same outfit as Holly.

"Now, Eve," Holly pleads, her hands quickly waving at me, vying for my focus. "You have to go."

I don't know this Holly, but given that she's turned up straight after I've found a hidden message, I'm too intrigued to sit and question her. I thought I was trapped here, but now might be my one and only chance to run for freedom. To take what life has given me and lead with love and clarity.

"Bring it with you," she commands.

I get to my feet and go to my bedroom door, knowing she's going to follow. Even though I have no idea of what's going on, I do know I don't have long. A sense of urgency burns inside me, my legs moving quicker by the second.

Throw me!

I know where I have to go.

Throw me!

I know what he wants me to do.

I run as fast as I can through the living quarters and the garden zones, my legs not stopping until I burst through the glass doors of the Drop and feel the warmth of the evening breeze hit me.

I look at the beautiful sight in front of me—the flawless blue skies on the brink of another glorious sunset, the same magnificent view I've loved for years.

Taking a deep breath, my chest heaving from the sprint, I launch myself forward. When I'm a few meters from the edge, I pull my arm back and around, letting go of the gift from Bram and sending it up into the heavens.

I watch it climb high into the sky before it eventually curves downward from gravity's pull, the colors spinning into a blur toward the world below.

Its journey is cut short with a loud bang. The cube bounces against an invisible force, changing its direction of movement, and ricochets uncontrollably before coming to an abrupt halt midair.

Midair.

I crouch at the edge of the Drop, getting as close to it as possible and trying to make sense of what is happening.

The initial patch of blue sky that made the first connection to the cube flickers. Lines of black-and-white static spread across a piece of perfection. After a couple of seconds it blinks into a black square, a hole in the view—a patch of nothing.

I gasp. Of course. I already knew Holly wasn't the only piece of fabricated reality I've been exposed to, a piece of advanced technology with which I've had a fake connection. But I wasn't expecting this.

"Are you serious?" I shout, turning to Holly, who's standing behind me, looking on with a face full of sorrow. "What is it?" I ask, my mind still unable to fathom the magnitude of the illusion in front of me. "Has everything been a lie?" I struggle to ask the question.

"Perhaps they just wanted to make you care," she offers back, her hands opening up to the fake sky above.

But she has no idea of what I've been exposed to lately, or how deep the lies run.

"It's to keep me here," I say, my voice low as my temper flares at the thought of the pretty prison they've stored me in until my body ripened and became useful to them.

"Perhaps," she concedes with a slight nod.

65

EVE

"EVE, WE DON'T HAVE MUCH TIME . . . ," SHE HISSES.

Looking past her, I see the glass doors of the Drop, which must have locked behind us as soon as we stepped out here. Already I can see security guards bashing their weapons against the panes, struggling to get in. Beyond them I see *her*, Vivian Silva, her face twisted in anger, shouting at them to work harder, get to me faster.

There's no way I'm going back through those doors ever again.

"What do I do?" I ask Holly, exhaling as I look back down at the sight beneath my feet—a huge drop into the clouds, then down into the unknown.

"It's only a couple of meters," she says, walking forward and joining me. "You've seen the cube. It's not real."

I nod to tell her I'm listening, but also to prepare myself for what I'm about to do.

"Lower your body as much as you can, and then it'll only be a very small drop."

"Really?"

"I promise," she says adamantly, crouching and leaning precariously, in my mind, over the edge as she gestures to something below.

"Thank you," I say, lowering myself onto my bottom and shuffling forward so that my legs dangle in the air—a position I'm used to here but will never adopt again. This is the end of my life in the Dome.

"What's it really like out there?" I ask, suddenly nervous. I've spent so long making up ideals in my head, having Vivian dream up her own version for me, that I've no idea what to expect, or why she wanted to hide the truth from me so badly. It was so terrible she decided to build all of this for me, but I don't believe reality could be any worse than the feeling of emptiness they've given me.

"I think you need to see it for yourself," she answers.

"I do. I really do." I turn onto my front, crawling backward on my forearms. "Are you coming with me?"

"There's no way I'm missing th—" She turns to the right, looking worried and expectant.

"What is it?" I hiss, edging myself back onto the ledge and running over to her, but I can't help. I'm not where she is.

"Jackson, man. What are you doing here?" she asks, as though talking to someone she knows, but there's no one here. A frown forms on her face as she becomes panicked. "You're wrong. She has a right to decide for herself. To choose—"

A force pushes her forward and cuts her off. There's a yelp of severe pain as her face contorts in agony.

"What's going on? What's happening?" I scream. Even though I know this isn't my Holly or any Holly I've met before, I'm aware of the torture happening to the person beyond the illusion. Her body glitches in and out of focus. Each time she reappears on the floor of the Drop, she does so in a different, agonizing position.

"Go, Eve. Now. Now!" she insists, unable to open her eyes even to look at me.

"Then what? Then what?" I scream.

But she can't hear me over her own cries.

I can't watch, yet I find it difficult to leave her.

A bang draws my attention to the glass doors, which have been blown apart, causing shards of glass to fly through the air.

"Stop her!" Vivian shouts above the commotion.

As a dozen feet start running in my direction, I turn and sprint. There's no time to lower myself down gently into the unknown. Instead, when my feet find the edge of the Drop, I jump into the air and prepare my body to land. The ground catches me far more quickly than I expect it to. I land on my chest, knocking the wind out of myself. Glancing up, I see the spot where I spent lazy childhood days, thinking I was looking out at the universe and dreaming up endless possibilities for the future. The thought saddens me. Not because I feel nostalgic for a time I once cherished, but because I feel sorry for that gullible little girl.

The view beneath my feet causes a sharp intake of breath to enter my lungs. Now I'm just like the Rubik's Cube, suspended in midair while standing on a hard surface that doesn't even buckle under my feet. It feels wrong to be standing still when my mind is telling me I should be helplessly falling to my death. I tell myself not to look down, but my brain is simply unable to compute the sight.

I focus on the task at hand. My freedom. My escape.

"Right, go right!" I hear Holly's voice stutter behind me.

I launch myself in that direction, running on air as I go, sprinting across the sky, the noise behind me filling my body with adrenaline. I'm like a machine, my mind determined and driven, fixated on finding a way out.

I have no choice but to keep close to the building, the curve of the sky making gravity pull me in, as though it's one of the men I can hear behind me, wanting to keep me here. But I won't have it. I won't be tied to this building and their storyline any longer. I have to find a way out. I have to leave. I want to leave.

I push as hard as I can, the soles of my feet pounding against the floor as I keep moving forward.

I'm aware of the men gaining on me—I can hear the rustle of their suits and the heaviness of their boots. I steal a glance behind me to see two men side by side, heading straight for me with determination on their faces. But I want this more, I tell myself.

"Keep going," a new voice beckons me, although this time it's my own.

I look up to see two versions of myself running in my direction. Whatever they use to create Holly must have been used to build me.

"What the—" I exclaim.

"Ignore us," shouts one. "Keep going!"

"They're getting closer," warns the other.

"When you get there, Eve, open your mouth," orders the first while sprinting past me. "Don't forget! Open your mouth."

I turn as one of the men leaps across the air after me, his arms wide to grab me as he descends.

I push up the incline and try to pick up speed, ignoring the burning sensation in my legs and lungs.

The guard lands next to me with a screech. Just as I'm about to feel relieved, his large muscular hand clamps onto my ankle.

"No!"

"I've got her. I've done it," he grunts, congratulating himself.

I look past him to find the other versions of me preoccupied with confusing the other guards. They can't help me.

I'm so close to freedom that it would be cruel to fail.

I look down at the man at my feet and mutter an apology, then stamp on his face with all my weight.

He howls in agony, letting go of me so he can grab hold of his broken nose.

Freed, I set off again, hoping I'll know salvation when I see it and that I have enough fight left in me.

The commotion behind me gets quieter the farther I run. I've managed to create a distance between us.

Ahead of me, I notice a black hole in the sky. The sight causes lightness to wash over me.

I sprint toward the one panel that's not trying to deceive me.

Without hesitation, my fist bashes against it. It swings open as though it were simply a door. This is definitely where I'm meant to be.

I take one last look behind me at the place that's been my home for as long as I can remember, then turn away.

It was never my home, just a prison.

I push myself into the hole and find a vertical ladder leading upward. I get on that first rung and don't look down as I climb higher and higher. Instead my eyes stay firmly on where I'm going.

"Up there!" I hear Vivian's voice boom from down below.

I don't look back, only forward.

When the steps end, I find myself at a circular handle, a wheel, begging me to turn it, to open the door it's sealing. Feeling as though I've won the biggest prize of all, I grip the cold metal and pull with all my strength, feeling the resistance give slowly as the wheel unscrews. I twist faster and faster. I'm ready to claim my freedom.

I open my mouth as instructed, instinctively knowing I'm in the right place, and push.

Suddenly I'm greeted by a deafening hiss and a huge gust of cold, wet wind, not pushing me back but dragging my feet into this new hole in the side of my sky, as though the world they've kept me from is willing me forward.

The heavy door slides open, pulling me with it into the brightest light of an unknown sky. I instinctively close my eyes tight, partly to shield them from the light, partly to prepare myself for what I think I'm about to see.

My hair sweeps across my face. The air is thin and uncomfortable in my throat, making it difficult to breathe. I suck in a lungful, preparing myself for whatever is out here. I'm tempted to take one last glimpse of the world they made for me. But I don't. I've seen enough of it. I've lived enough of that life.

It is time to move on.

I open my eyes.

Before me there is no flawless sky on the cusp of a perfect sunset. Instead murky gray storm clouds linger at varying heights, engulfing the building behind me and threatening a downpour in every direction I look.

From below comes a steady stream of bangs, sirens, and

loud explosions, which cause the walkway I'm on to wobble and shake.

It's terrifying and overwhelming, yet I feel my chest soar at the sight. This uncontrolled vision is what they've been keeping from me, but it's far more perfect than anything I've ever seen in the Dome.

This is what real life looks like—not an idyllic, fake utopia, but a world busy with energy and bustling with life.

As a gust of wind pushes against me, almost causing me to topple over, I have to suppress a hysterical giggle. It's as though Mother Nature were practically bursting at the seams to welcome me into her real arms and show me what she can do.

"Eve, I'm here," someone calls.

I turn and, through the clouds, I see him running toward me, his hand reaching out to grab mine.

Bram.

66

BRAM

I REACH THROUGH THE THICK CLOUDS BLOWING OVER THE outer surface of the Dome for the unmistakable silhouette of the girl I've been waiting for, the girl we've *all* been waiting for.

She reaches out, too, and we embrace. For the first time in our lives it's real. Her body trembles in my arms as I wrap them around her. Her head rests on my shoulder as she looks out at the world.

The real world.

My head spins with dizziness, caused not only by the ecstatic energy of finally holding Eve in my arms, but from waiting at this altitude for so long and the oxygen in my Oxynate running low. My body aches, but the tingling of adrenaline gives a fresh energy to my muscles.

"We need to go!" I say. "Here, put this in." I hand her a small plastic device and tilt my head back to show her my own. She quickly places it in her nose and takes a deep breath of fresh oxygen.

"Try to breathe normally!" I call, but my words are lost in the rush of wind that suddenly attacks us. She loosens her grip and tilts her head to face me. The last of the tears that have formed in her eyes escape over the rims and fall down her cheeks. Those eyes I've spent my life looking at through a visor are now staring back at me, more real, more beautiful, than I could ever have imagined. She smiles, and this gray reality is more beautiful than anything ever projected into that Dome.

A familiar sound cuts through the rush of air pounding on my eardrums. Drones.

They know we're out here.

"We don't have long!" I cry, but she can't hear me as my voice is blown back into my throat. I grab her hand and we run.

I lead her down the thin walkway around the edge of the Dome, hugging the curved outer surface like a rogue satellite orbiting a planet. I don't look down, but that doesn't make it easy to ignore the impossible height.

Suddenly I feel a burst of heat and a wave of energy pulse through us. It's followed by a deafening sound.

Eve drops to her knees instinctively, dragging me down with her. I try to pull her up, but her fingers grip through the holes in the walkway as she stares down, straight down.

Through a few gaps in the dark clouds, we catch glimpses of the ground below. The sight takes my breath away too.

Hundreds of thousands, maybe millions, of people have gathered at the base of the Tower, lapping at the perimeter wall like waves swelling at cliff formations on a coastline.

Another explosion and a wave of heat washes over us.

"They're nonlethal weapons!" I shout, hoping that some of my words will make it through the roaring of the wind to Eve's ears. "They won't risk losing you, Eve! They won't hurt you! We have to keep moving!"

She breathes hard and stands defiantly, raising her eyes to the swarm of EPO drones that can just be seen through the haze as they point their camera lenses in our direction. I see power on her face. I feel it radiating from her as her eyes widen at every new sight they're presented with. Like a newborn seeing for the first time.

I yank her arm and she follows. This time she's faster. She wants more, I can sense it. My heart is exploding with nerves, excitement, love . . . all terrifying.

"Down here!" I cry out, leaping down a short flight of steps to a lower level. Eve follows without hesitation.

As I look back at her I see the black shadows of soldiers following us through the clouds, weapons in hand, charging along the metal walkway behind us.

I grab Eve's arm again and pull her along.

Not much farther.

We can make it.

My brain has switched off its fear of heights. That's not important now. My feet have a new purpose, like they were designed for this moment and this moment alone as they stomp the steel beneath them, creating distance between us and those who threaten Eve.

"Eve, stop!" a sharp voice booms, slicing through the turbulent air like a blade, cutting right to our eardrums. Everyone pauses.

Us.

Soldiers.

Even the wind seems to take a moment.

I recognize the voice at once, and from the rigidity of Eve's body, I can tell she does too. Vivian.

"Eve," she says again, her voice reverberating around the metallic outer walls of the Dome, like some sort of god calling down from the heavens. "You must not leave, Eve."

Eve looks out at the world. She sees the dark outlines of the drones hovering. She sees the gaps in the smog and the tips of the cloudscrapers of Central in the distance. A city she's never seen before. A whole life she's never lived.

I squeeze her hand.

Even though this is only the second time we have ever met face to face, we've spent our whole lives together. I know how she thinks.

"That place, that world, it's not safe for you, Eve," Vivian says calmly. Confidently. As though she expects Eve to turn and run back in, like a scared child. "This is your home, Eve. Your world. It's yours and only yours. Perfection."

Eve returns my squeeze.

I look along the walkway and see the yellow box. We're almost there. I begin to move again and Eve follows.

We step slowly now.

The floor vibrates with the thudding of soldiers following us, but we're not scared anymore. It's they who should be scared.

"Eve, you cannot trust him," Vivian says, a quiver of panic in her voice. "He's leading you into a trap."

I stop at the box with my name, WELLS, written in black letters, and my father's face explodes into my mind. I know he's watching this.

I open the lock and pull out the bullet-shaped chrome glove inside. I look at Eve, who is staring along the walkway ahead of us. I follow her gaze and see the raised weapons of another group of soldiers.

"Weapons down!" Vivian cries. The men obey immediately.

I don't waste the moment. I unravel a long band of woven material from my pocket, loop it inside the Gauntlet, and pass it around the sturdy handlebar. I pull it over Eve's head and under her shoulders as a harness, then slip my hand inside the metal glove.

"Eve, that's enough," Vivian calls.

Eve looks into my eyes, and before I can ask if she's sure she wants to do this, she places her foot on the railing.

"Bram!" A voice blasts through the sky like thunder. My father. "Do you have any idea what you're doing? Think of everything we've done, how far we've come together."

Together. The word sits in my head as Eve kicks her legs over the metal safety barrier, and my stomach leaps with excited fear as she looks to me to join her. She is saving me as much as I'm saving her. I've spent my entire life following his orders, knowing they were wrong. Finally, I have a chance to do something right. To give the last girl on the planet, our only hope, a fighting chance at a life worth living. To show her that humankind is worth fighting for.

I grip the rail with one hand and steady my feet, not waiting for the logical side of my brain to intervene and stop me jumping off the side of the tallest building in the world, strapped to the most important human in history.

My heart is so loud it drowns every rational thought, numbing every doubt.

This is what I want.

This is what *she* wants.

This is what the world needs.

Eve wraps her arms around my neck, turning her back on

the watching drones and the waiting world below. I feel her body press up against mine as she pulls herself into me. I tighten my grip on the cold metal railing with one hand as the other lifts the Gauntlet over our heads.

"This is it," I say into Eve's ear. "Are you sure you want this?"

She pulls her face around, her nose touching mine, her electric eyes full of wonder.

She says nothing but presses her cold, trembling lips to mine.

This moment, this kiss, is everything.

I feel her hand slide down my arm, and as it finds my fist tightly clenched around the rail, she runs her fingers over my knuckles, melting my firm grip away. Through our kiss I feel her lips relax into a smile.

67

EVE

SO MUCH CAN HAPPEN IN THE BRIEFEST OF MOMENTS.

We kiss.

We smile.

We fall.

I am free.

To be continued . . .

Acknowledgments

It's been a long process from the first "what if" conversation to publication, and there have been so many people who have helped us along the way.

We would like to thank our incredible teams at Michael Joseph and Penguin Random House Children's, who came together like the Avengers of publishing to form a super-team for *Eve of Man*. There are a lot of you, so here we go . . . Tom Weldon, Francesca Dow, Louise Moore, Amanda Punter, Max Hitchcock, Holly Harris, Eve Hall, Yasmin Morrissey, Claire Bush, Emma Henderson, Ellie Hughes, Roz Hutchinson, Hannah Bourne, Lauren Hyett, Liz Smith, Michael Bedo, Camilla Borthwick, Susanne Evans, Maeve Banham, Zosia Knopp, Hazel Orme, Jacqui McDonough, Emily Smyth, Lee Motley, and every single person that had even the tiniest speckle of input into this book. We are so lucky to work with such brilliant people.

Thanks to our incredible agents Stephanie Thwaites and Hannah Ferguson, our managers Fletch and Happy Entertainment, Rebecca Burton, Claire Dundas, and all at James Grant.

Thanks to our lawyer, Kaz Gill. David Spearing, thanks for making another incredible trailer for the announcement of this book.

Thanks to all our friends who have had to sit through our "what if" conversations over the last five years and who have been so amazingly encouraging; to Bob and Debbie Fletcher for all the babysitting hours so we could actually write this; and to our unbelievably supportive families, who we don't see often enough, and when we do we're exhausted—thanks for putting up with us.

Thanks to our three boys, Buzz, Buddy, and Max, for being an endless source of inspiration and a much-needed distraction.

Finally, to anyone that reads this book and comes on this journey—thank you.